like family

By Erin White

Given Up for You: A Memoir of Love, Belonging and Belief

Erin White
like family

This edition first published in Great Britain in 2026 by
Serpent's Tail,
an imprint of Profile Books Ltd
29 Cloth Fair
London
EC1A 7JQ

www.serpentstail.com

First published in USA by The Dial Press, an imprint of Random House, 2025
First published in Great Britain in ebook by Serpent's Tail, 2025

Copyright © Erin O'Neill White, 2025

Book design by Elizabeth A. D. Eno

1 3 5 7 9 10 8 6 4 2

Printed and bound in Great Britain by
CPI Group (UK) Ltd, Croydon CR0 4YY

The moral right of the author has been asserted.

All rights reserved. Without limiting the rights under copyright reserved above, no part of this publication may be reproduced, stored or introduced into a retrieval system, or transmitted, in any form or by any means (electronic, mechanical, photocopying, recording or otherwise), without the prior written permission of both the copyright owner and the publisher of this book.

A CIP catalogue record for this book is available from the British Library.

Our product safety representative in the EU is Authorised Rep Compliance Ltd., Ground Floor, 71 Lower Baggot Street, Dublin, D02 P593, Ireland.
www.arccompliance.com

ISBN 978 1 80522 915 5
eISBN 978 1 80522 917 9

For Rebecca, beloved sister
and for Heather, treasured friend

Woe to those who get what they desire. Fulfillment leaves an empty space where your old self used to be . . . You furnish a dream house in your imagination, but how startling and final when that dream house is your own address. What is left to you?

—Laurie Colwin, *The Lone Pilgrim*

CAST OF CHARACTERS

THE SCHWARTZ-HUNTLEYS
Ruth and Wyn
Siddha
Gilly
Roz
Abe

THE CARUSO-GALLAGHERS
Caroline and Mike
Luca

THE GOLD-FYNCHES
Tobi and Evie
Nina
Jules

like family

1

Caroline Caruso was standing in waist-high water, adjusting her goggles and wondering why her friend Ruth was so late. Ruth was usually at the pond before her, sitting on the sandy beach and wearing a fleece over her bathing suit on even the warmest mornings. Ruth called this "super heating," and she'd taught Caroline that it was the trick to cold-water swimming. "You just get yourself so hot all you want to do is jump in the water," she'd instructed. Ruth was right about super heating, the same way she'd been right about pretty much every aspect of country living.

Ruth had lived in the Hudson Valley forever, while Caroline—a Manhattanite whose previous definition of a small town was Boston—had only been in Radclyffe for a few months when she met Ruth. She'd had a lot to learn, and Ruth had been a kind and candid teacher. Buy your corn from Lucerne's farm stand but drive the extra ten minutes to get your blueberries from Norlack's. Always go to the dump right before it closes so the manager will have no choice but to help unload your recycling. Volunteer at the community center tag sale if you want your kid to get a speaking part in the town play. Avoid all restaurants other than Dairy Barn between Memorial Day and Labor Day, and avoid even Dairy Barn over the Fourth of July. Caroline had lived here for almost seven years now, and Ruth had been right about everything.

Had Ruth texted to say she wasn't coming? Caroline considered getting out of the water to check her phone, but she knew there would be nothing—there was no cell service at the pond, even though it was only a few miles from town. Seven years in Radclyffe and Caroline was just now getting used to how much could change in a few miles, or even just a few blocks. In the ten-minute drive to the pond from her neighborhood of clapboard houses and yards filled with pollinator-friendly plants and lawn signs pledging allegiance to a wide range of both political causes and youth sporting teams, she passed a Michelin-starred restaurant, the library, an aura photography studio, a VFW club, and a Hannaford supermarket with mediocre produce but surprisingly decent cheese. Then the road narrowed and, crossing over a small bridge to follow a bend in the river, made a gentle turn toward low hills and fields dotted with weathered barns. As a child, Caroline had thought of valleys as fictional places (Rivendell) or cultural ones (Silicon, San Fernando), never quite understanding their actual geography. Now here she was, nestled between the Hudson River and the Catskill Mountains, and she felt—and this feeling still surprised her, every day—held in place by the landscape, comforted by its edges, the containment of its geological borders. How green was my valley, she'd often think as she drove, not ever having read the book or seen the film of that name, but knowing, somehow, the depth of sentiment the phrase conveyed.

Just as Caroline was getting ready to pack it in, Ruth came running down the path. "Sorry, sorry, sorry," she said, pulling off her sweatshirt. She rummaged in her bag and pulled out a swim cap and goggles, then knelt in the sand while she stuffed her wild curly hair under the cap. She waded in, gently splashing handfuls of water onto her chest and shoulders.

Caroline hugged Ruth. "You're warm," she said. "Did you superheat in the car?" Sometimes, when they were in a hurry, they'd just drive to the pond with the heat blasting. Less enjoyable than a warm chat on the beach, but still effective.

Ruth shook her head. "I was rushing," she said, a strange, stressed expression on her face.

"Are you okay?" Caroline asked.

"Not really," Ruth said.

Caroline's face must have shown her alarm because Ruth quickly said, "I mean—yes, I'm okay, I'm fine, everyone is fine, totally fine, it's just—well . . ." Ruth didn't seem to know where to begin.

"We don't have to swim," Caroline said. "Let's go back on the beach and talk."

"No, no, I want to," Ruth said. "This could be our last swim of the season. This water is already freezing." She lowered into the water up to her shoulders and shivered a little, then gently pushed off into a glide and kick, her head still above the calm water.

Caroline pulled her goggles down around her neck and began swimming sidestroke so she could look at Ruth. Her muscles fell into the ancient rhythm of "pick the apple, put it in the basket." After a few moments, Ruth switched from breast to sidestroke too.

"I have to tell you something and I don't want you to judge me," Ruth said.

"Okay," Caroline said, pulling her strokes a little harder to warm up.

"No, really—really don't judge me," Ruth said.

"Jesus, Ruth, what is it?"

"God, I don't know where to start."

"Start in the middle," Caroline suggested. This was something she and her husband, Mike, said to their son, Luca, who was seven years old and had an extremely underdeveloped sense of narrative timing. Caroline and Mike could often finish eating dinner *and* load the dishwasher before Luca got to the point, on the rare occasions that there was a point.

"Okay," Ruth said. She took a breath and exhaled a tiny batch of bubbles into the water. "So, you know how Siddha has a different donor than the other kids?" Ruth and her wife, Wyn, had four children, although Ruth had had their oldest, Siddha, on her own, a few years before she married Wyn.

"Yeah," Caroline said.

"And you know how I told you that Siddha's donor wasn't exactly a donor, I mean that I—"

Caroline interrupted, wanting to speed this along. "You had sex with him. Without meaning to get pregnant."

"Right, right," Ruth said. "But you know how I've always said I didn't know the man I'd slept with? The thing is, I did. I mean, I do—I mean, I did. I knew him. He knew Siddha when she was a baby."

"Oh, wow," Caroline said. She could hear the anxiety in Ruth's voice, and she wanted to be careful, but she also had a lot of questions. "Does Siddha want to meet him now?"

"The thing is, she can't, because he's dead. He died in September, but we just found out last night."

Caroline stopped swimming. "Oh, Ruth—oh god, Ruth! Why are you telling me this in the middle of the pond?"

Ruth stopped too, and they both started to tread water. "It gets worse."

Caroline made what she hoped was a calm and supportive face, although what she was really thinking was that she wished she had a pool noodle for the buoyancy this situation was beginning to require. She looked back at the shore, which seemed farther away than she would have liked.

Ruth said, "Siddha got a letter yesterday, from his attorney. I mean, Wyn and I got a letter, but Siddha opened it, and the letter says he left her something in his will. And so there we are, it's almost dinner and the little kids are in the kitchen, and Siddha bursts in with this letter, and she's like, Who's this guy who left me something in his will? And Wyn and I—"

"Can I ask who he is?" Caroline said. "I mean, what's his name?"

"Elliot Jenkins—no, wait." Ruth stopped. "It's Elliot Shepherd or something like that."

"You don't know his last name?"

"It used to be Jenkins, but then he changed it, I guess when he got married? I don't really know. He owned the hardware store in Barton Falls. Please tell me you didn't know him."

"I didn't know him," Caroline assured her. "But Barton Falls is so close. You never ran into him?"

"He moved to North Carolina when Siddha was one, and just moved back up here a few years ago."

"Did you know he was back?"

"Sort of. I mean yes, but I hadn't seen him. I knew that he was married and had two kids. I guess he'd cleaned himself up?"

"In what way?" Caroline asked cautiously.

Ruth sighed. "I think he got sober. He was a serious alcoholic. That was the reason I felt like I had to just cut it off. I mean, I always figured we'd tell Siddha eventually, like when she was eighteen, you know? The way the other kids can find out who their donor is then, which, of course, was stupid logic, a totally false equivalency, but it was working for us. Emphasis on *was*."

"Oh Ruth, I'm so sorry," Caroline said. "So what did you say, I mean when Siddha asked who he was?"

"We kind of stalled for a minute, until we could get the other kids to go play in the yard. Then we just sort of told her. At first, we really hedged, you know? At least we tried to hedge, but then we told her everything."

Caroline got the feeling that Ruth was hedging a bit with her too, which might have shown on her face because the next thing Ruth said was "I should have told you all this before now, I know, and I'm sorry. We just didn't talk about it with anyone, you know? Because we couldn't risk someone mentioning it at the wrong time, or, well—"

"Of course," Caroline said. "Of course I understand." She wasn't so sure she did, but she tried to push the uncertainty aside and focus on Ruth.

"Do you think I'm a terrible person?" Ruth asked.

"Ruth!" Caroline exclaimed. "I could never think that." And then, because she just couldn't help herself, she asked, "Was he an alcoholic when you met him?"

Ruth's face started to crumple.

"Never mind, never mind," Caroline said quickly. "You can fill me in later. You're most definitely not a terrible person."

"Do you think I did the wrong thing?" Ruth asked.

"No," Caroline said, firmly, although she wasn't sure what Ruth had done, exactly. Kept a big secret, that much was for sure. Caroline couldn't tell if she felt hurt, not knowing any of this before now. "I don't. But what are you going to do?"

"I don't know. Siddha's not talking to us. I mean, after we explained as much as we could, she just freaked."

"Well, that seems natural."

"I know, but it still feels terrible."

Caroline waited for a moment to see if Ruth was going to say anything else, and when she didn't, Caroline took a breath and said, "Ruth, I love you and I'm here for you, and you can tell me anything anytime, but I've got to swim back now before I freeze to death."

Ruth laughed. "Oh sorry! Let's swim back."

They both swam then, fast even strokes, and Caroline felt the relief of her body warming, her heart beating, her motion in the direction of the shore. She switched to breaststroke for a moment, as a thought occurred to her. She gently whacked Ruth's arm to get her attention. Ruth's head popped up.

"Should we cancel the party tomorrow?" Caroline asked. "I feel like we should. It's going to be too much. We could postpone?" Caroline kept kicking and pulling as she talked, and Ruth joined her.

"Maybe?" Ruth said. "But we can't postpone Sukkot. And the kids are excited about the whole 'eat outside in a temporary shelter like your nomadic ancestors' thing. Although all they really want is to roast marshmallows."

"So we can do it anytime," Caroline said.

"You know how much Mike wants us to meet Tobi and Evie."

Caroline laughed. "Oh, is that what Mike wants?"

Ruth stopped swimming long enough to swat Caroline on the arm. It was true that Mike wanted to introduce his cousin Tobi and her wife, Evie, to Ruth and her wife, Wyn, but it was really Ruth who'd been angling for the introduction. She was obsessed with their Instagram account. Caroline and Mike had tried to make it happen a few times, but Tobi and Evie had—to Caroline's annoyance—always ended up canceling.

Ruth went on. "Anyway, we need a party. A party is a good distraction." She laughed a little. "Look at me, look at what fourteen years of marriage to a WASP will do to a person. Distracting myself with parties." Then she started to cry.

"Oh, Ruth," Caroline said. "It's going to be okay. I know it is. But let's backstroke the rest of the way because if you choke on your tears and start drowning, I'm not sure I can save you."

Ruth laughed again, and, still crying, nodded her agreement. They both turned over, closing their eyes to the sun, windmilling their arms. Every few strokes Caroline stopped to make sure her friend was okay.

2

"Should we have canceled this party? I feel like maybe we should have canceled." Ruth was hosing off patio chairs and arranging them to dry in the sun while Wyn untangled strands of lights to string around the sukkah, which she still hadn't finished building even though the guests would be arriving in only a few hours. It had been a difficult morning with Siddha, who had emerged from her room at ten, come down to make herself a cup of tea, then gone back upstairs, all without a word. When Ruth followed, knocking gently on the closed door, Siddha didn't answer. And when Ruth knocked again, a little less gently, Siddha bellowed, "*Go away!*" That was four hours ago, and Ruth hadn't seen her since.

"It's a little late now," Wyn said.

"At first I thought it would be best to just keep on with life, but now I'm thinking, is it disrespectful?"

"To who? Siddha?"

"Yes, to Siddha," Ruth said, annoyed.

"I'm going to guess she won't even be around," Wyn said.

"I want her around!" Ruth cried. She put a hand over her eyes.

"I think we just need to give it some time," Wyn said.

"I keep waiting for her to ask us what Elliot was like, you know? Or to want some details about his life. She won't ask anything. I'm afraid she's just googling."

"Well, we both know there's not much there," Wyn reminded her.

THE NIGHT THE letter arrived, after Siddha told them she had no interest in whatever it was they wanted to say because they were liars and she didn't need any more lies, Ruth and Wyn had fallen into bed, exhausted, and searched Elliot's name on Wyn's iPad. They'd found his obituary, a few local news articles about the hardware store, and a quote from him about his kids' Little League team. That was about it. It seemed that Elliot and his wife, Hope, had created a portmanteau of their surnames when they married (Shepherd and Jenkins became Shepkins), which, under normal circumstances, Ruth would have found pretentious and performative, but in this anything-but-normal circumstance she found to be a great relief because it meant that Elliot *Jenkins*'s public record of multiple DUIs was, at least for now, hidden from Siddha's view. There was a part of Ruth that wanted Siddha to know about Elliot's past—it strengthened Ruth and Wyn's case for secrecy—but the better part of her knew that it would be confusing and painful, and as long as Siddha wasn't talking to them, Elliot's criminal record was the last thing Ruth wanted her to try to make sense of on her own.

"Do you want me to read the obituary?" Wyn had asked.

Ruth nodded. She closed her eyes and listened while Wyn read aloud: "Our beloved Elliot Russell Shepkins was born May 1, 1975. He is cherished and remembered by his wife, Hope, and twin sons, George and Theodore, age nine." Wyn stopped reading and looked at Ruth. "God, they're so young."

"I know," Ruth said. "It's a heartache."

Wyn continued reading about Elliot, how he'd worked as a cook, farrier, housepainter, roofer, and fire lookout until taking over Barton Falls Hardware with his wife in 2023. She stopped reading. "Elliot was a farrier?"

"Apparently so."

"Wow, cool. Was that before or after you knew him?"

"Are you being serious right now?"

Wyn squeezed Ruth's hand in apology and kept reading. "Private burial, with a public memorial to be scheduled at a later date."

This piqued Ruth's interest. She rolled over to look at Wyn. "Does it say anything about that? Did we miss it? Maybe we should go, and take Siddha? For some kind of closure?"

Wyn grimaced. "I think it would be more of an opening than a closure," she said.

Ruth got up to brush her teeth. When she came back, she could see that Wyn was now doing the *New York Times* crossword on her iPad.

"There was nothing," Wyn said.

"Did you check Facebook?"

"I did," Wyn said. "The hardware store doesn't have a page. And Hope's not on any socials. It's been a month, so maybe it already happened."

"Maybe," Ruth said, relieved at the thought, then guilty at her relief. She took off her robe, opened her bedside table, and pulled out a pair of socks.

"It's already time for socks?" Wyn asked.

"Yes, and don't put your cold feet on me."

"Author of *Five Children and It*? Six letters."

"Nesbit," Ruth said. She turned back to Wyn. "Can I look at the obituary again?"

"Have at it," Wyn said, handing her the iPad. She threw back the covers and went to the bathroom.

Ruth clicked on the tab of the obituary. How could there be an obituary for Elliot? In her mind, he was agile and young, light on his feet. Surely he'd aged, the way they all had, but he wasn't old. He'd been thirty-three when they met; she'd been twenty-three. Ruth had moved to Radclyffe when she was twenty-two, to take an assistant teacher position at Mott Valley Friends, a Quaker school that recruited teachers from Quaker colleges like Ruth's. She'd been a classics major and had no formal training in education, or in anything, really, having spent her senior year translating Ovid's *Amores* while her peers were studying for the LSAT and interning at nonprofits. But she'd volunteered at a local preschool during college and was a day camp counselor every summer, so she was confident she could do the job.

She'd been thrilled when the offer came, thrilled to go anywhere other than back to Madison, and she took to the work immediately. She loved the children and their rowdiness, their tender absurdities. During that first year she took night classes toward a teaching certification, and by her second year she had her own class of kindergartners, fifteen earnest near-babies to whom she read aloud an illustrated version of the *Odyssey* and buckled their overalls after they used the bathroom.

The night Ruth met Elliot she'd been out with friends to celebrate a birthday. She'd gone up to the bar to order more beers, pushing through the crowd that surrounded Elliot, a dozen or more people cheering him on as he caught stacks of quarters off his paint-stained elbows. When he flipped fifty-one, thus breaking the bar's previous record, the whole place erupted. Ruth was right next to him when he slapped all the quarters onto the bar, triumphant, and he picked her up and spun her around. Ruth had two thoughts at once, the first being, Who the hell is this person? And the second, My god, his arms.

Ruth told Elliot she was pregnant on a cold afternoon in late September, a few days after she made the decision to keep the pregnancy, and six weeks after they met. Before she noticed that her period was late, Ruth had been having the time of her life with Elliot. She felt both younger and older than she'd ever been. Ruth was a serious person, or at least that was how she thought of herself, and how others seemed to think of her too. She'd dated a few boys in college, but she'd never really enjoyed them, and she'd certainly never been in love.

Not that she was in love with Elliot, necessarily, although she loved being with him, loved the way he made her feel. Elliot was funny and wild; he was impulsive. "Want to swim?" he'd ask her when, after sex and before sleep, neither of them could cool down. And even though it was late, even though she had to be at work early the next morning, Ruth would always say yes. They'd drive to the pond in Elliot's truck, strip down on the beach, and swim naked in the moonlight. One night

Ruth got out of the water and walked back to the truck without even covering herself with a towel, and she thought, for the first time in her life, that her body was a beautiful thing. Elliot made her feel beautiful; he made her feel brave.

But in the week since Ruth had taken the pregnancy test, she had not been feeling particularly brave. She knew she wanted to keep the baby even though she wasn't sure what kind of father Elliot would be, or if he wanted to be a father at all. (If Ruth was being honest with herself, she did have a hunch about what kind of father Elliot would be, but she was trying to ignore it.) Once she'd decided to keep the baby, she knew she had to tell him before she lost her nerve.

One afternoon when school let out, she skipped a faculty meeting, saying she felt a cold coming on, and drove around Radclyffe looking for Elliot's truck. When she finally found it, she saw Elliot at the top of a ladder, repairing a second-story window frame. He waved at her, then started down, jumping off the ladder long before he reached the last rung. Ruth saw him jump, and for a second she thought maybe he *would* be a good father. She knew he didn't have much money; she knew that he drank too much, but maybe this baby would be the start of something new. Maybe he could teach this baby how to ride a bike and catch a fly ball and change a flat tire. Ruth's own father, whom she adored, was a research librarian who didn't own a single pair of sneakers but had taught Ruth the Dewey decimal system and the key Latin roots before she was eight years old. She knew that it didn't really matter what your dad taught you, but you needed him to teach you something, and maybe it would be good if Elliot taught this baby some things?

Elliot hugged her and gave her a long kiss that Ruth tried—and failed—not to return. It started to rain, and Elliot suggested they head for his truck. When Ruth opened the passenger-side door a landslide of beer cans fell at her feet. She felt a pain in her stomach, a twisting panic. Maybe Elliot didn't have anything good to teach this baby.

"I'm pregnant," Ruth blurted, before Elliot had even closed the driver's-side door. "And it's fine if you don't want to be involved, but I'm keeping it. And if you want to be involved but you're not ready to be a dad, then that's fine too, you can just—"

Elliot reached across the bench seat of the truck and pulled Ruth to him. He touched her face with his cold fingers, he kissed her lips, and her cheeks, and her hair, and then he held her with such strong solidity it was like being held by a tree.

Ruth, who'd promised herself that no matter what she wouldn't cry, folded herself into him and wept.

"LISTEN TO THIS," Ruth said, then read aloud from the obituary: "'In lieu of flowers, the family is requesting donations to the Barton Falls Recreation Department.' Why aren't they saying how he died?"

Wyn came to the door of the bathroom, rubbing a washcloth over her face. "It's an obituary, not a coroner's report."

"Still, I feel like they sometimes say something like 'after a long illness,' or 'lost a heroic battle to cancer.' Usually there's some clue."

"We can probably get more details when we talk to that lawyer."

Ruth groaned, tossing the iPad onto the bed next to her. "What do you think he left Siddha?"

"I don't know," Wyn said. She took off her shirt and came back to bed.

"I know you don't know, but what do you *think*? What do you imagine it could be?"

"His mother's engagement ring?"

Ruth gave Wyn a look. "That seems oddly specific."

Wyn shrugged. "I just feel like that's what people give their daughters."

Ruth felt cold. "She's not his daughter."

Wyn pulled Ruth in. "Ru, this is going to be okay. It really is. But in order for it to be okay, we—"

Ruth rolled her eyes.

"We," Wyn said again, "are going to have to stay calm."

Easy for you to say, Ruth thought. Although that wasn't fair, it wasn't easy for Wyn. She knew that. Wyn, who'd left behind her fancy Wall Street job to move upstate and join her fate to that of a single mother who taught kindergarten, who'd loved Siddha from the start. She'd claimed her with a ferocity that had nearly knocked Ruth breathless—and still did—with love and gratitude.

Ruth let Wyn hold her then, and she found that small warm spot between Wyn's neck and shoulder that made her feel safe, and happy, and the tiniest bit aroused. After a few moments, she felt Wyn relax into sleep. Ruth slid out of the embrace gently, put the iPad on the nightstand, and turned off the light.

RUTH TOSSED THE damp chair cushions onto a sunny patch on the patio, hoping they'd be dry before dinner. She looked at Wyn. "She hates us. She hates us so much. And I don't blame her. I'd hate us too."

"She doesn't hate us."

"What do we tell her about him?"

"Well, nothing right now, because she doesn't want to talk to us about him."

"But when she does? When she does want to talk, what do we tell her? Do we tell her about the drinking?"

Wyn sighed. "Probably? I don't know, hon. But we're not going to lead with that." Before Ruth could ask what, exactly, they were going to lead with, Wyn headed for the barn.

"Where are you going?" Ruth asked, aiming the hose at Wyn.

"I need to get back to building this sukkah," Wyn said, moving fast to avoid the water. "For you, my Jewish princess."

"Will you please stop pretending you don't know what that means?"

"Why do you think I don't know what it means?" Wyn said.

"I think we both know who the princess is around here," Ruth said.

"Roz?" Wyn asked.

Roz was their third child. She was ten years old, as beautiful as she was brilliant. She was also a diva, a terror, the center of all conflict, and the instigator of all mischief.

Ruth laughed. "Shh," she said. "She could be listening. She's out here somewhere."

"I don't think she'd disagree."

Holding the hose, water puddling in the grass next to her, Ruth said, "I'd say you don't have to bother with all this, but Tobi and Evie are real Jews. They're going to expect a sukkah."

"Yeah, well, we're real farmers, and here we are, offering a harvest celebration on a real farm. Maybe that's enough?" Wyn motioned toward the field where three sheep were grazing. There had been four, but a few weeks ago one had been attacked by a fox and sustained injuries so severe it had to be put down. Ruth wasn't so sure they were real farmers at all.

"It's not," Ruth said. "And even if we *are* farmers, I'm pretty sure Tobi and Evie grow way more of their own food than we do. I saw their root cellar on Instagram. It's bonkers."

"We have a root cellar! Feel free to post it on Instagram."

"It's stocked with Costco mixed nuts and LaCroix! I am not posting that on Instagram."

"Just wait until next fall. We'll put their root cellar to shame."

"It's not a competition," Ruth said.

"Oh, but it is," Wyn said.

"Well then it might be one you're going to lose."

"How funny," Wyn said. She made a quick move for Ruth and stole the hose out of her hand. "It seems you've forgotten a Huntley never loses."

Ruth laughed, a sharp exhaling "Ha!" as though warming up for choir practice. "Like a Huntley would ever let me forget that."

Wyn walked across the lawn with the hose. "And don't even worry. It's almost finished. I just need to find those two-by-tens that seem to have disappeared."

"Maybe we lost them in the move," Ruth said. This was Ruth's code for both "I threw that out before we moved" and "I am not going to help you find what you are looking for." She said it at least once a day to Wyn or one of their four children in the months since they'd left their little house in the center of Radclyffe and moved to this rambling farm with a drafty farmhouse, two barns, three pastures, and twenty acres of woodland.

"Nice try, but we didn't move the lumber," Wyn said. "I bought it when we got here, to build the chicken coops. It's got to be somewhere in the hay barn."

"Well then, you're on your own, because I don't go in there." Ruth pushed her sunglasses into her hair.

"Maybe I'll just ask Bex." Wyn turned off the hose's sprayer and reached into her pocket for her phone. "Hey Siri," she said. "Text Bex."

"You know what, I'll go check," Ruth said, motivated by a desire not to involve Bex in a day that already felt too complicated. Bex was a new friend of Wyn's—the two of them had met at the feed store—and now Bex seemed to always be around and helping Wyn, if helping meant sitting in old lawn chairs behind the barn and drinking beer with her.

Wyn was already dictating into her phone. "Hey bro," she said in a neutral, robotic voice. "Got any two-by-tens for desert tabernacle we're building in the yard question mark." She hit send.

"Seriously?" Ruth said. "Can't you just call it a pergola when you're talking WASP to WASP? Also, what's with the 'bro'?"

"How do you know Bex isn't Jewish?"

"Wild guess," Ruth said.

"You know, hon, I'm getting the idea that you don't like Bex."

"I love Bex!" Ruth lied. "I just don't love their whole 'I'm a sensitive folk singer but I'm also a butch ranch hand from Montana' schtick. Also, Caroline and I ran into them at Bread Euphoria a few weeks ago and they were over-the-top flirting with her."

"They *are* a folk singer and a ranch hand," Wyn said. "It's not a schtick. And everyone flirts with Caroline. A person who doesn't flirt with Caroline is a person without a pulse."

It was true that Caroline was objectively, undeniably, extremely beautiful. Movie-star beautiful, with full lips and glossy dark hair that was wavy in all the right places. She had smooth skin and dark eyes and a dazzling, disarming smile. Early in their friendship, Ruth had quickly realized that the world Caroline moved through was a different world. People were warmer to her, more attentive. Caroline got the best tables in restaurants, even without a reservation. She was offered the freshest pieces of fish at the fishmonger, an extra cinnamon bun at the bakery.

She asked people questions that Ruth would have just googled, and people were more than happy to stop what they were doing and give her the answers. People never asked Caroline to repeat herself—they heard her the first time.

"I don't flirt with Caroline," Ruth said. "You don't flirt with Caroline."

"That's because she's your best friend."

"Are you offering that as explanation for why I don't flirt with her, or why you don't?"

"Both," Wyn said. "But Bex is gonna flirt with her. It's a fact."

"Yes, fine, you're right, that's a fact. I can accept it. But honestly, it's more than that, it's just that they're so—oh, you know, so—" Ruth moved her hands around.

"You're smarter than Bex," Wyn said. "If that's what you want me to say."

Ruth made a face. "That's not what I want you to say," Ruth said. "I mean, clearly I'm smarter than they are."

"So then?"

"Oh, whatever," Ruth said, not wanting to get into all the things about Bex that bothered her, or more precisely not wanting to get into the one real reason she didn't like them, which was that she knew Wyn had a crush on them, and it was strange, Wyn crushing on someone who wasn't femme. Sure Bex was gorgeous—muscled and tattooed, but with a sweet, boyish face framed by spiky black hair, the combination of which was surprising and, yes, sexy. Ruth understood Wyn's attraction to Bex on aesthetic grounds, but she still didn't like it. The crush upset the balance of things. Wyn, with her short blond hair, strong legs, and ability to look sexy in both a suit and a pair of ripped basketball shorts, was a different sort of butch than Bex, but not *that* different. (Ruth's rule of attraction, which could be summed up as butch plus femme equals mutual desire, didn't allow for much nuance.)

"But now it's rude not to invite them to dinner," Ruth said.

"True," Wyn said. "But I can't build the sukkah without them."

Ruth groaned. "They're going to sing."

"No, they're not," Wyn said.

"Are you even serious? They are *always* singing." Sometimes Ruth wondered if Bex was going to start busking in her living room. Still, she had to admit that Bex was extremely helpful (it wasn't all beer and guitars) and the kids loved them, and it would be rude not to invite them. Before she could say something childish and hostile, like Okay, fine, but keep them away from Caroline, she was interrupted by their daughter Gilly calling to them from the house.

"*Mo-o-o-oms!*" Gilly yelled, standing on the back steps wearing only her underwear. "Where's my green leotard?"

"Check the dryer!" yelled Wyn.

Ruth winced. She hated yelling. But Wyn was a yeller, and now so were all their kids. Wyn didn't yell in an angry or violent way, just a very loud one. Ruth thought it was from too much time playing sports. Ruth thought everything she didn't like about Wyn was from too much time playing sports.

"I'll find it," Ruth said. "I need to start the beans. And thank you for building this thing. And when Bex gets here, tell them I said thank you, and that I hope they can stay for dinner."

Wyn smiled at her. "But leave your guitar in the truck."

Ruth smiled back. "Exactly."

3

Tobi Fynch and her wife, Evie Gold, were still working the crowd at Elliot Shepkins' memorial when the guys from the hardware store drove their truck onto the grass and started packing up the folding chairs. Tobi and Evie had been there for hours, although they'd barely seen each other since they arrived. They were committed to a divide-and-conquer approach to nearly every facet of their personal and professional lives, although once when Tobi had described it as such in an interview with *Ceramics Monthly,* Evie had interjected that she liked to think of their strategy more as "share and surmount." Evie liked to put her uniquely noncapitalist, postpatriarchal spin on everything she and Tobi did. Or at least she had. Now that their business, GoldFynch Pottery, was grossing three million dollars a year, Evie worried less about subverting the narrative and more about getting their warehouse expansion approved.

Which was why Evie was busy talking to the head of the county planning board while Tobi mingled, listening to new and old acquaintances share their memories of Elliot. She heard about the Christmas Eve when Elliot had unlocked the store at midnight after getting a frantic call from a customer in need of batteries, and a heroic early morning tarp delivery when the library ceiling caved under heavy snow. And then there were repeated stories of broken furnaces, broken sump pumps, broken washing machines, broken door handles. It seemed to Tobi that Elliot had fixed all the brokenness of this town, both real and metaphorical.

Tobi hadn't known Elliot well; she and Evie lived and ran their business in Radclyffe, which was only a few miles from Barton Falls as the bird flew but was separated from it by a river and a tangle of country roads, making travel between the two places as inconvenient as it was uncommon. Evie had met Elliot and his wife Hope at a meeting last year, something about changes to the industrial composting codes for the county. It had been one of those meetings that Tobi doubted Evie needed to attend until moments like this when, after raising a glass to a sweet man she barely knew, Evie was deep in conversation with a bureaucrat who hadn't returned a single one of her phone calls in the last six months. Evie was patient, and she knew how to get things done.

This gathering—which Hope had insisted was not a memorial but a celebration of life—had indeed filled Tobi with a sense of celebration; it made her feel grateful to be here, to be alive. It was a perfect day to be in the town park, out among the turning trees on the long, gentle hill down to the river, the water glinting and silver, the distant mountains evergreen and softly majestic. But there was also a shadowy feeling that Tobi couldn't quite shake, and that, of course, was death. Impermanence. The passage of time. The frailty of the human body. Because sure, this was a celebration of life, but they were all here because someone's life had ended. The music, the speeches, the sweet jokes, the sing-along, all of it was a declaration that none of this was going on forever. Elliot Shepkins was gone. And he wasn't even old! He was, in fact, only a few months older than Tobi.

She felt a damp panic at the thought of this man, one moment jumping for a rebound, the next moment dead on the YMCA basketball court. In just a few weeks, Tobi would turn fifty (fifty!), and while she knew fifty wasn't old, well, it also wasn't young. On a good day, that was a relief. She and Evie had worked like hell to get to where they were now, and Tobi wanted only distance between her and their years of barely scraping by. Even now they were still climbing the mountain of solvency, and maybe always would be. Owning a business was a thrill, but it was also terrifying, and while Tobi had gotten used to living this way, she knew she'd never stop worrying that they were only one bad quarter away from not being able to make payroll. It was Evie who had the stomach for it, Evie who could take the risk, who understood how to leverage what they had to get more.

Where was Evie, anyway? Tobi moved through the crowd trying to find her, hugging her goodbyes. As Tobi scanned for Evie, she made eye contact with the GoldFynch warehouse manager.

"Tobi!" she called, walking toward Tobi, grabbing the hand of the person next to her. "I want you to meet someone. Bex, this is my boss, Tobi."

"Tobi Fynch," Tobi said, putting out her hand. This Bex person looked familiar. Had she also worked for GoldFynch at some point? She was young, with short crow-black hair and an impish face, a long thin nose and jutting chin, and dark, lively eyes. She was what Evie would call adorable.

Bex took Tobi's hand in a strong handshake. "Bex Devereux."

"Oh," Tobi said, snapping her fingers. "I think we just saw you—I mean, my wife and I—did you open for Tegan and Sara last week? Was that you? You were amazing."

Bex put her hand on her heart, gave a little bow. "Thanks so much. I just moved here. In Deerville, off River Road."

"Oh wow," Tobi said. "Well, welcome. Are you staying for the winter?"

"Totally," Bex said. "I'm in it to win it. I did a real move, not just a summer thing. Or, as real as it can be. I got chickens, so . . ."

"So, pretty real," Tobi said.

"I'm building a recording studio," Bex went on, sliding her hand through her hair, leaving artfully disheveled spikes in its wake. "I bought a piece of land sight unseen, which might have been a mistake." She laughed, a laugh that was somehow both endearing and confident, in a way that suggested she didn't really think it was a mistake at all. "But Elliot and Hope had been setting me up." Bex shook her head. "Man, it's so sad." She put her thumbs in her pants pockets, the fingers of one hand latched around the neck of the beer bottle at her hip. The pulled-back lapels of her suit jacket revealed a pair of suspenders, under which her chest was gracefully, alluringly, flat.

Tobi took it all in: the beer bottle, the suspenders, the chest. The chest! She felt something in her own chest flip, and, startled, hoped she hadn't been staring. She looked away, scanning the park for Evie. Where was she? Tobi turned back to Bex, smiled in a way that she hoped seemed casual, friendly, and the tiniest bit apologetic for the leering, if it had seemed like she was leering. "I've heard so many great things about Elliot today," Tobi said, trying to stay on topic.

Evie appeared in the middle distance over Bex's shoulder, pointing to her watchless wrist. Tobi, relieved, nodded at her. "Great meeting you," she said to Bex. And then, before she could help herself, she added, "Let me know if you need anything, really. I was in your position once, getting started up here, I mean, I don't want to assume—"

"I very much need your help," Bex said. "All of it."

Tobi smiled. "I've got a whole crew, the best. I'd be happy to send anyone your way, really. I've gotta split, but just get my info from Hope, or come by GoldFynch anytime." And then the worry, the clench in her chest, was gone and the abundance returned, the brightening happiness to be here.

"Who was that?" Evie asked, not looking up from her phone as Tobi reached her.

Tobi looked over her shoulder, and waved again at Bex, who waved back. "Bex Devereux. From the concert the other night. Turns out she lives up here now."

"They." Evie was still typing.

"Oh, right. *They* just moved up here." Tobi panicked for a second, hoping she hadn't used the wrong pronouns when talking with Bex. Then she remembered that you didn't use a person's pronouns when talking directly to them, thank god. She looked back over at Bex, laughing with a young woman, their arm around the girl's tattooed neck, their bottle resting gently, sexily, on her shoulder. Wow, Bex could do a lot with a beer bottle.

"Well, I think we're set," Evie said. She stopped typing to look at Tobi over the top of her glasses. "I have to tell you, I wasn't sure this was really going to work. We were down to the fucking wire on this." She exhaled, hard. "God, I'm just so relieved. I'm going to text JP, tell him we can go ahead and draft the plans."

Tobi didn't answer. She was still looking at Bex.

Evie pushed her glasses into her hair. "Tob?"

"Yeah, yeah, I heard you, that's awesome." Tobi squeezed Evie's arm, pulled her in, kissed her head. "Really." She let go of Evie, took a little detour to put her empty beer bottle in a recycling bin. "By the way," she said, walking back again, "I told Bex we could help them out. They're trying to build a recording studio."

"God, can you imagine? Just starting out now? That first winter up here." Evie shook her head. "Remember how we'd just lie there listening to the mice running around in the walls? Wondering what the hell we'd done? Couldn't pay me to live through that again. I do not envy them."

"No, me either," Tobi said, distractedly. She wasn't thinking about mice and that first cold cabin where they'd lived all those years ago. She was thinking of Bex's shirt, the way it lay perfectly flat on their chest, all the buttons tucked neatly in their buttonholes. How beautiful they'd looked. How confident. Maybe that was just youth, but had Tobi ever been—or even appeared—so confident? Certainly not when she was young. She'd been a wreck most of the time, second-guessing herself, avoiding conversations, trying not to expose herself as the fraud she felt like. And sure, she had confidence now, she knew who she was, but it wasn't the same. It was hard won. She wanted to say all this to Evie but knew she couldn't, knew that Evie would just dismiss it all as the way of things, young people being young in a new and inaccessible way. She would plant herself, and by extension, Tobi, on the opposite shore, no traveling back. No chance of return. Normally Tobi was more than happy to keep her youth in the past. She'd worked so hard, had so much to show, such wild good fortune. How was it that all it took was a smoothly buttoned shirt to make her feel that she might not mind trying her luck at another go around, that, if she could, she'd do it differently, just to see what might happen?

4

"I'm too tired to go to this party," Caroline said. She'd just come out of the bathroom wrapped in a towel, her wet hair dripping on her shoulders. "I'm just not in the mood."

Mike was lying on the bed, shirtless and wearing boxers, looking at his phone. "It'll be fine, babe."

Caroline hated it when Mike told her it would be fine. And she hated it when he called her "babe." The problem was she'd once loved it, and she'd told him so, and now she didn't want to hurt his feelings by telling him to stop. It was heady and sexy before, but now, when it was mostly Mike standing in front of the open refrigerator asking Babe, where's the cream cheese? it felt a lot less sexy and a lot more Al Bundy.

But right now it wasn't making her angry, it was making her cry. And that made Mike look up from his phone. His face softened and he reached out his arm to her, beckoning. Caroline unwrapped the towel and lay down on top of him.

"It's been such a long week," Caroline said. "I just want to go over there and sit on their fancy patio and drink Wyn's expensive wine and have a nice time. I don't want to be worried about Luca and what he's doing. Or not doing. I just want to be with our people, and not worry about everybody else."

"Who's everybody else?" Mike said.

"Tobi and Evie."

"You mean my actual family?" Mike said. He was clearly annoyed, which made Caroline annoyed, which pretty much summed up their dynamic when it came to Tobi and Evie. "You don't think Ruth and Wyn are going to like Tobi and Evie."

"I just don't think the fact that they're all lesbians is a reason we need to introduce them."

"Well, there's also the Jewish thing—"

"Okay, now you're just profiling." Caroline stood and went to the mirror to comb her hair.

Mike shrugged. "Maybe, but I still think they're going to get along."

"Which will be nice for you," Caroline said, in a not-very-nice voice.

"Yeah, it will be nice for me. It will be nice for the people I love to know each other." He paused for a moment. "To like each other. I don't think that's strange."

"It's not strange," Caroline conceded. She knew she was being ridiculous. But did Mike really need to see more of Tobi? They seemed to see each other most weekends and even sometimes during the week, especially now that they were training for the Rod Sullivan Run Aground—also known as "the Rod"—which was some sort of relay triathlon in which one person (Tobi) biked, another person (Mike) ran, and the two of them paddled (in a double canoe) around Hazelboro Lake. Tobi had been trying to get Mike to do the Rod with her since Caroline and Mike had moved to Radclyffe seven years ago. Caroline had finally run out of reasons why this wasn't the year, and now Mike was spending most of his free time either preparing to exercise, exercising, or recovering from exercising. Which was probably the reason that Tobi was putting her in a bad mood.

"Luca will be fine," Mike said. "I promise. I'll be on him. You're off duty tonight. I promise."

"You swear?" Caroline said, lifting her pinkie. Instead of wrapping his own pinkie around Caroline's, Mike kissed it.

"I just—" Caroline stopped talking and closed the bedroom door. She picked up a T-shirt of Mike's from the edge of the bed, smelled it, and pulled it over her head. She sat down next to Mike, pulled her knees into her chest, and said in a quieter voice, "I just can't stop thinking about what Ms. Shantelle said yesterday, how Luca seemed lonely to her. And sad. Sad and lonely."

"She said a lot of really nice things, too," Mike said.

Caroline put her hands over her eyes for a moment. Then she looked at Mike. "Yeah, I don't think 'He's got a talent for coding' exactly balances out 'I'm not sure he has any friends.' Honestly it just makes it worse." Ever since the teacher had said that about Luca, Caroline had been imagining him as a grown man, alone in a room surrounded by computers and vape pens and empty Soylent bottles. She felt herself starting to cry again but tried to stop—she would not cry about this. She would not cry about Luca's teacher saying that Luca seemed sad and lonely, the two things she'd been as a child.

"He has Victor," Mike said.

"He *had* Victor," Caroline said, "and now Victor is gone."

Victor was a sweet boy who Luca had known since preschool. Victor and Luca had been inseparable for years. They both loved anime and Pokémon, were terrible at sports, and were eagerly awaiting their eighth birthdays, when they'd be old enough to join the library's Saturday morning Dungeons and Dragons club. Victor's birthday was a month before Luca's, but he'd valiantly vowed to wait until they could both walk through the door of meeting room B together. They quizzed each other endlessly on the things they would need to know when that momentous day arrived. "We're going to want to hit the ground running," Victor would always say, which made Caroline and Mike crack up. They loved Victor so much. They were—although they didn't like to admit it and didn't really talk about it with each other—deeply grateful to Victor for being Luca's friend. But last spring Victor's parents had divorced, and over the summer Victor's mom had moved the family back to Brooklyn, to be closer to grandparents. Luca was bereft, although perhaps not as bereft as Caroline and Mike. "Who'd you sit with at lunch today?" Caroline would ask, casually, and Luca wouldn't answer. Mike told her this was bound to happen, it was just a matter of time, a kid can't have just one friend, and Caroline said, "Of course a kid can have just one friend, one friend is all you need, and why are you blaming Luca for his bad luck?"

After all, Caroline only had one friend. Well, two if you counted Mike, which Caroline didn't. Caroline found it deeply annoying when women would say things like "I married my best friend." A husband—a spouse of any gender—was, in Caroline's opinion, not a friend. Why would you bother to put up with all the challenges of married life for a friend? She also didn't like the idea of spouses as soulmates, or the idea of soulmates in general. When Caroline thought of her soul—and she did believe she had one—she thought that its whole point, its entire reason for existing, was that it didn't need a mate. It was the one thing about a person that was entirely whole, peerless, complete. No, Mike was not a soulmate, and Mike was not a friend. Mike was her husband. But god, how she loved *that* word! She knew she wasn't supposed to, the patriarchy and all that, but she loved saying it. The gentle hum of the first syllable, the embrace of the second. This is my husband, she liked to say. Or Have you met Mike, my husband? Have you met my light, my optimism, my banisher of loneliness? Have you met the keeper of all my secrets, even the ones I didn't know I had?

Caroline had been thirty-three years old when she met Mike. After years of making her living as a performer and accompanist in New York, she'd moved to Boston to study early music and performance at Boston Conservatory. On a cold afternoon in winter, she slipped into a restaurant on her way home from a particularly exhausting rehearsal. Her quartet was playing Mozart's Piano Quartet in G Minor and her fellow musicians were repeatedly asking her to lighten the piano part, to let it catch the air it was meant to catch, but air wasn't easy for Caroline. She'd agreed to the piece because she thought restraint was what it required, and Caroline was very good at restraint. The cellist had yelled; Caroline had cried. She'd never been more discouraged.

Mike was drying glasses behind the bar when she pushed open the door and asked if they were open. Sure, he'd said, even though they didn't open until five. She asked for a whiskey and soda, and Mike gave her one, and then another, and then brought her a bowl of spaghetti Bolognese without asking if she was hungry. That was his first kindness. His second was that he barely spoke to her, just worked the bar, filled his garnish trays, and carried in buckets of ice from the kitchen to fill the undercounter bins. He was industrious. He was graceful. He was good company. But soon enough the restaurant was officially open and getting crowded, so Caroline paid her check and left without saying goodbye. She went back the next afternoon, but Mike wasn't there. The new bartender asked if Caroline wanted to leave a message. No, she said. And then, changing her mind, she rummaged around in her purse for a piece of paper. *Thanks for the Bolognese. —Caroline,* she wrote, and added her phone number.

A few days passed, and a few more, and Mike didn't call. Maybe he hadn't gotten her note? Bars were busy places, after all. It hadn't really occurred to Caroline that he wouldn't call. Men called her. But the week passed, and still nothing. So she put him out of her mind and focused on her concert. When she walked into the hushed performance room, there he was, in the front row.

"How did you know?" she asked him when he walked her home that night.

"You left me a flyer," he said.

"I left you a message on *the back* of the flyer," Caroline said. "With my phone number. Did you not see my number?"

"I did," he said. "But I thought it would be more romantic if I just showed up."

"How did you know I'd be playing?" Caroline asked. The flyer was just a stock photo of a piano and a violin, and the name of her ensemble, the Falstad Quartet.

"I didn't," Mike said. "But I figured the concert would be good either way."

Mike wasn't musical, and music was Caroline's life. She was a terrible cook, and Mike lived for food. He was a full two inches shorter than she was, and eight years older. He rode a motorcycle, which Caroline found terrifying. Caroline didn't have a driver's license, which Mike found ridiculous. There were serious questions, too. Would he work in a bar forever? Was that okay with Caroline? Was it okay with Mike? Would Caroline ever admit that she didn't really want a PhD in early music? Would Mike become an alcoholic, like his father? Would Caroline become depressed, like her mother? They didn't know. They didn't know anything really, just that the days when they woke together and fell asleep together were the best days.

That first summer they were together, Caroline discovered she was pregnant. They were both entirely, unequivocally, thrilled. They married the week before Christmas, and Caroline passed her master's exams in January. She would take a year off, she decided, before getting back to it.

But then Luca was born, and Caroline knew there was no getting back to it. She officially withdrew from school. She wasn't going to finish her PhD.

Mike worked extra shifts at the restaurant and for a friend's landscaping company, although it still wasn't enough money, and when Luca was barely three months old, they were dangerously close to using up their cash reserves. When Caroline's former advisor emailed her about a last-minute opening for the fall semester at Gorman College in Radclyffe, New York, Caroline jumped at the chance. She'd teach one class and give private lessons. "We'd be near Tobi," Caroline had said, when she told Mike about the job. And then, trying to preempt any concerns, "I think we can do it. I think we can just figure it out as we go."

SHE AND MIKE did figure it out. They adapted to living in a new place as married people, and as parents. They were good at figuring things out, together. All her life, Caroline had played so many games with people. Tried to impress them, to play it cool, to act smart, to act clueless. With Mike, she just wanted to be herself, make things work, and have a good time. Mike wasn't perfect, far from it. Caroline wished he made more money, had a little more ambition, wasn't quite so satisfied with their perfectly satisfactory life—but he was her light. And more than just that, Mike had shown Caroline how to find her own light, so that Caroline wasn't just less lonely when he was around, she was less lonely even when she was alone. Mike was her happiness. She knew she wasn't supposed to say this, or to depend on him for that, but what could she say? It was true.

But now it seemed like it was Luca who needed some light, and Mike didn't know what to do any more than she did. She felt let down. She felt scared. She wished someone had told her that when it was your kid's loneliness, well, that was the worst possible darkness.

5

Ruth sent the kids outside to set the table just as the sun was setting. Gilly and Roz had made place cards, and Abe was going to construct a tiny natural diorama at each place.

Earlier that afternoon, Ruth had sent him on a scavenger hunt (mostly to get him out of her hair), telling him to forage a few objects for each person. "Then you can share your reasons for choosing them," Ruth said. "But nothing dead," she added quickly.

"And no nests and no bird eggs," said Gilly. She was twelve and deeply protective of birds. "You never know if they're coming back."

"And no poop," said Roz.

"Maybe stick with leaves, Abe," said Ruth.

"But don't pull them off the trees," said Roz. "That's literally murder."

"Actually," Gilly said, pronouncing it "act-chew-al-ly" and drawing out each syllable, "that is not lit-er-al-ly murder, it is figuratively murder."

"It's neither," Ruth said. "It's just something we shouldn't do. And Abie knows that. Right, Abie?"

Abe groaned and slammed out the back door. Ruth's heart swelled for him. Her boy, the only one in a house where even the dogs were female. She worried about how the outside world treated him, she worried that he felt out of place in their family, misunderstood. But more than all this she was—irrationally, unfairly, secretly—thrilled to have been the one who bore him, their only son, their little prince, their heir.

When everyone was gone and the house quiet for a moment, Ruth pulled out her phone and went back to a tab she'd kept open, a page of photos accompanying Elliot's obituary. She'd looked at them a dozen times since the letter had arrived on Thursday, studying his face and body, the way both had been altered—and not—by time. At first, she'd told herself she was looking for resemblance to Siddha, but that wasn't true; Siddha was her clone, always had been. Ruth was just looking at Elliot. His red hair and beard, graying in the later photos, but no less thick. His broad shoulders, his broad smile. There was a wedding photo, and a picture of him with a newborn baby in each arm, the bright shine of delight in his eyes. There was Elliot in a kayak, and Elliot behind the counter at the hardware store. Always smiling, always that open, kind face.

When Ruth had walked out of that bar with Elliot—a bar long since closed and replaced by a store called Flowerkraut that sold houseplants and fermented foods—she walked out a different person. She'd gone in a cautious, practical girl who considered her true talents to be Latin translation and ping-pong and gone out a woman about to have sex with a man who didn't know her last name. As she and Elliot stood talking at the bar, she'd given him many opportunities to walk away from her, to find someone sexier, better at flirting, better at sex, better at everything than she was, but Elliot wasn't interested in finding someone else. He wrapped a ringlet of her hair around his finger and asked what she did to make it curl like that, and when she said Nothing, he'd looked at her in a way that made her crotch throb. He asked her questions about things that had nothing to do with her job or where she'd gone to college, or any of the usual topics men seemed to like. The topic Ruth was most accustomed to discussing with a man was the man himself, and Elliot was notable in his deflection of her questions. He touched her with a gentleness that she found dizzying, and when he put his hand on her back and asked if she wanted to get out of there, she could only nod in response.

She thought now of how it had felt—she could still feel it!—to have Elliot's arm around her shoulders as they went to his truck, how he'd opened the door for her, and how, when he'd gone around to the other side and gotten in, he'd pulled her to him and she'd slid across the bench seat of the old truck, and they'd kissed, the scratch of his beard oddly, wonderfully, pleasurable.

"Come home with me?" he whispered, his breath warm on her mouth. Again, she nodded yes, and he drove the few blocks to his apartment with an arm around her, her head on his chest. He smelled of beer and paint and cigarettes; his arm was warm on her bare skin. When they got to his apartment, they raced up the stairs, laughing, and there was none of the nervousness she'd felt before with men, only excitement. Elliot pushed open the unlocked door, pressed Ruth against the wall, lifted her skirt, and pushed down her underwear while she unbuttoned his jeans. They had sex twice before they even made it to the bedroom.

In the morning, Ruth woke with a start, her mind flooded with all the things she'd said the night before, the parts of her that this stranger had seen. She felt a dark rush of embarrassment. She wanted to sneak out somehow, the way people did in movies, but when she tried to get out of bed, Elliot reached for her.

When Ruth was with Elliot, she was astonished by her appetites, her boldness. Elliot asked her what she liked, and she told him, and the sound of the words coming out of her mouth was as thrilling as the acts themselves. She was distracted at work, counting the minutes until she could rush to his apartment, where she'd unbutton her dress before she'd even made it through the front door. They ate pizza in bed, played cards at Elliot's kitchen table, took walks late at night, stopping to kiss in the middle of the wide, empty streets. Ruth barely knew Elliot, although somehow it seemed she'd never known anyone better. And she knew herself, in a different way. She was desirous; she was desired. She was sexy. Ruth had always told herself that Siddha was Elliot's one gift to her. But there had been other gifts, too.

RUTH HEARD THE mudroom door open and quickly slid her phone into her back pocket. "Hello, hello!" she called cheerfully.

Siddha walked into the kitchen and looked at Ruth. "Hello?"

Ruth remembered this tone, this petulant, sullen, not-really-a-question questioning tone. It had been Siddha's default form of communication from age thirteen to fifteen. Everything Siddha had said in those years seemed to just be a different phrasing of the question Why are you even talking to me? God, how Ruth hated it! How they all hated it.

Wyn in particular had zero tolerance for Siddha's bad attitude, having been raised in a house where talking back of any kind wasn't tolerated. "If I ever did that to my mother . . ." Wyn would say when she'd ask Siddha about her homework or if she'd unloaded the dishwasher, and Siddha would roll her eyes and walk away.

"She'd what?" Ruth had asked once, taking the bait. "Send you to boarding school? Leave you with a babysitter while she went to Europe for six weeks? I'm not interested in parenting advice from your mother, Wyn." Wyn had fumed then, stormed out of the room just as Siddha had a few moments before, and Ruth, enraged, had broken a dish by throwing it in the sink.

This time was different, though. This time Wyn wasn't asking any more of Siddha than Ruth was, and they were both much more worried than they were angry.

Ruth smiled at Siddha, a smile that she hoped conveyed a sort of warm neutrality. "Hey there, sweetie."

"Did you think I was someone else?" Siddha asked, incredulous.

Ruth shrugged and kept smiling. "Oh, you know, Mike and Caroline are headed over for dinner."

"I won't be here."

"No?" Ruth asked, gently.

"Yeah, no. I'm going out."

Ruth turned to the fridge to get the salad greens, resisting the urge to ask her daughter what "out" meant. "Oh, well—dinner will be early, and I know everyone would love to see you, so if you wanted to just pop down for a few before you head out, I'd love to feed you and—"

Siddha cut her off. "You're acting weird."

Ruth laughed a fake laugh that sounded much sharper than she'd intended. "Just trying to get it all done!"

"Yeah, well, you didn't have to have this party."

"Oh, hon," Ruth said. She dropped the greens on the counter and looked at Siddha. "Did you want us to cancel it? Because—? Oh, we would have, of course we—"

Siddha interrupted, scowling. "I meant because it's stressing you out."

"I'm not stressed out, hon. Truly. Are *you* okay?"

Before Siddha could answer (not that she was going to), Ruth heard the mudroom door open. "Hello, hello!" Mike called.

"Hello, hello!" Caroline echoed.

"Hi!" Ruth called. "Come in!" And then, quietly: "Sid, look—"

Siddha just shook her head and went up the back stairs.

Luca came bursting into the kitchen, wearing a baseball hat and a cape. "Moadim l'simcha-cha!" he said, adding an extra "cha" to the greeting.

"He googled that on the way here," Caroline said, coming in behind them at a notably calmer pace. "To impress Evie and Tobi. The real Jews."

Ruth laughed. She opened her arms to hug Caroline, resting, for a moment, in her dependable embrace.

"I think we brought everything you asked for," Mike said, putting a mesh bag of lemons on the counter and a lidded ceramic container next to it. "These are still warm," he said, tapping the container's lid.

Caroline pulled her phone out of her bag. "Oh, wait, we didn't see this last text. Do you still need marshmallows?"

"We'll find some," Ruth said. She started slicing apples at a furious pace and tossing them into a bowl. "Or, Mike, can you text Tobi and see if they have any?"

"They don't do sugar," Caroline said.

Ruth laughed. She stopped her chopping. "Remember that post Evie did last winter about making lemonade with Meyer lemons and how the twins love it even without sugar? She must have used the word 'Meyer' fifteen times. God forbid we think her kids eat regular lemons."

Caroline nodded and groaned. "Also, who drinks lemonade out of a ceramic mug?"

Mike pulled Caroline in, kissed her on the cheek. "Be nice."

Caroline rolled her eyes at Ruth. Ruth laughed a little, but didn't want Mike to feel bad. Mike was the dearest, kindest man she'd ever known, and she loved him. And not just that, she was grateful that he'd pushed for this dinner, because she'd been dying to meet Tobi and Evie.

"Mikey, we're just teasing," Ruth said. "Teasing ourselves, more than them. We're just jealous."

Before Caroline could say anything to protest, Ruth said, "I'm sure Caroline told you about Siddha."

Mike nodded. "I'm really sorry, I mean—"

Ruth put out her hand. "It's okay, truly. I just wanted to make sure you knew. I'm just so glad you're all here. This will be a good distraction." She gave them both a wide smile, and hoped it looked genuine and not frantic. Or at least, a little more genuine than frantic. "We all just need a nice evening."

"Our specialty," Mike said. His phone pinged and he looked down at it. "She'll bring the marshmallows!"

"They'll probably be those vegan ones," Caroline said. "Gray and hard."

Mike handed Caroline a glass of wine. "Please drink this, for all of our sakes."

Caroline took the glass. "Sorry, sorry," she said. "All around." She raised her glass to Mike, and then Ruth. "I was up half the night trying to finish those supplements for my Rome proposal."

Ruth clapped her hands. "I can't believe you're going to Rome!"

"Well, we'll see," Caroline said. "I'm not going anywhere without the money."

"You'll get it!" Mike and Ruth said at the same time.

Ruth turned back to the oven and pulled out a sheet pan of roasted squash. She lightly touched one to check for doneness, then licked her finger to cool it. "Will you play something?"

"That I can do," Caroline said. She walked through the kitchen into the living room and sat down at the piano. "What is this?" she called. "*Mother Earth News?*"

Ruth came into the doorway to see Caroline holding up a magazine with a flock of sheep on the cover. "It's Wyn's. In case that didn't seem obvious."

"Well, I'm using it as a coaster." She put the magazine down on top of the piano, put her wineglass on it, and sat down. "What do you want to hear?"

"The usuals," Ruth said, going back into the kitchen.

THE FIRST TIME Caroline had come to Ruth's house, she'd seen the piano right away and, taken by its beauty (it was a Steinway, Wyn's great-grandmother's), she asked if she could play it before she'd even taken off her coat.

"Of course," Ruth had said that day. "Play anything." She knew that Caroline was a classically trained musician, and so she expected something from Bach's *The Well-Tempered Clavier* or some other vaguely recognizable piece. But instead, Caroline started the gentle plinking and hum of "The Way We Were," only to, over the course of the next few minutes, belt out an astonishingly Streisandesque rendition of the entire song. Ruth plopped down in the armchair next to the piano and cried. Ruth's mother had died suddenly of a pulmonary embolism when she was eleven years old. This had been her favorite song. "How did you know?" Ruth asked, teary-eyed, when Caroline finished.

Caroline smiled. "Oh, it's everyone's mother's favorite song," she said. "That's why I like to play it. I love mother music. Probably more than I love my mother." Caroline laughed then, and Ruth laughed too, in a way that she never laughed about mothers, never allowed herself to, but that felt truly wonderful.

Caroline played all through that first afternoon, every song Ruth could think of. "Send in the Clowns," "The Circle Game," "California Dreamin'," "Who Knows Where the Time Goes?"—all of it. Caroline knew every song, every word. All the mother music. The kids played, running around inside the house, and then outside, and then inside again. Ruth made spaghetti at some point, and Wyn came home, and everyone ate, and the kids played, and when it was time for Caroline to leave, Ruth said, "Let's be friends forever," and Caroline had said, in the sweetest, most serious voice, "Oh yes, let's do that."

"DID YOU PUT chilies in the beans?" Caroline called from the living room.

Ruth laughed. "I did." And then, more quietly, to Mike, "She's still not going to like them." Ruth tended to cook for her own Midwestern palate, which meant everyone else needed to douse the food she'd made in a lot of chili crisp and hot sauce. "I hope she brought hot sauce."

"She doesn't leave home without it."

"Hey, Mikey—" Wyn was standing at the kitchen window, holding a beer and a pair of tongs. "Come out and see this baby!" Wyn was referring to her new meat smoker, which she'd bought from a childhood friend in Tennessee and had shipped up North. It had taken her three days to assemble it. Ruth was terrified that it was going to burn down their house.

Mike grabbed his beer and headed for the mudroom. "Go out this way," Ruth said, motioning toward the sunporch. "It's easier." The kitchen, for reasons Ruth didn't quite understand, had four points of entry: sunporch, mudroom, hallway to the living room, and a door out to the front yard which Ruth had repeatedly and futilely asked the kids not to use because it would hit the fridge (and a person, if a person happened to be standing at the fridge) when it opened. Last week, after Roz had slammed into her while she was holding a bowl of pudding and a plate of defrosting chicken breasts, both of which she dropped and the dogs proceeded to devour, Ruth had locked the door and hidden the key. Later, when Ruth had asked Wyn if she'd noticed that this new house seemed to have multiples of a lot of things that they only needed one of—stairways, fireplaces, living rooms—Wyn had pretended not to hear her.

Ruth was at the sink filling a pitcher with water for the table when two kids she recognized from Instagram as Tobi and Evie's twins—on the internet they were unnamed, referred to only as "our mudlarks," but Ruth knew from Caroline that their names were Nina and Jules—ran into the kitchen and up the back stairs.

"Hey, hey, you little cuties," she called after them. "Everybody's outside!" And just like that, they came running down the stairs and out again, all without a word.

Ruth laughed. "Did you see that? I think Tobi and Evie are here," she called to Caroline, but Caroline didn't answer. She was deep into a rendition of Carly Simon's "Let the River Run."

Ruth felt a flip of excitement in her stomach. She wiped her hands on a dishtowel and went to the mudroom, where Tobi was dutifully removing her shoes. "Oh, leave them!" Ruth said. "No need!" She reached out to shake Tobi's hand. "I'm Ruth." It was strange to see Tobi in real life, she thought. She looked younger on Instagram.

"Hey, I'm Tobi, thanks so much for having us."

"Oh, we're so glad you all could come."

Evie came in the door, a bottle of wine in each hand. Her hair was pulled back from her face and she was wearing a striped blouse with a deep V-neck tucked into wide-leg jeans. "Hi there," she said, handing the wine to Tobi. She pushed her oversize glasses into her hair before hugging Ruth. "I feel like we already know each other!"

Before Ruth could think of how to respond, Evie said, "Oh shit! I forgot the marshmallows. Hey Tob, did you by chance grab those marshmallows I left out on the counter?"

"I did not," Tobi said, making a sort of grimace at Ruth. "Sorry."

Ruth waved away the apology. Okay, she thought, they're cute, but they're just regular people. Of course, the Instagram thing is just an act. It always is. "Come in the kitchen, let me get you a drink."

Caroline stopped playing and came into the kitchen to greet Tobi and Evie. "Nice haircut," she said to Tobi. She hugged her, then hugged Evie.

Tobi ran her hand over her hair, which was black with glinting strands of silver, closely shaved on one side. She smiled, a wide smile that animated her whole face, snapped her jawline to attention. "Evie did it. One of her many talents."

Evie smiled a bit lasciviously at Tobi.

Okaaay, Ruth thought. She didn't like it when married lesbians were performative with their lust. It was like they were trying to say No lesbian bed death here! It annoyed Ruth. She also still had good sex, but she liked to keep it private.

What Ruth really didn't like (but couldn't turn away from) was the way certain lesbians liked to perform the post-heteropatriarchal family unit. And that was what Evie and Tobi were famous for. Well, maybe not exactly famous, but it was their schtick, and it was all over their company's Instagram, which had something like two hundred thousand followers, and that, at least to Ruth, made them pretty famous.

GoldFynch Pottery—Tobi and Evie, really—took up a lot of space in Ruth's psyche. How she studied those posts! She marveled at the way Evie managed to cultivate a sense of intimacy and collusion with her audience, as though she were telling all two hundred thousand of them something she'd never told anyone before. And about . . . pottery? But that was the thing: the posts were about so much more. They were about being a Jewish lesbian mother in upstate New York, and that was where Evie had Ruth. Their account was the first one Ruth checked when she opened Instagram, not even bothering to scroll through her feed. She'd see a new post and get a delicious wave of dopamine, followed—instantly—by a hot mess of feelings: connection, envy, insecurity, smugness, wanting. So much wanting.

It wasn't that Ruth wanted any of Evie's possessions, and god knows she didn't want her children. She was mildly jealous of Evie's looks—her wavy auburn hair and angular face with its light dusting of freckles—but, having spent more years than she cared to admit cursing her own dark, tight curls and moon-shaped face, didn't feel much more than her companionable lifelong jealousy of any woman with compliant hair and prominent cheekbones. No, the true root of Ruth's desire was Evie's life force, her ambition, her orientation toward the world. Evie seemed to get up every morning and do a day in an entirely different way than Ruth, and Ruth wanted—oh how she wanted!—to know what it felt like to have a day like Evie's.

Ruth knew so much more about Tobi and Evie's lives than she should, and yet there it all was, on a public account—generated for the sole purpose of public display—so why did she feel as though she was stalking them? She'd asked Caroline many times if it was all true, or if they were faking in some way, and Caroline said that she hated to disappoint Ruth as much as she hated to say positive things about Tobi and Evie, but she was pretty sure it was real. They were the Platonic ideal of lesbians, the sort of couple *The New York Times* and straight women who didn't know how to make their husbands do more housework liked to trot out as proof that it's much easier for queer couples to achieve domestic equality. A proposition that, in Ruth's experience, was entirely untrue. But Tobi and Evie were here to prove her wrong. They did everything fifty-fifty: they ran a business together and had even managed to have twins so that each of them could always be caring for a child. Caroline had told Ruth that Evie didn't even breastfeed because it was inherently unequal. They worked tirelessly to rid their marriage of the scourge of inequality. Meanwhile, Ruth sometimes thought that she and Wyn went out of their way to foster it.

In all fairness, though, Ruth and Wyn had shared the supreme domestic burden: childbearing. Much to the surprise of the people who met them now, Ruth had not carried all their children. Before she met Ruth, Wyn hadn't planned on getting pregnant, although she was adamant about wanting a large family. She was great with kids, and from the moment they met at a party hosted by a co-worker of Ruth's who happened to be Wyn's college roommate, Wyn was smitten with Siddha. She'd spent most of the party trying to convince Ruth to let Siddha have ice cream. ("I love watching kids eat ice cream," Wyn had said, which made Ruth love her instantly. Well, that and her gorgeous legs.) During their courtship she'd told Ruth she was planning on at least four kids. "I can give you one, but how are you planning to get those other three?" Ruth had asked her. "I'm hoping my future wife will want to carry them," Wyn said. Ruth laughed. "This potential future wife is done having babies," she'd said. "So you might want to rethink that."

And Wyn did. She rethought it, adjusted course, and a few months after they married, she started taking prenatal vitamins and sending Ruth links to potential donor profiles. When they settled on a plan, Wyn stopped her two-day-a-week commute into the city and joined a tech start-up in Radclyffe as their CFO. Ruth had to hand it to Wyn, she could be very flexible when it resulted in getting what she wanted.

The pee was barely dry on the pregnancy test stick when Ruth started panicking that she'd made a huge mistake. It would have been much easier to be pregnant herself than to endure Wyn's pregnancy. Wyn hated being pregnant (Ruth could have told her—and did tell her, many times—that she would), and complained ceaselessly. For nine months, as Wyn recited a litany of discomforts and an exhaustive catalog of psychological and sensory responses to pregnancy (The amazing smell of wet bricks! The sweating! The size of her nipples!), Ruth wanted to scream This is not news! I have done this! But she knew that you can't yell at a pregnant woman.

But then Gilly was born, and it turned out Wyn was built for birth. It was the ultimate athletic event. She squatted, she breathed, she sweated, she pushed out that nine-pound baby in five pushes. And as soon as she did, Ruth forgave Wyn all her complaining, because Gilly was a miracle: a perfect miniature Wyn, blond and green-eyed and entirely irresistible.

"Thank you so much for Gilly," Ruth would say in tearful gratitude, when, after having driven Siddha to preschool, she'd take sweet little Gilly from Wyn and walk the dogs with the baby in a carrier strapped to her chest—a chest that was not swollen with pooling breast milk. When Gilly started to fuss, she'd just turn back for home and hand the squawking, starving baby to Wyn. Then Ruth could go in the kitchen and make herself a double espresso that would have no bearing on Gilly's sleep cycles. Even better, she could manage Siddha's adjustment to big sisterhood without the fog of postpartum hormones. She felt competent, she felt solid. Siblings were a blessing; Siddha would grow to love Gilly; a little tension was to be expected. Ruth had never been a happier mother. And as it turned out, the birth had an amnesiac effect on Wyn, who seemed to have no recollection of how much she'd hated pregnancy. She was ready to try for another when Gilly was a year old. Why not? Ruth thought. We're really in it now. Roz was born just two weeks after Gilly's second birthday.

But Roz's birth was more complicated than Gilly's, and Wyn announced she was done, despite being one baby short of her self-determined destiny. Ruth asked, Couldn't they be happy with three? But the truth was, by then, Ruth was fully in the thrall of the large-family mythology. She loved her three children and was astounded by the good fortune of being able to give Siddha not one, but two sisters. Ruth was an only child, and she'd thought that Siddha would be too, and that had seemed sweetly fated to her, a nesting-doll replication of her own only-child childhood. But once Gilly arrived, and then Roz, Ruth saw how the three children were a little pack, how they turned to each other for comfort and for entertainment.

She began to see siblings as a seawall against the ocean of life's hardships, and she decided to take up the task of completing theirs. When Roz was two, Ruth said she'd do it, she'd be the one to have their fourth. She was only thirty-three, after all. What was one more baby? The answer to this question turned out to be debilitating morning sickness that sent Ruth to the hospital for IV fluids twice, and sciatic pain so intense she had to sleep in a recliner. Roz and Gilly were always sick, Ruth was exhausted, and she felt like she was neglecting Siddha, who was now a busy and complicated ten-year-old. No more, she vowed. Absolutely no more.

Abe was born two weeks early, tiny and sleepy. He grew fast on the love of his siblings, who doted on him; even Roz, who was only three years old when he was born, would stroke his head when he fussed. And Ruth, exhausted, dazed, was the happiest she had ever been. They'd done it. They'd made a family. Two weeks after Abe was born, Ruth called her head of school and resigned. I'll take a year or two, she thought, and let things settle a bit. That was seven years ago.

"BEHOLD!" WYN SAID, bursting into the kitchen with a platter of smoked ribs, as though they were a newborn king and not just one of the many dishes they (Ruth) had made for the party. But Ruth did have to admit they looked pretty good. And so did Wyn. She'd changed out of her work clothes and was wearing a pair of jeans and a faded denim shirt with the top buttons undone. Her hair was a bit damp (had she somehow managed to take a shower in the last fifteen minutes?), and she had the look of effortless, confident sexiness that could still make Ruth go weak, or at the very least (and much more important), let go of the day's grievances.

Ruth took the platter of ribs from Wyn and slid the tray into the warm oven. "Meet Tobi and Evie," she said. "And grab them some beers?"

"Welcome to Sugar Hill!" Wyn said. She handed Tobi and then Evie each a beer from the fridge. "Want a tour?"

"Very much!" Evie said, clinking her bottle against Wyn's. She peered through the kitchen into the dining room. "This place is just amazing. And what a gorgeous drive. I didn't know this part of Radclyffe even existed. It's so close to town but it feels like you're in the woods."

"That's what we couldn't pass up," Wyn said.

"Your neighbors have horses?" Tobi asked, pointing out the window to the far pasture where horses were grazing.

"They're actually ours," Wyn said.

"Wow," Tobi said in a tone that, it seemed to Ruth, was saying a lot more than wow.

"They belonged to Wyn's sister," Ruth said quickly. "Her kids left home; she didn't have time to take care of them anymore." Ruth heard her own intentional vagueness, the way that "left home" sounded as though the kids had just gone off to college, when all Wyn's nieces and nephews had left home at fourteen to go to boarding school, just like Wyn and her siblings had, and their parents before them. On Ruth and Wyn's first official date—Reuben sandwiches and beers at a dive bar—Ruth had said, "Just so you know, as an educator, I don't believe in boarding school." Wyn had just nodded and said, "Duly noted." Later when they'd fucked and Ruth's head had spun with what Wyn had done to her, and Ruth had rhapsodized about Wyn's skill, her range, Wyn had laughed and said, "Hate to break it to you, babe, but all that was brought to you courtesy of boarding school."

Evie and Tobi walked from the kitchen into the living room, oohing and ahhing over the wide floorboards, the original woodwork, all beautifully restored, the windows, the built-in bookcases flanking the enormous stone fireplace. "God, it's all so gorgeous," Tobi said.

"Thank you," Ruth said. "It all needs a lot of work."

"Are you going to keep the pool?"

"Definitely," Wyn said, while at the same time Ruth said, "Probably not."

Everyone laughed.

"It's low on the list," Ruth said. "There's a lot to do."

"Which I see as a great adventure," Wyn said. "Ruth isn't so sure."

Ruth felt her face get hot. Before she could say anything, Evie asked, "And you really left Cavalier Tech altogether? I hope you got a decent buyout."

"Quite decent," Wyn said. "Best decision I've ever made. I had to give this a try, and now that the kids are older, it just seemed like the right time."

Ruth went back in the kitchen. She wasn't in the mood for this story again, the myth of Wyn's sticking it to the man and heading back to the land to do the one thing she truly loved in this life. It was true that Wyn had always loved rural life; she'd grown up in the suburbs of D.C., where her father worked for the World Bank, but she'd spent every summer—the happiest days of her childhood—at her grandparents' horse farm near Nashville. Wyn had been her grandfather's favorite, and he taught her to ride and care for horses, and to hunt. He was a gentleman farmer, a term that had always seemed problematic to Ruth, although she couldn't exactly explain why. Wyn worked alongside her grandmother in the garden, took care of animals, built fences, stacked hay, fixed the tractor. It was lovely in the recounting, in the way that it seemed to Ruth most childhoods except hers were. (Ruth's childhood had been more of a Grimms' fairy tale, in which the mother, once golden and loving and warm, vanished.)

When the pandemic started and the kids' school had closed, the family, including their two dogs, one hamster, and two goldfish—three if you count Veronica, who died en route and was buried in a shallow grave dug with a camping spoon at a rest stop on I-80—temporarily moved to Wyn's family farm in Tennessee. For the first time in her life, Ruth experienced rural living. After the first harrowing months passed and they'd settled into a strange rhythm of life, Ruth enjoyed it, enjoyed the space, the green, the animals. Still, when Wyn suggested they start looking for a farm of their own when they returned to Radclyffe, Ruth balked. She loved their house on Olive Street; she'd had enough upheaval and wanted to settle back in, even though Wyn was right, they'd outgrown the house in more ways than one. Luckily for Ruth, Wyn's list of farm "must haves" was absurdly long, so they had a few more happily crowded years in their house before the real estate agent told them about Sugar Hill.

The first time they saw it, Ruth knew they were moving. Sugar Hill was exactly what Wyn had been waiting for: a small farm with just enough space for animals, two well-built barns, a few established garden plots, plus a grand, rambling farmhouse. Ruth couldn't say no, even though she wanted to (and not just because she couldn't bear the idea of living somewhere that had a name). Instead, she asked questions. What about Siddha? Is a farm really the best place for a teenager? Wyn had talked with Siddha; she was thrilled by the idea. Then: What about the drive? We both hate to drive. Wyn had clocked the drive, and it was only fifteen minutes from their old house, in the direction of the kids' school. They'd be driving less!

The real problem was, Ruth didn't have a competing dream. What was she going to say? I really want to stay in this little house we've entirely outgrown and drink my morning coffee in silence and think a little bit about my future, but mostly about what I'll make for dinner? That was the hard part of being married to Wyn: the forcefulness of who she was, and what she wanted. It was hard to want anything big enough to measure up. So they'd bought the farm, and Wyn had quit her job. And they were, for the first time in their married life, living solely on Wyn's family money. Which, honestly, Ruth wished was the part of all this that bothered her. In the months since they'd moved to the farmhouse, Ruth had been consumed with a restlessness, trying, and for the most part failing, to come up with a plan for what she wanted to do next.

She felt out of practice thinking about herself, and oddly unfamiliar with time and how to use it. The last few years had passed at such a strange and inconsistent pace. When she'd quit her job, assuming she'd go back to teaching when Abe was a little older, she'd had no real sense of what "a little older" was. Now she was pretty sure it was somewhere around eighteen. Because these kids—these *four* kids—were so much work. Had someone told her that it would get easier as they got older? Had that been Wyn, or maybe Wyn's mother? Either way, they'd been wrong. The work increased at the same rate as the laundry. And the dishes. And the dentist appointments. Throw in a pandemic, a move to Tennessee, a move back home eighteen months later, and then—just when everything was evening out again—another move, this time to their own farm, and Ruth was left spinning. Abe was seven and Ruth was no closer to figuring out what she wanted to do next.

CAROLINE WAS AT the stove, stirring the brussels sprouts. She smiled, kindly, at Ruth. "It's quite a story," she said. "Are you tired of it?"

Ruth peeked back into the living room before she spoke, making sure the tour had moved on. "Sort of."

"It really is a beautiful house," Caroline said.

"Yeah," Ruth said. "It really is." She went to the fridge and took out the butter. "The thing is, and I know you've heard me say this a million times, I miss our Olive Street house so much. I know it's crazy, I mean there was no way we could keep living there, it was way too small, but this—this is a lot." Ruth felt a stab of sadness, thinking of the last night they'd all slept in the old house together. It had been late June, just after school was out, and Siddha—whose attic room was already emptied—had slept next to Abe, squeezed into his twin bed. When

Ruth had checked on them before going to bed herself and seen the tangle of their bodies, Abe's arm flung across Siddha's back, the mess of Siddha's curls on Abe's pillow, she hadn't been able to hold back the tears.

Caroline took the butter from Ruth and unwrapped a stick, put it on a plate with a spreader. "It's a lot. Have you still not listed it?"

"Not yet," Ruth said. "It's so dumb. Of course we need to sell it. We can't have an empty house sitting there. But that's the problem with all the work the farm needed, how it made the move from Olive Street drag out for so long. There's still furniture over there. I mean, the other day I stopped by on my way home because we were out of toilet paper and I thought there might be a stash in the linen closet. How ridiculous is that?"

"Was there?"

"There was!" Ruth said. "Twelve rolls. And a bag of dog food. It's like my own private Costco."

Caroline laughed. "Tell me when you go next time, and I'll give you my list."

"Will do," Ruth said. "Anyway, now I've got this Siddha situation and"—she lowered her voice to a whisper—"a dead Elliot on my hands."

"No time for real estate," Caroline agreed.

As Wyn led Tobi and Evie back through the kitchen, Ruth handed each of them a bowl of food. "Let's head out!" she said in a chipper voice, knowing that she sounded a little controlling and a little shrill. Wyn gave her a look, which she ignored. She mouthed, Siddha? to Wyn, but Wyn just shrugged.

Everyone spilled out into the yard and made their way to the sukkah, which, in the end, was beautiful. Wyn and Bex had given it a latticed roof by crisscrossing the beams with leafy branches, then strung the whole thing with lights. Ruth's heart swelled at the sight of Siddha laughing with Mike under the lights, her curls still wet from the shower, the dark gloss of them dampening the straps of her dress. She saw Caroline walk over and put her arm around Siddha, then kiss her gently on the head, and saw how Siddha leaned into Caroline, and Ruth felt tears behind her eyes. She blinked them away as she walked toward them.

"Siddha, have you met Tobi and Evie?" Ruth asked, extending an arm toward her. Siddha gave her the tiniest, dirtiest look, which Ruth read as Why the fuck are you asking me that? You know I haven't. But because Siddha was also Wyn's daughter, and Wyn believed in instilling social graces in children with the same fervor that evangelicals believed in instilling doctrinal obedience, Siddha turned her face to Tobi and Evie, smiling, and said, "No, but I love your pottery."

Evie laughed and said, "You're sitting with me, doll."

"Oh, sorry, but I'm going out," Siddha said.

"Stay just for a minute or two?" Ruth said, hoping she didn't sound too needy.

Siddha glared at her. But she didn't leave, which felt like a victory.

As everyone was finding spots at the table, Ruth realized the candles weren't lit and she needed matches. She dashed into the house, bumping into Wyn in the mudroom, a pair of tongs in each of her hands.

Wyn leaned in and kissed her. "Hi," she whispered. "You okay?"

"Totally," Ruth said.

"You seem a little frantic."

"You seem a little buzzed."

Wyn laughed. "I might be." She kissed Ruth again. "Bex is here. They're out in the barn taking a call but they're staying for dinner. I need to grab another plate."

"I had the kids set a place for them," Ruth said. "I need matches."

"I have a lighter in my pocket."

Ruth slid her hand into Wyn's back pocket and pulled out the lighter. She kissed her again and went back outside. She gave the lighter to Siddha, and a few moments later, the table was dotted with lit candles of all heights casting a warm glow on the plates and bowls of food, mismatched napkins, pint jars of water and lemonade for the kids, and Abe's odd naturalist decor. He'd been obedient, at least: no poop, and nothing dead. Mostly it looked to Ruth like an assortment of rocks from the driveway. The places were set with GoldFynch plates of varied earth tones. The dishes were a few years old, but in pristine condition, because Wyn didn't like using them—something about the sound of cutlery on the ceramic. Ruth agreed, although that hadn't stopped her from buying service for twenty. She would never admit it, but she was indifferent to the pottery. It was the Gold-Fynches themselves that kept Ruth coming back for more.

"Nice dishes," Tobi said, smiling.

Ruth smiled. Tobi really was cute. "We love them," Ruth lied. "We use them all the time."

When everyone was gathered, Ruth motioned for Gilly to plug in the last strand of lights and Nina and Jules, whose lives, Ruth guessed, were devoid of anything even vaguely representative of Christmas, cheered and clapped.

"Sit, sit," Ruth said. "Everyone sit." Everyone did, and then just as quickly everyone stood up again: Mike ran inside for more beer, Evie went back to her car to grab the biscuits she'd brought from Bread Euphoria. The kids switched places, then cried because they wanted their original seats back, then their parents told them to please just sit down. Abe was having a hard time keeping up with moving his personalized rock and leaf formations. Ruth put her hand on his shoulder. "It's okay, Abie," she whispered. "You can let it go. That's the beauty of nature, it'll work for anybody."

When everyone was finally seated, Mike stood. Ruth groaned. "Not again!"

Mike laughed. "I just want to make a toast," he said.

Ruth put her hand over her heart. She mouthed, Sorry!

"To Ruth and Wyn, for hosting, for bringing us together."

"To Ruth and Wyn!" Everyone raised their glasses.

"To the harvest," Tobi said. "Moadim l'simcha."

Ruth winked at Luca. He winked back, although he had to hold his eye closed to do it.

There was much clinking of glasses and bottles, and as everyone was drinking, Bex came to the table, an apologetic smile on their face. "Hey, sorry about that, had to take a quick call."

Wyn clapped them on the back. "Do you know Tobi and Evie?"

"Tobi!" Bex reached out their hand to shake Tobi's, and then Evie's. "We met right before I came over here. At Elliot Shepkins' memorial. Small world up here, I love it."

Ruth froze. Wyn froze. The memorial had been earlier today? Siddha did not freeze, but instead, when Evie stood to shake Bex's hand, she also stood, and left the table. Ruth watched her walk across the grass to the house.

"Oh boy," Roz said.

"Oh boy, what?" Luca said. Caroline shook her head gently at him.

Ruth got up to follow Siddha, but Wyn reached out and put her hand on her arm to still her. Wyn gave Bex her beer bottle and raised her own water glass. "Bear with me one moment, before all this beautiful food gets cold, while we thank you all, beloved friends and family, for helping us mark the first harvest at Sugar Hill. In the words of Thoreau—"

Oh Jesus, Wyn, really? Ruth thought. She felt panicked. She needed to get to Siddha.

"Let us live in each season as it passes; breathe the air, drink the drink, taste the fruit, and resign ourselves to the influences of each."

"Here's to resigning myself to the influences," Tobi said, taking a long swig of beer.

Everyone's faces were shining in the glow of candles, of booze, of Wyn smoothing things over. But Ruth was not shining. She was annoyed. She shook off Wyn's hand and left the table without a word, because what was she going to say? Excuse me, I'm just going to run inside and tell my daughter that even though we've lied to her all her life, she can believe me when I say we had no idea there was a memorial for her dead father today?

Of course Wyn and Ruth would have told Siddha about the memorial if they'd known about it. Of course they would have taken her. This last part might not be true, but Ruth was going to say it, she most definitely was going to say it. She was going to start—somehow, somewhere—to clean this whole thing up. She wasn't going to keep waiting. She wasn't going to give Siddha space. Wyn was wrong about that, and Ruth knew it.

She went inside and called for Siddha, but there was no answer. Ruth went upstairs; Siddha wasn't in her room. She went to the attic, but Siddha wasn't there, either. Ruth looked out the attic window at the driveway, and saw that Siddha's car was gone. She reached into her pocket for her phone to check Siddha's location. Siddha had turned off location sharing. "Fuck," Ruth whispered. She sent Siddha a text. *Are you going to Eliza's?* She looked at the phone for a few moments, waiting for the three dots to appear, but the screen was blank. Ruth groaned and went back to the party.

No one seemed to have noticed her absence, or if they did, no one mentioned it. Wyn tried to make eye contact with her a few times, but Ruth avoided her. She was angry. Why hadn't Wyn let her go to Siddha? Ruth drank a glass of wine, and half of another, and felt herself relax a little. She saw that everyone was warming to each other, having a nice time. Despite the mess of things, she was glad.

Before long, the kids, sated and tired of sitting, abandoned the table for the trampoline. The candles burned down. Evie squeezed the orange peel from her drink over the flames and the air filled with a warm citrusy smell. Wyn brought out two bottles of scotch. And when they could no longer put off the children's begging for a fire, Tobi went down behind the barn to manage the operation. After a while, Ruth thought maybe she or Wyn should go down and take a turn, but Jules and Nina were the youngest kids down there, and the unspoken rule was that the parents of the youngest were de facto in charge. It wasn't fair, but nothing about parenthood was. Besides, Ruth felt she'd done enough. She'd even found an old bag of stale marshmallows in the pantry. And it wasn't like Mike and Wyn were so worried about taking their turn. They'd gone off to the barn with Bex, bringing dinner to the horses and, Ruth assumed, smoking pot. The kids kept running back and forth across the lawn, going in and out of the house, slamming the door each time.

Ruth felt her phone buzz in her pocket. She pulled it out, and saw there was a text from Siddha.

there now

Well, Ruth thought, at least she told me where she is. I guess that's something. She was choosing to ignore the very real possibility that Siddha was lying. She hearted the message, then put the phone back in her pocket.

"So," Ruth said to Evie, "did you do anything fun this summer?"

"Oh, you know, we work so much," Evie said. "It's a busy season for us. But we did manage to get away to this amazing camp for queer families."

Ruth nodded and made a quiet "how interesting" noise, although the truth was, she knew all about their summer camp: the adventure-loving families, the intergenerational kitchen workers, the folk songs, the zine making, the overnight canoe trips. It sounded like fun to Ruth, who'd grown up reading books about summer camp but had never been. After reading Evie's posts, Ruth had searched the camp website for last-minute openings (there were none). When Ruth asked Wyn if maybe she'd want to go next year, she'd said, "No way. I did my time at camp."

"But you loved it!" Ruth said.

"Not as much as I love sending our kids to camp without us."

Ruth wouldn't press the point. Because as much as Evie's posts made her feel like she should want to go to family camp, Wyn was right. They were not a family camp kind of family. And those two weeks when all their kids' camps overlapped? They were the best two weeks of the year. Wyn was not wrong about this. Wyn was not wrong about many things, which was why Ruth loved her, and also why she found her maddening.

Ruth looked over at Caroline. What did she think of this amazing camp? But Caroline wasn't paying attention to the conversation. She had pulled a distressed Luca onto her lap and was trying to convince him to go back down to the fire with the other kids.

Evie went on, "Gilly and Roz are the sweetest names. How did you two come up with those?"

Caroline stood, Luca's hand in hers. "Luca and I are going to check out the fire," she said.

"Great idea," Ruth said. "There are loads of marshmallows down there, Luca."

Luca gave Ruth the sweetest little thumbs-up.

Ruth turned back to Evie. "They're our moms' names. Well, sort of. Our moms are Gilda and Rosalynn, which are the girls' full names, but we never call them that. And by some crazy coincidence we both have a grandfather named Abraham, so that was easy, although we've only ever called him Abe, every day of his life. Wyn's real name is Winifred, so she's the one who made a good case for giving everyone strange names but never using them. WASPs excel at nicknames."

Evie laughed. "Well, they have to, because they're always naming their kids after people who are still alive."

"Oh, well, my mom's dead," Ruth said. "So there's not a lot of confusion there."

"Oh god," Evie said. "I'm so sorry, I—"

"No, no," Ruth said. "No, don't be. Long ago. I was just a girl." She smiled. "I absolutely love that Gilly has her name."

"And Siddha?" Evie asked, gently.

Ruth wondered if she knew something. "Oh, well, I was a real Jew-Bu in those days," she said. "I regret nothing, but Siddha's not so happy about it. Cultural appropriation and all that."

Evie laughed. "Nina is named after Nina Simone, so we're in trouble on that front too."

"I recommend not telling her. Maybe just say you liked the name."

"Smart," Evie said. "And it also aligns with my main parenting philosophy, which is to keep information sharing to a minimum."

Ruth felt herself, surprisingly, loosen as she chatted with Evie. She was fun. Ruth had known that Evie was older (by about ten years, she thought, according to her Instagram math) but their age difference hadn't really registered until now. Ruth liked to say that you were only as old as your youngest child, which was probably because having a seven-year-old made her feel younger than having a sixteen-year-old, and Ruth liked feeling young. Evie didn't act like the mother of five-year-olds, and she also didn't seem like she was particularly interested in feeling or appearing young, although now that Ruth could see Evie's auburn hair in real life it was clearly just an expensive (and gorgeous) dye job. But it really wasn't anything physical, just that Evie wasn't as animated as Ruth might have expected, as lively. She seemed quieter, and more real.

Caroline came back to the table. Ruth wanted to ask her how it was all going down there, but she knew she wouldn't want to talk about Luca in front of Evie.

"I should probably relieve Tobi," Evie said. "It's my turn."

Ruth avoided Caroline's eyes. "Sounds good," she said.

Evie stood to go and Caroline started gathering dishes.

"Oh, leave it all," Ruth said. "Sit with me."

"I'd guess I have about four minutes before Luca's back here, crying."

Ruth put her hand over Caroline's. "Only mom," she said.

"Best mom," Caroline said, and put her hand over Ruth's.

This was a joke between them, their origin joke. Ruth and Caroline had met at a Music Together class when Abe and Luca were a year old. Ruth had taken Abe because she realized she'd never done a single thing with him other than schlep him around to his sisters' activities, and she was feeling bad about it. Before the class started, two women were talking loudly about a book they'd just read, something radical about how a mother needed to understand that she—despite being imperfect, flawed, and inexperienced—was the only mother her child needed. It was imperative to banish "best mom" thoughts and worries, which were harming your child. Your kid only needs you, their one mother.

Ruth, who was feeling annoyed, sleep deprived, and generally unseen as a lesbian lately, interrupted the women's gushing. "Yeah, well, the thing is, I'm married to a woman, so I actually have a lot invested in being the *best* mom." Caroline had laughed, loudly, and no one else had, and Ruth had decided they would be friends. She never went back to the music class.

"Are Mike and Wyn still smoking in the barn?" Caroline asked.

"I have no idea, but I think it's safe to say yes."

"Mike was supposed to be on Luca duty," Caroline said.

"Oh, Luca is fine," Ruth said.

"So is Siddha," Caroline said, in a tone that matched Ruth's own benignly dishonest reassurance.

They looked at each other and laughed.

6

Caroline was wild with feelings as they drove home from the party. She was driving because Mike was not only in no state to drive, but also asleep in the passenger seat, which annoyed her. And Luca was asleep in the backseat, which gutted her. She kept looking at him in the rearview mirror, his head thrown back, his mouth wide open, snuffling out tiny snores with each rise and fall of his little chest. In the darkness and shadow of the car, he could have been any age. Little boy, teenager, old man. She thought of how quickly these seven years had gone, and how quickly the next seven would, and how then she'd be the only woman in a house of men, their huge feet, their smells, their mysterious, unplumbable depths. How lonely she'd be! She thought of Ruth in her enormous house with all its bookshelves and couches, pianos (okay, only one piano, but what a piano it was!), fireplaces, and all the children, all the animals. Life was always so loud at Ruth's, in the best way. And Caroline's life was loud too, she supposed, but not at all in the best way. She looked at Luca again, her one beautiful boy, and thought of him leaving, and her eyes welled.

Caroline had a habit of borrowing future loneliness. She'd spent most of her life feeling lonely, and even at times when the loneliness receded, she would feel herself heading toward it again. Loneliness was familiar, it was its own uncomfortable comfort. But Ruth had been a great antidote for Caroline's loneliness. From the beginning, she had claimed Caroline, in a way that no other woman ever had. Ruth said things like, "Women like us don't see it that way," or "When you're like us," and Caroline's heart would sing, although sometimes Caroline wasn't really sure Ruth's declarations rang true. Was Caroline the sort of woman who wouldn't even consider lip fillers? Had no interest in ziplining? Would never make her own hummus? Caroline didn't know, but she also didn't care. She loved Ruth, loved being claimed by her. There was just something a little different about tonight, something that had left Caroline feeling unsure, and now, driving home in this car of sleeping males, Caroline was lonely.

She pulled into their driveway and just as she was turning off the car, Luca, who she'd thought was still asleep, startled her with a question.

"Is Siddha's dad dead?"

Caroline felt a sickly warmth rise in her throat. "Oh, um, well—" Caroline said, whacking Mike's leg to wake him up. She coughed a little before she spoke, trying to clear her throat, to calm her voice. "Well, Siddha doesn't really have a dad, but, um—yes. Yes, the person who helped Ruth and Wyn—well, really just Ruth actually—um, but also Wyn in a way, if you think about it, although not to make Gilly and Roz. I mean, they had another helper . . . I mean, actually, really—um, yes. That person—that person died."

"So Siddha's helper died? Or her dad? Because Roz told me that Bex was at Siddha's dad's funeral today."

Caroline looked at Mike. She didn't like where this was going.

Mike ran his hand through his hair, opened his eyes wide, trying to wake himself up. He turned and looked at Luca. "He was Siddha's helper, buddy. Her helper. Siddha has two moms, just like Jules and Nina."

Caroline pinched Mike's hand. Seriously? Why did you bring them up?

"A helper isn't a dad," Luca said.

"That is absolutely right," Caroline said. "And another word for helper is 'donor,' like we've talked about, but a donor isn't a dad, either."

"Then why did Roz say it was her dad?"

"Oh, maybe she was just a little confused."

"About the dad part or the dead part?"

"Um, the dad part. But yes, he is dead. Her donor is dead."

"Did you know him?"

"No," Caroline said at the same moment that Mike said "Just a little."

You can't be serious, Caroline telepathed. When she'd come home from the pond two days ago and told Mike all about Ruth and Elliot, then asked if Mike had known him, he said he'd once stopped by Barton Falls Hardware on his way home from Boston because they'd been out of duct tape. Caroline didn't see how buying a roll of duct tape from somebody counted as knowing him, even "a little."

"Oh," Luca said. Caroline could almost see his brain working, shuffling the facts around like puzzle pieces on a card table. Only this puzzle, to complete the metaphor, was one of those ratty old ones you find on the shelf at a beach house with lots of missing pieces.

"Any more questions?" Caroline said, as though she'd just done an upstanding job of clearly and honestly answering the ones he'd already asked.

"No," Luca said.

"Okay then!" Caroline said. "Let's get those teeth brushed." She opened her car door.

Luca slowly unbuckled his seatbelt, then climbed out of the car. "So Dad isn't Jules and Nina's dad?"

"No!" Caroline and Mike answered. With a hand on each of his shoulders, Caroline ushered Luca up the front walk and into the house.

They went inside, where Caroline steered Luca into the bathroom, wiped his face with a warm washcloth, put toothpaste on his toothbrush, and reminded him to pee before he got into bed. She walked down the hall to his bedroom, where Mike had already pulled back the covers and cued up Luca's audiobook, *The Cricket in Times Square*, which he listened to every night. When Luca came in, Caroline gave him half a melatonin gummy, wondering for the one-thousandth time why they didn't give him the gummy before he brushed his teeth, but oh well, there was no changing the ritual now. She kissed Luca good night, turned off the light, and closed the door.

When Caroline got to her own bedroom, Mike was lying on the bed with his eyes closed. She stood next to him. Without opening his eyes, he said, "We need to talk about that."

"We sure do," Caroline said. "But not now."

Mike squeezed her hand in thanks, and an instant later he was asleep. Caroline changed into her pajamas and went back downstairs to make herself a cup of tea. She filled the kettle and sorted some mail while she waited for the water to boil. She flipped through *Bon Appétit* and dog-eared a few recipes for Mike, then pinned a mailer advertising a gutter cleaning service to the bulletin board. She couldn't stop thinking about Luca, and his questions. He'd been five years old when they'd first told him that Mike had given Tobi and Evie the sperm they needed to make the twins, and he'd taken it in stride. He'd had a few questions about the logistics of getting the sperm out of Mike's body and into Evie's, but even those weren't terribly hard to answer.

The question that Caroline couldn't seem to answer right now was *Why*. Why had she and Mike agreed to give Tobi and Evie Mike's sperm, and why had Tobi and Evie asked? Why had any of them thought it was a reasonable idea, let alone a good one? The answer, Caroline reminded herself, was what Mike had told her all those years ago, when she'd first asked him about his parents and if he had any siblings. "I don't have parents," he said. "Or siblings. But I have my aunt Lynne and my cousin Tobi and they're all I need. They're everything."

When Mike was fifteen years old, his mother walked out, leaving Mike with his dad, an alcoholic who worked the night shift at the GE plant in Pittsfield, Massachusetts. Mike's mother had been a cleaner at a yoga retreat center in the Berkshires. When the weather was bad, she would stay over at the center, which meant she was often away from home for days at a time. When she finally returned, she'd bring Mike food from the dining room, strange things like tofu and seitan and millet bread. Mike, who lived on egg noodles and butter when she was away, would inhale the food.

One night, when Mike's dad was at work and Mike was tucking into a plate of pureed squash with kale and pepitas, his mom told him that she'd been offered a job as head of housekeeping at a newly built satellite retreat center in India. Did he want to come with her? She understood if he wanted to stay, especially since he'd just made the varsity basketball team. "She wasn't really asking me to go with her," Mike had said when he first recounted the heartbreaking story to Caroline. "I don't even think she could have taken me." That was the worst part as far as Caroline was concerned, that his mother had made it seem like his choice. How she hated this woman she'd never known!

Mike's mom was gone the next morning, and Mike never saw her again. He kept going to school, rifled around in kitchen drawers for enough cash to buy peanut butter and Hamburger Helper at Price Chopper, and tried to stay away from his dad, which wasn't too hard, considering that he was mostly either at work or passed out on the couch.

This was when Tobi and her mother, Lynne, who was Mike's father's sister, had come into the picture. About a month after his mom left, Mike came home from basketball practice to find Lynne sitting at the kitchen table. "Pack your stuff," she'd said. "You're coming to live with Tobi and me in Boston." As the story went, Mike said, "No way," and Lynne said, "Don't talk back to me, young man, you either pack your bag or I will." And with that, Mike felt, for the first time in his life, the force of parental love.

He moved into Lynne and Tobi's house, where he slept in an unheated sunporch in the warm months, and on the living room pull-out couch in winter. It was a small, worn-out house, but a peaceful one. Lynne's AA *Little Red Book* was always out on the coffee table in the living room, and the serenity prayer was taped on the front of a cabinet in both the kitchen and the bathroom. There were lit candles on the dinner table every night, even though dinner was rarely more than spaghetti with meatballs or chicken à la king, and all the plates were chipped, the silverware mismatched. Mike had had no idea it was possible to live this way, to fall asleep at night with the assurance that nothing would wake him before morning. He enrolled in Tobi's high school and made the basketball team after Lynne convinced the coach to let him try out mid-season. He got a dishwashing job at a restaurant owned by a friend of Lynne's. Three years later, Mike and Tobi both graduated with honors and went off to UMass, where they lived together in an off-campus apartment.

Lynne had come to Caroline and Mike's wedding, an entirely secular affair held at the Jamaica Plain courthouse. When the judge pronounced them husband and wife, Lynne stood and, to the horror of Caroline's parents—a horror that stemmed more from a devotion to social norms than to a Judeo-Christian God—performed a traditional Hopi wedding chant she'd learned at a sober-living retreat in Sedona. It was the first time Caroline had ever seen Mike cry.

The love Mike had for his family—small as that family was—was grand and ferocious and mutual. It was like nothing Caroline had ever seen before, and certainly nothing she'd experienced. She'd heard plenty of stories of neglect and abandonment, but she'd never known anyone who'd lost as much as Mike had, and then turned around and been loved—and loved in return—so completely. Every time they were all together, Caroline marveled at the sweet balance they struck: the raucous but intimate teasing, the way they cared without being overbearing, were honest without being critical. And they were always, always doing things for each other. Caroline had once heard someone say that love is a verb, and while at the time she'd sort of understood what the person had meant, it was Mike's family that brought the aphorism to life. Lynne, Tobi, and Mike seemed to exist in a Möbius strip of offering and care.

Caroline and Mike lived in Boston, just a few miles away from Lynne, and the logistics and details of their lives remained intertwined even after Mike and Caroline were married. Lynne's car was in the shop? Mike drove her to work. Mike was flying in late? Lynne met him at the airport with a sandwich. And when Tobi came into town from Radclyffe, well, it was an all-out festival of mutual attention. Concert tickets, pot roasts, a new coat of paint in Lynne's bathroom. Mike was just as attentive—if not more so—to Caroline, but Tobi and Lynne showed very little interest in enlarging their circle of care to include her. And when she tried to ease her way into the dynamic, making her famous banana bread for Lynne's drum circle, buying Tobi's pottery for all her friends and family at Christmas, they were both grateful, but in a cool, polite way.

Caroline knew what Tobi thought of her. She'd seen the look Tobi gave Mike when he introduced them—it was a look she'd seen pass between men and their friends many times before, and it was some version of "Nice work." As they began to spend more time with Mike's family, every time Caroline would begin talking about something Tobi's eyes would glaze slightly, and then as soon as Mike started talking Tobi would spring to life again. Caroline found the whole situation confusing; she wasn't accustomed to people dismissing her so readily. She made jokes, she made more banana bread. She went to see the bands Mike and Tobi loved, she went to Celtics games. And still the glazed look from Tobi, the cool distance from Lynne. Was it because she was younger than Mike and Tobi by almost ten years? Did they think she was good enough for Mike? Maybe, and maybe not. Either way, they weren't interested in Caroline. It was Mike they wanted: Mike's love, Mike's attention.

Years later, when Caroline became friends with Ruth and still hadn't cracked the Tobi code, Ruth told her to let it go. "I'm not sure it's personal," she said. "Tobi's just the kind of lesbian who doesn't like straight women."

"But straight men are fine?" Caroline asked. "I mean, that's what's so fucking annoying. I keep wanting to say, 'I'm *Mike's* wife. Your beloved bro is married to *me*. It takes two to maintain this heteronormative status quo that you're so down on."

"Yeah, except she's probably not down on it. I mean, she probably doesn't even care. I think what she really cares about is making sure that the world, when it looks at her, thinks she's more like Mike than like you. Which means she sort of wants to steer clear of you."

"Ouch."

"Yeah," Ruth said. "Misogyny's everywhere, sadly. Even on the Isle of Lesbos. I think Tobi wants to be one of the guys, you know? You're a reminder of all the ways in which that's just not entirely possible."

Had Caroline gotten these insights from Ruth sooner, she might not have been so eager to do whatever it took to win Tobi over. She might not have said Yes, of course, please take my husband's sperm and use it to make a baby.

The day Tobi and Evie asked for Mike's sperm there was no pretext, no fancy brunch, no nice bottle of wine. Tobi had texted both Mike and Caroline, asking if she and Evie could stop by. "We were wondering," Tobi said as they all stood in the kitchen, Caroline cutting up avocados and putting them on Luca's high-chair tray, "if the two of you would be willing to donate Mike's sperm?"

Caroline looked at Mike, and Mike looked at Caroline, but before either of them could say anything, Tobi said, "Don't answer now."

Evie nodded her agreement, and seemed almost fearful that one of them would speak. "Think about it," she said. "Take as long as you need."

How careful they were to include her! Caroline thought. She was touched, which of course Tobi and Evie had known she would be, but Caroline had been too wrapped up in the familial moment that had finally arrived—it had arrived!—to think about their angle. She felt—at last—Tobi and Evie's solidarity with her, their understanding of her natural attachment to Mike's sperm, her place in the order of things.

In those days, Caroline was happier than she'd ever been. She was finally out of Boston, out of her PhD program, working her dream job, married to her tender-hearted, hunky husband who made her pasta with truffle cream sauce whenever she wanted, was the primary caregiver for their darling boy, and who was also working nights as a bartender and making great money. Their rental house had loads of charm and a sweet backyard, with a baby swing in a tree and tomato plants in the raised beds. And all set in motion by her own pregnancy. If Caroline believed in anything, she believed in pregnancy. And while she didn't know all the details, she knew that Evie and Tobi had been trying to conceive for a very long time without success. Before Caroline and

Mike moved to Radclyffe, Evie had had two miscarriages. She and Tobi had taken a year to reassess, and now, they explained, they were ready to try again, only this time with a known donor. Live sperm, Tobi explained, would increase their chances of conception. "Fresh is better than frozen," she'd said.

"Like salmon," Mike said, and they all laughed and made corny jokes about swimming upstream. Caroline felt buoyed by this potential for a shared purpose, a familial connection. She was also—and this she would never admit to anyone, barely even herself—buoyed by the thought that Evie, at forty-three, didn't have the greatest odds of getting pregnant, and this grand gesture would, perhaps, be just that.

Later, when they were alone and discussing the request, Mike said he wasn't sure. Of course you are, Caroline thought. You're just afraid to say it. Would it be his kid? he asked. How much would it look like him? And how would Luca feel about it? Caroline didn't so much answer Mike's endless stream of questions as just listen to him ask the same things, over and over. Caroline knew she had an opening here—she could play up the downsides, the risks, the absurdities of giving away his sperm, but in the end, she knew that saying no would be a mistake. If Caroline pushed Mike toward saying no, he'd feel tortured by the idea of not helping his beloved Tobi, and Caroline would be out of the tribe, forever. And if Evie and Tobi wanted a baby, well, of course they should do everything they could to have one.

Saying yes had been a joy. Everyone cried, and they danced around with Luca, and drank a lot of wine. Caroline was happy, and newly optimistic. Soon there'll be another baby! Soon this family would take a new shape, and she'd know her place in it. But when they found out that Evie was carrying twins, it was Caroline who started waking up nauseous every morning. Evie and Tobi had been adamant about only wanting one child, better for their marriage, better for the planet. But now they would have two children, while Caroline and Mike had only one.

Did Caroline want another child? Yes and no. Luca was one and a half when Evie found out she was pregnant. Life was much more complicated than it had been when they made their agreement. Caroline's boss had suddenly retired, and she was asked to step into the role of director of the college's Collegium Musicum, the early music ensemble. She had to take the job: Mike was working as a sales rep for a local winery and picking up shifts at a bar in town, which meant Luca was in childcare. And they wanted to buy a house, not just rent.

Caroline was tired. And Luca was hard. When he started biting his toddler classmates, they had to take him out of his childcare and put him in a new one that was known for its commitment to creativity and the natural world. Mike called it "Burning Man for toddlers," a joke that helped to ease the pain of its monthly fee. This was all happening in early 2020; by the end of March, Luca was home, Caroline was teaching college freshmen how to play the hurdy-gurdy over Zoom, and Mike—suddenly jobless—had gone in on a distillery-turned-hand-sanitizer-operation with the bar's local aquavit supplier and was working eighteen hours a day. The idea of another child was no longer just complicated, it was laughable.

Luca was two when the twins were born in the fall of 2020. Tobi and Evie disappeared into a pandemic haze of caring for newborns and keeping their business afloat, and Mike and Caroline barely saw them until all their kids were vaccinated, at which point the twins were almost two years old. Even then they didn't socialize much; because Caroline managed their social calendar, she made plans with Wyn and Ruth instead. Their big family and their chaotic and messy house were, oddly enough, very calming to Caroline. She felt safe and accepted, and loved how Luca could just blend into the crowd, that even if he wasn't playing with Abe, he could play with Gilly and Roz, or even Siddha, sweet Siddha, who would play cards with him for hours on end. They all just absorbed him, which freed Caroline. It was an entirely different energy than at Tobi and Evie's, where, in contrast to their placid toddlers, Luca seemed like a wild animal.

Sometimes Caroline looked at Tobi and Evie, their successful business, their two kids, their perfect division of labor, and she wanted to scream You don't get to have it all! No one does. But more than that, what she really wanted to say was: What could I have possibly thought I owed the two of you?

7

Ruth was walking the dogs in the woods behind Sugar Hill, trying to pay attention to a podcast Caroline had sent her about microdosing psychedelics. *Maybe we try this??* Caroline had texted, attaching the link. *Maybe?* Ruth had texted back, knowing there was a zero percent chance they would. Ruth and Caroline loved to send each other slightly zany ideas for things they might do or places they might go together: a new sauna-and-cold-plunge spa, a community choir, an Ayurvedic foot massage workshop, a strategy for gamifying clutter clearing. They rarely followed through on any of their shared suggestions, although they had gone as far as registering and paying for the foot massage workshop, but ended up going to the movies instead when, in the car on the way to the wellness center, Caroline admitted that she hated touching her own feet.

When Ruth reached the stream on the edge of their property, she threw a few sticks into the water, watching the dogs as they splashed and tumbled over each other in the shallows. She sat down on a wide, flat boulder and took out her phone to turn off the podcast. But instead of putting it back in her pocket, she tapped on her phone's browser and went to a page she'd been opening and closing all morning. It was the website for Howe Real Estate, and right there on the home page was a photograph of the agency's founding owner, Florence Howe. Florence was Elliot's best friend. Or at least she had been, in the years when Ruth knew him. Florence had been Ruth's friend too, although they'd parted ways when Ruth ended things with Elliot. Ruth would sometimes drive past a bus bench advertising Florence as the Hudson Valley's best real estate agent, but when she did, the sight barely registered with her. How had she done it? Ruth wondered. How had she simply decided that part of her life was over? Had she really thought it was possible, to make that decision and then make it her—and her family's—reality?

Ruth had been looking at this website so intently that she'd memorized the promotional text and Florence's face, which was remarkably similar to the face in Ruth's memory, although Florence's hair was gray now.

Was she going to call Florence or wasn't she? Ruth quickly closed her phone, shoved it in her coat pocket. Then, just as quickly, she pulled it out again. She opened the page and tapped the phone number under Florence's picture. A second later, she heard Florence's voice.

"Florence Howe."

Oh shit, Ruth thought. Oh shit! What was she going to say? All this time trying to decide if she was going to call Florence without a single thought about what she was going to say.

Florence spoke again. "Hello?"

"Florence!" Ruth said, trying to sound both relaxed and cheerful, and then, worried that she might sound too relaxed and cheerful, changed to a more neutral tone of voice. "It's Ruth. Ruth Schwartz."

"Ruthie Schwartz," Florence said in a pleased tone. "I've been thinking of you."

Ruthie. "I've been thinking of you too," Ruth said. "That's why I wanted to call. I just found out—we just found out—about Elliot. I mean we just, well, I . . ." Ruth stopped speaking. Why could she not settle on a pronoun? Who was this "we" she heard herself referring to? Siddha and her? Wyn and her? All six of them? She cleared her throat. "I didn't know Elliot had died. I didn't know about the memorial."

"Ah, I wondered about that, when I didn't see you. Well, Hope wanted it to be small, you know. A grassroots, word-of-mouth kind of thing. Oh, Hope is Elliot's wife. Or she was Elliot's wife. No, she *is* his wife. Jesus, it's all so much."

"I know, it really is." Ruth took a breath. "I so wish we'd been there, at the memorial. I mean, we would have gone, we definitely would have." Again with the pronouns! What was wrong with her? "Not that we'd been in touch. I mean we hadn't seen Elliot, but we would have, of course we would . . ." Ruth unzipped her coat. She was suddenly very warm.

"Of course you would have," Florence said kindly. "How is Siddha?"

"She's sixteen, if you can believe it. Seventeen in March."

Florence groaned. "Time, you thief."

Ruth laughed. Between the cool air on her skin and Florence's joke she was beginning to feel better. "Yeah, well, time also gave me three more kids, you might remember."

The last time Ruth had run into Florence was at the Radclyffe Sheep and Wool Festival, just a few weeks after Abe was born. She and Wyn had been there with all four kids. Abe was strapped to Ruth's chest, Siddha and Gilly were sitting on hay bales, holding Holland lop rabbits that, after much begging, Ruth and Wyn had agreed they could take home as pets. Roz was on Wyn's shoulders, eating maple cotton candy and making a sticky mess of Wyn's baseball hat. Ruth remembered the day so well, even though she hadn't thought of it in years. She could still see Florence's face, the way she took in the whole scene—all the children, all the mess—with a look of surprised amusement. She also remembered that it was the fact of Wyn that seemed to surprise Florence most.

"Right, right," Florence said. "Four kids. And how's your wife? Remind me of her name?"

"Wyn," Ruth said. "And she's great."

"I'm glad," Florence said.

Ruth wondered if Florence was married. She hadn't seemed the marrying kind, but that was long ago. Ruth wanted to ask but didn't. Instead, she said, "I know how much you loved Elliot."

"Oh, I did. I did love him. Which was easy, except when it wasn't."

"I really am so sorry, Florence."

"I'm so sorry, too, Ruthie."

There it was again! *Ruthie*. This was why she'd called. She hadn't been wrong to reach out to Florence. Ruth felt almost calm for the first time in days. She also felt a new puncture of grief as her mind brimmed with memories she wanted to talk about and questions she wanted to ask, all of it tinged with confusion and the strange warp of time, but also with an unexpected pleasure. Ruth could not believe she was talking to Florence; she could not make sense of all the years she'd spent not talking to her. She didn't want to hang up. And then she had an idea.

"At the risk of being totally inappropriate," Ruth said, "can I ask you a real estate question?"

8

"What are we thinking in there? Any of those workable?"

Tobi was standing behind a canvas curtain in a makeshift dressing room in the corner of a loft in Radclyffe, trying on white T-shirts and trying to fend off the interference of a twenty-something editorial assistant wearing a jumpsuit the color of bubble gum and a mullet the color of a cherry Slurpee. "Um, yeah? I think so?"

"We can shoot some with a flannel over it too, if you want, and maybe some kind of apron? We're going to want some contrast with the other artists, you know, something sort of defining? Something that says 'I'm a potter'?"

"I don't really wear an apron in the studio," Tobi said.

"Sure, okay, maybe some kind of smock, then?"

"Not that either." Tobi didn't want to be difficult, but there was also no way she was going to be on the front cover of *Hudson Quarterly* in a smock. "I think the T-shirt will work. Just give me a sec."

Her phone buzzed with Evie's signature text tone.

How's it going?

Tobi texted thumbs-up.

I wish I'd come!

Me too! Tobi texted back.

This was a lie. Tobi didn't wish Evie were there. Tobi was enjoying handling this photo shoot on her own, and she didn't want to involve Evie. In the past year, Evie had really hit her groove with the business end of things, which was great for GoldFynch but complicated for Tobi. Tobi liked to make pots, full stop. Evie, on the other hand, was a little tired of making pots, but she loved a strategy session, she loved to negotiate. She loved to promote. As they'd begun to rely on social media to create a certain vibe around their work and to drive national sales, Evie had cultivated a distinct online persona that had gotten the company an enormous—and in Tobi's opinion, outsized—social media following.

In true Evie form, her online presence wasn't fake or insincere, it was just Evie—brilliant, political, funny, a little crass, sexy—but with the volume turned up. There were long manifestos on the broken childcare system accompanying photos of Evie in the bath, a mug in hand and a bottle of locally distilled whiskey on the edge of the tub. There were multi-photo posts of their kids having tea parties in the woods with their stuffed animals, serving leaf and twig sandwiches on GoldFynch plates. There was once even a mirror selfie of Evie taken in their bedroom, and if you zoomed in you could see Tobi's underwear on a chair. It was all a little much if you asked Tobi. But no one did. And that was fine. Evie was having fun, and it was amplifying GoldFynch, getting them gigs like the cover of *Hudson Quarterly*.

"Hey," the assistant called to Tobi from the other side of the curtain. "So, we're gonna change course a bit here—thinking we might do a little food styling for a few of these shots. Someone just ran out to grab some figs and nuts from the Creamery. Are you good to hold tight for a bit? You want to come on out? I can get you a coffee?"

Figs and nuts? "I'm all good. I'll just stay in here." Tobi realized this must have sounded ridiculous. Why would she want to stay in this dressing room indefinitely? But she didn't care. She wasn't coming out.

"Cool," said the assistant.

Tobi reached for her phone to ask Evie what she thought of figs and nuts, but then decided she'd just let it go. Whenever she was involved in something like this—a photo shoot, an interview, a press event—without Evie, Tobi felt like an impostor. She tried to remind herself that this time, she was here to highlight her own new studio endeavor, Few&Far, although just as quickly she reminded herself that Few&Far had been Evie's idea. After an argument they'd had last winter about how little time Tobi was spending in the studio, Evie hatched a plan: Tobi would produce small batches of wheel-thrown pots that were sold, in limited numbers and for high prices, a few times a year. Evie floated the idea on a Monday, and by Friday she had a business plan, a build-out strategy, and a crew. Tobi was thrilled, but she was also a little stunned. It seemed to be exactly what Tobi wanted, but was it? And how did it happen so quickly? Lately, being around Evie was sort of like having a permanent case of jet lag.

Evie and Tobi had met when they were just out of college and were both apprentices to a potter in rural Indiana. They'd come from opposite coasts: Evie from Portland, and Tobi from Boston. The potter, an illustrious and ornery man in his late sixties, was famous for his enormous pottery, vases, and urns that required extraordinary strength, which was something both Evie and Tobi had. They'd both studied ceramics in college, working on landscape crews in the summers to build upper body strength. The apprentice work was grueling, and the pay nearly nonexistent. Evie and Tobi didn't mind, though, in large part because they were falling in love.

They'd only been in Indiana a few weeks when they were assigned to the night shift on the kiln (it was a wood-burning kiln, which required constant monitoring). They were already fantasizing about their future together, only in their case it wasn't the apartment they'd move into, it was the pottery they'd create. "Entirely functional," Evie said. "I want people to use it until it breaks, you know? I want that to be the whole point. I mean, isn't that always the whole point? That a pot's going to break? That from the very first moment you hold it, you know it can't last, not in its original form. It contains its own ending. That's what makes it a living thing."

"Oh my god, you are so stoned," Tobi said, laughing. But she also loved what Evie had said, and they made a pact that someday they would have their own studio. The following spring there was a for-sale posting on their pottery listserv, a house and workshop in Radclyffe, New York. They'd never been to upstate New York, but that didn't matter. What mattered was that the pottery studio was incredibly cheap, and it came with a house, of all things. Granted, the kiln was nearly beyond repair and the house was a one-room cabin, but they knew they could make something of it.

Tobi and Evie left Indiana for Radclyffe in June, and spent the summer fixing the kiln, mouse-proofing the cabin, swimming in the ponds and the rivers, and laughing about the summer people. They marveled at how fancy things could be even though this was the country, and how funny it was that everyone called it "upstate," and wouldn't it be hilarious if people called northern Indiana "upstate," and my god, everyone here was such a snob. But honestly, they said, over and over to each other, who wouldn't be a snob if you lived here, here where they could spend the morning in their ramshackle cabin, fixing pipes and rebuilding the kiln and listening to birdsong, then swim naked in a river and stop by a bakery on the way home—a bakery that sold croissants that were so flaky and sweet and slightly salty that, after they ate them, they licked their fingers to pick up every crumb from the bottom of the paper bag.

After much debate, they decided to begin with a bowl. A bowl was all a person really needed. They spent a year perfecting its shape, and when they weren't throwing pots they were doing odd jobs, landscaping, dishwashing, even working construction. They were adamant about not selling any of their prototypes or practice pots, even though it would have been easy enough to rent a booth at the Saturday flea market and offload every bit of it for a pretty good price. But no, they'd only have one chance to make a name in Radclyffe, in the land of rich tourists and extraordinary talent. They'd have to put their best possible form forward, right from the start.

After a year they were satisfied, and so they made a run of fifty bowls. They took five to Capricorn, the buzziest restaurant in Radclyffe, and asked the owners if they'd like to buy twenty-five more at a price so low it made Tobi's stomach hurt to say it. But Evie had a hunch that if restaurant patrons saw a bowl they'd never seen before, they'd ask about it, and want to buy it.

What we want, Evie explained, over and over to a doubting Tobi, is for people to go into a store and ask for the bowl, and for the shop keeper *not* to have it. Tobi thought this was bonkers, but Evie was insistent. She'd felt something in the air of this place. She'd felt the wanting and the good taste and the drive to get a new, beautiful, unobtainable thing. People didn't want to see the bowl coming and going, in every shop window and restaurant. They wanted to have to figure out how to get it.

And Evie had been right. The calls from shop owners started to come in, and when they did, Evie and Tobi were ready. They had inventory; they had a plan. They'd deliver fifty bowls to three stores in Radclyffe on the fifteenth of each month. When those bowls were gone, they were gone. No preorders, no waiting lists.

That bowl was the beginning of GoldFynch Pottery. People went crazy for that bowl. More than one woman—it was always women—cried when Evie told her they were out of stock. After a few years, they started making plates and mugs, and then a serving platter. They opened a store in Radclyffe. People wanted them to open a store in Brooklyn, but then what was the point? Evie and Tobi had come to the Hudson Valley by way of another river, the mighty Ohio, and they hadn't set their sights on New York. They never even went to the city. Evie didn't like noise and Tobi didn't like crowds.

After ten years they were operating at a level of success that their mentors could only have dreamed of. They had sold the cabin and the pottery studio, moving their work to a two-story studio in a renovated factory and their home to a Queen Anne Victorian in the center of Radclyffe. After ten more years they'd taken over the whole factory building, and now they were ready to expand again.

Neither of them had been making pots much anymore, which was okay with Evie. She was manifesting her vision. But Tobi wasn't in it for the vision. She was in it for the clay, the physical act of making. And so

Few&Far was born. When Tobi had finished a sizable inventory, Evie would announce an online drop, and every single piece would sell in a matter of minutes. Evie liked to say that scarcity was the soul of desire.

Lately that phrase, the soul of desire, had been coming back to Tobi at the oddest moments. It came to her when she thought of Bex Devereux. And it came to her now. Because a few moments ago, when she'd heard the room outside the curtain go quiet, she'd taken off her shirt, unclipped her bra, and was now standing, topless, in front of the mirror. Tobi was looking at her breasts; she was trying to remember the last time she had actually looked at them. In a few weeks, Tobi would be fifty years old, which meant that for approximately thirty-eight years she had lived with these breasts. She had rubbed soap across them in the shower, settled them into the cups of a bra, covered them with towels, covered them with T-shirts and sweatshirts and tank tops. She had never once wanted to be desired because of them; she had never once wanted them to be the object of anyone's desire. Tobi loved Evie's breasts, and Evie loved Evie's breasts, and this shared love had allowed them both to be contentedly agnostic about Tobi's.

Tobi's breasts had become, in the way that so many things had in the last ten years, invisible. She didn't think of them. She didn't think of how she'd once hated them; she didn't think about how many people seemed to now be getting rid of their breasts. She thought, if she'd thought about it at all, that her breasts were a problem she'd already solved with sports bras and busyness. She had a wife, two five-year-olds, and an all-consuming job. Besides, the people who had top surgery, they were truly suffering, dysphoric. Tobi didn't love that word—dysphoria—primarily because her brain couldn't tease it out from the word "dystopian," with its attending images of burning cities and zombies and viruses. Even if she did meet the criteria for gender dysphoria (did she?), it wasn't a word she'd use to describe her feelings.

But what if a person didn't change their body because of torment, but because of desire? *The soul of desire.* Tobi had been thinking about her soul, and where it resided. She had been thinking about desire, and where that resided, too. Where it came from, how long it stayed. When she'd seen Bex, she'd felt a super bloom of wanting inside her, a field of wildflowers opening in her chest. Or maybe the feeling was even more dramatic than that, more unexpected. It was like a sapling breaking through soil, sprouting branches, unfurling leaves, a full-grown tree inside her.

All her life Tobi had wanted women, had desired them, and she'd loved that wanting, and loved the women. That was the entirety of how she'd allowed herself to express and experience desire. It was a one-way street, an arrow, a periscope. And the object had always been a woman. But then she stood next to Bex, and felt the same familiar rush of wanting, the same intensity, the same arousal—only it wasn't to possess or be close to them. It was to *be* them.

It wasn't that Tobi hadn't felt, abstractly, some piece of this desire before. She had. Of course she had. For as long as she could remember there had been a part of her that wanted, in some way, to be a man, but that wanting was always tinged with real sadness, because she didn't want *not* to be a woman. She didn't feel like a man, she didn't think her body was a mistake, or at least not entirely. But to alter this body? To mold it, even slightly? To compress it here, expand it there, to smooth it, to form it like warm clay in her hands? That was a thrilling idea. And mostly it was thrilling because it wasn't chased by the gut punch of loss she'd felt whenever she had thought about being a boy. She'd feel nearly desperate in those moments, desperate to keep herself, to keep all of what she loved—to be herself, only different. But how?

For a long time, she hadn't really known, and then for an even longer time, when in some far reach of her mind she *did* know, life was coming at her too fast, one desire after another fulfilled, and—whatever else she might have wanted, whoever else she might have been—there wasn't time, there wasn't space. Until Bex. Because Bex, well, they took up *all* the space. Right there, right in front of Tobi, was a person who hadn't waited, who wasn't distracted, who wasn't trying to do everything right before they made things right for themselves.

Which was what had led Tobi to go home, that night after the memorial, after the Sukkot party, and—after Evie and the kids were asleep—go on the computer and order a binder. I just want to see, she'd told herself. I just want to see what it looks like. She'd had the binder sent to her pottery studio, but she'd left it in the mailing envelope until today. There had been lots of choices, but she'd gone with one from a company called Tomboys, which was what her mother had always—and lovingly—called her. A tomboy. Later she'd understood that the word was no longer used, although Tobi wouldn't have been able to say what the problem was. Evie would have been able to explain it to her, but she wasn't going to ask. And anyway, Tobi didn't care. She still loved the word as much as she'd loved it when she was young. *Tomboy.* She loved that word the way she loved clay and kiln. It conjured cool wind and solitude, the feeling she'd get as a child when she'd jump to reach the lowest thick branch on a tree and her hands would find solid purchase, her feet would leave the ground, and she would think, *The whole world is mine.*

But now, standing in a dressing room and holding this Tomboys binder, Tobi was not feeling very expansive. She'd measured carefully before she ordered, but it looked really, really small, and almost improbably tight. She wished the binder had clasps, the way a bra would, but she knew then it wouldn't work the way it was supposed to. The back (at least she thought it was the back) was stretchy, like a bathing suit, but the front felt more like a tarp. It had no give. Tobi took a breath and tried putting it on over her head, but then once it was around her neck, there wasn't enough space to get an arm up and through. She realized she'd have to put both her arms through while it was still above her head, and then shimmy it down. She tried that, only to get it stuck over her neck and shoulders. It was like wearing a piece of PVC pipe. Shit, Tobi thought. After some gyrations and contortions that made her think of those inflatable gumby-men in the parking lot of car dealerships, she finally managed to undulate her torso enough to get the thing up around her face, and then off. She rummaged around for her phone, googled "putting on binder" and there, in a list of bullet points, she saw *Step into binder and pull up over waist.* Genius! she thought, scrambling to take off her shoes and peel off her pants. And that was when she heard the door to the loft open and the voices of the assistant and photographer. Tobi started to sweat.

The assistant knocked playfully on the wall outside the curtain. "How are we doing in there? Everything cool?"

Jesus fucking Christ, Tobi thought. She was really sweating now, so much sweating. She almost asked for a towel, but then thought better of it. "Yep," she said, wiping her face with her sweatshirt. "All cool. I'll be out in just a minute."

Tobi pulled the binder up over her butt and torso, hoisted one strap and then the other over her shoulder. She tucked one breast and then the other into the binder, careful to keep her nipples facing forward as the website had directed. She put the fresh T-shirt over her head, tousled her hair back into place.

And there it was, her chest. Level and even. Smooth. But it wasn't just her chest, somehow her neck seemed longer, and her arms too. Was her torso longer? She was having the strangest sensation, the most disorienting funhouse mirror feeling, looking at herself. Only it wasn't distortion that she saw, it was the body she'd always imagined she had, it was the body she'd seen, always, in her mind's eye. She felt a rush of excitement, then a warm flash of shame. Because if this binder had changed her body in this way, that meant that her body, all along, had been something else. What had she convinced herself of? What a fool she'd been! She should have started binding years ago. Didn't she know she wanted this? Shouldn't she have figured that out by now, now being almost *fifty* years old? Tobi rubbed her hands over her face, turned away from the mirror for a moment. Dude, chill, she said to herself. Be here now.

"Not to rush you, but the figs are starting to sweat and that's not great for our lighting." The assistant was no longer trying to hide her agitation. "Are we all set?"

Tobi turned sideways in the mirror. She put her open palms against her chest. She tried to take a deep breath, but the binder made that impossible, so she took a few shallow, slow breaths, wiped her face with her old T-shirt. Tobi smiled at herself. "We are," she said, and pushed back the curtain.

9

Ruth arrived early at the Olive Street house, thinking she'd take some time to spruce it up a bit, but when she got there, she couldn't make herself go inside. She deadheaded the marigolds in the front yard, picked a few weeds, swept the steps with a porch broom they'd left behind. She was nervous about seeing Florence. She'd thought of canceling a few times this week, but she wanted to do something to prove to Florence that she wasn't a total flake. Why she needed to prove anything to Florence was the question, although it wasn't a question Ruth knew how to answer.

Ruth had met Florence a few days after she'd met Elliot. She'd burst into his apartment after work only to be startled by the sight of a woman lying on the couch, reading the newspaper. She had long, shiny black hair that hung over the arm of the couch, bright red polish on her bare toes, and perfect rips in her jeans. Ruth had no idea who this woman was, but she knew she was very, very cool. Before she could gather herself enough to say hello, Elliot came in from the kitchen with two beers. "Hey, beautiful," he said, leaning in to kiss Ruth. "This is Florence."

When Ruth didn't kiss him back, Elliot just laughed. "Flo and I are old friends, we go way back." And then, in a loud whisper he added, "She plays for the other team, if you catch my drift."

Ruth felt herself blush.

Florence laughed, reaching out her hand for a beer. "Jesus, Elliot, really? You're embarrassing the girl."

"It's fine," Ruth said, wishing she could disappear. How she hated that Florence had called her a girl!

"Lemme grab another beer," Elliot said.

"No need," Florence said, getting up from the couch and handing hers back to Elliot, although not before she took a long swig. "I've got class in an hour anyway." She pulled on a sweatshirt. "And I've got practice tonight, if you catch my drift." She winked, and swatted Elliot on the arm.

Elliot laughed. Ruth smiled, and tried to look cooler, older, and more relaxed than she was. "Have fun," she said, and immediately regretted it.

Later Ruth would learn that Elliot and Florence had gone to high school together and dropped out of college at the same time. Ruth would also learn that she liked Florence, a lot. Elliot and Florence were best friends, although their dynamic was different than the one Ruth would later see between lesbians and straight men. Florence wasn't trying to be like Elliot; if anything, he aspired to be more like her. When Florence was around, Elliot was quieter, more considerate. He kept a bag of apples in his fridge because she liked to eat one every night after dinner and bought her word search books because she liked to solve puzzles when she watched TV.

One of the things Ruth had liked most about Florence was her ambition, which was unlike that of anyone else she'd known. In Ruth's world, ambition looked like LSATs and unpaid internships. Florence's ambition looked like buying a duplex with money she'd earned by working three jobs, then living in one side while she renovated the other. Florence had skills; Florence had grit before grit was a thing.

"RUTHIE!" A VOICE called from behind her. Ruth turned on the step, broom in hand. There was Florence in a black blazer with gold buttons, expensive-looking jeans, and even more expensive-looking loafers.

"You look amazing!" Ruth said.

"So do you!" Florence said, walking up the steps and hugging her. "I already love this house. Look at this blue porch ceiling. Did you do that?"

Ruth propped the broom by the front door. "That was Wyn," Ruth said. "I guess it's a thing in the South. For bugs, maybe?"

"Evil spirits," Florence said. "They can't cross water, so the blue is to keep them out of the house. It's called 'haint blue.'"

"Look at you," Ruth said. "A veritable fount of real estate knowledge. And we're not even inside yet!" She looked up. It really was the prettiest shade of blue, an antique, milky turquoise.

"I can see why you didn't want to leave," Florence said.

When they'd spoken on the phone last week, Ruth had explained her reluctance to move out of the house, and how that reluctance had made it hard for her to put it on the market, even though they didn't live there anymore.

"I know," Ruth said. "Honestly, I don't know why we did."

"Well, this might jog your memory," Florence said, handing Ruth the spec sheet she'd printed. "It's fifteen hundred square feet, Ruthie. I can't believe you lived here with four kids."

Ruth took the paper. "Well, they were four very little kids. I mean, other than Siddha. But eventually we renovated the attic for her."

"And only one full bath?" Florence said. "How did that even work, logistically?"

"There's a half downstairs," Ruth pointed out, feeling a little defensive, the way she had when Wyn's family came to visit and could not believe they lived there. The small house had become a point of pride for Ruth. Which, admittedly, was another reason she'd wanted to stay in it long past the time they should have left.

"Well, regardless of the half bath, we can't list it for more than six ten—I mean, that is, if you're ready to sell it. I don't want to be the one to rush you."

"Wow, that still seems like a lot," Ruth said. "I mean, we bought it for three-something." She handed the paper back to Florence. "Okay, I'm feeling brave. Let's do it. Let's see what you think."

They went inside and Florence walked through the downstairs, which was essentially a circle of rooms: tiny front hall to tiny kitchen, tiny kitchen to tiny dining room, tiny dining room to tiny living room, which was off the front hall. "Sweet as can be," she said, coming back around to Ruth in the front hallway. "Let's say six flat, and maybe get a war going. That is, if you don't want to do any reno other than the basic fluff."

"What's the basic fluff?"

"Paint, maybe redo the powder room? Put in some new countertops, rebuild the porch steps. Not much, really."

Ruth laughed. "That's 'not much'? I'd hate to think of what a lot is. I thought it was a seller's market?"

"It is, but you still have to make an effort. It's like getting the house ready for a party. A nice blowout and some lipstick. That's all we're talking here."

Ruth smoothed her slightly matted hair. Florence laughed. "That was not code. You're perfect. You're Ruth."

Ruth smiled. Oh how nice it was, seeing Florence!

"I think I might have just the buyer for this place," Florence said, excitement in her voice. She took off her jacket and hung it on the newel post.

Ruth smiled at her. "You really do love this, don't you? Real estate, I mean."

"I do," Florence said. "I never thought I would stick with it for so long, you know? Spend so many years doing the same thing. But then the beauty of real estate is that it's so many things. And it's so much about the psychology of people and their needs, which, it turns out, I'm very good at." Florence opened the closet door and turned on the light. She made a face that Ruth couldn't quite decipher and then went on, "People come to me, delusional and filled with wanting, and, as my granny used to say, I get them sorted. I show them what's possible, I give them the set and setting for a new life—more peaceful, more exciting, whatever it is—and if they can't see it we just keep looking until they can. And honestly, you can say it's shallow, but nice countertops can make a person happy. So can windows, or a yard, or a bathtub. There are a lot of ways to make a life better."

"And your life," Ruth said. "How is it?"

Florence smiled. "My life is good." She turned and walked toward the kitchen. "What happened here?" She pointed to the kitchen doorway, where a piece of molding was missing.

"Oh, that was where we marked all the kids' heights," Ruth said. "We ripped it out when we moved. To take it with us."

"Well, that's sweet, but you can add 'new kitchen doorway' to your punch list."

"Will do," Ruth said, although she was keeping no such list. She walked into the dining room, its bay window a perfect frame for the neighbors' ornamental cherry trees that had been a balm to Ruth in every season. She felt her heart catch a bit. "I gave birth to Abe right here," she said, "and those trees were covered in blossoms. It was the most beautiful thing."

Florence looked alarmed. "You gave birth in the dining room? Jesus, Ruth, why?"

Ruth shrugged. "Things were so easy with Siddha. I mean, relatively, and I knew I could do it. I didn't want to be in a hospital. We had an inflatable birthing tub and everything. Wyn's mom almost had a heart attack when she found out. That might have been half the reason I did it."

"That I can understand," Florence said.

"Do you have a mother-in-law?" Ruth asked.

Florence seemed to be considering the question. "Not exactly," she said. "My girlfriend has a mother, but I've only met her a few times."

"Do you live together? I mean, you and your girlfriend, not you and your sort-of-mother-in-law." Ruth knew she was asking too many personal questions, but she couldn't help herself.

Florence laughed. "No, I don't live with either of them. Katrina, that's my girlfriend, she lives in Brooklyn."

Before Ruth could open her mouth to ask yet another question,

Florence said, "I've been thinking of the morning Siddha was born. How we came to see you."

"Oh wow," Ruth said, surprised. They were going to go there? Suddenly she needed a glass of water. She went to the kitchen for a glass. "I haven't thought of that in a long time."

"You were very brave," Florence said.

"I don't think I felt very brave."

Ruth remembered how she'd cried when her labor started, how she'd panicked. She'd called Elliot but he hadn't picked up, so she called Florence, who told her not to worry, she'd find him. The three of them had become close in the months since Ruth discovered she was pregnant. Her pregnancy—and her decision to keep the baby—had complicated the few friendships Ruth had in Radclyffe, and she had quickly grown tired of explaining her situation. She'd also grown tired of the concerns and antics of other people her age. She was gestating a baby! She had very little interest in discussions about dating or roommates or graduate school. She was counting grams of protein and going to bed early. It was just easier to hang with Elliot and Florence, the only other two people in the world who understood—and were happy about—Ruth's decision.

Ruth and Elliot had decided (well, Ruth had decided and Elliot had happily agreed) that while she would be this child's primary parent, they would still be a family, and Elliot would be a vital part of the baby's life. Ruth was enlivened by her plan, which, to her twenty-three-year-old deeply naïve self, felt radical and exciting. She would do this! She would do it so well. This arrangement—if you could even call it an arrangement—suited Elliot just fine. He wasn't ready for full-time fatherhood or marriage. "Maybe you'll be more like a fun uncle," Ruth had suggested. "And you can be her fun aunt," she'd said to Florence, who'd responded with an actual squeal of happiness at the thought.

Then Ruth and Florence laughed about "Aunt Flo," and when Elliot asked what was so funny, Florence just rolled her eyes. "My god, Elliot," she said. "You are so clueless. Might be how you got yourself into this situation in the first place." It was a joke, of course, because this situation they were in, this waiting for a baby to arrive, a new person to love, was—

for all of them—a happy one. Elliot was still drinking his beers and Florence was still drinking her red wine, but no one ever seemed drunk, and Ruth (for whom Elliot kept a stash of seltzer and orange juice in his fridge) made the mostly arbitrary decision that it was all okay.

Over the course of her pregnancy, Ruth made a lot of arbitrary decisions. They didn't seem that way to her at the time, of course; in fact, they felt like important reflections of how her future with Elliot and the baby would play out. Elliot helped her paint the nursery (which was technically not a room but a corner of her apartment that she'd cordoned off with velvet floor-to-ceiling drapes she'd found at Goodwill) and install the car seat, but she went to her midwife and doula appointments alone. Elliot assembled the crib, but didn't come to the meeting with the pediatrician. Ruth wasn't exactly transparent in her decisions—and she certainly wasn't discussing other options with Elliot—but he didn't seem to mind. Ruth had a feeling, which made her both grateful and uneasy, that Elliot didn't want to be more involved, and that he wasn't giving much thought to what it really meant to have a baby.

Still, he was deeply loving to Ruth, deeply attentive. He spent a lot of time with his lips pressed to Ruth's belly, singing sea chanteys and teaching the baby how a knock-knock joke worked. He addressed the baby with a string of nonsensical endearments—Mookie, Slushie, Twinkie—and when Ruth told him she thought the baby's name should be Siddha, he started calling the baby "El Cid, our fearless knight and warrior," and referring to Ruth as the Queen Mother. "I'm getting the sense you have a very weak grasp of European history," Ruth said. But her annoyance was feigned. Elliot made her laugh; he made her happy.

That is, until Ruth's water broke ten days before her due date and Elliot was nowhere to be found, and Ruth couldn't stop crying. Ruth's father had paid for her to have a doula, and it was the doula who, after tolerating two hours of Ruth crying and checking her phone, got real with her. "Look at me," she said to Ruth, holding her firmly by the shoulders. "Stop crying and listen very closely." She told Ruth that this was no time for phones, no time for anyone but this baby, and that Ruth needed to shut out the noise and get down to business. Ruth was startled. Wasn't a doula supposed to flood the room with kindness and warmth? Wasn't she just supposed to do whatever Ruth asked her to do? Luckily for Ruth, this doula had a different orientation toward her work. Ruth stopped crying. She drank a glass of water and took a shower. The doula French-braided Ruth's wet hair, stopping to press on her lower back when a contraction came. Three hours after the tough-love pep talk, Siddha was born.

When Siddha was settled and the doula had gone home to get some sleep, Ruth looked at her phone and saw a waterfall of missed calls from Florence. Ruth called back and Elliot was the one who picked up. "Ruthie!" he exclaimed.

"She's here," Ruth whispered, not yet aware of the fact that newborn babies weren't bothered by noise. "You can come and see her in the morning."

"I'm in the waiting room. With Florence."

Ruth laughed. She was still high on birth endorphins and brimming with love and forgiveness. She could have said Where were you? Instead, she asked, "Well, what are you waiting for?" Barely a minute later the two of them burst into the hospital room. Ruth handed Siddha to Elliot, who held her so tenderly you'd have thought she was made of spun glass.

"You won't break her," Florence said, reaching in to take her turn. Ruth took pictures of them with the camera she'd packed in her hospital bag. She was so happy, she didn't even mind when Florence said she thought Siddha looked like Elliot. When the sun came up, Florence went out for coffee and food, and they ate egg sandwiches while Siddha slept in the plastic bassinet.

And then it was time for Ruth to learn to nurse, and for Siddha to have a bath. Elliot and Florence left. Ruth had been alone with Siddha then, and she had what she remembered as her first moment of real clarity about the situation she was in—the actual situation, with the actual baby.

THINKING OF ALL this, Ruth felt a dizzying disorientation, like she'd just stepped out of a boat. She finished her water. "We should go upstairs and take a look at the bedrooms," she said. "I'm just warning you, there's a trapeze in the kids' room. And a drinking fountain."

"A drinking fountain? Were you running a preschool?"

"Wyn was tired of the kids always asking for a drink of water. They'd call downstairs like a hundred times a night before they went to sleep."

"Well, god love Wyn, but I can tell you without even seeing it that it has to go."

"Come up anyway," Ruth said, "come see the rest of our destruction." She led the way to the front staircase. When they got to the second floor, Ruth asked Florence if she wanted to start in the attic. "It's actually really cute."

"Lead the way," Florence said.

As they went up the stairs, Ruth felt the stuffy warmth of attic air hit her, then the glow of the room's pink walls.

"Oh, sweetness," Florence said.

Ruth smiled. "Wyn did it," Ruth said. "When Abe was born and we were running out of space she told Siddha to make a list of everything she wanted in a bedroom and Wyn would make as much of it happen as she could."

"Wow," Florence said, gesturing to a hand-painted mural on the wall. "Actual rainbows and unicorns."

"Wyn has some very unusual talents," Ruth said.

"Indeed," Florence said. She sat down on the deep windowsill and looked at Ruth. "How is your Siddha?"

There was that question again. Ruth knew there was no getting away from it this time. "She's okay."

"I'm glad," Florence said. "And I'm sorry, about how it all turned out. I'm sorry if I overstepped or—"

"You didn't," Ruth said.

"Well, I did," Florence said, with a little laugh.

Ruth laughed too, but she turned away, opened the dormer closet's door, and pretended to investigate its far reaches, even though she knew it was empty.

Florence had overstepped, it was true. She had tried, unsuccessfully, to usher Elliot into dedicated fatherhood. Elliot was overwhelmed by newborn Siddha. He didn't like to hold her, and as soon as she cried, he handed her back to Ruth, which was exactly what Ruth wanted him to do. Florence often tagged along when Elliot came to see Siddha, always saying that she just wanted to pop in and say hello, although it was clear to Ruth that these visits were Florence's idea. "Look at her, El," she'd say, cooing at Siddha, taking her gently from Elliot's arms when she fussed, but instead of handing her back to Ruth, she'd quiet Siddha herself, then hand her back to Elliot. Ruth saw what Florence was trying to do; Ruth saw that Elliot needed to build his confidence, to find his way with Siddha, but as she watched them together, all she wanted to do was grab Siddha. Whatever vague sense she'd once had of the seriousness of Elliot's drinking had crystalized now that Siddha was here. Elliot drank too much, and Ruth knew it. What she didn't know was what it meant, exactly, about her and Siddha's future. She had a feeling, though, and it wasn't a good one.

In those early months of Siddha's life, nothing had been like Ruth had hoped, or what she'd planned for. Ruth had been undone and knocked over by Siddha—the ferocious love, the unrelenting work, the rupture of time, the renovation of her own body. Elliot had been knocked over too, although it certainly wasn't from the strain of caretaking. In the first days he'd been attentive and helpful; he was staying at Ruth's apartment and waking with each feeding, if only to bring Ruth a glass of water or a sandwich.

After a week of this schedule, Elliot felt himself doze off at the wheel on his way to work, and Ruth told him to go back to his apartment and get some rest, which was the end of the overnight help. Then Ruth's dad came to town for a few weeks, which was a respite for Elliot, who—wisely—thought it best to keep his distance from Ruth's father.

Ruth's father went back to Madison when Siddha was a month old and Ruth was a changed woman. She'd endured the excruciating pain of early breastfeeding. She could calm Siddha with just the sound of her voice. She could bathe Siddha without panicking. She could wear Siddha in a sling while she bought her own groceries and scrambled her own eggs. The ideas she and Elliot had once had about being a different kind of family, the whole "fun uncle" bit, it all seemed ridiculous to

Ruth. Siddha was no longer just a silent creature swimming under her heart. She was a human being; she was Ruth's child. Did Ruth still love Elliot? Did she want to be a family with him? She didn't know, and she wasn't sure it mattered. The only thing that mattered was Siddha.

In the months that followed, Ruth prepared herself to go back to work. She'd once thought that maybe Elliot and even Florence would do some Siddha care when Ruth returned to teaching, but the idea of creating some sort of schedule—let alone some sort of mutual dependence and accountability—left Ruth feeling exhausted. She enrolled Siddha in full-time childcare using the small inheritance her mother had left her. There was only enough money for two years of childcare, but Ruth decided she'd worry about that later. All she knew for certain was that she wasn't going to leave Siddha with Elliot.

Perhaps as self-fulfilling prophecy, or perhaps as anyone at all could have prophesized, Elliot became more erratic as Ruth became more guarded. He stopped showing up when he said he would, or he showed up late, or said he had to leave just a few minutes after he'd arrived. The worst—and least surprising—change was that he seemed to be drinking more. Soon enough, Ruth started to notice a pattern. When she'd get pissed at Elliot for drinking or being flaky, Florence would intercede and try to patch things up. One Saturday afternoon, Ruth sent Elliot home when he'd shown up smelling like beer, but the next morning he came by with a basket of strawberries, offering to hang out with Siddha while Ruth took a nap, and Ruth knew it was Florence who'd told him to do it. The interference made Ruth angry, and it confused her. Could Elliot even be in Siddha's life without Florence's coaching?

A few weeks before Siddha's first birthday, a coveted faculty house became available on the campus of Ruth's school, and she jumped at the chance to move. Now Elliot was twenty minutes away. This felt like a relief to Ruth, which made her feel guilty. "We'll just schedule our visits," she said, brightly, when she told Elliot about the move. "It won't be as easy to just stop by, but you can stay longer or take her for the afternoon. You could even take her to the park."

One afternoon in March, right after Siddha's first birthday, Elliot was on his way to see her when he drove through a four-way stop and hit a tree. He was mercifully unhurt, but his blood alcohol level was twice the legal limit. He was arrested, released on bail, and because it was not his first offense (which was news to Ruth), he was sentenced to two months in prison.

The day after Elliot was sentenced, Florence called Ruth, but she didn't take the call. It pained Ruth, but she didn't want to hear Florence try to convince her to give Elliot another shot. He was driving drunk, Ruth thought. On his way to see Siddha. For days the words were a hot pan she made herself touch over and over, and she would shiver in what felt like actual pain, reminding herself what had almost happened. What could have happened. She'd make a noise, a quiet involuntary wail when she thought of it, which sometimes startled Siddha, which then made Ruth cry.

Florence called her every day for a week. Ruth didn't call her back. Ruth used her money—now there would only be enough for one more year of childcare—to hire a lawyer and file the papers for sole custody of Siddha, and then, six months later, for full parental rights. Elliot signed all the papers, and Florence didn't call.

RUTH SAT DOWN next to Florence on the window seat. "I blocked out so many things, things that are coming back to me a little bit at a time. And right now, I'm thinking about how kind you were. How kind you were to me, and how I just left you behind."

"You had to," Florence said. "I know that."

"I did," Ruth said. "But I'm still sorry."

"I shouldn't have gotten involved," Florence said. "That's the truth. There was this part of me that knew Elliot could be a great dad, and I thought that maybe if I helped him, he could show you that he had it together. I was his enabler. I mean, I didn't know what that word meant then. I didn't know how impossible it was to have a healthy relationship with an alcoholic. I didn't even know Elliot was an alcoholic! I just thought he drank a little more than he should. And I thought I was just being loyal. I thought I was paying him back for everything he'd done for me. He really protected me when I came out, and then all those years after when my family had basically disowned me. And there was this part of me that thought we could be a little family, you know? The four of us. It was misguided, to say the least."

Ruth wanted to say more then, to tell Florence the terrible way she'd found out about Elliot's death, the whole mess with Siddha, but she couldn't. She didn't know how to explain that they hadn't told Siddha about Elliot, that the right time—when Siddha was ready, when Ruth and Wyn were ready, when they knew what to say, when Siddha could grasp the complexities of Elliot's role—had been an ever-distant horizon they would surely reach someday, although it never seemed to grow closer. And how could it? The conversation would require surgical precision. They would need to explain that Elliot was somewhere between a father and a donor, but much closer to a donor than a father, although not a donor in the "let me help you make a baby" sense because technically Elliot hadn't offered his sperm for the purpose of conception and Ruth certainly hadn't been asking for it. Quite the opposite, really. It was a lot for a young child to understand.

And then, well, life came at them fast. Siddha was barely two years old when Ruth and Wyn married, and only four when Gilly was born. The next decade had been a blur of pregnancies, babies, toddlers, kids. There was never a moment to think about anything but sleep and diapers, preschool registration, spelling words, ear infections, multiplication tables, soccer practice, summer camp, and dinner, dinner, dinner. When they returned from Tennessee after the pandemic, Siddha's adolescence rolled in like a desert thunderstorm, and suddenly—bafflingly—there were vape pens in her backpack, tanking grades, skipped classes. In a (misguided) attempt to change Siddha's channel, Wyn and Ruth sent her to an alternative performing-arts middle school two towns over. When that move proved to be an abject failure, they dragged her back to Mott Valley.

It was during this chaos that Ruth received a letter from Elliot. He said he was living in Barton Falls now, that he was married and had twin sons. He told her he'd gotten his life together and would like to see Siddha. Ruth wrote back and told him that she and Wyn were open to the idea, but it wasn't a good time. She'd reach out when things settled down. Things had settled down, but Ruth had never written to Elliot.

Ruth took Florence down the attic stairs, and they went through the second floor: the bathroom, the hall closets, the little kids' bedroom, a quick look into the bedroom Ruth had shared with Wyn and, at any given time, at least one of their children and both of their dogs. They went back downstairs once again so Florence could inspect the appliances. She found them acceptable. Ruth found them perfect and worthy of great levels of nostalgia. She loved that refrigerator.

"So, what do you think, Ruthie?" Florence asked, tapping her nails on the kitchen counter. "Are you ready to let it go? Site of the inflatable birthing tub?"

Ruth laughed. She wasn't ready, not at all. She would like to keep this house, just the way it was, for the rest of her life, so that she could walk back into it whenever she wanted. So that she could walk back into her children's babyhoods, her and Wyn's foolish and delightful youth. But she wasn't going to say any of those things to Florence. Instead, she said, "Seems like it needs some work first. Want to do it with me? I mean, help me with the fluff, or whatever you called it? We could figure something out with the commission, so you'd get paid for it, of course."

"I'd be delighted. I love a project."

"You always did," Ruth said.

"Are you referring to Elliot?" Florence asked.

"Oh god, no!" Ruth said, reaching out to put a hand on Florence's bare arm. "I meant house renovations!" Her arm felt warm and strong. A charge went through Ruth, and she thought she'd lost her balance, but her feet were firmly on the ground.

Florence put her hand on Ruth's, which did nothing to steady her. "I knew what you meant," Florence said. "I was just kidding."

Ruth laughed nervously. "Okay, good." She turned off the lights, reached into her pocket for the key. "I'll just talk to Wyn," she said. "I'll see what she thinks."

"Keep me posted, hon," Florence said, already walking out the door. "I'm here whenever you're ready."

10

The sun had barely set on Halloween night and already Caroline was done. She'd stayed late at rehearsal, having had to push out the start time so she could attend the Halloween parade at Luca's school, an event she found both dull and excruciatingly, existentially painful. Luca seemed even more vulnerable than usual in his costume, and she'd felt her heart catch at the sight of him, her little wizard in a wrinkled cape, poking his wand into the dirt.

At four o'clock, Ruth, Wyn, and their kids had come over for a quick chili dinner before they all went trick-or-treating, and by five there had already been multiple bouts of tears over ripped, uncomfortable, or just disappointing costumes; UN-level negotiations over how many bites of chili constituted dinner; and Abe choking so violently on a roasted pumpkin seed that Ruth had to do the Heimlich on him. And through all the chaos, Wyn and Mike had been sitting at one end of the table, laughing, talking animatedly about mountain bikes, some kind of walking tour through the Hebrides they were both "stoked" to take when all the kids were older.

Caroline could no longer contain her annoyance. "Okay, okay," she called out, clapping her hands. "Attention, everyone, change of plans. Dads are taking the kids trick-or-treating, and moms are staying home. And I'm defining 'dad' loosely tonight," Caroline said, looking at Wyn. "Lest you think you're off the hook. It's anyone drinking a beer."

"Or cracking bad jokes," Ruth added.

"Or having side conversations while the moms are safety-pinning the children's costumes and making sure they've all ingested a decent amount of protein." Caroline fake-smiled at Wyn and Mike.

"And saving their lives," Ruth added.

"I asked if he was okay," Wyn said.

Ruth glared at her.

"But yeah, yeah, okay—guilty on all counts," Wyn said, her hands up in surrender.

"Seems like these womenfolk could use a little break," Mike said.

"Get out," Caroline said, thrusting Luca's plastic pumpkin pail at him. "Get out now."

The kids ran for the back door, spilling out into the yard. Mike grabbed a coat, handed a flashlight and another beer to Wyn, and headed out. "Babe, we've got this!" he called from the porch. "You two just enjoy some peace and—"

Before he could say anything else, Caroline slammed the door. She leaned back against it, basking in the sudden quiet. "Why is this my least favorite holiday?" She looked at Ruth, who was already collecting chili bowls and scraping the contents into the compost. "And why do you not hate it?"

"It's my only chance to give my kids some enchantment," Ruth said. "To lift the veil, peer under it with them. You have Christmas, and Santa, and the Easter bunny."

"You have Santa," Caroline said. "I mean, you do Christmas." She opened the dishwasher. "Just throw everything in here," she said, rinsing a sponge under the running tap.

"Will do," Ruth said, loading the dishwasher with impressive speed. "I don't *really* have Christmas. I mean, we do it, and I love it, but I feel bad about it. It makes me feel like a bad Jew, so that's not great. And I never celebrated it when I was young, so I have no memories. Halloween is what I remember. I remember all the strangeness, the thrill of being out in the dark, of transforming yourself. And it's guilt free. I mean, not entirely guilt free, with all the sugar, but it's as close as I'm going to get." She put in the last plate, reached under the sink for a soap pod, and started the dishwasher.

Caroline nodded. "I get that. Honestly, I think I'm just tired. And annoyed with Mike and Wyn, the way they're always having those side conversations."

"I know," Ruth said, holding her hand out for a turn with the counter sponge. "I mean, if you enjoy each other's company so much, make your own damn plans!"

"It's like how they went off to the barn at your party, when Mike had told me he'd be on Luca all night."

"Oh god, that party!" Ruth said, shaking her head. "What was I thinking?"

"It was lovely," Caroline said. "Although I do have to ask you something, about the kids."

Ruth put down the sponge and looked at Caroline. "Did Roz do something?"

"No, no one did anything," Caroline said. Technically this wasn't a lie, seeing that speech wasn't the same as action. "I think the kids must have been talking about dads and donors at the firepit—under Tobi's watch, by the way." Caroline rolled her eyes. "Because when we got home, Luca had a bunch of questions."

"Ah," Ruth said.

"So now we have some cleanup to do. But I'm not sure how. I mean, I feel bad even bringing this up right now, with the whole Siddha situation."

"It's fine. Really, it's fine. I was actually looking at Mike and the twins the other night and thinking how nice it is for them to know him. It's sweet. I mean, I was just thinking of Siddha, of course, and how she can't have that now . . ."

Caroline didn't love this comparison between Mike and Elliot. She shouldn't have brought this up! But it was too late. "I guess it *is* sweet for the twins," she said, cautiously. "But I'm not sure it's so sweet for Luca."

"Totally," Ruth said. "I get that."

Caroline went on, "The thing is, Roz told Luca that Siddha's dad was dead, and then he asked us if this was true, and before we could really explain, he asked us if Mike was Jules and Nina's dad."

"Oh god, Rozzie," Ruth said. "She used the word 'dad'?"

"I mean, that was Luca's interpretation. I have no idea if she actually used that word." This was a lie. Caroline was entirely certain that Roz had used the word "dad." Luca couldn't remember where his lunchbox was if his life depended on it, but the child had an uncanny memory for conversation. "I know this is a very tender subject for you right now, and we don't have to talk about it—"

Ruth interrupted, putting her hand on Caroline's arm. "It's fine, really. At this point I'm feeling pretty unflappable. Hit me."

"Okay, thank you. So, I just don't know what to do about Luca's question. I mean, when he asked that question, about Mike being the twins' dad, I was like, Should we have been clearer? I thought we were very clear. But maybe we were kidding ourselves. Maybe we were just repeating the same small piece of the story over and over. We never talked about genetics, or DNA, or any of that. We just kept saying Dad helped them! Dad was their helper! And it's not like Jules and Nina are strangers, or even distant friends. They're Luca's cousins! And they live in our town!"

"That's not a bad thing," Ruth said.

"I'm not saying it is, I'm just saying Luca is too old for us not to have thought this through, to have considered all the nuances. And now I have no idea how to approach it with him."

"Maybe you should talk to someone," Ruth said. "I mean," she added quickly, "not because I don't want to talk about it with you, I do, I really do! But I am hardly a reliable source of advice right now."

"Do you mean some kind of professional?"

"I don't know, maybe?" Ruth said. "I mean, I really don't think there's anything to worry about here, but again—" She pointed to her chest. "Unreliable."

Caroline laughed.

"Do you think about it when you see them?" Ruth asked. "The twins, I mean. Do you think about them being Mike's kids?"

"They're not Mike's kids!"

"I meant genetically," Ruth said. "Do you see Mike in them? At all?"

"Never," Caroline said. "Isn't that so weird? I mean," she went on, not waiting for Ruth to confirm or deny the weirdness, "they don't look anything like him. They're sort of just clones of Evie."

"Like Luca is of you," Ruth pointed out.

"Right? Poor Mike. He seems to have very weak genetic material."

"It's those WASPs. They're like water. Everywhere, but invisible."

Caroline laughed, happy to be laughing. "My not-so-tall glass of water," she said. "Anyway, maybe that's part of the problem. I just haven't thought of the twins much over the years."

"Has Mike?"

"I don't think so. I mean, I can't be sure, but he hasn't said much about it, really at all." She shrugged. "My god, what is wrong with us?"

Ruth laughed. "There's nothing wrong with you. You don't ruminate."

"Oh, that's rich," Caroline said. "Like I don't ruminate." She rolled her eyes. "I think you're right, though. We need someone, some kind of expert of some kind."

"Well, you could call a therapist, maybe? One who specializes in this sort of thing."

"No," Caroline said. "Not therapy. I know you love therapy, but I'll never get Mike to go to therapy." She shook her head. "No, I'd need something different, just a book or a group or some kind of instruction from an expert. You know, we just need help figuring out what to say."

"Could you ask at Luca's school?"

Caroline shook her head. "The psychologist there already knows a little too much about Luca from all the 'does he have a friend' conversations. She thinks we're too involved already."

"School psychologists are tricky that way." But then Ruth's face lit with a thought. "Wait! I do know someone! The psychologist at Mott Valley retired last spring, and now she's got some sort of private practice, or she's some kind of educational consultant or something like that. She's amazing. I mean really amazing. Not your typical school psychologist at all. She created this incredible culture in the school . . ."

Caroline tuned out. She didn't like hearing about Mott Valley. Everything about it seemed like a dream: gorgeous old buildings surrounded by fields and forests, small classes, endless enrichment activities. She wanted, so much, to send Luca there, but they just didn't have the money. Once, when she'd admitted to Ruth that she was jealous of her because her kids went there, Ruth had said, "Oh, don't be. It's not that great. I mean, trust me, it's got plenty of problems. Probably more than your average school." Well, then, Caroline had wanted to say, why do you send your kids there instead of the public school? But she didn't.

Sometimes Caroline wished Ruth wouldn't do so much leveling, so much converging of their wildly disparate lives. Sometimes she wished Ruth would just say, I get it. I'd be jealous too. It was tricky, because Caroline loved Ruth for all the ways she brought her in, all the ways she claimed her. Still, when it came to the very big difference between them—all of Ruth's money, which was actually Wyn's money—Caroline wanted Ruth to acknowledge it. She just wanted her to say Yeah, I know. Money is a real mindfuck, isn't it? Caroline knew this was a tall order, that people who had money mostly just felt bad about it, but still. She couldn't muster much sympathy for rich people, mainly because it seemed they didn't need her to. They could console themselves with their money.

"Anyway," Ruth continued, "I think you could just call her. Marcia Glassie-Greene is her name. I can look her up right now." She reached into her back pocket for her phone.

"Oh, no, that's okay," Caroline said. "I'll do it later." Would she? She wasn't sure she wanted to talk to this Marcia Glassie-whatever. Caroline worried she'd think they should have done more for Luca, sent him to Mott Valley Friends, or some fancy summer camp where kids build robots out of Legos.

"Or I can call her for you," Ruth offered, "to make the connection."

The doorbell rang before Caroline could answer. She grabbed the mixing bowl of candy from the kitchen table and headed down the hall to the front door. "Here we go!" she said. But when she opened the door, there were no trick-or-treaters, just a short woman with gray hair and bright-red lipstick, wearing a long camel coat and carrying a bottle of wine.

"You came!" Ruth said, coming down the hall with her arms open. "I'm so glad." Ruth hugged the woman, then turned to Caroline. "I told Florence to stop by if she wanted to see some costumes."

Ruth had told Caroline all about Florence, how Ruth had called her after Elliot's memorial, how they'd met up at the Olive Street house. Caroline had a lot of questions about Florence—she had a lot of questions about the whole Elliot era, which was a piece of Ruth's past she knew virtually nothing about. And while Caroline knew it really wasn't about her, she still found herself feeling like she'd just woken from one of those dreams where you discover a room in your house you never knew was there.

Florence smiled at Caroline and handed her the bottle of wine. "Thank you for having me," she said. "I don't get any trick or treaters now that I've moved to a quiet side street, and I've missed seeing all the costumes! All the festivities."

"Oh, well, the kids are out right now, so we're a little short on festive," Caroline said, motioning to the living room, which had been decimated by the kids in their pre-Halloween mania. There weren't even cushions on the couch. Caroline started tidying, putting books back on the shelf, tossing Playmobil people into bins, making a pile of socks for the laundry. Why were there always so many socks?

"Oooh, it's Italian," Ruth said, looking at the label on the bottle of wine Florence had brought. "Caroline's on her way to Italy in the spring."

"Where?" Florence asked.

"Oh, Rome, hopefully," Caroline said.

"Oh, gorgeous. I rented a villa in Tuscany for my fiftieth birthday last year, which I know, I *know,* is the most cliché fiftieth-birthday celebration ever, but I can tell you it's cliché for a reason."

Ruth looked at Caroline. "Oh my god, we're doing that."

"I'm in," Caroline said.

"We were just talking about child psychologists," Ruth said. She unscrewed the top of the wine bottle and filled a glass from the hallway bar cart.

Caroline looked at Ruth, but she was looking at Florence. Ruth! Caroline thought. I just met this woman!

"Oh, I just sold a house to one, actually," Florence said, taking the wineglass. "Marcia Glassie-Greene."

"Ah!" Ruth exclaimed, holding up a second full glass for Caroline. Caroline motioned for her to just put it down on the cart. "Small world! That's who we were talking about."

"She seemed great," Florence said.

"She *is* great," Ruth said. "She really helped us with Roz."

Caroline stopped reassembling the couch. "Wait, you went to her? You didn't say that." Had Ruth said that? Had Caroline not been listening?

"Yeah, yeah, we went to see her. Roz's teacher suggested it. More than suggested, really." Ruth made a pained face. "Anyway, she was great. Super helpful."

"What did she say, I mean about Roz?" Caroline asked, reaching for the wine now.

Ruth poured her own glass and turned to Florence. "Roz has a bit of a mean girl tendency," she explained. "And we'd done a crappy job of dealing with it. We'd sort of written it off, you know? Like oh, she's a middle child, or she's just assertive. Meanwhile, she's a total biatch."

Florence laughed. "I can't believe you—Ruthie, of all people—are the mother of a mean girl."

"I know, right? I'd love to blame Wyn's genes, but then look at Gilly. Blessed angel. And she's still wielding some power over Roz, but honestly, she's just sort of coasting on her age. Roz is going to lap her pretty soon, I think. And then we're all screwed. I mean really screwed. We need Gilly to work on holding her own. But that was one of the things that was so awesome about Marcia. She was just like, Uh, no, that's not how it works. You can't lean on Gilly here. It's not her job to make Roz a nicer person. That's on you. Which is a daunting task. We were scared of Roz. We still are, honestly." Ruth laughed. "But we're getting better, sort of."

Florence laughed. She looked at Caroline. "And what's your issue, if I may ask?"

No, Caroline wanted to say. You can't ask. "Oh, well, my husband, he donated sperm to his cousin, and now our kid has some questions."

"Oh wow," Florence said. "Wow."

"It really was so generous," Ruth said, quickly. She smiled at Caroline, in apology. "A truly generous act."

Okay, Caroline wanted to say. Enough. It wasn't a kidney for god's sake. Although a kidney would have been a lot easier in the long run.

The doorbell rang then, and Caroline went to get it. Florence and Ruth were on the couch and didn't get up. Just chatting away, Caroline thought, annoyed. Why was Florence even here? It was strange being with her and Ruth. Ruth was different around Florence. Different than with Wyn, different than with her. She seemed younger, more energized. Flirtatious. Caroline felt a subtle flush in her body, a charge. My god, she thought. I'm jealous. Because Ruth had never acted this way around her. Which, Caroline was thinking now, meant that Ruth had never been attracted to her, not even in the beginning. Had she wanted Ruth to want her, even just the tiniest bit? Even if they would never, ever do anything about it? Even if Caroline didn't feel the same way? And then, the thought Caroline rarely allowed herself to have: everyone was attracted to her! So was Ruth really not? Not at all?

"Do you mind if I sneak out back for a smoke?" Florence reached into her purse.

"You're still smoking?" Ruth asked.

"One a day, baby," Florence said. "Never more and never less. Best five minutes of my day." She held up the cigarette pack. "Anyone care to join me?"

A cigarette sounded fantastic to Caroline, but she didn't feel like bonding with Florence. "You two go," she said. "I'll man the door."

And so off they went, laughing like teenagers, with their cigarettes and wine bottle. Caroline stood at the door, giving candy to the kids, commenting on their costumes. Hating this night even more than she usually did. She was thinking about Ruth, and about this Marcia person, and about how Ruth was so good at finding people to help her. She had an endless list of fantastic recommendations: the babysitter who drives and does the dishes, the dentist who juggles after every exam, the swim teacher who can convince even the most hydrophobic child to put their head underwater. The list went on and on. Ruth got what she needed, the best of what she needed, and Caroline envied her for that. Part of it, of course, was her money. But part of it was that she just knew how to ask. Her kids needed help and she got it, from amazing people. Although honestly, Caroline didn't know what was so wrong with Roz. Sure, she was a little bossy, but all Ruth's kids seemed a little bossy. They were strong-willed and smart, talkative and confident in that private-school way, the way of children who'd been told their whole lives that what they thought and what they said was of utmost interest and importance. Caroline loved that about Ruth's kids, loved how lively and creative they were. She even loved Roz's smart-aleck side. At least she usually did. Right now, all she could feel was jealous.

Maybe stop being jealous and just do something, Caroline thought. She put the bowl of candy on the top porch step and went back inside. Ruth and Florence were still out back. She reached into her purse for her phone and googled "Marcia Glassie-Greene child psychologist Radclyffe." And there she was, a bright-eyed woman in a black turtleneck, with silver hair cut in a chin-length bob. Was that the law, Caroline wondered, that psychologists had to have chin-length silver bobs? But she did look smart. Before she could lose her nerve, Caroline hit *call* on the Google listing.

"You've reached the office of Dr. Marcia Glassie-Greene. Please leave a message." The voice was serious but warm. Caroline liked the sound of it. She left a message asking Marcia to call her back. Then she grabbed her wineglass and headed for the back porch.

IT WAS ALMOST eight o'clock when Caroline heard the kids burst through the front door, in a great cloud of commotion. They dumped all their candy onto the floor before she could get inside and tell them not to. Luca, overjoyed by the bounty, was throwing pieces up in the air, trying to catch them in his mouth.

"Luca, buddy, careful," Mike said, taking off his coat. Luca ignored him.

Ruth and Florence followed Caroline inside. Caroline saw Florence take in the chaos, wide-eyed.

Ruth reached for Wyn. "Wyn, you remember Florence?"

"Of course," Wyn said, opening her arms to hug her.

Caroline wondered when Wyn had last seen Florence, and what she thought of her. Caroline wondered so many things!

Then Ruth introduced Florence to Mike, and after a quick "Hello, nice to meet you," Florence pulled on her jacket and headed for the door. "I'm going to dash," she said, giving Ruth a hug. She squeezed Caroline's arm. "Thank you for a lovely evening." And just like that, she was out the front door.

"Sort of like a reverse Mary Poppins," Caroline said to Ruth when the door closed.

"This might be a little more Halloween than she's up for," Ruth said.

Caroline took a drink of her wine. "Yeah, well that makes two of us," she said.

"Who's ready to make their pile for the switch witch?" Ruth said in a teachery voice. The switch witch was sort of like the tooth fairy, only instead of taking away teeth and leaving cash, she took away Halloween candy and left board games and yo-yos. It had worked for a few years, but now the kids were on to Ruth. Nothing was better than candy.

"*No!*" the children shrieked in unison. Roz threw her body over her pile of candy. Abe started shoving his down the front of his Batman costume, and Luca put two Snickers bars in his mouth at once.

"Relax, kiddos! Mama's only teasing," Wyn said.

"Thanks, fun mom!" Ruth said, whacking Wyn's arm.

"Yeah, thanks, fun mom!" Luca said, chocolate-tinged spittle dripping out of his mouth.

All the adults laughed, and Caroline felt her heart swell. The truth was, she wasn't over this scene, not at all. She'd never be over seeing her boy—her beautiful, guileless boy with his utter inability to detect sarcasm—in this scrum of children who loved him. All her annoyance, all her jealousy and expectations, evaporated in the warmth of this loud, sugary, joyful moment. *This* is your family, Caroline reminded herself. And they are Luca's, too.

11

Tobi worked late every Monday night, and not just until seven, but late late, a young potter's hours. She worked until midnight, one or two in the morning. She came home quietly, slept in the attic guest room so as not to disturb Evie and the kids, and—more important—not to be disturbed by their morning noise. When they'd started Few&Far, Tobi's one nonnegotiable was that she could work at least one all-nighter every week.

On this particular Monday, after everyone else left the studio, Tobi had rummaged around in her work bag for the binder. She'd been wearing it more often now, although still only when she was alone, and mostly while she worked. She could get it on with less struggle than that first attempt at the photo shoot. Still, it was a significant, sweaty effort. Tobi had told herself these days of secret binder wearing were an experiment: she'd see how it felt, if it became more natural over time.

So far, binding was making Tobi feel a strange combination of invincible and tortured. She always managed to keep it on for a few hours, despite the discomfort and the distraction, the tightness, the itch. The compression was no joke, and it made taking a deep breath hard. Yet it also created space, altering the physical distance between her and the wheel.

How strange it felt, the expanse that was now between her arms and her chest. Just a few more inches, sure, but why did it suddenly seem like an entirely different body? The problem was, when Tobi wore the binder, she threw pots just as quickly and skillfully as she always did, but she never really lost herself in the flow. She could think only about her shallow breathing, her achy breasts, her arms. This was the paradox of binding: it diminished her physical breasts but brought them, maddeningly, front and center in her consciousness.

And then at times when Tobi couldn't safely bind—like when she was canoeing with Mike—all she could think about was how good it would feel to move her arms and not feel her breasts. What range she'd have! How smooth her strokes would be. With each dip of the paddle into the water, she'd feel it, the possibility. After an hour of rhythmic paddling, a rhythm that could have been—should have been—meditative, Tobi's brain had carved a deep mantric rut of "Not this. Not this." In this way the binder—when she wore it, when she didn't wear it—had become a splinter. Barely visible, but wildly distracting. Maybe it will get better, Tobi thought. Would it get better?

She heard a knock at the studio's fire escape window and turned to see Mike, smiling and holding a six-pack. Tobi waved, then motioned for him to wait. She grabbed a sweatshirt off a hook by the door and pulled it over her head. Mike wasn't the most observant guy, but Tobi wanted to avoid any questions or conversations about the binder.

"Dude," Tobi said, opening the window for Mike to climb through. "What are you doing here?"

"I was on my way home and remembered that Monday was your night. But I'll split if you're in the flow."

"I very much am not," Tobi said. This was true, but even if it weren't she'd never send Mike away. Tobi was always happy to see him, always ready to stop whatever she was in the middle of to go anywhere he wanted to go, do anything he wanted to do.

Before Mike had come to live with Tobi and her mom, she'd both loved and feared the idea of men. Her father had been brilliant and loving, but he was a terrible drunk, and a violent one. Tobi shared a name with her father: she was the fifth in a line of Tobias Fynchs, and the first girl to be given the family name, an inheritance that was both a great gift and a total mindfuck for boyish Tobi. She'd had no idea how, or who, to be.

She was ten years old when her dad left, and sixteen when Mike came to live with them. Mike was strong-willed, but his temperament was even. He was funny, he was kind. He was wildly protective of Tobi's mom, and of Tobi too. A few months after Mike moved in, Tobi started sleeping through the night for the first time in her life. She ate two helpings of dinner every night, finished her homework, played basketball in the park with Mike and his friends, the friends he made after just a few weeks at school, friends who became Tobi's friends too.

When Mike moved into Tobi's house, he'd brought a duffle bag of clothes, a backpack of books, and a cast-iron skillet that had belonged to his mom. That was the entirety of his possessions. One night at dinner, after he'd been living there for a few months, he quietly asked Lynne if he could clear out some space in the garage. One of his fellow dishwashers had offered to sell Mike his motorcycle. It didn't run, not yet, but Mike knew he could get it going.

"Of course," Lynne said, as she stood to clear the dishes from the table. "Tobi will help you."

Later that night, Tobi went into her mother's bedroom and told her that it wasn't fair. Tobi had always wanted a motorcycle, and Lynne had forbidden it. Lynne was a hospital social worker and had spent much of her career in the ER, where she'd seen too many accidents. "You mean a donorcycle?" Lynne asked, when fourteen-year-old Tobi had said she was saving her money to buy one someday.

Tobi didn't care what her mother called them; she desperately wanted a motorcycle. She collected secondhand Haynes manuals the way other kids collected comic books, and she pored over them while she ate breakfast, and when she was supposed to be doing her homework in the afternoon. But no matter how much Tobi begged, her mother forbade it.

"You hate motorcycles," Tobi said, standing next to her mother's bed. "Why does Mike get to have one?"

"He's an orphan now," Lynne said. She patted the empty space on the bed next to her, an invitation for Tobi to sit down. Tobi ignored it. "He needs to get lost in something. It will take him years to get that thing running, if he ever does. But it will help him stay busy, while he figures out his place. It will make it easier for him to feel like he belongs, and that's what we want. We want him to feel like he belongs."

"And what do I get? To make me feel like I belong?"

Tobi's mother gave her a look that said Don't be ridiculous.

"I'm not helping him clean out the garage," Tobi said.

"Okay," said her mother. And so ended another fight between them, the way they always ended: a negligible win for Tobi, overall victory for her mother.

After the motorcycle arrived, Tobi started avoiding Mike. This was a particularly painful (and foolish) way of getting back at her mother, seeing as the only thing Tobi wanted more than to work on a motorcycle was to spend time with Mike. But now she lingered at school so she could walk home alone, and went in through the front door to bypass the garage.

One afternoon, Mike came into the kitchen where Tobi was eating her after-school cereal and asked if she would come outside and help him. "I just need another set of hands," he said.

"I'm a little busy," Tobi said.

"No, you're not," he said.

"Okay, fine," Tobi said, and slammed up from the table and out the door to the garage.

Mike told her he just needed her to hold the bike steady while he tried to get the carburetor out, but right away Tobi could see that the carburetor was the least of the bike's problems. The hoses were deteriorated, the brakes corroded. She picked up a spark plug from the workbench and its wires broke apart in her hand. "Do you have the electrical schematic?" Tobi asked.

Mike gave her a blank look.

"Hang on a sec," Tobi said. "I'll be right back." The motorcycle was a 1983 Norton, and while Tobi didn't have the exact manual for this model, she knew she had something similar. She brought her milk crate of manuals out to the garage and found one for a 1979 model. She showed Mike the exploded view of the engine and explained that what he really needed to do was get inside it, to see what was up with the ignition, and to clean out the air system, which she could see was clogged with dirt and dust. "When a bike doesn't run, it's always one of three things," Tobi said. "Fuel, spark, or air. Have you drained the fuel tank?"

Mike shook his head. "I haven't done shit, obviously."

"How much did you pay for this thing?" Tobi asked.

"Nothing," Mike said.

Tobi laughed. "I can help you," she said, quietly. "I mean, I think I can help you."

Mike put his hand on Tobi's shoulder. "Dude, I *know* you can help me. And when we get it running, it's half yours. Totally. We share it, right down the middle."

They got to work then, the two of them. Tobi explained the engine to Mike, how they'd start by cleaning it, putting in new gaskets, replacing the spark plugs. "We'll follow the machine," she said, "and it will tell us what to do." She didn't really know what this meant, but she'd read it in one of her motorcycle magazines, and she liked the sound of it. They worked until dark.

The next day was a Saturday, and at breakfast Mike asked Tobi if she had time to work on the bike. "Sure," Tobi said, and looked over at her mother, who seemed to be pretending not to hear.

It took them the better part of a year to get that bike running, but they did it. They learned—both of them—how to follow the machine, to understand what it needed from them. And then they rode it all around Boston, and even out to Walden Pond and to the beach in Winthrop. Lynne made them both swear up and down that they'd never take it on the highway, or go over fifty miles an hour. They kept their word, riding it all the way to Amherst on back roads when they went to UMass for college. They kept it in a barn behind the old house where they shared a third-floor apartment and took it out for long rides through the tobacco fields on fall weekends. After college, Tobi went right to Indiana, and Mike went back to Boston and took the bike with him.

Mike sold the motorcycle when Luca was born. Tobi assumed Caroline had made him do it, but Mike said no, he'd made the decision himself. "Gotta stick around for this kid," he said. This was something Mike said a lot when Luca was a baby. Mike had very strong feelings about sticking around. Tobi understood. She had strong feelings too. So strong, in fact, that in those days, when she and Evie were trying to start a family, she often woke in the night, panicked that she wouldn't be able to keep herself from leaving the way her own father had.

Tobi felt like Caroline didn't know how lucky she was, the way that Mike was so intent on making sure Luca knew he was always there for him. Once when Luca was a baby, Tobi stopped by on a Saturday afternoon to find Mike vacuuming the house while wearing Luca in a Baby-Björn, a bottle of milk in his back pocket. Mike seemed to always have Luca attached to him: in a sling, a backpack, a bike seat he'd ordered from Holland that situated Luca squarely between the handlebars, his little helmeted head bobbling when they went over a bump. Tobi had felt funny alternating surges of jealousy in those days: part of her wanting to be Mike, part of her wishing she were Luca.

"SO HEY," MIKE said, hopping up to sit on one of the worktables. He opened a beer and handed it to Tobi. "Shit's gotten a little weird over at my house since that dinner at Ruth and Wyn's."

"Oh man, I know," Tobi said. "That whole Elliot Shepkins thing. I can't believe he's Siddha's dad. Did you get any more details on that?"

"Not really," Mike said. "But it seems like the kids were talking that night, and Luca has some questions. About me and the twins. Did your kids say anything?"

Tobi shook her head. "It might have gone over their heads. And it's not like we're going to bring it up."

Mike took a swig of his beer. "Don't ask, don't tell?"

"More like, don't care until they do."

"Got it," Mike said. "I'm not sure if Luca cares, but I think Caroline does. I mean, I know she cares. Or she's worried."

"About what?" Tobi asked.

"Well," Mike said, "any of the many things one might worry about when their husband is a sperm donor, Tob."

"Like we're going to pressure you into paying for college?"

"It's more likely to go the other way on that one," Mike said. "You know what Nana used to say."

"Where's my Pinot?"

Mike laughed. "Can't get blood from a stone."

Tobi held out her bottle, and they both drank to Nana, which was fitting, because drinking had been their nana's main pastime. Mike and Tobi's family tree was just one liquor-soaked branch after another, but their unspoken understanding was that if they talked about it, joked about it, watched each other, well, then they would be okay.

"Caroline's worried that we've oversimplified the whole thing. That we've stuck to this same story, and now Luca is older and maybe he needs a little more nuance. And I'm like, Shit, I don't know if nuance is so good here. I mean, you just have to peel it back a bit and then the whole thing is really complicated."

"It really doesn't need to be," Tobi said. She put her hand to her chest for a moment, the flatness of it a strange, beautiful thrill.

"Do you think about it much?" Mike asked. "I mean, it's kinda weird, how we never talk about it."

"Is it? I think it's nice that it's just a fact. It's a given. I mean, I get it, there was a time when I thought it would be a lot for all of us to hold in our heads. But then—the kids, they take up so much space as actual people, there's not much time to see them as anything else. I mean, they're a lot of work. Our life is kind of chaotic, I don't have that much time to think." She took a long drink of her beer.

"Does it help that they don't look like me?" Mike said. Was that the tiniest bit of disappointment in his voice?

"Seriously, Mikey? I'd love it if they looked like you," Tobi said. "We never would have asked you to do this if I didn't love the idea of my kids looking like you. And anyway, they do. They have a lot of Mike mannerisms."

"Those are probably from you," Mike said.

"They're from both of us."

Mike nodded. They didn't talk for a while, just drank their beers. Silence was the most familiar sound in the world to the two of them. "The thing is," Mike said, finally. "Caroline thinks we should go and talk to someone about it, about how to help Luca understand. To clarify."

"Like a shrink?"

"More like a consultant, I think. Someone who used to work at Mott Valley Friends. Only the best, right?" He rolled his eyes.

"Only the best," Tobi concurred, a bit sheepishly. She hadn't yet told Mike that the twins would be going to Mott Valley next year. She'd been putting it off, seeing as she had enjoyed knocking private schools (and private-school kids) with Mike since just about forever. She needed to gently break the news to him that the twins would soon be those very kids.

Mike ran his fingers through his hair, smoothed his hand over his beard. "I don't want to go."

"That tracks," Tobi said.

"Like *you'd* want to?"

"Definitely not. But I've done my fair share of therapy."

"It's not therapy," Mike said.

Tobi held up her hands in surrender. "Got it," she said. "It's not therapy."

"Should I go?" Mike asked.

"Yes," Tobi said, without hesitation. "I speak from experience here, Mikey. You have to go. Your wife wants you to go to therapy, you go." If Evie could hear me right now, Tobi thought, she'd kill me. She'd pick up one of those urns from the curing shelf and smash it over my head.

Evie didn't like the word "wife," but Tobi loved it. Evie had only agreed to get married for the tax benefits. And she didn't like the idea of Tobi doing anything out of marital obligation. Or any kind of obligation, for that matter. But Tobi loved calling Evie her wife. She loved having a wife. It was, to her, the most extraordinary thing in the world. If someone had told her, when she was a teenager and split open with hormones and lust and confusion, that someday she would have a wife, well, she wouldn't have been able to believe it.

Evie didn't want a wife, she just wanted Tobi to want all the same things she did. Would Evie want them to do therapy now? Tobi wondered. If she knew that I was wearing this binder? No, Tobi thought. Or not because of the binder. She'd want to go because of the secret.

When was she going to tell Evie, anyway? That was the question. Tobi felt herself moving dangerously past the time when she could be truthful about the binder, when her questioning, her experimenting, could unfold in real time with any kind of transparency. Even now she'd have to pretend she'd just ordered the thing, pretend to be debating about whether she wanted to wear it, when the truth was, Tobi was already moving past the binder. This was what she needed to admit: the results from her binder experiment were already in. Tobi didn't want to be compressed. She wanted to expand. She wanted more chest, more space, more breath. That was what she'd seen—what she saw—in Bex.

You need to slow down, Tobi told herself, until Evie can get on board. Of course, it would be hard for Evie to get on board if Tobi hadn't even told her about the binder, or why she wanted to wear it. Tobi felt the heat of her own impatience. What if she woke up every morning and just put on a T-shirt and went to work? It was such an old desire, one she'd long ago filed away as simple nostalgia for her prepubescent childhood, her once boyish body, the ancient pleasure of being mistaken for her mother's son. She'd forgotten to even want it, forgotten until she saw Bex. And now she was turning fifty—fifty!—and had money and health insurance. And she lived in a world where people had top surgery all the time. She could do what she wanted. She could do what she wanted! But then—and here it was, the loop, starting over again like an old CD stuck in a car stereo—what about Evie?

"Tobi, dude, are you listening?"

"Yeah, yeah, sorry," Tobi said, snapping her mind back to attention. "I'm listening. I'm right here."

12

When Caroline and Mike arrived at Marcia Glassie-Greene's office suite, the door from the waiting area to her office was open. Caroline saw her sitting behind a desk, typing.

"Come on in," Marcia said, taking off her glasses and rising to greet them. She had a warm smile and a pleasant, symmetrical face that was framed by full gray bangs. The rest of her hair was pulled back in a chignon, and she wore a red scarf tied jauntily above the neckline of a black jumpsuit. She was barely five feet tall.

I guess she grew out the bob, Caroline thought. She also thought, Wow, this woman has style. She looked at Marcia's left hand for a wedding ring, and when she saw one she felt relief, although she wasn't sure why.

"Please, sit down," Marcia said, taking her own seat in an Eames chair and motioning toward a white linen couch. "Let me apologize in advance for my seating arrangements. That couch is terribly uncomfortable, and you don't have to pretend otherwise. I ordered a new one, but did you know how long it takes for furniture to arrive?" She laughed. "When I placed the order I thought, well, I hope it comes before I retire!"

"It's cool," Mike said. Caroline could hear the nerves in his voice. She squeezed his hand, but he didn't squeeze back.

"So," Marcia said, and then took a sip from her coffee mug. It was a GoldFynch mug, which annoyed Caroline. She wondered if Mike would say anything about the mug, but he didn't.

"Luca," Marcia said, putting down the mug. She smiled again. "You said in your message that he's seven? Second grade, then?"

Caroline nodded. "That's right. His birthday is in March."

"I love seven," Marcia said. "The age of reason."

"Yeah, well," Mike said. Caroline dug her nails into his thigh.

"What's he like?" Marcia asked.

"Oh—" Caroline looked at Mike, who, after that nail dig, was definitely going to keep his mouth shut. "He's a very sweet kid. Very sensitive, very smart." Caroline went on, telling Marcia all about Luca, about the things he was good at, the things that were harder for him. And then, when she was warmed up and feeling a brave sort of emotional momentum spurred by Marcia's kind face, her openness, her interest, Caroline said the thing she had promised herself she wouldn't say. "Luca doesn't have a lot of friends. Friends have always been hard."

"He has a friend," Mike said. "A really good one."

Marcia smiled. "Well, that's really all a child, or any of us, needs."

"Yes, well," Caroline said, "the problem is, that friend moved away over the summer." Caroline was, somewhere in the back of her mind, aware of the fact that the conversation seemed to be heading farther and farther from the whole sperm donor topic, but maybe this was just how it worked? Maybe they had to lay the groundwork? Either way, Marcia's face conveyed such kindness, such interest, that Caroline decided she'd just follow Marcia's lead and tell her the story—the whole story—of Luca and Victor.

"Well, Victor sounds wonderful," Marcia said when Caroline had finished. "But he's moved away."

Mike said, "We've taken Luca a few times to hang with Victor in the city."

"Really?" Marcia said. "Well, that's very generous of you."

"Oh, it's our pleasure," Caroline said. "I mean, we love Victor. We're happy to do whatever we can to support their friendship."

"Still, that's quite a commitment on your part. And not very sustainable, over the long term."

Caroline looked at Mike. "It's fine," she said. "We really don't mind."

"You know," Marcia said, slowly, in a tone that suggested she didn't really think Caroline and Mike knew, not at all, "the thing is, parents can often overthink the friendship dynamics of young children, and place too much emphasis on the relationships, expect them to be permanent or meaningful in a way they oftentimes aren't. Adults often see their old childhood friendships through the lens of later, more intimate friendships, and imbue them with that same level of meaning, when in reality, it's just not like that for children."

"Well then, what is it like for children?" Caroline asked.

"Oh, that varies, of course, but friends are quite fungible. So now your task is to teach Luca that Victor, while a very wonderful friend, can be replaced. He doesn't need to go to the city to visit him. He can find someone here. You need to show him that you think he can do that."

"So what do we say?" Caroline asked.

"You simply say, Now that Victor has moved away, it's a good time to start finding a new friend."

"He's deeply attached to Victor."

"Who wouldn't be? *I'm* attached to Victor and I haven't even met him!" Marcia said with a laugh. "But at the end of the day, that attachment is Luca's, not yours. You need to stick with the facts, the circumstance at hand. Luca's friend has moved away, and he needs a new one. It's really a very ordinary situation."

"It doesn't feel very ordinary," Caroline said. She felt the prick of tears.

"Oh, I understand," Marcia said. "There's nothing ordinary about our own children's lives." She smiled at Caroline. "And I know this friendship is very important to Luca. But you're making it important to you, which is making it very hard for you to help him do what we all must do when we grieve, which is to ask ourselves, What next? And to do what we can to bring joy back into our lives. You're giving Luca the message that he's not capable of that, that his joy was singular and irreplaceable. That's a tough message to get."

"So you're saying it's our fault," Mike said. Caroline didn't squeeze his hand this time, or pinch his leg. Yeah, she wanted to say. You think this is our fault?

"I'm saying that if you'd like to help Luca make a new friend, and it sounds like you would, then perhaps the thing to do is to take some logical, practical steps toward that end. You have some agency to help that happen. Use it, and then step back."

"What do we say?" Caroline asked.

"You say, I've invited such-and-such child to go bowling with us on Saturday. Would you like to eat pizza or Chinese after?"

"The whole meaningless-choice-to-feel-powerful thing," Caroline said.

Marcia shrugged and laughed a little. "Hey, it works. And also, the choices aren't meaningless. They're well within the scope of what feels like real agency to a kid."

"And if they don't have a good time?"

"Then move on to another candidate. One of them will stick."

"Victor is a really special kid."

"But even special kids are replaceable."

"And Luca is—" Caroline's voice broke a little. "Luca is special too."

"Yes," Marcia said. "I can see that. I really can." She smiled. "Which is why he can find a new friend. I am quite confident about that." She smiled at both of them, paused for a moment, a perfect beat shorter than would have been awkward. Caroline marveled at her timing. "Do you have many friends?"

"You mean now?" Caroline asked.

"Now, or in your past."

"Sure," Caroline said. "I mean some. I mean—" She laughed nervously. "Not a lot of friends, no. But Mike does," she said, looking at Mike. He looked back at her. He wasn't going to say anything. "But he doesn't care as much as I do. I mean, he's not as worried as I am about Luca not having friends."

"Well, that makes sense," Marcia said.

"Really?" Caroline said. "I thought it would be the opposite. I mean, I thought Mike would want Luca to have more friends. I thought he'd want to help him more."

"Mike?" Marcia said. "Do you want to add anything here?"

"I think Caroline covered it. I mean, yeah, I have a lot of friends, and I'm not worried about Luca." Mike closed his mouth then, as though he was afraid another thought might pop out.

Marcia nodded. "I'd guess that's because Mike doesn't really see friendship as a struggle. If you haven't had to work at something, you don't really know how to begin, or what life is like without it. Mike might just be thinking that if Luca wanted more friends, he'd get them. He might be thinking that Luca is pretty content. He might also have a better sense of the fact, and I do think this is a fact, that friends don't solve all your problems."

Marcia looked directly at Mike and smiled. She said, "And please, Mike—please correct me if I'm wrong. The last thing I want to do is make an assumption about your feelings."

"No, it's cool," Mike said. "I mean, yeah, it's sort of exactly what you said."

Caroline was dumbfounded. *Really?* she thought. *It's exactly what she said? How had they never talked about this before?*

"But you, Caroline," Marcia continued, "you might be more well-acquainted with loneliness."

Caroline nodded, willing herself not to cry.

"The trick would be for both of you to be able to put aside your own experiences and really look at Luca, without fear, with genuine curiosity. To really just be with him, to watch how he works, to listen to what he says, to meet him where he's at, so to speak."

Caroline wanted to say, *I'm not curious about Luca.* Instead, she said, "I think the only thing I really want to know about Luca is that he's okay."

"Oh, he's most definitely okay," Marcia said. "That we can know for sure." She smiled warmly at Caroline. "That," she said, taking off her glasses and resting them on her lap, "that's just a fact."

EXACTLY FIFTY-ONE MINUTES after Caroline and Mike had walked into Marcia's office, they stumbled out onto the street. The sun was bright, and they squinted, as though they'd been in a movie theater all afternoon. "Wow," Caroline said.

"Yeah," Mike said. "Wow."

Caroline put her arm through Mike's. She knew him well enough to know that their "wows" didn't mean the same thing.

"I thought we were going to talk about the sperm donor situation," Mike said.

"I did too," Caroline said. "I guess we never really got past explaining who Luca is." It had felt wonderful, explaining Luca to Marcia. For the first time in all her years of being Luca's mother, she felt a sense of lightness, of optimism, although she wasn't quite sure why.

It wasn't as though she liked what Marcia had said. The opposite, in fact. She found it upsetting, frightening. But it was more the way she'd said it, the confidence and warmth, the way she'd made it seem that what they were doing was so vital. When did Caroline ever feel that? Only when she played music. She never felt that way as Luca's mother. But now, in that office, Marcia had made it seem as though they were engaged in such essential work. She had made Caroline feel, for the very first time, that she had the chance to do something beautiful and creative and meaningful for Luca's development. Until now all the advice had been sticker charts and consequences. But Marcia was all love and revolution. Not that Caroline had any idea what to do next, not really. But right now, that didn't seem to matter. Luca was okay.

13

On the first Friday in November, Ruth spent the day as she had spent every first Friday in November: setting up for the annual Mott Valley silent auction. After many exhausting hours of assembling folding tables, finalizing price lists, and plating the five hundred brownies donated by Bread Euphoria, she rounded up the kids and drove them home, stopping at the grocery store on the way. When she pulled into the driveway, her heart fell a bit at the absence of Siddha's car.

Before Elliot died, just the sight of the car—a blazing red Volkswagen GTI—had been enough to put Ruth in a bad mood. The car had been a gift from Wyn's mother, and because Grandma Rosalynn had been a little fuzzy on the New York driving age, it had arrived six months earlier than Siddha's license.

All the kids had been in the driveway when the car came, watching with fascination as the driver unloaded the car from the rig. Siddha was wild with happiness, jumping up and down, hugging Ruth, hugging Wyn, taking a video with her phone. Not wanting to look like a total monster, Ruth waited until all the kids were in bed to lay into Wyn about the car. "You can't just send a child a car," Ruth said. "Who does that?"

Wyn had just shrugged. "My mother," she said. "And her mother before her. It's the Rosalynn way. There's no use fighting it."

"You know what I think of the Rosalynn way?" Ruth said. "I think—"

Wyn interrupted. "I do, hon. I know exactly what you think of it. But clearly this car isn't going anywhere. So let's make a plan."

At breakfast the next morning, Ruth had laid the ground rules for the car. "Once you have your license," she'd told Siddha, "you can have limited access to the car until you turn seventeen. Then, if you show us that you can handle the responsibility, it's yours." Before Siddha could respond, Ruth added, "And you'll have to get a job, to cover gas and insurance."

"Fun," Siddha said.

But ever since the letter had arrived from Elliot's lawyers, Siddha was driving the car whenever and wherever she wanted, and Ruth wasn't saying a word. She'd hardly been home at all this week, and when Ruth would ask where she was going, she'd tell Ruth she was babysitting or studying with friends. Ruth doubted she was doing either, but she hadn't said anything.

"Why don't you all go out to the barn and find Mom?" Ruth said to the kids. She turned off the car and started gathering her things. "I know she wants to see you."

This was a little trick Ruth and Wyn played on each other, always sending the kids in search of the other parent. It was how they bought, or stole, some alone time. Although right now it wasn't alone time Ruth wanted so much as a chance to check in with Siddha. She texted her. *Hey hon, how was your day?*

Siddha texted right back. *It was fine I'm at debate and then I'm going to Nyla's for dinner*

Earlier in the week, Ruth had asked Siddha if she could take care of her siblings that night. "We have the auction at school," she'd explained to Siddha. "And I'd rather not get a sitter. Can you handle it?"

Siddha had made a face that suggested she was considering it, then a face that suggested she'd realized, sadly, that she wouldn't be able to do it. Ruth knew that both faces were purely performance. "I have this thing at school," Siddha said.

"What thing?" Ruth said.

"For yearbook?" Siddha said, her questioning tone suggesting that either she wasn't sure, or that she'd told Ruth already and she should remember.

On a Friday? Ruth had thought. She'd sighed. "Okay, Sid, I'll see if Lola is free."

Now, just a few days later, Siddha had clearly forgotten the details of her original excuse and had fabricated a new one. Ruth was about to text Wyn and ask her to get some more information out of Siddha—she was much better at that these days—when the kids came bounding into the kitchen.

"Mom told us to ask you for a snack," Abe said, breathless from the run across the yard.

"How thoughtful of Mom," Ruth said. "Go wash your hands. Gilly, can you make something? Maybe cheesy toast?" Ruth went into the living room, where Roz followed her, crying. Ruth sat down on the couch and beckoned Roz to her, then half listened to her rage about some injustice that had befallen her on the playground at lunch—which was most likely just Roz's friends trying to exercise their basic human right to self-determination.

Jesus, Wyn, you've been home all day, Ruth thought, trying to ignore the sound of Gilly and Abe fighting over the toaster oven settings. *Why can't you come inside and make the kids a snack?* Or why hadn't she made the snack already, and left it in the fridge, the way Ruth had always done when she was planning to be out when the kids came home? How was it that if Ruth was out for the day and Wyn was home, Wyn was still somehow the working parent? Was it because Ruth wasn't *actually* working? But then again, neither was Wyn, not technically. Although Wyn seemed to think she was.

Over the summer, Ruth had talked about this ambiguity with Caroline, who'd suggested that maybe the solution was to get a job. Caroline loved working; Ruth knew this about her. She'd had her first job at thirteen, sorting out-of-date magazines at her neighborhood newsstand, and aside from her maternity leave, she'd been working ever since.

"Look, Ruth," Caroline had said when Ruth was venting her frustrations. "Freud said it best: life is love and work. Or something like that. *And* is the operative word there. You can't have a life with one and not the other. You've got love to spare, god knows, but you really, really need some work. And at the risk of sounding gross and capitalist, it needs to be work that pays you. In money. The problem is, and I hope it's okay that I say this"—Ruth nodded her permission for whatever was to come—"you don't *need* money." Caroline shrugged then, and Ruth appreciated the way she was acting as though they always spoke frankly about the wealth Ruth had married into, which they didn't.

Caroline continued. "But you know what? You kind of do need the money. Because everyone does. Everyone needs the reductionist, problematic clarity of being a wage earner. It might crush the soul, but it really bolsters the mood."

"But where?" Ruth asked. "And doing what? I can't go back in the classroom. At this point I think it would kill me."

"Definitely not the classroom," Caroline had agreed. "But there are plenty of other jobs out there."

Ruth knew that Caroline was right. Wyn was going to be home all day, and Ruth needed to get out. That, ultimately, was the reason that Ruth had to get a job. She couldn't be home all day with Wyn. Did she resent that now, just as the kids were old enough to be out of the house, was the time when Wyn suddenly needed to live a new dream, dashing Ruth's chance for some hard-earned solitude? Well, yes, yes she did. But the truth was, Wyn had the gift of good timing. She lived the very definition of a charmed life. That had been true when Ruth met her, and it was even more true now.

Long ago Ruth had asked herself: Can you look past Wyn's good luck and love her anyway? Can you see who she really is, and can you hold on to that? Can you loosen your jealousy, even if you can't entirely let it go? Ruth had decided, after much deliberation, that she could. She could see Wyn as a wounded, vulnerable, sensitive, deeply generous person who loved Ruth like crazy. She was also an incredibly good time. But even so, Ruth still resented her sometimes. Sometimes she resented Wyn so much it made her stomach hurt.

Because that's what resentment really was, a discomfort that Ruth had to live with. It was all on her, not Wyn. And when it flared, it was up to Ruth to figure out how to fix it. But this time around, all her usual fixes were out of reach. She wasn't going to take a trip, because leaving Siddha felt impossible. She wasn't going to dive into a project, like reupholstering the living room couch or wallpapering the dining room, because their house and their lives were too full of Wyn's projects.

Ruth knew there was no logic to this, that of course she could spend her days doing those or any number of other things. She could volunteer more at the kids' school, she could go back to school herself. She could work at Bread Euphoria, for god's sake. Wyn didn't care how Ruth spent her time, and money certainly wasn't the issue. And if she didn't want to do any of these things, well, Wyn would love having Ruth at home, would love seeing her multiple times during the day. What she would really love was for Ruth to join her in the project of this farm, to help her move electric fences, muck the horse barn, deworm the sheep. There was no way in hell Ruth was going to do any of that, but even if Wyn's daily tasks were more palatable to Ruth, she still wouldn't have wanted to participate. Ruth needed space from Wyn, she always had. She needed privacy; she needed solitude. She needed these things to quiet the jealousy, the disbelief she still felt sometimes when she thought of Wyn's life, her temperament, her audacity. To love Wyn, Ruth needed space from her. But resentment, a powerful centrifugal force, could really immobilize a person. Since they'd made the move to the farm Ruth had felt like she was on one of those fair rides that spun around so fast that you were flattened against it, the floor dropping out, unable to lift even your arm. She was spinning under the force of her own anger.

"Rozzy," Ruth said now, gently interrupting Roz's tirade about Loretta and Asa's transgressions, "I have to go upstairs and take a shower. Eat some cheese toast and watch some TV and you'll feel so much better."

Roz muttered (how did she have a ten-year-old who muttered?) something about no one caring about her life, then went into the kitchen. Ruth heard her yell at Gilly for making her toast too bubbly.

My god, enough with the yelling, Ruth thought, quickly stealing up the stairs before anyone else could find her. She had just turned on the shower and was peeling off her clothes when she heard her phone ring from her bedroom. She went in to see who it was. Caroline. She went back in the bathroom and turned off the water, wrapped a towel around herself, and lay down on the bed.

The whole world hated talking on the phone now, but not Ruth. She was still happy to stop whatever she was doing to talk. Phone calls reminded her of her own mother, who had loved nothing more than a good phone call. Nearly any time her mother was home, Ruth could find her in the kitchen, the long coil of phone cord hanging like a jump rope across the room from the phone on the wall to her mother at the sink, or the stove, or the kitchen table where she liked to sit with her feet up on a chair, flipping through a magazine. The phone seemed to Ruth a perfect form of communication. You could be doing whatever you wanted, in whatever state of dishevelment or, as was the case right now, undress, and hear the voice of someone you loved.

"Hey there," Ruth said. "Did you go to Marcia?"

"We did," Caroline said. "My god, she is amazing. I mean, really amazing. If I'd known a psychologist could be like that, I'd have gone a lot sooner."

"Right?" Ruth said. "She just tells you what to do! At first, I was kind of gobsmacked, and then I was like, Wait, tell me more!"

"It's the dream. It really is. I keep thinking about how things could be different if I'd gone sooner. I have zero parenting intuition—"

"Not true," Ruth interrupted. "You have great intuition."

"That is so kind and such a lie. I'm a hard worker and I do a lot of research. But anyway, now who even cares about intuition! Now I've got Marcia."

"So you're going back?"

"If I can convince Mike," Caroline said. "I mean we didn't even get to the whole donor thing, we were just talking about Luca." She laughed a little. "Which, if you'd told me was going to happen, I'd be like, No way am I ever going there—but it was fine. It was more than fine. It was kind of great. And now it's like I have one thousand more things to ask her about. Although I'm sort of torn because part of me doesn't want to know how badly I've fucked up in the past, and the other part of me is like, Tell me now! While there's still time."

Ruth laughed. "There is plenty of time," she said. "I promise." She leaned over to the bedside table in search of a nail clipper. "I'm putting you on speaker so I can cut my fingernails. Isn't her office just so gorgeous? It's like a set for a movie about therapy. Starring Diane Keaton."

"Right? It made me covetous. Those rugs and paintings, which, by the way, were all real, not prints. Do you think she did them? Do you think she's a painter?"

"Maybe," Ruth said. "She seems to have a good eye. And she wears those big earrings."

"Oh, she had on studs when we saw her. Diamonds."

"Nice," Ruth said. "Very classic. I admire women with the time and energy to change their earrings. What was her outfit?"

"This great black jumpsuit. I'd expected her to be in some sort of Eileen Fisher getup. That's sort of the law, isn't it?"

Ruth laughed. "I think when we saw her she was in black cigarette pants and a button-down. She's very fit. Do you think she does Pilates?"

"She seems more yoga to me," Caroline said.

"Or lap swimming. Maybe she swims laps every morning."

"God, I can't wait to be sixty and on my second career and swimming laps every morning."

"Right? I bet she swims and then sits in the sauna."

"I could see that," Caroline said. "I mean, her skin is great. It's the skin of someone who steams."

"Speaking of which, I'm supposed to be taking a shower. Call me tomorrow?"

AFTER HER SHOWER, Ruth went down the back stairs and into the kitchen where the kids were still making rounds of cheese toast. "I think you're all set," she said, shooing them out of the kitchen. "We're having an early dinner."

Wyn came in just then. "I love an early dinner," she said. "I think Ma Ingalls called it 'supper.'"

"Because she and Pa Ingalls had to leave at six for the fundraiser auction at the private one-room schoolhouse?"

"Oh, shit," Wyn said. "That's tonight?"

"I reminded you this morning," Ruth said. "When I left to spend my entire day setting it up."

"I'm sure you did," Wyn said. "It's just been a crazy day."

Has it? Ruth wanted to ask. But she didn't. "You know, I can go without you." There was no way in hell she was going without Wyn.

"Nah," said Wyn. "Let's go." She kissed Ruth. "It's basically as close as we get to a date right now."

"We can go on an actual date," Ruth said. She didn't like it when Wyn suggested they were too busy or preoccupied for each other, even though Wyn wasn't saying it as a criticism, or a complaint. Wyn was as honest as she was content.

"We can," Wyn said, "but will we?"

"Probably not," Ruth said. "Hey, did I tell you that the Petersons donated a week in their apartment in Montreal?" Montreal was an old joke between Ruth and Wyn. They'd once had an awful getaway weekend there, Ruth newly pregnant with Abe and barfing into trash cans all over the city.

"Seriously?" Wyn said. She was looking at her phone, cracking pistachios, and drinking a beer. She wasn't listening.

"Bidding starts at two grand. I'm thinking we should go for it," Ruth said, resting her chin on her hands, her eyes open wide and gazing right at Wyn. Would this get her attention? It would not. Ruth sniffed loudly. "Hey hon, you really smell like barn." She picked up Wyn's beer, holding it between Wyn's eyes and her phone. "Maybe finish this in the shower?"

LESS THAN AN hour later, they were on their way, driving west toward Mott Valley Friends, Ruth's second trip of the day. At least Wyn drove this time, and Ruth played around with the music, trying to find something loud and sexy. Despite the rushing and driving and general annoyance, it was nice to venture out into the evening together. Sure, it was to a school event, but still, they were out, and the kids would be asleep by the time they got home. That was all that really mattered.

Ruth settled on a song, then checked her phone for a text from Siddha. Nothing. *Hey Sid,* she texted. *Mom and I are headed to the auction. Be home by 11?* She deleted the question mark, replacing it with a period. Then she switched it back to a question mark again. Was she actually asking her sixteen-year-old the favor of coming home at a reasonable hour? She guessed she was. She hit send and waited for a reply. When she didn't get one, she turned her phone over.

"Siddha turned off her location," Ruth said.

"I know," Wyn said.

"You do?"

"Yeah. I've been checking. It was my idea, remember?"

Ruth did remember. She remembered how she'd said she didn't want to surveil her kid, and Wyn had said that it wasn't surveilling and anyway, yes you do. They'd reached an agreement with Siddha, saying they'd always text her first, and only check her location if she didn't answer in fifteen minutes.

"Do you think it's because she's doing meth in the Circle K parking lot?"

"No," Wyn said. "I think it's because she's mad."

Ruth's phone buzzed with a text and she felt a wash of relief, but it was only Caroline.

just made another appt—we're going back

yay! Ruth typed.

"Is it Sid?" Wyn asked.

"Caroline," Ruth said, not looking up.

"I thought we were on a date."

You can't be serious, Ruth thought, after the way you ignored me in the kitchen? But she didn't say that. She just put her phone back in her bag. "She and Mike went to see Marcia Glassie-Greene about the whole sperm donor thing, and now they're basically in therapy."

Wyn laughed. "Suckers."

Ruth laughed, but she felt defensive, both of Caroline and herself. "Would you ever want to go to therapy? I think it might not be a bad idea, especially right now."

"I don't like talking about my feelings with anyone but you." Wyn put her hand on Ruth's leg.

Ruth closed her eyes. There was a time when this would have thrilled Ruth, when it *did* in fact thrill Ruth, made her dizzy with feelings of intimacy and importance. But now it made her feel tired.

"I know you love therapy," Wyn said, "but I—"

"Why is everyone saying I love therapy? I haven't been in therapy for twenty years."

"Yes, but you loved it."

"It's not that I loved therapy, I loved Dr. Lippman. That's not the same thing."

Wyn, who knew just how far to go with Ruth, and who knew that Ruth's deepest wound—her mother's death—was, and always would be, tender to the touch, squeezed Ruth's leg. "I know."

Oh, Dr. Lippman! Ruth thought. If only she could talk to her about Siddha. Or better yet, send Siddha to her. She would know what to say, how to make sense of it all. She felt an ache of missing Dr. Lippman, a great swell of longing.

Dr. Lippman had been formidable in every way. Nearly six feet tall, with an enormous head of curly silver hair, she wore strangely beautiful, almost costume-like clothes, sweeping dirndl skirts, enormous earrings and rings. She told Ruth stories about Joni Mitchell and Martha Graham, about Frida Kahlo and Golda Meir, as though they were her old friends. She complained about Madison, its provincialism and snow, its collective obsession with football and its dearth of decent Thai food. She treated Ruth with exceptional kindness, but never pity.

Over the many years Ruth saw her, Dr. Lippman helped Ruth to internalize two basic truths. The first was that the worst possible thing that can happen to a child had happened to Ruth. The second was that Ruth's life was going to be amazing. It would all be more wonderful and more interesting than Ruth could imagine. And this amazing life that was, beyond a doubt, coming her way was not despite Ruth's early loss of her mother, and it was not because of it.

With Dr. Lippman, there were no equations, no tradeoffs, no silver linings. There was just the great, gorgeous mess of being a human. She expanded Ruth's mind and her heart. She did away with superstition, with Faustian bargains and magical thinking. Reality with Dr. Lippman was magical enough. She stretched Ruth, gently, until she could contain all the sadness and all the thrill.

Ruth would never really understand how she'd done it. She could never explain how she felt about Dr. Lippman, or what was so special about her, until one day in high school when Ruth had to go to church after a sleepover with her Catholic friend Emily, and she'd listened, sleepily, to a long, repetitive chant of a psalm about the merciful Lord, and Ruth thought, That's Dr. Lippman. Merciful. Even then she was aware that maybe this was a little problematic, giving her therapist an attribute assigned to God, but Ruth didn't care. She loved Dr. Lippman.

Ruth had gone through a period, two or three years after her mother died, when she would bring gifts to Dr. Lippman. Small things, like a painting she'd done in art class, or a bracelet she'd made at camp. She'd even saved enough allowance to buy Dr. Lippman a scarf she thought she'd like, a cheap imitation of the type of clothes Dr. Lippman wore. She accepted all of Ruth's gifts with a kind enthusiasm. She hung the painting in her office, she put the bracelet on right away, and the scarf. Later it would make Ruth cringe to think about the things she'd given her, but at the time the sight of Dr. Lippman opening the gifts had filled Ruth with joy.

Ruth had seen Dr. Lippman once a week from the time she was eleven years old until she went to college, and then again when she came home for winter and summer vacations. In the summer after her junior year, Dr. Lippman told her she would be retiring and moving to Israel, where her grandchildren lived. Israel? Ruth thought. Grandchildren? She'd had no idea. In her last session, Ruth pointed to the painting she'd given Dr. Lippman all those years ago. She couldn't believe it was still hanging there, that Dr. Lippman hadn't taken it down. "I'm so embarrassed by that," Ruth said. "By all the gifts I gave you when I was little. I think I was pretending you were my mom."

Dr. Lippman turned to look at the painting. "I love that painting! I loved all your gifts." She turned back around to look at Ruth. "How lucky your mom was, to have had you as her daughter."

Ruth cried then, for the last time, in a room so full of a decade of her tears that they might have ended their final session together floating out the door in a canoe.

When the hour was over, Dr. Lippman hugged Ruth, and handed her a piece of paper with all her contact information on it. She told Ruth she could write to her—email or letter—and she would always write back. Or Ruth could never write. Either way was fine, she'd said, either way she would be grateful, for the rest of her days, that she'd had the chance to know Ruth.

Ruth had never planned to write Dr. Lippman. How could it be the same as talking to her? But when Ruth was twenty-three and had taken six pregnancy tests in a span of forty-eight hours, finally surrendering to the reality of all those pink lines, she rummaged around in a box of things from home and found that piece of paper Dr. Lippman had given her when they'd last met.

Shalom from the past! Ruth wrote in the subject line of that first email. And then, thinking better of it, deleted the line and wrote *Hi from your patient Ruth Schwartz*. She started the email with newsy updates: she'd graduated from Haverford with a degree in classics and taken a job teaching kindergarten at a Quaker school in the Catskills. *Not very good Thai food here, either!* she joked. And then, gathering her courage, she typed *The real news is that I'm pregnant*. For a long moment Ruth sat and watched the cursor blink on the screen, studying those words. She deleted them, then typed them again, then deleted them. She typed them a third time, then added *and I'm not sure what to do*.

The next morning there was a response from Dr. Lippman. *Dear Ruth*, she wrote. *We knew this life of yours was going to be a big one, didn't we? It makes sense that you don't yet know what to do. But you will. Write me back anytime, tell me anything you want me to know.*

Over the next week, Ruth wrote to Dr. Lippman nearly every day. One day she'd write and say she knew she should have an abortion, the next day she'd write and say there was no way she was having an abortion. Dr. Lippman didn't say much about the pregnancy, or what Ruth should do about it. *Tell me about your job,* Dr. Lippman wrote. *What's your apartment like?* Ruth told Dr. Lippman about her wily and precocious kindergartners, how she'd devised a stream survey project that had them out in the woods behind the school every day, collecting stones and drawing pictures of moss on small clipboards. She described her apartment, how happy she was to live alone after four years of roommates and housemates, how she'd bought herself a sewing machine, and a bicycle.

It all sounds perfect, Dr. Lippman wrote. *How is your father?* Ruth knew that Dr. Lippman was asking what he thought of all this, or if Ruth planned on telling him. She hadn't yet, but she knew that if she decided to keep the baby he would support her, because Ruth's father always supported her. Her father hadn't really recovered from her mother's death, but he had been a good father to Ruth, a solid, reliable presence. He hadn't been overly protective, or needy. He was serious in a way that made Ruth feel sad, and her sadness made her feel guilty, and her guilt made her not want to see him very often, which made her feel even more guilty. Still, she loved him, and knew he loved her.

It sounds like you've made a beautiful life for yourself, Dr. Lippman wrote in response to all this news. Was she saying, So don't ruin it by having a baby? Did she mean, You're doing a beautiful job, so you can handle having a baby? Ruth knew she couldn't ask Dr. Lippman to clarify, because Dr. Lippman wasn't going to tell her what to do.

I don't really know the father, Ruth wrote late one night. *Not exactly. I mean, I know him, but we're not in a committed relationship. And I don't think we should try to be. I guess what I'm saying is, I might have to do it all on my own. And I don't even have a mother myself.*

Having this baby would be so, so hard, Dr. Lippman responded. *Harder than either of us can imagine right now. But you do have a mother, Ruth. I say "have" in the present tense because I believe now that mothers aren't subject to the laws of time and space. Maybe it's getting older, maybe* it's having grandchildren, maybe it's all the sunshine and bougainvillea and pita bread here that's allowed my brain to expand, but I don't think us mothers really go anywhere.

"Us mothers." What had she meant by that, just herself and Ruth's mother, or did she mean Ruth too? *Us mothers.* Ruth read the line over and over. She felt the charge of it. She felt its claim.

Thank you, Ruth wrote. That was the entirety of her message, and she didn't write to Dr. Lippman again until she sent her a picture of newborn Siddha.

RUTH PUSHED AGAINST her seatbelt and turned to Wyn. "Hey, wanna just go to Lyle's and shoot pool?" she asked. "We haven't done that in ages."

"What?" Wyn said. "Now?"

"Yes, now."

"And skip the auction? Aren't you the chair of the committee or something?"

Ruth shrugged. "Secretary."

Wyn was not one to ask questions at a time like this. "Hell, yes," she said. "That is exactly what I want to do. Although," she said, sliding her hand up Ruth's leg until it rested on the crease of her thigh and crotch. "There's this one other thing I want to do first." She looked in the rearview mirror, then slowed the car, pulled over onto the wide shoulder.

Ruth laughed. They'd done this dozens of times before, roadside sex, on the way to a date or on the way home. They were good at it, agile. It was, Wyn always liked to say, one of the perks of country living. Ruth unfastened her seatbelt, unbuttoned her jeans. Wyn slid her hand under the waistband of Ruth's underwear.

She came fast, thinking of Florence.

14

Tobi had been meaning to stop by the Shepkins' hardware store ever since Elliot's memorial, but Barton Falls wasn't really on the way to anything, so it was early November before she made it to the store. Evie had registered the kids and two of their friends for a cardboard-sword-making class at the Barton Falls rec center, and since it was Tobi's weekend for driving (yes, Evie had a system for carpool shifts too), Tobi found herself just a few blocks from the hardware store with plenty of time to kill. She swung into the parking lot and, before she could think better of it, she texted Bex. *Hey I'm at Barton Falls Hardware. Need anything?*

As soon as she hit send Tobi thought, Shit, was that weird? It wasn't like she and Bex were close, or even friends really, and they were definitely not the kind of friends who ran errands for each other. It was just that the hardware store was a point of connection between the two of them, and Tobi couldn't keep herself from taking advantage of it. She wanted to connect with Bex. She'd taken a quick dip into the online pool of testimonials and informational websites about top surgery, but she'd jumped right out again just as fast. It was all too much. There was too much information, too many photos, too many recommendations and options. Tobi needed someone—an actual person—to talk to.

Tobi had learned a few encouraging things from her internet deep dive, the main one being that she could get the surgery without being on T, which was great because Tobi didn't want to take hormones. She didn't even like to take Advil or the vitamin D capsules Evie left out for her every morning. Tobi didn't want a deeper voice, or facial hair, or a redistribution of body fat. While she was glad for the clarity on this point, it did make her feel a bit unsure. Was it okay not to want T but to want top surgery? Was it okay not to want to change her pronouns, or at least not change them now? These were the questions she had for Bex, despite her fear that the questions would make Tobi seem old and clueless, with no idea of how all this worked, of what she *should* want. It was hard to admit, but Tobi wanted Bex's permission; she wanted their blessing. She knew it was wrong to want that from Bex, or from anyone for that matter, but she couldn't help it.

Tobi's phone pinged with a text: *Cool of you to ask! All good*

She pushed the hardware store door open and heard the sweet, nostalgic jingle of the bells tied to the handle. Hope, who was behind the counter, looked up at the sound and smiled. Her hair hung in two neat braids, and in her sweatshirt and jeans she looked competent and ageless, the sort of woman Tobi always thought would make a good lesbian but with whom there was no charge, not even a hint of attraction.

"Hi," she said. "I'm Tobi Fynch, Evie Gold's wi—"

"I know who you are!" Hope interrupted. She came out from behind the counter and gave Tobi a hug. "What are you doing over here? Is Evie with you?"

"Sadly no," Tobi said. "But she sends her love. I was just dropping the kids off at the rec center, and I realized I needed—" She paused for a second, then motioned at an endcap display of inflatable turkeys and ceramic cornucopias. "A few of these?"

Hope laughed. "I know, it's all ridiculous, isn't it? Elliot would have thrown a fit. But I've got so many people in here just wanting to be supportive, which is super sweet, but you can only sell so many pairs of scissors, you know what I mean? So then I had the idea to branch out a little, at least while we're getting the sympathy traffic. And it turns out people love a theme. They come in for a tube of superglue, but then they see a plastic turkey and they can't resist. And the markup on this crap is fantastic." Hope waved her hand over the pile of lawn inflatables, table decorations, and leaf flags. "I'm never going back. I already told my wholesaler to sign me up for all of it. Christmas, Hanukkah, St. Patrick's Day—you celebrate it, I'm gonna sell you some crap for it."

"Well, Evie would be very proud," Tobi said. "And she'd be dying to get you on Instagram."

"Oh, we both know that's never happening." Hope clapped her hands together, pointing at Tobi. "Now, what can I help you with? And you'd better not say scissors."

Tobi laughed. "Um, duct tape?"

Hope groaned. "You're as bad as the rest of them. It's in aisle five."

Tobi took the long way to aisle five, thinking maybe she could pick up a few snow shovels and some windshield wiper fluid. At the back wall she ran into a young employee pricing bird feeders. "Oh hey," she said.

"Hey," the girl said.

Tobi looked at her more closely, then read her name tag. *Siddha.* "I thought you looked familiar," Tobi said. "You're Ruth and Wyn's daughter."

Siddha looked a little nervous. "Yeah," she said. "Can I help you find something?"

"I'm all good," Tobi said. "Just grabbing a shovel."

Siddha stepped aside, letting Tobi go by. "Nice to see you," she said, then went back to the bird feeders with what seemed like significantly more concentration than the task warranted.

Tobi took the shovels to the counter, along with a bottle of Goo Gone, a package of Magic Erasers, two nut rolls, and a handsaw.

Hope looked at Tobi's pile on the counter. "I thought you needed duct tape."

"Right!" Tobi ran back to aisle five and grabbed three rolls, plus a roll of packing tape, just in case.

"This is a very eclectic sympathy purchase," Hope said.

Tobi grinned at her. "I try. And don't worry, the kids' class is every Saturday until January. I'll be back for whatever Hanukkah items you get in stock."

"Oh, bring the kids next time, will you?"

Tobi nodded. "Speaking of kids, Wyn and Ruth's kid is working here now? Seems a little far from home."

"She's a good worker. We love having her." Hope smiled then, although she seemed to be looking behind Tobi, and when Tobi turned she saw Siddha looking at Hope, smiling back at her.

Tobi felt her phone buzz. She reached into her pocket and saw a text from Bex: *Hey, still at hardware? If so, can you grab corded drill? Mine just died. I'm good for it*

Sure thing, Tobi texted back.

"Hey," Tobi said. "Looks like I need one more thing. A corded drill, for a friend."

Hope laughed and handed Tobi her bag of purchases. "Oh seriously, Tobi? For a friend?"

15

Caroline had just come in the door from work when Mike came up the basement stairs with his life jacket.

"Oh, awesome!" he said. "You're home."

Caroline didn't like the sound of this. "Awesome because?"

"I need you to take Luca to archery."

"Why can't you?"

"It finally stopped raining and Tobi's free, so we have a shot at getting out on the lake before dark."

"The Rod isn't until July. What's the rush?"

"Canoeing is our weak spot," Mike said. "Neither one of us has done it before, so we have to keep at it until the lake freezes."

"Maybe you should just ask someone to join your team and do the canoeing," Caroline suggested. She made a show of taking off her coat and her shoes, as if to say, I'm not going to archery. "Aren't you allowed to have three team members? You could ask Wyn. Didn't she row in college? I bet she'd be great."

"I think we're good just the two of us."

Of course you are, Caroline thought. "Is it even safe? I don't want you falling in and getting hypothermia."

"Tobi got us drysuits."

"You can't be serious."

"I am very serious."

"You have drysuits? For canoeing?"

"You just said you didn't want me to get hypothermia." Mike pulled on his boots. "Thank you, Cece. I'll make it up to you, promise." He kissed her then, and she didn't kiss him back. He pulled away and looked at her questioningly.

Caroline held his gaze. "You said you'd be on Luca."

Mike looked confused. "What do you mean? I've taken him to every archery lesson since—"

"At Ruth and Wyn's party," Caroline interrupted. "You promised me you'd be on him, so I could have a nice time, and you weren't. You weren't on him."

Mike sighed, rubbed his hand over his beard. "Jesus, Caroline, that was like a month ago. And he was fine."

"'Fine,' really?"

"Yeah, he was," Mike said. "Look, the donor issue, I get it, we have to deal with that, and we will, but he's clearly okay. The kid's going to have to deal with a lot in this life, and I hardly think that's going to be the worst of it."

The kid. Caroline felt heat rise in her body. She hated it when Mike called Luca "the kid." There was a harshness to it that she didn't like, and it seemed like lately he'd been using the word more often. When Luca was a baby, even when he was a toddler, Mike had been unfailingly tender with him, bouncing him to sleep on a yoga ball, scooping him up when he fell, pressing cold washcloths against his feverish forehead. But now that Luca was a little older, Mike's tenderness seemed to be cooling. He responded differently to Caroline's worries, saying things like *He needs to learn*, or *Life is rough sometimes*. It wasn't that Caroline didn't agree (Although did she, really? Did Luca's life have to be so rough?), it was that she didn't like to be reminded of how rough Mike's life had been, all the terrible things *he'd* had to learn. It made her worry that it was a risk to have a child with someone who'd been so wounded, not to mention that he was almost a decade older than she was. Their age difference was one of the things that made their marriage work—Caroline had needed a partner who knew himself and what he wanted—but it wasn't always ideal when it came to parenting. Mike's ideas could feel a little outdated. "I feel like you're not really taking any of this seriously," she said.

"Any of what, exactly?"

"Luca," Caroline said, lowering her voice. She knew he was upstairs with headphones on (it was three-thirty, smack in the middle of the sacred screen time hour), but she didn't want him to hear her say his name.

"When are we ever doing anything but taking him extremely seriously? And dealing with every single thing this kid needs?"

"Will you please stop calling him that!"

"Calling him what?"

"*Kid!* Stop calling him kid!"

Mike groaned. "That's what he is! He's a fucking kid! And you know what? Childhood isn't always so easy. We can't make everything perfect for him. I mean look at my childhood! And I turned out okay."

Caroline didn't say anything.

"What? I didn't?"

"He's not like you," Caroline said.

"Yeah, that's obvious," Mike said.

"What's that supposed to mean?"

"It means he wouldn't have lasted a day in my house."

"And that's the goal?" Caroline said. "To toughen him up?"

"A little resilience might not be a bad thing," Mike said.

"Oh my god, I hate that word," Caroline said. "It's basically justification for all the ways our society has abandoned children."

Mike opened his mouth to answer, but before he could speak, there was a scream from upstairs. "*Mama!*"

"*What?*" both Caroline and Mike yelled.

"There's a daddy longlegs on my wall! It's going toward the bed! *Come fast!*"

Mike looked at Caroline.

Seething, she grabbed a paper towel and headed for the stairs. "They actually bite, you know."

WHEN CAROLINE AND Luca got to archery, he ran off to join the other kids, and Caroline sat down in one of the folding chairs set up against the wall for parents. Luca had told her she didn't have to stay and watch ("Dad never does," he'd said, cheerfully), but Caroline, still angry, was going to prove a point, if only to herself.

This was a foolish stance for any number of reasons, the primary one being that Caroline hated watching Luca's activities. She'd put Mike in charge of anything that might invite an audience: swimming lessons, modern dance (not that Luca had lasted through more than one session of that), jujitsu (also only one session), that sort of thing. Caroline preferred drop-off activities, like the library's Lego club, or the art class Luca took on Wednesdays at the community center, where there was never any suggestion that parents stay and watch their children paint. Watching Luca out in the world, figuring out how to be a human among humans, it was more than her heart could bear. Caroline was a better mother in private. She could tend, listen, comfort, encourage, all with love and patience.

But then she'd end up somewhere like this middle school gymnasium filled with kids and all bets were off. She was too raw with love and worry for Luca; she couldn't manage it. The only reason she hadn't just convinced him to skip archery and go for hamburgers was that Wyn had set up an archery range in one of their fields and Luca was dying to do target practice with Roz and Abe. Caroline could withstand pretty much anything if it meant Luca keeping up with the Schwartz-Huntleys.

A few minutes before class was scheduled to start, Bex Devereux walked into the gym. They waved at Caroline. She waved back. She'd forgotten that Bex was the assistant teacher in the archery class. Ruth was right, Caroline thought, remembering Ruth's recent complaint about the ubiquity of Bex, they really are everywhere. And they were also, somehow, good at everything. Ruth pulled out her phone and pretended to study it. Please don't come over, she telepathed. But apparently the one thing Bex wasn't good at was receiving telepathic messages, because they were headed right for her.

"Hey there, Caroline." When Bex said her name, they somehow gave it a bunch of extra syllables which came out sounding like they'd had a really good time in Bex's mouth.

"Hey," Caroline said. She untied the scarf from around her neck, hoping she didn't already look flushed. Bex made her sweat. They were the rare person who flustered Caroline. They were so sexy, so everything-all-at-once. Caroline agreed with Ruth that Bex was a bit annoying (more than a bit annoying to Ruth), in the way that young and childless people could feel tedious, prattling on about how busy and tired they were.

"Do you think Bex even knows what day of the week it is?" Ruth had asked Caroline recently. The two of them had been standing in front of the giant wall calendar in Ruth's kitchen, trying to find a single evening in the next month when they were both free to take Abe and Luca to see the Perseus show at the planetarium, when Bex had popped in, a camera and tripod in hand, saying they wanted to grab a few potential album pics in the attic before the sun went down. "I was up there the other day and the light is really cool," they said. "In this fractured, ethereal sort of way, you know?"

"You mean dusty?" Ruth asked.

Bex seemed to consider this description. "Maybe," they said. And then, with that smile: "Yeah, a little dusty. Like, nostalgia, but in the form of light."

Caroline could sense Ruth was about to laugh, and she nudged her. "Sounds gorgeous," Caroline said. "Can't wait to see how it turns out."

Bex gave Caroline a little salute and bounded up the back stairs.

"Admit it," Caroline said, laughing now too. "They are so cute."

"Are they?" Ruth asked, rolling her eyes.

In that moment, Caroline had felt a bit confused. Did Ruth not think Bex was cute? Was it strange that Caroline did? Was it Bex's boyishness that Caroline was attracted to, and was that offensive to Ruth in some way? Before Caroline could push, Ruth had made the comment about Bex not knowing the date and turned her attention back to the calendar.

BEX SAT DOWN in the folding chair next to Caroline and smiled at her. That smile! Somehow both cunning and guileless, and entirely disarming. And that was saying something, as Caroline prided herself on being impossible to disarm. She'd said that to Mike once, and he'd said, That makes it sound like you're always carrying a weapon, and she'd said, In a way I am, and he'd left it at that.

"Luca is doing awesome," Bex said. "I think he'll be ready to join the Monday night Heracles class before spring."

"Great," Caroline said. "Is that Abe's class?"

"Yup, but it looks like Abie will be moving into the Apollos after Christmas."

Seriously? Caroline thought. There was another level? What were these kids preparing for? Living off the land by sixth grade?

Bex put her hand on Caroline's leg. Wow, Caroline thought. Bold. But also so gentle, as though their hand were a leaf, or a flower. This was what she'd wanted to discuss with Ruth, the gentle boldness of Bex.

"He'll be hunting rabbits in the woods with Abie and the rest of them in no time, don't you worry," Bex said.

Caroline wanted to say, Rabbit hunting is not my goal here. My goal is drinking wine on the patio with Ruth while Luca is occupied for more than fifteen minutes. But she didn't want to say anything that might jeopardize the placement of Bex's hand on her leg. "Can't wait," she said.

Bex jumped up. "Okay, gotta get this show on the road. Lovely as always, Lady Caroline."

As class started, Bex and the other teacher corralled the kids into groups. Caroline pretended to be interested for as long as she could, practicing her anxiety-reducing breathing techniques as she watched a kid walk away from Luca while he was still talking. When it seemed like Luca was settled in a group and participating in the warm-ups, Caroline pulled out her phone. She scrolled Instagram for a while, did the crossword. She checked her personal email, and her work email. And that's when she saw the email about the grant. The subject line was *Tate Fund Grantees*. She opened it. *Thank you for your application to the Tate Fund. This fall, we received over fifty applications from Gorman professors, each proposal worthy of funding. Unfortunately . . .*

Shit, Caroline thought, turning over her phone. She didn't want to read the rest. She hadn't gotten the grant. She hadn't gotten the grant! She was a shoo-in for the grant. People always got the Tate. The application was just a formality. That's what everyone had told her. Just a formality. But it wasn't just a formality! Not for Caroline. Was this because she didn't have her PhD? Was it because she'd balked at her department chair's suggestion that she teach an additional class next year, on top of the three she was already teaching? Whatever it was, now Caroline didn't have the money. She wasn't going to Rome.

16

"Happy birthday, my love," Evie said, reaching her martini coupe across the table to clink Tobi's pint glass. "Here's to another trip around the sun."

Tobi and Evie were having dinner at Capricorn to celebrate Tobi's birthday. It was a small celebration, despite the magnitude of turning fifty; but several months ago they'd decided ("they" meaning Evie) to throw a joint birthday party in the spring, when Evie would also turn fifty. The plan was fine with Tobi. She wasn't much for birthdays, but Evie loved them. Evie loved to marvel at the passage of time, to take account of what had happened, plan for what would come. She loved horoscopes, birth charts, the Enneagram. She liked to pull tarot cards. For Evie, a birthday was a day to reflect, to take stock, to dream big. For Tobi, it was a time to spring for the expensive wine and have more-adventurous-than-usual sex.

In the early years of their relationship they'd often fought on Tobi's birthday, Evie asking Tobi too many questions about what she hoped the year would hold, what her goals were, how she wanted to manifest her visions—questions that bored and annoyed Tobi and only made her want to be more of a Neanderthal, saying things like, I hope to bang you in an elevator, which would make Evie feel hurt and unseen. But while these differences—and what they suggested about their divergent temperaments and worldviews—had once riled them up, now neither of them cared. They'd made their peace with birthdays.

Tobi had wasted a lot of time in the early days of her relationship with Evie by trying to deepen whatever contrasts she could find between the two of them. This was mostly because there appeared to be so few and this made Tobi uncomfortable. Tobi didn't know if it was the straight world or the queer one telling her this—most likely it was both—but Tobi had felt very strongly that the girls (and later, women) in her life should be as different from her as possible. By the time she met Evie, Tobi was fully invested in the femme/butch dichotomy, even though she wasn't entirely sure she was butch. But she didn't overthink it, mostly because the assumption had really worked for her—sexually, sartorially, and emotionally.

In high school, Tobi dated (or, more accurately, had furtive bathroom sex with) the head of the cheerleading squad. In college, Tobi dated nursing students with French manicures. She dated business majors with dry-cleaning bills. Tobi had an artistic temperament, so her girlfriends were rational and organized. Tobi wore her hair short; her girlfriends wore theirs long. And they always had more money than Tobi. That was the easiest contrast to manifest, because, well, it seemed to Tobi that everyone in the world had more money than she did.

But then she went to Indiana and fell in love with Evie, and all the old dichotomies fell in on each other. Evie was also an artist. She had long, honey-colored hair, but she pulled it back into a messy ponytail or a bun on the top of her head that she secured with a pencil. She wore black tank tops and Carhartts and had a scattering of tattoos (which were now, as Tobi's own were for her, a source of pride and regret in equal measure). But she also wore big hoop earrings and a necklace with a diamond pendant. She listened to Sleater-Kinney, but also Patsy Cline. Evie liked to talk about feelings, which was a familiarly femme characteristic, but unlike other girlfriends, she didn't buy Tobi's insistence that feelings just weren't her thing. "Oh, don't tell me you've bought into that whole stoic butch bullshit," Evie had said when Tobi told her she really didn't think much about how it felt when her dad walked out on her and her mom.

And then there was the question of money. How much did Evie have? When they met, Evie had just graduated from some private college in Oregon, one of those schools without grades where students create their own majors in subjects like West Indian diaspora textiles. But then Evie started telling Tobi stories about her childhood, about how her parents drove an old car with such badly ripped upholstery that Evie sat on a beach towel in the backseat, and that she'd taken her lunch to school in a bread bag. To make it all more complicated, the old car was a Saab, and the bread bag lunch was whitefish salad in a pita.

"How'd you end up at the crazy college?" Tobi asked once, after Evie regaled her with the story of selling all her brother's old soccer gear at a consignment shop to make the money she needed for a spring break trip to Baja.

"Oh, I got a scholarship," Evie said. "A full ride."

"For what?" Tobi asked.

"For being smart," Evie said.

Tobi fell a little more in love with her then. How amazing, her confidence! Still, she pressed on. "But how did you even know about that place?"

"My grandfather was a professor there."

Evie's grandfather was a professor? How could you have a grandfather with a PhD and not have money? How had she grown up reading *The New Yorker* at the breakfast table and spending her summers at a Vermont sleepaway camp but had to use all her babysitting money to buy the winter coat she wanted? It was all so confusing!

Evie laughed when Tobi finally blurted, "Are you rich or not? I mean, I've never known anyone like you before."

"I think what you're saying is you haven't known any Jews," Evie had said. And she was right. When Tobi converted to Judaism in the months before their wedding, Evie got her a subscription to *The New Yorker* as a present. In the years that followed, Tobi came to understand that the gift was only partially in jest. It was also Evie's way of saying—

consciously or not—We'll be doing things my way. Tobi had been, and still was, all in, but sometimes their life—her life—seemed crazy. What sense did it make that they washed out their ziplock bags and hung them on a handmade wooden dryer next to the sink but had taken the twins to Japan when they were three years old?

Tobi had fallen in love with Evie the moment she met her, and had felt then, in a moment of crystalline clarity, that Evie was the woman she wanted to be with forever, the woman to end all searching. If she'd had slightly better self-esteem, she might have allowed herself to be certain that they were destined for each other, but she wasn't there yet. It was Evie who would help her get there, Evie who would love Tobi so entirely, so confidently, and who would demand more of Tobi than anyone ever had, because Evie knew what she herself was worth. And that was the real thrill. That was the cliff's edge Evie invited Tobi to walk, a place where Tobi could use words like "destined" without laughing nervously, without trying to sound cool.

And tonight, on this birthday, Tobi wanted Evie to ask her some of the old questions. Because this year, Tobi had goals. She had a vision that needed manifesting. She wanted Evie to pull tarot cards for her, or at the very least, pull a notebook out of her purse and make a list of her hopes for the year, then tape it to their bedroom mirror when they got home. But Evie was tucking into the steak in front of her and sipping her second martini and looking content. Which Evie really was these days. She was content. She wasn't asking a lot of Tobi, on the emotional front. She was happy to chat about TV shows and gossip about co-workers. She was happy to sit in silence. Was this what marriage was, Tobi wondered? Just one long run of not getting the timing right?

And then, just when Tobi was feeling dejected and, quite honestly, bored, Evie nodded slightly, leaned in, and said, "I think someone wants to say hello."

Tobi looked back over her shoulder and there was Bex Devereux.

"Hey," Bex said, smiling their adorable smile. "I thought that was you."

Evie put down her drink and looked at Tobi, a bit mischievously.

Tobi didn't return the look. She turned to Bex. "It *is* me," she said, with a shy smile that she hoped didn't seem too shy, or too smiley.

"I can't thank you enough for sending Trevor my way," Bex said. "He's amazing. He was in the studio all day and for the first time I feel like this crazy scheme of mine might actually work."

"Trevor is very good at making you feel like that," Evie said, still looking at Tobi.

"You remember Evie, my wife?" Tobi asked.

Bex pivoted slightly toward Evie. They closed their eyes for the briefest moment, putting a hand over their heart, gently bending at the knees, then tilting toward Evie in a sort of prayer stance. "Totally. Hey, Evie. Sorry to interrupt."

"Not at all," Evie said, her smile broad with enjoyment.

"I sent Trevor over to Bex's," Tobi explained. "To help with their studio build-out." Had she told Evie? She couldn't remember.

"A godsend," Bex said.

"Truly," Evie said, still smiling.

"I'm going to let you two get back to your dinner," Bex said, pointing at them simultaneously. They pivoted then, turning toward Tobi. "But I owe you a beer."

Tobi raised her hand in silent protest, but thought, also silently, Yes, please. Let's have a beer.

Bex walked away. "She paid Trevor," Tobi said.

"They," Evie corrected.

"Right, right, they," Tobi said. "I didn't want you to think I sent him over on our dime."

Evie took a bite of her steak. Her mouth full, she motioned with her fork to the air behind Tobi. Bex appeared again at the table.

"Back again!" they said. "One quick thing, I'm having a listening party, on the twentieth. Really casual, just a few people. I'd be psyched if you came. Both of you. I'm just trying out some new stuff."

Evie smiled.

"Great," Tobi said. "Awesome. Thank you. We'd love it."

And then they were gone again, but Evie was still smiling. "What is it about them?" she asked Tobi.

"What do you mean?" Tobi said.

"That makes you turn red."

"I'm not red," Tobi said.

Evie pointed to Tobi's chest, which, without even looking down, Tobi knew was blotchy. Tobi put her hand over it. Fifty years old and still betrayed by her pale Irish skin. Would it ever stop?

"I'm not into them," Tobi said.

"Oh, I know," Evie said. She pushed her plate forward a bit. She rested her elbows on the table. "But you're something. Does it freak you out? The top surgery? I know it's not your thing, but—"

"It doesn't," Tobi said. "It really doesn't." And here it was, the opening, the doorway. But now that it had appeared, Tobi could not walk through it. She wanted to tell Evie that there was nothing about Bex that freaked her out, or if she was freaked out it was only because she wanted—so badly—to be like Bex. To do what they had done. Tobi wanted to reach her hand across the table and take Evie's. She wanted to say, Will you help me be brave? The way you always have? Can I borrow your confidence, the way I used to? Can I draft on your speed, can I follow your directions? But Tobi couldn't say those things, she realized now, because Evie wasn't going where Tobi was going. And that was terrifying. It was scary. It was sad. It was thrilling. All she wanted was for Evie to tell her she could do it. To give her permission. Give her courage. But now that she had this opening, she knew she couldn't take it. She knew she couldn't ask these things of Evie. Tobi knew that she had to do this—or at least decide to do this—without Evie's permission. She was going to have to keep the secret a little longer.

"They just make me feel old," Tobi said. "You know, the times they are a-changin'."

Evie sighed. "Yeah, I hear you. Does it help that you've never been hotter?"

No, Tobi wanted to say. It doesn't help at all. She took a long drink of her beer, then reached out for Evie's hand. She kissed it. "Yes," she said. "It does."

17

"Well," Marcia said, "you won't be surprised to see that I still have the same couch."

Caroline smiled. She sat down, put her purse next to her on one side, her coat on the other. She fussed with the throw pillow, casually looking for a tag. "After my parents' divorce, my father married a woman with the most amazing couch." Caroline had no idea why she'd said this.

"Really," Marcia said, her tone resting somewhere between statement and question.

Caroline nodded. She didn't know what to say then. She thought of that couch, Darcy's couch, and how she'd once sat on it with her own mother, when—during one of Caroline's visits home from Boston—Darcy and her father invited them for dinner. Caroline's parents had divorced while she was in college, after twenty-five years of marriage. They'd told Caroline they simply didn't love each other anymore, as though their twenty-five-year marriage was a painting they were tired of looking at, a dinner they'd grown tired of eating. Caroline had been stunned when it happened, although not as stunned as she was when her parents remained friends even after her father married Darcy, a blond fifty-five-year-old dental hygienist.

"What an apartment!" Caroline's mother had exclaimed to Caroline when the two of them were in a taxi back downtown after dinner. "I needed a winch to get me out of that couch. Who could possibly want such a behemoth in their living room?"

"Well, Dad, obviously," Caroline said.

"Oh, sweetie," Caroline's mother said. "Your father doesn't give a shit about Darcy's couch." And then she patted Caroline's arm. "But you, on the other hand, love a nice couch. I know that." She leaned over and kissed Caroline. "You have my blessing to love Darcy's couch."

"I don't need your blessing to love Darcy's couch," Caroline said, petulantly, although of course she did.

That dinner had been terrible for Caroline, sad and surreal, and she'd just wanted to forget all about it. She was newly pregnant and had come to the city to shop for wedding dresses with her mother, which was supposed to be a joyous errand. But she hadn't found a single dress she liked, and her mother had done a poor job of hiding her disappointment that Caroline wasn't having a church wedding. That night in the cab all she'd wanted was to get back to Mike and make him promise that he would not wait twenty-five years to tell her he didn't love her.

"IS THAT COUCH making you think of something?" Marcia asked.

"Oh, no," Caroline lied, wondering if she'd been silent for a long time. She smiled at Marcia, crossed and uncrossed her legs, looked out the window. "Not really."

Marcia smiled at her. "It certainly is nice to see you again," she said.

"It's nice to be here," Caroline said. This was all feeling very awkward now. Where was the ease of the last visit?

"It's okay if it's not nice," Marcia said. "It can be hard to come on your own once you've come with your spouse." She smiled. "A different dynamic."

Caroline nodded. When she'd left the message on the answering machine for Marcia confirming the appointment, she said it would just be her, and she hoped that Marcia wouldn't ask why, especially since she'd already lied—a minuscule lie, a barely white lie—to Ruth when she said she'd convinced Mike to go back to Marcia. She hadn't convinced Mike of anything. She hadn't even asked him.

The night after that first appointment, Caroline, who had been weeping off and on all day for reasons she couldn't explain, had crawled into bed early with a score she needed to learn. She could barely keep her eyes open by the time Mike came in from the bathroom. On his chin there was a small bit of the charcoal toothpaste he'd recently started using that was slowly staining their sink gray. He leaned down to kiss her, and Caroline reached out to wipe his chin, then wiped the toothpaste on his T-shirt. "Thanks," he whispered. "Super sexy move."

"Super sexy look," she said. She put aside the score and pulled him onto her, turning her head so that his face was against her neck. He kissed behind her ear, gently ran his lips down her neck. She started to cry.

"What is it, babe?" he whispered between kisses. "Are you sad?"

Caroline gently pushed Mike off her, then rolled onto her side, his face so close to hers their noses were almost touching. She closed her eyes, felt tears roll down her cheeks. She didn't wipe them away. "Just relieved, I think."

"Me too," Mike said, pressing his thumb gently to one of her cheeks and then the other, extinguishing her tears.

"I don't mean relieved because the appointment is over."

Mike didn't say anything.

"I mean relieved because I think we might have finally met the person who can help us with Luca. She seems so smart! And positive. I kept thinking about what she would say about Luca, you know? About his friend problem."

Mike rolled over onto his back. "Can't we just take today's win? Can't we just leave it at that for a while?"

Caroline rolled onto her back. No, she thought. We can't. *You* can, and you will. But I'm not going to. Because that's not how it works. Parenting isn't basketball. Or maybe it was for some people, but it wasn't for Caroline. Parenting was an Ironman. Parenting was one of those races that people did where you had to climb over a wall and crawl through mud under barbed wire. And Caroline was tired. She was ready to tap out. This exhaustion was frightening, this desire to somehow get a break from a relentless task. But now that she'd been to see Marcia, she could imagine sitting in that office, right there on that couch, and saying to Marcia, "I'm tired." And she didn't know exactly what Marcia would say, but Caroline had a feeling it would be something really lovely.

"Luca is okay," Mike said. "That's what she'd tell us. That's what she did tell us. I'm not sure we need to pay her another two hundred bucks for her to tell us the same thing in a different way."

"Well, maybe it *is* worth two hundred bucks, to me. Maybe that's how much I need to hear it. And we didn't even talk about the whole donor dad thing," Caroline said. "Which was the reason we wanted to go."

"Right," Mike said. He squeezed her hand and rolled over. "Can we talk about it tomorrow?"

This was Mike's way of saying Go, spend the money, just please don't make me do anything else. Fine, Caroline thought, I'll take the win. And she had.

NOW THAT THE couch discussion was out of the way, Caroline felt the impulse to tell Marcia about her fight with Mike, but she didn't know how, or where, to begin. Mike's traumatic childhood? Her fears about the reach of said trauma into their own child's life? It all seemed too dark and complex, and she wasn't sure how she'd talk fast enough to explain it all while then quickly—very quickly—assuring Marcia that Mike was a great dad, and she hadn't made a world-class mistake by marrying and having a child with him.

So, instead, Caroline told Marcia a little bit of this, a little bit of that. Marcia nodded encouragingly, asked a few gentle and smart questions. The conversation bounced along for a while, until finally Caroline was able to speak without censoring herself. "I applied for a grant to go to Rome," she said. "To take my students to Rome, and I didn't get it."

"Oh," Marcia said.

"And you're the first person I've told. I haven't told Mike, I haven't told Ruth, I haven't even told my department chair, although I'm sure he already knows. Now I'll have to tell my students, who were all planning on going to Rome for their spring break. They thought they'd be busking in St. Peter's Square and eating gelato. And now who knows what they'll be doing?"

"That does sound like a lot to lose," Marcia said. "I can certainly understand your disappointment."

"I don't even know if I'm disappointed," Caroline said tartly. She pulled her hair back into a ponytail and held it in one hand while she rummaged in her purse for a hair tie with the other. When she couldn't find one, she let her hair fall again, zipping her purse closed. "When would I have the time to know that? I'm too busy feeling guilty. And like a failure. And embarrassed. Did you know I don't have my PhD?"

Caroline wondered if Marcia would say something encouraging then, like, Of course you're not a failure or Who even needs a PhD? but she didn't say anything. Caroline wondered if anyone, ever, had listened to her say such things about herself and not rushed to assuage her self-doubt. It was so kind, she thought, surprised, that Marcia didn't try. She'd always thought the opposite was true, but it wasn't. Reassurance wasn't kind. It was dismissive. And Caroline—her feelings—had so often been dismissed. How could she feel anything but content? She had no business feeling any other way.

"I'm tired," Caroline went on, when it seemed clear that Marcia wasn't going to console her. "I am so, so tired. I am tired when I wake up, and I'm tired when I go to bed, and it's not my iron levels and it's not my hormones, or maybe it is my hormones, who knows, but what it really feels like is my mind. My mind is so tired, like I could walk all day and never need to rest but if I have to make one more decision or figure out one more thing I'm just going to have to lie down and I'll never, ever be able to get back up."

"Of course you're tired," Marcia said. She spoke with the calmest, quietest, kindest voice Caroline had ever heard.

Caroline closed her eyes for a moment. "Can I ask you something crazy?"

"Please," Marcia said.

"A favor, not a question."

Marcia nodded.

"Can I just sit here for a little while, and can we not talk?"

"Yes," Marcia said. "For as long as you like. Or at least for the rest of your hour." She smiled at Caroline.

Caroline leaned back into the couch. She felt the tears come, but she didn't wipe them away. She closed her eyes, and she cried. She cried and cried. Not sobs, not wails. Just quiet tears steadily streaming down her cheeks. Marcia rose from her chair and gracefully placed a box of tissues on the couch next to Caroline, but Caroline didn't take one. She just kept crying. Every once in a while, Caroline thought she might try to speak, but then she thought better of it. She really didn't have anything to say. Or she had too much to say. Either way, it didn't seem to matter. What she was doing now was crying, and there was nothing to be done about that, and so she just kept doing it. She just kept crying. After a while—maybe five minutes, maybe twenty, Caroline had no idea—she sat up, gathered her things, said goodbye to Marcia, and left.

18

Thursday dinner in the Schwartz-Huntley household was referred to as "pick-and-poke," which meant that everyone would fend for themselves. Cereal, cheese and crackers, frozen tortellini, it was all fair game. Thursday was everyone's favorite night of the week, and Ruth greeted pick-and-poke with a mix of relief and annoyance. Relief that she didn't have to make dinner, and annoyance that everyone was so happy she wasn't making dinner. Her own mother had been a real stickler for family dinner; the three of them sat down together every night at exactly six-thirty. After she died, Ruth's father had held to their dinner ritual with an almost superstitious faithfulness, as though those fifteen minutes were the single thing keeping the two of them afloat. And they might have been.

This Thursday was going to be a deviation from the usual schedule, because that morning Ruth had asked Siddha when she'd be home, and Siddha had said at dinner time, because she was going to Bex's listening party with Wyn. This plan—which was news to Ruth—had made her happy, and also a little jealous. She wanted to get in on some quality time with Siddha too, so she'd made an executive decision to make Siddha's favorite dinner, chicken pot pie. Besides, Thanksgiving was next week and they'd be picking and poking at the leftovers for days.

"I thought it was pick-and-poke," Gilly said when she saw the pot pie cooling on the stove. Ruth answered by handing her a bunch of forks for the table.

"Uh, Mama, FYI it's pick-and-poke," Roz said, a minute later, when she came into the kitchen. Ruth handed her the plates without answering.

"We're not picking and poking?" Wyn asked.

"Oh my god!" Ruth finally responded. "We are not. We are eating chicken pot pie."

"We're potting and pie-ing!" Abe said. "I helped."

"Yes, you did," Ruth said. And he had, if helping could be defined as lying on the floor with the dogs and narrating the plot of *Star Wars* in excruciatingly precise detail.

Siddha came in then, and Ruth tried not to make too big a deal of her presence. "Hi, hon," she said. Siddha gave her a cool hello.

The little kids jumped up at the sight of her, which made Ruth both happy and heartbroken. Siddha really had been avoiding the family. They all wanted to be next to her. As everyone sat down, Ruth spooned pot pie onto plates and passed them around.

Wyn filled the little kids' glasses with milk. "What's new, Sid?" she asked.

"I'm thinking of getting a tattoo."

Ruth looked at Wyn but didn't say anything.

"*What?*" Roz said, dropping her fork with a clang. "Like a real tattoo?"

"Yup," Siddha said.

"If you're Jewish, you can't get a tattoo," Roz said, straightening her back with authority, an authority that was undermined not only by her age but by her milk moustache.

"Yes, you can," Ruth said. "Where did you hear that? Never mind, I don't want to know. Jews can get tattoos, but Siddha can't. She's not old enough." She put a spoonful of brussels sprouts on her plate and handed the bowl to Gilly. "Sprouts, everyone."

"I have salad," Abe said, and passed the bowl to Roz, who passed it to Wyn without taking any.

"I can get one with parental permission," Siddha said. "A tattoo is really not a big deal."

Ruth didn't want this to turn into an argument. But there was also no way she was giving parental permission for a tattoo. "People really regret their tattoos," she said. "Roz, sprouts." She pointed at the bowl. Roz pretended not to hear her.

"Do you regret yours?" Roz asked Wyn.

"Definitely," Wyn said.

Siddha groaned. "No you don't."

"Okay, I don't," Wyn said. "At least not all of them. But I can tell you right now that if I'd gotten the tattoos I wanted when I was sixteen, I would most definitely regret them now."

"What tattoos did you want when you were sixteen?" Gilly asked.

"Gilly, eat more pot pie," Ruth said.

"The Chinese character for 'fearless,' and Michael Jordan's face," Wyn said.

"Next to each other?" Gilly asked.

Wyn made a wondering face, suggesting she hadn't thought about placement.

"Okay, well I don't want anything like that," Siddha said.

"The tattoos you have now are very pretty," Abe said to Wyn. "I'm done, can I sit in your lap?" Wyn nodded yes, and Abe climbed out of his seat and onto her.

"And romantic," Roz said, cattily.

Abe pulled back the sleeve of Wyn's shirt to expose an ink daisy growing on the inside of her forearm, a tribute to Wyn's college girlfriend, Daisy. Everyone in the family knew the story: how when their moms had fallen in love, Wyn had pledged to get the tattoo lasered off, or have it made into a bouquet with all Ruth's favorite flowers, or get a whole smattering of other tattoos as a testament to her love for Ruth, but Ruth had just waved it all off. "I like daisies," she'd said.

"What kind of a tattoo do you want, hon?" Ruth asked, leaning on her elbows toward Siddha, trying to make it seem like she was one hundred percent supportive of her while also one hundred percent not going to let her get a tattoo.

"Oh, I don't know," Siddha said in a voice that Ruth could tell meant that she did know and wasn't going to say.

"Well, you've got plenty of time to decide," Ruth said. She stood from the table, bringing her plate to the sink. "In the meantime, who wants brownies?"

19

Bex's listening party was at Herbe Sainte, a fancy cocktail bar that Evie liked to call "Herb's Saints." Conveniently, it was on a Thursday, which was Tobi's night to be out of the house. Evie's night was Wednesday, and they had a standing babysitter every Friday. They divided the rest of the week's bedtimes equally.

Bedtime, the scourge of modern parenting. Who knew? Every modern parent, of course, but until they had their own kids, Tobi and Evie hadn't fully understood how torturous it could be. When the twins were a year old, Evie had insisted they codify their bedtime plan. "We both hate doing it," she said. "So we need to figure out some way not to use it against each other."

Evie was very good at acknowledging their weaknesses, and was just as insistent that getting out from under them was the only way to go. At first Tobi would protest, say No, no, it was okay, really, but then when it became clear there was no real upside to pretending that she was above feeling resentful, jealous, and angry, she'd see the wisdom of Evie's transparency.

Tobi herself wasn't being so transparent these days. When Evie asked about her plans for the evening, Tobi told her she'd be working late. But at nine, Tobi cleaned up and headed out. The show had started early, at eight or maybe even before, but Tobi hadn't wanted to arrive in time to hear Bex sing. She couldn't bear the thought of just sitting there listening to Bex play their new music for what they'd said in the text would be an intimate crowd. For Tobi, anything that could be described as "intimate" that wasn't sex with Evie was something she very much didn't want to do. But Bex hadn't been home when Tobi stopped by with the drill, so she hadn't had a chance to talk with them. She was going to give it another shot tonight, after the show.

Tobi walked in and headed right for the bar, but then she saw Wyn Huntley and her teenage daughter. Wyn waved at her.

"Oh hey," Tobi said. She held out her hand to Wyn, who took it with a firmness Tobi admired.

"Hey, Tobi! You remember our daughter, Siddha?"

"Oh yeah, totally, I just saw you at—"

"Great to see you again," Siddha interrupted, and held out her hand to offer an equally firm shake.

Impressive, Tobi thought. She made a mental note to make sure her kids knew how to shake hands.

"You missed the show," Wyn said.

Tobi grimaced. "I thought that might be the case," she said. "I was working."

"It was pretty great," Wyn said. Siddha rolled her eyes, the tiniest, fastest eye roll Tobi had ever seen.

Tobi stifled a laugh. "I hope I didn't miss Bex," she said.

"Are you kidding? They'll be working the crowd for hours." Wyn motioned to the bar. "Go get a drink and find them."

Tobi headed for the bar and ordered a beer. The bartender had once worked at GoldFynch, and she was just catching up with him when Bex appeared next to her.

"Hey," Bex said, their face flushed with what Tobi assumed to be the excitement of playing a show. "You came."

Tobi put down her beer and turned to give Bex a hug. "I did, but I'm so sorry to say I totally missed the show." She said this in a way that belied how intentional missing it had been, and the statement left her a little breathless. "I got caught up in the studio."

"Never apologize for that," Bex said. "That's golden time. That's the whole point. Making the art. Meeting the muse." They shook their head. "That's the whole reason we're here."

Tobi didn't want to say, Actually, I was weighing one hundred blocks of precut clay because my assistant's kid has the flu. Instead, she just said, "Yeah. It really is. How did it go?"

"Eh," Bex said, making a sort of half grimace. "I think a lot of it bombed, TBH. But that's okay." They shrugged. "I might not have been ready for this. I was just antsy, you know, to get some shit out there. I'll take it back, fix it up. Play it for the chickens, see what they think."

Tobi laughed and took a long drink of her beer. "How are those chickens?"

"Rockin," Bex said. "They're still laying, like, a dozen eggs a day even in this cold. I just love those ladies. So much in fact that I almost turned down a last-minute chance to tour with May Erlewine. She needed someone to sub her opener, who's got some kind of gallbladder something or other, and anyway, I almost said no because I didn't want to leave the hens."

"I hope you thought better of it," Tobi said.

"I did," Bex said. "I leave tomorrow."

Tobi laughed. "They'll be here when you get back," she said. She saw the bartender head back to the kitchen. It was just the two of them. Well, what the hell, Tobi thought, and taking a swig of beer for confidence, asked Bex, "Hey, can I ask you what is maybe a really inappropriate question?"

"My favorite kind," Bex said.

"Did you have top surgery?"

"That's your inappropriate question?" Bex asked. "I'm underwhelmed. Yeah. I had top surgery."

Tobi wasn't sure if she should act surprised or just get on with her actual question. She decided to just get on with it. "And was it—" She stopped. She was sweaty and losing her nerve.

"Painful? Expensive? The best thing I've ever done?" Bex said, grinning.

There was that smile again. God, Tobi thought. Is that smile what I want? Is this whole thing some stupid midlife attempt to be as delighted by life as Bex appears to be?

"Yes, yes it was," Bex continued, laughing at their own joke.

Tobi laughed with them, and felt herself relax the tiniest bit. "Good to know." She looked down at her beer. "It's strange," she said, "I know it sounds crazy, but I just never really let myself think about it until I saw you. Isn't that weird? I mean, it's not like I live in a cave, or that I haven't seen a lot of nonbinary people, or that I have a problem with it, or anything like that, it's just—"

"It doesn't seem crazy at all," Bex said. "I don't think life is linear, you know? I mean, being here, walking around in this meat suit, we're always wanting different things, new shit. We're in flux. That's cool. That's being animals. Nothing wrong with that."

Meat suit? Tobi thought. God, how she wished she could recount this conversation to Evie! She'd get such a kick out of it. "Yeah, I guess not," Tobi said. "I think it's always just seemed like, if I were going to do something about this"—she motioned to her chest—"it would be such a big deal. Logistically. I mean, you have to recuperate, right? And I have kids, and a business—a job that requires me to use my body."

Bex nodded. "I get it. Not to be entered into lightly." She looked at Tobi's chest. "Are you binding?"

Tobi felt herself blush. She took a drink of her beer. "Uh, yeah. I mean, some of the time."

"Fucking torture, am I right?"

Tobi nodded. "You are not wrong."

"Anyway, it's not really *that* big of a deal. Especially when you consider how shitty binding is. You'd be back to it in no time." And then Bex asked, "Do you want to see?"

"Oh god no, I mean, that's okay, I mean—" Tobi looked around, panicked. "No, really."

Bex laughed, already unbuttoning their shirt.

Tobi didn't say anything. She knew she shouldn't look away, but the sight of Bex's chest—smooth, nippled, bare—made her feel lecherous, and old. And the scars, faint as they were, made her a little queasy.

"It's okay," Bex said, quietly, as though they'd read Tobi's mind. "The whole point of this is that it's just my chest now." They shrugged. "No big deal. That's why I did it."

Tobi nodded. "Right."

"But you still think I should button my shirt," Bex said, laughing.

"Yeah," Tobi said.

Bex started buttoning. "Look, you can call my surgeon. He's the best of the best. He's in the city. I'll text you his number."

"Oh, thanks, but I'm not really at that point yet."

"Well, if you do get there, let me know."

Tobi ran her hand through her hair. "Great, yeah, great. Thanks. Thanks so much. And hey, I'm sure you were great tonight . . ." She trailed off, and, unsure of what to do next, put out her hand. Bex took it and pulled it to their chest, putting their other arm around Tobi in a half embrace. For a moment Tobi's hand rested on Bex's chest, and she thought about what Bex had said, about all this not being linear, and she found it comforting. It was the permission she knew she shouldn't have to ask for, but was so, so happy to have.

TOBI WENT RIGHT into the downstairs bathroom when she got home, to take off the binder. She stuffed it back in her work bag, then went upstairs to check on the kids. As she reached the second level, she could hear the fan blowing on high in their room, and she groaned. One night last summer, the twins had discovered that with their box fan turned up to the highest setting, they could inflate one of their duvet covers to create a sort of wind tunnel/hot air balloon big enough for both of them to stand up in. Now they liked to make it on nights when they weren't tired, and they'd play in there, then eventually fall asleep. They'd crawl out in the morning, their hair matted and snarled like birds' nests, their little cheeks chapped from the wind. The problem—

which was the twins' delight—was that Tobi and Evie couldn't turn off the fan when the two of them were inside. They just had to wait until morning.

Tobi closed the door again and went down the hall to her bedroom. She was hoping Evie would be asleep. She wanted a shower and some time to think. But the light was on. "Oh, hey," Evie said when Tobi came in. She put down her book.

"You let them make the wind tunnel?" Tobi unbuttoned her jeans.

"I didn't *let* them do anything," Evie said. "I just put them to bed and closed the door and then ignored every sound I heard that wasn't screaming." She smiled. "How was your night? Did you end up going to Bex's thing?"

"Yeah," Tobi said. She stepped out of her jeans, hung them on the back of the door. "I stopped by."

"I want to hear how it was, but first I want to show you something." Evie reached for her laptop. "They sent the photos from the *Hudson Quarterly* shoot today," she said, pulling her glasses down from her head.

"Oh?" Tobi went into the bathroom, casually took out her toothbrush from the cabinet. "How are they?" She avoided her own eyes in the bathroom mirror. Shit, she thought. She had told herself she would talk to Evie before the photos came back, but she kept putting it off. It never seemed like the right time. Mostly because Evie would, in that conversation, cut right through it all and ask the questions that Tobi still couldn't answer.

"They're amazing," Evie said, smiling as she scrolled. "You look so hot, babe. I mean, really hot. Come see." She held out the laptop to Tobi as she came back to the bedroom. "What shirt are you wearing? Was it one of theirs?"

Tobi took the computer and looked at the pictures. Was the binder obvious? To her it was, but maybe not to Evie. Maybe you had to be looking for it. "Uh, it was one of theirs, I think." She handed the computer back to Evie and went back to the bathroom to rinse her mouth.

"Well, you should get one of whatever it was," Evie said. "It looks great on you."

Tobi laughed, but a thrill ran through her. She felt like a gun had just gone off at the start of a race, and she was finally free to run. But where? Part of her wanted to tell Evie everything. Tell her about ordering the binder, how comical it had been trying to get it on, how terrible it felt to wear. She wanted to lay it all out: all the complications, the paradox of how much she hated wearing the binder but how incredible it made her feel, that when she was wearing it, she felt both more uncomfortable and happier than she could ever remember feeling. She wanted to tell her about the panic that accompanied her feelings, the no-man's-land where they left her. What could she do now? Only one thing, it seemed, and that thing was terrifying, and Tobi had no idea how she'd gotten here so fast, but she also had no idea what had taken her so long. She wanted to tell Evie that she feared she was going to have to do something drastic now, and she would be, in a way, doing it to both of them. These were all the things she wanted, so much, to say.

But not now, not tonight. Because what Evie had just told her was the answer to every question worth asking, and she wanted to live here for a moment. She wanted her wife to love what she saw. Tobi pushed down the top of the computer and put it on the bedside table. She lifted Evie's glasses from her face and put those on the table, too. And when Evie pulled Tobi onto her and slid her hand under Tobi's shirt, Tobi shook her head, the slightest, tiniest shake. Tobi took Evie's hand and kissed it, as gently as she could, then pressed it against the mattress. Holding it there, she began her slow way down Evie's body.

20

"I guess what I really want to know is, does she have kids?" Caroline asked.

Ruth and Caroline were in Ruth's kitchen, sorting through Wyn's squash harvest. The counters were piled high with butternuts and acorns, delicatas and kabochas, and a handful of varieties that even Caroline, who prided herself on being a squash connoisseur, claimed she'd never seen before. All the kids were scattered to their various Saturday morning activities: Gilly and Abe were at the stable for riding lessons; Luca and Roz were at Lego club. And, after much cajoling on Wyn's part, Siddha and Wyn were playing tennis.

Tennis had always been their thing. Wyn had taught Siddha to play when she was a preschooler by using oversize balls and a special miniature net she'd bought from a tennis camp she and her siblings had gone to when they were young. Wyn had claimed that Siddha had real talent even then, although Ruth hadn't been so sure. Wyn had said, With tennis you play the long game, to which Ruth had replied, Please don't use a sports metaphor to explain a sport to me.

Ruth's doubts and obliviousness aside, Wyn had been right—Siddha became a fantastic tennis player. She was fast, she was strong, and she had an uncanny ability to read the court. She was also on track to be ranked as the number one singles player on the Mott Valley team next spring if she worked hard enough over the winter.

This morning Ruth had been carrying the laundry down the hallway when she'd overheard Wyn and Siddha talking about tennis. They were in Siddha's bedroom, and the door was only partially closed. Ruth stopped, leaning against the wall to listen. "It's in reach, Sid," she heard Wyn say. "And I know you want it. I know you want first singles. And I know you're pissed and upset at us, but I also know you want to play with me even though you're saying you don't. So let's take all those feelings to the court and you can use them to beat my ass."

Normally this sort of talk would have made Ruth roll her eyes, but not this morning. This morning it gave her hope. And later, when she saw Wyn and Siddha walking across the driveway, Siddha in her tennis skirt, her hair tamed into a tight braid, and Wyn in her ancient K-Swiss tennis shoes, both of them with racket bags slung over their shoulders, she'd thought, Well, maybe we are going to survive this.

"OH, I'M SURE she has kids. I mean, they're old by now, but she must have them. Otherwise how would she know so much?" Ruth handed Caroline a delicata whose stem seemed suspiciously soft. "Or not even that, really. How could she care?"

Caroline smelled the squash, then tossed it on the discard pile. "And a husband? I mean she wears a ring, so I assumed yes."

"You assumed she was straight," Ruth said.

"Oh, no, I mean—no, I—" Caroline fumbled.

"I'm totally kidding," Ruth said, laughing. "She said she has a husband when we saw her."

Caroline wiped her hands on a dishtowel and looked at Ruth. "She told you she has a husband? I feel like she hasn't told me anything about herself."

"Oh, just in that small-talk way, you know? Like, my husband is a miser about the heat, something like that." Ruth was secretly thrilled by the idea that Marcia Glassie-Greene had small-talked with her and not with Caroline. What is wrong with me? she thought.

"Where do you think she lives?" Caroline asked.

"No idea. I could ask Florence?"

"Oh, have you seen her again?"

"A little bit. She's been helping me with Olive Street."

Ruth was aware that this was a great understatement, barely a sliver of the truth. Yes, Florence was helping her at Olive Street, but Ruth was also texting with her multiple times a day. And when she wasn't actively texting Florence, she was either waiting for a new text to arrive or scrolling through their old texts. Ruth had always been adamant about plugging her phone in downstairs before going to bed, but she'd started putting it on her bedside table instead, so that she could wake up and see if Florence had texted her.

At first, Ruth had told herself this was fine, this was fun, this was no big deal. She'd told herself she was healing her relationship with the past, making sense of what had happened, making peace. It felt good to talk about the old times with Florence. There were so many things she'd forgotten! She'd worked so hard to put that time behind her, but now she was excavating it, gently, with Florence as company and guide.

Ruth kept checking in with herself: How would I feel if Wyn saw these texts? Fine, she decided. Wyn wouldn't care. Wyn didn't like to text this way. Wyn didn't enjoy reminiscing; she wasn't much for chatting. But was this just chatting? When did chatting become banter, banter become witty repartee? And when did witty repartee become flirting? When did flirting become proposition? And at what point was every bit of it inappropriate?

Ruth had thought of deleting the text chain with Florence, but scrolling through it gave her such delight. She loved seeing how the texts had gotten longer, funnier, more frequent. She didn't want to lose them. In fact, they'd had a delightful exchange right before Caroline had come over, one that had started with a heated debate over wallpaper choices and had ended, somehow, with Florence comparing Ruth's ass to a brioche. To which Ruth had replied *did this just become a sext thread?* To which Florence replied with the needle-and-thread emoji. Ruth hadn't known if this was an affirmation or simply a way to clear the word "sext" from the bubbles on their screens. Both possibilities left her breathless. They also prompted her to change her phone's passcode, which was a new answer to the question of how she'd feel if Wyn read the texts.

And now here she was, not telling Caroline any of this. And that silence, that forbearance—a rarity in their friendship, at least on Ruth's end—felt, even more than changing her phone's password, like an answer to the question of what, exactly, was going on between her and Florence.

"WELL, YES," CAROLINE said, "please do ask Florence where Marcia lives, and then tell me right away. I have my theories, and I want to know if they're right."

"I can see her off Millstream, in one of those bungalows right by the farmers' market," Ruth said.

"Or up on Mount Shelby, with a view."

"Do you think she'd want to be so far out of town? Maybe she likes walking to work."

"Or maybe she used to live in a neighborhood, and now she wants the consolations of the natural world," Caroline said. "Like you."

"Very funny. Call me crazy but I don't find fifty pounds of wormy squash very consoling." Ruth handed Caroline another questionable-looking squash, although this time Caroline put it in the save pile.

"Okay, I have to admit something," Caroline said.

"That squash isn't actually worth saving?"

"No," Caroline said.

"Okay, but it isn't," Ruth said, leaning across the counter for it.

Caroline moved the squash out of Ruth's reach. "It's fine for soup," she said. And then, "It's about my last appointment with Marcia."

"Mike didn't go back with you," Ruth said.

Caroline looked at her, astounded. "How did you know?"

"Um, I know Mike, and I know therapy."

"It's not therapy, really," Caroline said.

"Okay, well, whatever it is, it doesn't seem like Mike's cup of tea."

"True," Caroline said. "There's one more thing. I basically just cried. I mean, I was sort of crying about not getting the Rome grant, which is a stupid thing to cry about—"

"It's not at all stupid."

"Honestly I was crying about everything. And I was crying a lot."

"Oh, everybody cries a lot in therapy."

"Well, maybe not like this. I mean, I really cried. Like, there was snot."

Ruth laughed.

"I'm feeling a little embarrassed. Like maybe I shouldn't go back."

"Oh no, no. Crying is Therapy 101. It's like breathing to a therapist. Marcia Glassie-Greene doesn't care. I promise you she doesn't care."

"I wouldn't be so sure—"

Ruth interrupted. "Look, you can't think about trying to keep up appearances or impressing her. First, it doesn't work, she can see right through you. And second, she really, really doesn't care. She doesn't want to be impressed. Every therapist knows that every single person in the world is at least a little fucked up, so it's best not to waste your money trying to appear hyper-functional, or even functional for that matter."

"Okay, but there's something else." Caroline sat down on the kitchen stool.

"You have a crush on her," Ruth said.

"Oh wow, this whole thing is so predictable, I guess. I feel really basic."

"Basic in the best way! As in fully human. And yeah, it's just sort of the drill. It fades. Transference."

"Yeah, but I don't just have a crush on her. I mean, I actually might not have a crush on her at all, not exactly. Can you have transference for throw pillows? I get that a crush on Marcia might fade, but my god, I'll be in love with her throw pillows forever. They're made of some gorgeous old antique rugs or something. Can you make pillows from rugs?"

"Maybe," Ruth said. "I'll never know. Because whatever they're made of, my children would destroy them in about seven seconds."

Wyn walked into the kitchen. "What would our children destroy?"

"My therapist's throw pillows," Caroline said.

"How was tennis?" Ruth asked Wyn.

Wyn took an apple from the fruit bowl on the counter and bit into it. "Great," she said.

"Where's Sid?" Ruth asked.

"She said she was going to Eliza's."

"Without changing? Or coming inside?"

Wyn shrugged. "I guess so." She took another bite of the apple. "Why are you two talking about Caroline's therapist's throw pillows?"

Ruth pushed her glasses up on her nose with her index finger and looked at Wyn. She wanted to hear about tennis with Siddha, but didn't want to get into it while Caroline was there. "Caroline is seeing Marcia Glassie-Greene, remember her? The Roz Whisperer? We're just enjoying speculating about her life. You know, what her marriage is like, where she lives. Where do you think she lives?"

Wyn's face was blank. "Caroline's therapist?"

"Don't look so incredulous," Ruth said. "It's an important question."

"Is it?" Wyn asked. "Or is it just gossip?"

"You know," Caroline said, "in a historical context, gossip is an essential part of building and maintaining the social fabric. There are studies that show that gossiping is actually very healthy."

"Studies?" Wyn said. "Really? Like what kind of studies?"

"Ignore her," Ruth said to Caroline. Then she turned to Wyn. "It's just that Caroline's curious. We're both curious, actually. And curiosity is a good thing. It's empathy-building." She tilted her head and raised her eyebrows at Wyn.

It was a fact universally acknowledged that Wyn had zero curiosity about anyone other than herself. She was loving, she was devoted, but she wasn't particularly interested in plumbing anyone's depths but her own. And not only that, Wyn also had zero recall when it came to the details of people's lives, or people themselves, for that matter. It was impossible for Ruth to have a conversation with her about anyone. Ruth would always start in with some juicy detail, and then Wyn would interrupt her, saying, Wait, who's Amara again? And then Ruth would say, If you don't know who she is, this story will be meaningless to you, and Wyn would say, Just remind me, and then Ruth would sigh, and say, She's Frieda's mom, married to that weird guy who sells rare books out of the warehouse behind the feed store, and then Wyn would nod and say, Ah, or Right, or some other utterance suggesting she had a small inkling of who they were talking about (although she didn't), and then walk out of the room, forgetting that Ruth was telling an actual story about these people she was pretending to know.

"You know," Wyn said, "Eleanor Roosevelt once said, 'Small people talk about people, and big people talk about ideas.'"

"Was she referring to people's actual size?" Ruth asked.

"She was referring to moral stature," Wyn said.

"Oh, well I'm definitely on the short side when it comes to that," Ruth said.

Caroline laughed. "That's why we're friends." She pointed at Wyn with a delicata. "Maybe Eleanor Roosevelt was just trying to get people to stop talking about her philandering husband."

"Or her girlfriend," Wyn said. "Wasn't she having an affair with that journalist?"

"Anyway," Ruth said, suddenly eager to change the subject, "speaking of gossip, I just ran into Liz Levy at Walgreens, and did you know she's homeschooling her kids this year?"

"What?" Caroline said. "I thought she was a hand surgeon."

"Right?" Ruth said.

"Do I know this Liz person?" Wyn asked.

"Out!" Ruth yelled, throwing a dishtowel at Wyn.

21

Tobi was piling boxes and hauling old recycling to the curb to make space in her garage for Mike. He'd texted her that morning asking if he could keep a Vespa at her house. It was a barn find, and he'd bought it for Caroline as a surprise. He just needed a place to work on it, get it running. He'd borrowed a friend's truck to pick it up, he'd be there in an hour, if that worked? A scooter seemed like a strange present for Caroline, but Tobi just texted back *Sure man, bring it over.* Had she ever said no to Mike?

Mike pulled into the driveway just as Tobi was trying to decide if she should trash the twins' inflatable swimming pool or figure out a way to patch it. Evie wasn't home, so she settled on trashing it.

Mike hopped out of the truck. "Caroline wants a Vespa?" Tobi said, by way of greeting.

"She was supposed to go to Rome in the spring, with her students. But she didn't get the grant, so she's not going. And she's really bummed. I thought this might cheer her up, you know? Like, you can't be in Rome, but you can ride a Vespa! What do you think?"

Tobi thought giving a disconsolate Caroline a Vespa was a terrible idea, but she wasn't going to get involved. And Mike seemed so excited. Tobi didn't want to, as the kids said, "yuck his yum."

"I cleaned out some space," she said, turning toward the garage.

"Awesome," Mike said. "I think it just needs a once-over and it'll run like a dream. But you're the expert. Let's open her up."

Let's. God, it could still slay Tobi, the way he asked her to join him. To be a "we" with Mike was to know a taste of heaven. "Oh," she said, "okay, sweet."

"Totally cool if you don't have time, I just thought—"

"Nothing but time," Tobi said. Evie had taken the twins to a birthday party, and Tobi was off duty until dinner. She'd planned on going into the studio, but that could wait. Mike opened the tailgate, positioned a piece of twelve-inch lumber as a ramp, and climbed into the bed, and together they wheeled it off.

"It's a beauty," Tobi said. She rubbed the dust and grime away from the odometer. "Jesus, only five hundred and sixty miles?"

"Now you know why I couldn't resist. Mostly I think it's just mouse damage. Chewed wires, that sort of thing."

Tobi nodded. "Does it start?"

"Yeah," Mike said. "But it needs new tires."

So they got to work. Mike held the steering column while Tobi cranked off the front tire; Tobi flushed the carburetor while Mike disconnected the brake cables and readied the new ones. It was all just like it had been before. They talked about the Celtics, the Patriots, the Bruins. And then they worked in a silence that was sweeter even than the memory of their old silence, risen and doubled as it was now from the passage of time, the complications and busyness of life, the rarity of uninterrupted hours together. Tobi felt young and not young, she felt ageless. She felt the old worries of youth, the weightlessness of them now, and she felt the new worries of middle age, and those felt weightless too.

All this might have been why, after a long silence that Mike broke with a request for a socket wrench, Tobi said, "Hey, crazy thing I've been meaning to tell you. I might have breast surgery." She cringed, cursed herself silently. Why had she said that? Had she ever said the word "breast" to Mike before? God, it sounded so weird. "Top surgery," she quickly clarified. "I might have top surgery."

For a second Mike didn't say anything and Tobi thought maybe he hadn't heard her, and in that moment she was relieved. A bullet dodged. And then, in the next instant, when he still hadn't answered but the shape of his face had changed ever so slightly, she flushed with regret. But then Mike smiled and said, "Honestly, I think your tits are big enough already." And then she reached over to punch him in the arm, and he howled, and punched her back, and she laughed and felt a happiness so deep she could have cried.

"Oh man," Mike said, shaking his head a little, and then, after a second. "Wait, are we talking oh *man* here? Actually?"

"No. Just me. Without this." She put her hands on her chest.

"Damn, Tob, that's awesome." He smiled, looking straight-on at her chest, in a way that would have seemed inappropriate if it weren't Mike. "Yeah, I can see it," he said, stepping back to see the whole of her. "I really can."

"Okay," Tobi said, although it was so much more than okay. Tobi was buzzing, exuberant. "Okay!" she said again, not knowing what else to say. *He can see it.* That was all she wanted to hear. That was what Evie had told her, too, wasn't it? The other night, when she'd looked at the *Hudson Quarterly* photographs. Evie might not have known, exactly, what she was looking at, but she'd liked what she saw.

"Will it hurt? I mean, I know it's going to hurt, but will it be a big thing?" he asked.

"Honestly, I have no idea. I'm just starting to think about it. So I don't really know anything. I've been sort of avoiding doing much research, because I don't want to freak myself out. I mean, I'm sure there's a recovery, and pain meds, and drains, and all that, but . . ." Even saying those words was making Tobi feel queasy. "But people do it all the time, right? I mean, yeah, I think it will be fine." She was reassuring herself now.

"It will be awesome," Mike said. And then he paused, looking at her in a way that left her unsure of what to do. Were they going to hug? He was looking at her expectantly. Did he want her to say something else?

"The bolts?" Mike asked.

"Oh, yeah. Yeah," Tobi said, "right here." She reached into her pocket, handing them to Mike. "Well, I think Caroline is really going to love this."

"No you don't," Mike said.

"No, I don't," Tobi said.

WHEN IT STARTED getting dark, Mike left and Tobi headed inside. Evie and the kids had come home; Evie was at the dining room table with her laptop and the kids were in the living room watching *The Sound of Music*. It was their favorite movie; they watched it in daily thirty-minute increments, and then started over as soon as they were done. When they'd watched it the first time, Tobi had suggested they maybe turn it off after the captain and Maria's wedding, to avoid all the complexities of the Nazi scenes, but Evie dismissed the idea. "Nazis are a part of life," she'd said. Tobi wasn't entirely sure she agreed. Of course, yes, Nazis were a part of life, but did they have to be a part of their preschoolers' lives? But she didn't fight it. And anyway, she liked the way the brave nuns triumphed over evil in the end. Tobi was Jewish now, but there was a part of her that would always be rooting for the nuns.

"Hey," Evie said, without looking up. "Do you want to just take them to La Casita for dinner? I'm not feeling anything else."

"Yeah, sure," Tobi said.

"What did Mikey want? You were out there a while."

Tobi opened the fridge, looking for a beer. "He got Caroline a scooter for Christmas."

Now Evie looked up. "Seriously? What kind of scooter? Like a Razor scooter?"

Tobi laughed. "Not a Razor. A real scooter, a Vespa. He needed somewhere to work on it in secret. It's a surprise."

"He got a Vespa for Caroline? That doesn't really seem like the ideal gift for her."

Even though Tobi had already said as much to Mike, Evie's criticism made her feel defensive of Mike. "I think it's thoughtful."

"Sounds like more of a gift Mike is giving himself," Evie went on. "Kind of reminds me of how my brother would always give me baseball cards for my birthday because he wanted me to have something to trade with him."

"He's trying to do something nice for her," Tobi said, sharply.

Evie looked at her, puzzled. "Why are you getting all worked up?"

"I'm not worked up, I just think he's really trying hard to make her happy, and it's nice."

"I wasn't saying he wasn't trying, I was just saying it seems a little misguided. To assume your spouse wants what you want."

"Like you don't assume that all the time?"

"Okay, you need to chill."

Tobi took a long drink of her beer.

"And no, actually, I don't assume that all the time." Evie gave Tobi a what-the-hell-is-going-on look. "And you know that. So please don't get all weird with me." She picked up her laptop from the table and stood. "And you know what? Don't talk to me like that. Like you and Mike are the team. I don't know how Caroline feels about that, and I don't honestly care, but it doesn't work for me." She motioned across the space between them. "It's you and me, Tob, we're the team. Remember?"

Tobi turned away for a moment. This was an old fight, one they hadn't had in a long time: Evie vs. Mike. Evie's insistence that she be the one, the primary, the chosen. Tobi was careful, most of the time. But just then, in the garage, she hadn't been careful. She'd told Mike about the top surgery without telling Evie first. Tobi felt a prick of worry, the fear she often felt when they had this fight, when she wanted to reassure Evie, to forcefully, truthfully, tell her that it was always Evie first, Mike second. But that was a hard—and often impossible—thing to do. Tobi knew it was supposed to be easy to name Evie as her primary alliance, but it wasn't. She'd thought that over the years, and especially once they had kids, it would get easier, clearer, that Evie would edge ahead of Mike and stay there. But still they were mostly neck and neck. And in the end—and this was what sometimes scared Tobi—in the end, she knew it was Mike who took the prize.

22

Caroline came home just a few minutes after nine P.M., saying a silent prayer that Luca was asleep. She'd had a late rehearsal, and because Mike was working until end of service, she'd asked Siddha to babysit. The rehearsal went well, and Caroline let everyone out a little early. She picked up takeout from Thai and Stop Me on her way home, in case Siddha was hungry. But when she walked into the kitchen, it was clear that Siddha had other things on her mind. She was sitting at the kitchen table, her skirt pulled up, tending to what looked like a very new—and rather amateur—tattoo on her thigh with a tube of Neosporin and a pile of Band-Aid wrappers.

"You're home!" Siddha pulled down her skirt and tried to slide the Band-Aid wrappers off the table and onto her lap, but instead they fluttered to the ground around her. She attempted to kick them under the table while maintaining eye contact with Caroline.

Caroline resisted the urge to laugh. "What are you doing?" she asked.

"Nothing," Siddha said.

"Is that a tattoo?" Caroline pointed to the creep of red below Siddha's skirt.

Siddha tried to pull her skirt lower. "No," she said.

Caroline just looked at her, not saying anything.

"It's a stick-and-poke."

"I think that's sort of the same thing, isn't it?" Caroline put the take-out bags on the table. "Can I see it?" she said. "I just want to make sure it looks okay, infection-wise."

Siddha shook her head. She looked like she was trying very hard not to cry.

"Look, Sid, it's okay. Really." Caroline went to the sink to wash her hands. "I'm not going to tell your moms. I mean, I'm going to strongly encourage *you* to tell your moms. But I do need to see it. I can't let you leave without knowing you're okay."

Siddha started crying. "I really fucked it up. I knew I shouldn't have tried to do it myself. And now it's really bad."

Caroline reached for a Kleenex and handed it to Siddha. "I'm sure it's not that bad," she said. "Show me."

Siddha pulled up her skirt. On her thigh there was a red blotch and a faint inky outline. At first Caroline couldn't tell what it was. A daffodil? A microphone? She looked more closely. Maybe a hammer? "A hammer?" she guessed, hoping she'd gone with the right choice.

"That's what it's supposed to be, but I screwed it up."

"No, no," Caroline said. "You didn't screw it up at all." She couldn't believe she was reassuring Siddha about the accuracy of her DIY tattoo. "I can see it now. You did a nice job."

Siddha took an audible breath. Caroline stood. "Let me get you a glass of water."

When she came back to the table, with a glass of water for Siddha and a glass of wine for herself, Caroline said, "I brought home some curry. Why don't we eat a little, and then think about what to do next?"

"I should really get going," Siddha said.

"You need a minute," Caroline said. "You need to eat." She put a bowl of curry in front of Siddha and handed her a spoon. They ate in silence. Siddha started crying a few times, and when she did, Caroline would just give her another Kleenex.

When they were done, Caroline said, "Can I take another look?"

Siddha lifted her skirt. Her skin was still red and angry, but it didn't look much different than any other new tattoo. And because she was married to someone in the restaurant industry, Caroline had seen a lot of new tattoos.

"You're going to want to keep a bandage on it for a few days," Caroline said. "And then, after that, the key is moisturizer. Something nice and thick, like Aquaphor. But no Vaseline. And no antibiotic ointment. That's not what it needs. It really just needs time."

"Do you have a tattoo?" Siddha asked.

"Not a one," Caroline said. "But have you seen my husband? I know what I'm doing here."

Siddha laughed.

Caroline loved the sound of that laugh. She took a sip of her wine. "The hammer, is that, I mean . . ." Caroline wasn't sure how far she should go. She didn't want to overstep. "Is it for Elliot? For his hardware store?"

"Yeah," Siddha said. "But it was such a dumb idea. It was too hard. I should have just done his initials or something."

"Oh no," Caroline said. "Where's the poetry in that? A hammer is good. I like it. Very mythical." She smiled.

Siddha smiled back. "You're not going to tell my mom?"

Caroline shook her head. "I'm not. But you are."

Siddha started to protest, but Caroline stopped her. "You don't have to tell her tonight, or even this week. You can let it heal a little more if that's your worry. But you do have to tell her."

Siddha sighed. "Okay," she said. "I will."

Caroline stood to get her wallet from her purse. She pulled out two twenties for Siddha and handed them to her. Then she handed her a third. "That one's for the Aquaphor."

23

It was almost ten when Ruth came home, and she'd expected everyone to be in bed. But Wyn was still in the kitchen, doing the dishes.

"Do you want the good news or the bad news?" Wyn asked.

Ruth was tired. She'd made the mistake of volunteering to set up Mott Valley's Beanfeast, a Thanksgiving-week gathering that—quite craftily, Ruth had to admit—managed to not involve a single Pilgrim, indigenous person, or turkey while still satisfying the ubiquitous American need to mark the harvest season. Beanfeast was a celebration of beans, in all their forms. There was bean art, both two- and three-dimensional; original songwriting and skits; and of course endless stews, burgers, and chilis. Ruth had been at Mott Valley all evening, inventorying crockery, testing the sound equipment, hanging artwork, and completing a multitude of other tasks that she had no real aptitude for or interest in.

"The good news," Ruth said. She pulled a stool back from the island counter and sat down.

"There's pie."

"Why did you buy pie?"

"I didn't. Florence Howe dropped it off."

"Oh," Ruth said. That *was* good news. "And the bad news?"

Wyn sighed. She turned around at the sink. "It seems that Siddha went ahead and gave herself a tattoo."

"What? A tattoo? How do you give yourself a tattoo? Are you fucking kidding?" Ruth stood up, headed for the stairs. "Is she home? Where is she?"

"She said she was going to the library with Eliza and—"

"It's ten o'clock," Ruth interrupted. "Pretty sure the library is closed."

"Yeah, pretty sure they never went to the library," Wyn said.

Ruth didn't say anything.

"Look, wherever she went, she'll be back soon, and there's something you should know."

Ruth went to the fridge. She needed some wine.

"The tattoo's a hammer," Wyn said.

Ruth turned from the fridge. "A hammer? Why in god's name would she want a hammer tattoo?"

"I think it's for Elliot," Wyn said quietly. "Because of the hardware store."

"Seriously?" Ruth said. "Did she tell you that?"

"No, but I can't really see another explanation."

"This is bad," Ruth said. "I don't know how we're going to get ourselves out of this. I should have agreed to see him. I should have let him see her."

"Do you mean 'we'?" Wyn was angry.

Before Ruth could respond, Siddha burst in through the mudroom door, bringing the cold with her. She walked through the mudroom still in her coat and boots, looking puffed up and defiant.

Ruth looked back at her, hard, and Siddha did not deflate. "You got a tattoo?"

Siddha nodded.

"Can I see it?"

"Why?" Siddha asked.

"I want to make sure it's okay."

"I've got it," Siddha said.

"I suppose I'd say I agree with you, that if you're old enough to get a tattoo, you're old enough to care for it, but as the case is, you're *not* old enough to get a tattoo! But that's all water under the bridge now, so I'd like to at least make sure you don't get a staph infection."

"It's fine," Siddha said. "Caroline said it looks fine."

Ruth was confused. She looked at Wyn, who just shrugged at her. "Caroline? You showed it to Caroline?"

"Never mind," Siddha said.

Ruth went to the sink to get herself some water. *Caroline?* "Hon," she said, telling herself to stay focused and worry later about why Caroline knew about this and didn't tell her, "I know you keep saying you don't want to talk about this, but we can contact Elliot's lawyer anytime. You don't have to worry about hurting my feelings, or Mom's."

"Hurting *your* feelings?" Siddha yelled. "You seriously think I'm worried about your feelings? When it turns out you didn't even think once about my feelings, my whole life?"

"Come on now, Sid," Wyn said at the same time that Ruth said, "You know, Sid—" but then they both stopped.

"What?" Siddha asked. "What do I know? What do you think you can tell me that I don't already know? Because you're not the only one who knows things. I know *everything*."

"Oh, do you?" Ruth said. She felt herself getting warm.

"Ruth," Wyn cautioned. She put her hand on Ruth's arm.

"Oh my god!" Siddha yelled, heading for the backstairs. "You're so crazy! You're always like, 'Oh, hon, whatever you want,' and 'Oh, hon, whatever you need.'" Her voice was high and syrupy. "But really, you're just an authoritarian asshole who thinks she's in charge of every single human. I fucking hate you."

"Siddha!" Wyn yelled. "Knock it off!"

For once, Ruth didn't feel the need to temper Wyn. I fucking hate you too, Ruth wanted to say. She wanted, so badly, to scream at Siddha, to tell her what a beast she was, how terrible she was being. And more than that, she wanted to tell her everything about Elliot. Every stupid thing he did, every mistake. She wanted to tell her that he'd gone to jail. Jail! And a quieter part of Ruth wanted to tell Siddha that she was sad, so sad, and she knew that Siddha was sad too, and she wished there was a way for them to be sad together. But Ruth didn't say any of these things. "Hate me all you want," she called to Siddha, who was storming up the stairs. "I'm not going anywhere."

"Yeah, well I am!" Siddha yelled.

The next thing they heard was the slam of Siddha's door; a moment later, Abe called out. Ruth groaned. She put her head in her hands. "One night," she says. "I'm gone one night, and this happens."

Wyn ran her hands over her face and through her hair. She pulled Ruth in for a moment, but Ruth was too rattled to be held, and pulled away. Wyn sighed. "I've gotta get to the barn," she said, reaching for her hat on the counter. She put it on and headed for the door.

Ruth reached across the kitchen counter for the pie box. She sliced the tape with a knife and opened the top. "Key lime," she said.

"Your favorite," Wyn said. She was in the mudroom, putting on her boots.

There was something in Wyn's voice, the tiniest bit of friction, the grit of the finest sandpaper. Ruth could hear it, although no one else would have. Ruth felt a little heat in her neck. She went to the cabinet for a plate. "Yours too," she said, although they both knew this wasn't true. Wyn loved chess pie; Ruth made it for her every year on her birthday. Key lime was a far second for Wyn, or even third, after tart cherry. But Ruth loved key lime, and Florence remembered. She remembered.

24

"It's actually called 'Beanfeast'?"

Tobi and Evie were at the breakfast table with the twins, going over the plans for the day. Evie was meeting with the design team to settle on next year's seasonal colors and Tobi was taking the twins to some event at Mott Valley Friends, where they would be going to kindergarten next year.

"It is indeed," Evie said, finishing up her coffee. "And you need to be there at eleven. That's when all the prospective kindergartners are meeting up."

"'Prospective kindergartners'? Seriously? How can that even be a thing?"

Evie sighed. "It's a private school, Tob. That's just how they roll. We're going to have to get used to it."

They'd had a million conversations about this, the whole public-school-versus-private-school decision, and how much they both wanted to support the public schools and weave themselves into the fabric of their community, but the truth was they didn't want either of those things as much as they wanted to send the kids to Mott Valley. It was a great school, and they could afford it, so why not? Being able to afford the tuition was a benefit of having children late in life and Evie, who had suffered mightily to get these children, liked to point out that they'd be fools not to take the good breaks with the bad. Especially because this good break meant sending their kids to a school that wasn't only academically enriching, but also very queer. Even the head of school was gay. The place was a dream, and Tobi was happy to be dreaming it, although she wasn't happy to be going to Beanfeast. Still, Wednesdays were her official days for school events and doctor's appointments, and so she'd do it.

When they arrived at Mott Valley it was 11:05 and Tobi had no idea where to park, so she just swung into the first open spot she saw and told the kids they'd walk the rest of the way. Getting out of the car, the twins instinctively grabbed each other's hands, which they did when they were nervous or unsure. Tobi had been watching them reach for each other since they were a few minutes old, but something about this moment, when they stood on the precipice of elementary school and yet still wanted each other above everyone else, made her heart catch.

Being the parent of twins was its own thing, and Tobi was bowled over by the luck of it. When people asked her about the chaos of twins, the work, she couldn't even feign hardship. In fact, she couldn't imagine having only one baby at a time. Twins seemed to her the most natural, and certainly the most logical, way to have children. Their twin-ness made them both sturdier, more solid, less vulnerable. They had a primary, physical attachment to each other, which had made it easier for Tobi and Evie to remain aligned, since it was two against two right from the start. Whatever the increase in effort, it was well worth it.

Tobi walked behind the twins, so lost in her own thoughts that she didn't realize she had no idea where she was going. "Hey you two!" she called to the twins. "Where are you going?" Jules and Nina started running back to Tobi just as she heard someone call her name. She turned and saw Ruth Schwartz. Did her kids go here too? Had Evie told her this and she'd forgotten?

"Oh hey, I thought that was you!" Ruth said when she'd caught up to Tobi. And then, to Jules and Nina, "Don't tell me you two are coming to Mott Valley next year!"

"We are!" Nina said. Jules nodded his agreement, the Red Sox cap he'd insisted on wearing bobbing over his eyes.

"Incredible," Ruth said. "You're going to love it. Do you want to know something crazy?"

Now they both nodded.

"I used to be a kindergarten teacher here."

"Really?" Tobi asked.

"About a million years ago," Ruth said to her, and then to Nina and Jules: "Well, seven years ago, to be exact. In case you were worried I was a dinosaur."

"I'm glad we ran into you, dinosaur or not, because we're a little lost," Tobi said. "We're supposed to meet up with the other"—she paused for a moment, unable to say the words "prospective kindergartners"—"little kids? In the meeting hall?"

Ruth nodded. "Walk across the lawn and then around that red brick building, and you'll see it on your left. I'd take you, but I've been here all morning and I'm trying to make my getaway."

Tobi laughed. "Go, be free," she said.

The twins took off running across the lawn and Tobi followed. She realized she wanted to tell Ruth she'd seen Siddha at the hardware store, how nice it was that she was working for Hope now. Oh well, Tobi thought. I'll tell Mike to tell her for me.

Tobi took in the beauty of the campus as they walked. She'd known that the school was kindergarten through twelfth grade (Evie, in fact, had had to put her hand over Tobi's phone when she'd started using it to calculate the cumulative tuition they'd be paying over the next thirteen years), but still it was much larger and grander than Tobi had expected. It looked more like a college, and a fancy one at that. The buildings were old—the school had been founded before the Civil War—and the trees and gardens were mature and stately. In just the five-minute walk to the meeting hall, they passed a medieval herb garden which, according to the engraved plaque, had been tended by every fifth-grade class since 1950 as part of their yearlong study of medicinal plants; a bronze statue of a crow by Leonard Baskin; and a hand-printed sign hung over the bare branches of a rhododendron which read *Be Mindful and Cautious Please There Are Bunnies Nesting Here.*

It was a lot to take in.

When they reached the meeting hall, Jules and Nina, still staying close to each other, were swept up in a group of other excited and nervous children and led out the door and over to the kindergarten building, where they'd join in a series of bean-centric activities carefully designed to foster connections and settle nerves, while parents stayed behind for their own activities (which had the same objectives).

After the parents had mingled a bit, the head of school invited everyone to take a seat. He was just as warm and gently distinguished-looking as he appeared in the website photographs. "Welcome to Mott Valley," he said, gently tapping the mic attached to the lapel of his wool sports coat. He raised his arms in invocation. "This is where it will all begin for your children. A life of inquiry, of both self and world; a life of contemplation and action, of exploration and joyful adventure."

Wow, thought Tobi. Seemed pretty ambitious considering she wasn't even sure her kids had remembered to put on underwear today.

The head of school went on, regaling the parents with stories of the lower-school musical, the beloved sledding hill, the annual birthday party held for Lucretia Mott, during which students recited original poems and historical speeches on abolition. Tobi felt her sarcasm fall away. As he talked about the second-grade salamander study and the sixth-grade trip to Montreal, the Appalachian folk dancing, the monthly Ghanaian drumming circle, she felt tears in her eyes. Her children would do these things. Her children! There was a time when even those words—the possessive, the plural—would have been enough to knock the air out of Tobi, and now here she was, listening to this man tell her of the wonders that awaited them. Adventure, knowledge, power. It really was incredible.

Then why, Tobi wondered, was it also making her stomach hurt? She took a drink from the water bottle she'd been given at the registration table. It was, of course, a metal reusable one, printed with the school's seal, an image of a gender-ambiguous nightgown-clad angel bursting through an ancient-looking doorway, framed by the school's motto: *Behold, I have set before thee an open door.*

And then Tobi knew what was happening. She knew why her stomach hurt. She was jealous. Here she was, fifty years old, listening to these grand plans for the lives of children, two of them hers. What about her life? She didn't want fancy trips or scratch-cooked lunches, she didn't even wish she'd gone to a school like this one. Tobi wanted someone to set before her an open door.

"Now, enough of all that," the head of school said, rousing Tobi from her thoughts. "Let's find your children and see what sort of fun they've been having. Our student guides will escort you to the kindergarten rooms." He gestured toward a scrum of earnest teenagers wearing name tags.

The kindergarten classrooms were in their own building on the edge of campus. The façade was entirely windows, which meant that each classroom had a floor-to-ceiling view of the pond and fields across the road. Tobi walked inside, where a warm, vegetal smell filled the hallway. She found the room where Jules and Nina were and entered quietly, standing near the wall. Her heart lurched at the sight of them, sitting next to each other at a tiny table, surrounded by other tiny people, all wearing felted crowns that said *My First Beanfeast.* Jules was wearing his over his cap. All the children were eating bowls of soup and drinking apple cider, and on a table near the door there were rows of drying bean collages. She saw her children's names on their projects, and she thought of them, sitting together, carefully gluing beans on card stock.

Tears filled Tobi's eyes then; she was absurdly, entirely, bowled over with love for them. Oh, these children! Her children. They were the light of Tobi's life. And she would not—she would not!—be jealous of them. She would not poison her love for them with envy of the lives that lay ahead of them, lives of self-knowledge and choice. She would be brave; she would remember that it was never too late; she would tell Evie what she needed to do.

I have set before thee an open door.

Jules and Nina saw her and waved. Tobi waved back, smiling. Jules beckoned her to them. "Try some stew," he said, raising a spoon to Tobi's mouth as she knelt next to him. Tobi took a bite of the tepid soup and smiled at Jules. "Amazing, right?" he said.

"Truly," Tobi said, adjusting Jules's crown and baseball hat so he could see. "Truly amazing."

25

It was almost noon when Ruth finally escaped Beanfeast. She texted Wyn to say she was going to do some holiday shopping before she headed home. Because she was trying to maintain a modicum of honesty in her deceit, she stopped by CVS and bought four rolls of wrapping paper and a bag of holiday peppermint patties before she headed to the Olive Street house, where she had a date to meet Florence at one.

Ruth and Florence had been meeting up at the Olive Street house every few days, talking over the renovation plans, next steps, the lists of people to call. The thing was, Ruth never made anything happen between their rendezvous. She didn't order a new front door, didn't price the countertops. The only task she could be counted on to complete was texting Florence to see if she was free. And Florence always was.

This was less good luck than a result of Ruth's concerted efforts to learn Florence's schedule and habits. Showings were in the morning and new listings went live on Thursdays, so Florence was never free Friday or Saturday. She had a standing lunch with a few real estate friends on Tuesdays, then did Pilates in the late afternoon, and saw a physical therapist for her knee on Wednesday mornings. So when Ruth texted Florence to see if she was free on a Tuesday at two, or a Wednesday at one, she was.

And Ruth—well, Ruth was always free. At least from nine A.M. to four P.M. There was both rigidity and freedom to her schedule. Before she'd gotten reacquainted with Florence, she'd resented having Wyn around the house during her free hours, but now Ruth just left. She told Wyn she was going to the drugstore, or the library, or to get groceries. And all this was true. Before she met up with Florence, Ruth would rush to the drugstore, or to the library, or the grocery store. And then she'd go to the Olive Street house to meet Florence, silently begging the clock to move slower, to stop altogether. There was so much to say, so much to catch up on. Although mostly what they did was examine the faraway past, and mull over their lives now. There was very little to say about what had transpired between them.

The day was relatively mild, and so Ruth and Florence were sitting on an old wicker loveseat in the backyard, drinking wine out of chipped coffee mugs Ruth had found in the back of a cabinet. Last week, when she'd asked Florence to stop by and look at the water heater, Ruth had wiped off the loveseat and rummaged around in the garage for the cushions. Her family's half-assed moving job was continuing to prove convenient.

"I have a question for you," Ruth said.

"Hit me."

"Do you have any idea what Elliot might have left Siddha in his will?"

"I really don't," Florence said. "Have you called the lawyer?"

"No, not yet. We told Siddha the timing was entirely up to her, that she could just tell us when she wanted to make an appointment and we'd go. We didn't want to rush her into anything. But now I'm beginning to wonder why she's stalling, and if there's something we're supposed to be doing that we're not."

"I don't think you're supposed to be doing anything, really."

Ruth put her head on Florence's shoulder. "Flo, I do *not* know what

I'm doing right now. This whole thing with Sid, with Elliot, it's such a mess. It was not in the brochure."

Florence laughed. "And what brochure was that, exactly? *So You've Decided to Have a Baby Daddy?*"

Ruth playfully hit Florence's leg and lifted her head. "It's just that I had no plan. I mean, after the official, legal plan. I had no idea how to proceed as Siddha got older."

"You had your instincts," Florence said. "Which is all any of us have."

"Elliot wanted to see her," Ruth said. "Did you know that?"

Florence shook her head. "I didn't."

Ruth looked at her. There was something she'd been wanting to ask but hadn't known how. "Flo, did something happen between the two of you?"

"You mean other than the accident?" Florence said.

It hadn't occurred to Ruth that the accident would have been the end of Florence's relationship with Elliot too.

"I mean, if I'm being honest, *you* happened to us," Florence said. "You and Siddha." She smiled, a little sadly, at Ruth. "I wanted him to get it together for Siddha. And then, when he couldn't, I lost my patience. I was sad; I was sad to lose Siddha." She looked at Ruth for a moment. "I was sad to lose you."

Ruth felt a thrill, a spark in her arms, her chest.

Florence went on, "Once he left for North Carolina we didn't really talk. I needed space. I went to some Al-Anon meetings, tried to get some sense of what had been going on, what my role was. He reached out when he came back and I was happy to hear from him, and we said we'd get together, but we never did. I think I reminded him of a painful time. We sort of let each other go. What did he say to you when he reached out? In his letter?"

"He said he wanted to know Siddha before she was grown up and gone."

"And you said?"

"I said it was a bad time, but I'd think about it and get back to him." Ruth shook her head. "That's what I said. I said I'd think about it."

"And did you?"

"Yeah, sort of. I mean, I thought about it, and I talked to Wyn, and we decided it wasn't a good time, and then it never seemed to be a good time. We'd just made it through the pandemic, and Siddha wasn't transitioning back to regular life very well. I think part of me was waiting for him to reach out again, you know? To see how serious he really was. That was shitty of me."

"Did he reach out again?"

Ruth shook her head.

Florence sighed. "It's heartbreaking, Ruthie. But that doesn't mean you did the wrong thing."

"I don't know about that," Ruth said. She rubbed her forehead. "How am I ever going to explain it to Siddha? I should have just moved to California. I should have taken her away from here, so there was no chance of our lives getting all tangled up again."

"There was no way you were moving to California. You were set on this place. You loved it. You said it was the home you'd been dreaming of all your life."

"I did?"

"Remember those little dresses you sewed for Siddha? And the way you always carried her on your back, and how you fed her mashed tofu and—what was it—flaxseed?"

"Oh Jesus," Ruth said. "You're making me sound psychotic."

Florence laughed, shook her head gently. "Ruthie, you were the best. The best I've ever seen, before or since. You knew what Siddha needed. You always have."

Ruth didn't know what to say to that. "You have a good memory."

"For the important things," Florence said.

How good it felt, Ruth thought, to be an important thing. "Can I tell you the strangest part of Siddha and the tattoo?"

"Please," Florence said.

"The first feeling, the strongest feeling, it's not even anger. I was jealous. Isn't that so fucked up?" Ruth went on, not waiting for Florence to confirm or deny. "It's not that I want a tattoo—or who knows, maybe I do want a tattoo. It was just the acting out, the doing what she wanted.

I've been thinking so much about the past lately, of course, you know—taking it all apart, thinking of all the, oh, what do they call them, opening doors moments—"

"Sliding doors," Florence corrected.

"Right, right, sliding doors, and thinking about what if *we'd* gotten together?"

Florence looked at her, confused. "You and me?"

Ruth laughed. "Yes, you and me! I mean, I didn't know I was gay then, although I think I probably did know—but anyway, either way, what if we had?"

"And then what, we moved to California?" Florence laughed. "This is a lot of magical thinking, Ruthie."

Ruth sighed. "I know."

"You'd have gotten very tired of me," Florence said. "You'd have outgrown me."

"Oh, I don't know about that."

"Well, I do, and so would anyone else who looked at your four children and your farmhouse, and those donkeys you have. That is not a life I could have made with you."

"They're alpacas," Ruth said.

"Whatever they are, they are a long way from what I was offering."

"You weren't offering anything," Ruth pointed out.

"And wasn't that lucky for you? Because it sent you looking, and you found Wyn. And she's quite a find." Florence gave Ruth a mischievous look.

"I didn't marry Wyn for her money."

"I know you didn't, but the money is a boon, isn't it? I mean money is freedom, it's a life force. It allows you to ask questions, to make a life of your own desiring."

"Well, of Wyn's own desiring."

"Is that really true, though? I mean, I think I still know you well enough to not entirely believe you."

"Yes. No. I mean—I don't know. Look, I needed Wyn. You're right about that. After Elliot, I needed her stability, and her money. I needed her work ethic and her drive. And she gave it to me, in spades. For a long time that was great. But now, now I'm like, everything's on her schedule. Everything she does, it's like it's the first time anyone's done it. She's always being transformed. She's always wanting things desperately. For a long time I thought, when she said that, that it was some sort of emergency, you know? Like she was in some sort of crisis. She was desperate to leave J.P. Morgan for Cavalier Tech. She was desperate to have a big family. Then she was desperate to leave Cavalier. But now I'm beginning to think it's just the way she talks. I mean, she wants things, sure, but we all want things. She's not that different. All these years, I've been dropping everything to make sure her desperate desires are actualized. I'm sort of tired of it."

Florence laughed. "Hence the farm?"

"Exactly. She was like, I'm desperate to farm. And so I was like, Okay! We'll get a farm. When in reality, it was just that she thought it might be great. And you know what I thought might be great? To drink a cup of coffee in my kitchen, by myself. You know what I'm desperate for? Wyn to go to work. I'm desperate to be back in this house. The six of us, all crammed in on top of each other. I loved that. I loved that the little ones all slept in the same room, and Siddha slept in the attic. It felt like we lived in a children's book, a wild and cozy story that I didn't want to end. I mean I wanted it to keep changing, a little bit at a time. I wanted the kids to get older and go to school, but really that was just because I wanted to stand at the counter in that kitchen and drink that cup of coffee."

Ruth laughed, knowing how ridiculous it was that she continued to boil down her existential crisis into a single cup of coffee when in reality she didn't even like coffee that much. "I wanted to hear myself think and know that everyone I loved was out there in the world, close, but not too close, doing their thing. I wanted a little solitude inside the great togetherness of our lives, you know? I wanted to rest, knowing that we were all okay, we were all a family. That's what I used to fantasize about. That's what I never got to do. That's what I'm desperate for."

"Oh, Ruthie."

Ruth felt like maybe she'd said too much, or complained too much, or painted a strangely bleak picture of what were wildly luxurious circumstances. "I just needed to be alone. And think about what I wanted to do next. And I never got that chance."

"Because Wyn took it."

"Because Wyn didn't need to sit and think. She never does. She knows what she wants to do next. And because she knew, she got to do it, and I'm stuck. And not only am I stuck, I'm fucking everything up with Siddha."

"You're going to figure it out. And okay, you're a little stuck. But we're all a little stuck sometimes," Florence said.

"It's been a long time now," Ruth said. "We've been married for fourteen years! But you want to know what's so strange? People are always like, Fourteen years, and look at the two of you, what's your secret? And honestly, I have no idea. Sometimes, a lot of the time really, I think I don't know a thing about being married. Not one thing. Sometimes I think, everyone else is married, everyone else has a marriage, and I—well, I have something else."

"What kind of something else?"

"I don't know, Wyn's momentum, maybe? Maybe that's what we have. I mean, that's what I attached myself to, what I signed on for. I knew what I wanted, and I had no idea how to get it. But she knew everything."

"Ruthie, don't sell yourself short. You were the wisest twenty-three-year-old I've ever met."

Ruth shook her head. "That may have just been an act. I wasn't really so wise. And I didn't know anything about being married fourteen years ago. I thought Wyn did, but did she? It's just that marriage seems so serious, so deep, so—oh I don't know, so *something*, and I think—is that what Wyn and I have? Maybe we don't."

"Oh, I think you do," Florence said.

"I just don't know."

"Well, that much has been clear in this discussion." Florence seemed amused.

"Are you making fun of me?"

"You seem to be having a hard time figuring out what you want,

Ruthie. I think you need to get on it. I think it's time. What are you desperate for?"

Maybe it was the wine, and maybe it was the anger, or the fresh air, or the tattoo, or just being so entirely fed up with everything and everyone. Maybe it was all this talk of Elliot—Elliot the screwup, Elliot the drinker, Elliot the redeemed—but no talk of the Elliot who'd lit her fire, no talk of a place deep inside her where she was no one's mother and no one's wife, just a woman who was terribly sad that he was gone, along with her youth, along with her optimism, her foolish, foolish optimism. Ruth didn't answer Florence. She just put down her mug and reached for the edge of Florence's coat collar and pulled her in, hard, and she put her mouth on Florence's mouth, tasting wine and lipstick and an entirely, thrillingly new mouth. She was floating above her body, she was her in her body, she was the best of being young and the best of being old, and she was kissing Florence, and oh god, how good it felt! How desperately she wanted to never, ever stop.

26

It was Black Friday, and Caroline was not marking the day as Luca—who had just learned about Black Friday by reading the weekend ad circular from the newspaper—had begged her to, which was to say she was not standing in the cold outside Target to get a deal on a new PlayStation. Instead, she was standing in the cold foyer of the Radclyffe library, helping kids wrap the jumble sale presents they'd bought for their families and friends. It was a tradition: every year, Ruth and Caroline would work the wrapping table, holding tape dispensers and securing bows, cutting wrapping paper and taking gift-tag dictation from the littlest shoppers. The gifts were all old, donated junk, kitschy sorts of things kids love and think (mistakenly) their parents will love too. Hand-painted wineglasses, five-hundred-piece puzzles of kittens in wagons, brooches and bracelets, clip-on bow ties, needlepointed tote bags, dog-eared atlases and cookbooks.

It was a sweet way to spend the morning, although Caroline was having less fun than usual this year because Ruth, who'd texted an hour ago to say she'd gotten held up and she'd be there as soon as she could, still wasn't there. It wasn't like Ruth to be late for a volunteer shift; it was usually Caroline who was dragging her feet. Was Ruth upset about something? They'd texted about Siddha's tattoo late Wednesday night; Caroline had apologized for not telling her right away, and tried to assure Ruth that she would have told her eventually, she just wanted Siddha to have the chance to tell her and Wyn herself. Ruth had told her not to worry, it was all fine. *Well, as fine as it can be when your kid gives herself a tattoo in honor of her dead dad!* she'd texted. Caroline hadn't quite known how to respond to that, so she just went with a row of black hearts.

At eleven o'clock, Caroline saw Ruth hurrying across the library lawn, holding a bag and two coffee cups. "Oh my god, I'm so, so sorry I'm late," she said, as she walked into the foyer. "So sorry. I got held up at the tile store." And then, with a bright smile and a tilt of her head, she held up the bakery bag. "But I brought morning buns!"

Caroline opened the bag and handed Ruth a bun. "You were buying tile?"

Ruth nodded, breaking off a piece of bun and popping it in her mouth. "At some wholesale place in Langham, with Florence. But we shouldn't have gone today, the traffic was insane."

"Oh," Caroline said. "Fun, though. I love tile." Did Ruth know this? That Caroline loved tile? That she would have happily gone to the tile store with her?

"Sort of fun," Ruth said, rolling her eyes, then taking a long sip of her coffee. "I'm getting decision fatigue, for sure. I mean, that's why I asked Florence to go with me, she's in the business. She's got an eye, you know, and can think fast."

"Right," Caroline said. "You know—"

"Oh god, it's Evie," Ruth interrupted, motioning to the door.

Caroline turned around to see Evie walking toward them with a box of pottery. "Oh hey," Evie said, seeming surprised in that way she always did when she ran into Caroline. As though the encounter was not exactly a surprise, and not at all exciting.

"Hey," Ruth and Caroline said in unison.

"Do y'all know where I can drop these off?"

Caroline groaned silently. Evie was from Portland and had lived upstate for twenty-five years. She needed to knock it off with the "y'alls."

"You can just take them inside," Caroline said. "Someone in there will tell you where to put them."

"Oooh, can I get a quick peek?" Ruth asked, peering over the edge of the open box.

"Oh sure," Evie said. "It's just a bunch of seconds, mostly mugs."

"Any Few&Far?"

Evie looked at Ruth, a pleased expression on her face. "No," she said. "But we have a sale going up in two weeks."

"Oh, fun," Ruth said casually, like this was news to her, though Caroline knew it wasn't. "I'll have to check it out."

Evie went inside with her box. When she was out of earshot, Caroline laughed. "Why do you pretend to not know anything?"

"It's embarrassing!" Ruth said. "It's like I'm stalking her. I shouldn't have even said that thing about Few&Far seconds, but it would have been such a coup to score some, I couldn't resist."

"You could just say, 'Oh yeah, I saw that on your socials,' or whatever it is people say."

"I could, but the thing is, it's not like I just look at the socials and then move on," Ruth said. "I mean, I heavily google."

"Well, you don't have to tell her that," Caroline pointed out.

"Right," Ruth said. She finished off the last bite of her bun, then wiped her hands on her jeans. "But at this point I'm not sure I can keep track of what I'm supposed to know and what's just weird. Like, it's okay to know there's a pottery sale going live in two weeks, but is it okay to know that the clogs she's wearing are handmade in San Francisco, come in celery, topaz, and celestine, and cost four hundred dollars?"

Caroline took a sip of her coffee. "No," she said. "It's not okay to know that."

"So I have to pretend!"

"Or stop googling."

"Yeah, that's not happening," Ruth said. "I know you hate it when I say this, but they're just so fascinating. The branding—the branding is genius."

Just then a bunch of kids came over, and Ruth and Caroline helped them wrap. A tiny girl that Caroline recognized from Luca's class worked slowly and carefully, winding a ribbon around a small cardboard jewelry box. "What did you find?" Caroline asked her.

The tiny girl didn't look up from her work. "A button. For my mom."

"Oh, lovely," Caroline said. "Do you mean a brooch?"

"No," she said. "It's a button."

Caroline tried not to laugh. "Oh, well, I'm sure she'll love it. Here, let me put my finger on your ribbon, and you can tie your bow around it."

The girl began to focus even more intently. Finally she finished, and moved along with her siblings.

Caroline and Ruth stood for a few moments in silence. Then Caroline spoke. "This house project is really a lot of work. It's good you have Florence to help you."

Ruth nodded. "It really is. She's very knowledgeable."

"How is it? I mean, how is hanging out with her?"

"Actually, really nice," Ruth said. She was blowing on the top of her coffee even though it wasn't warm anymore.

"Yeah?" Caroline said. "What's really nice about it?"

"Should we do roses-and-thorns?"

Caroline laughed.

Ruth leaned in. "Okay, can I tell you something? I kissed her. I mean, she kissed me?" Ruth shook her head. "No, no. I very much kissed her first. But she kissed me back. I mean, we kissed."

"Wow," Caroline said.

"I didn't mean for it to happen," Ruth said. "I mean . . ." She stopped.

Caroline didn't know what to say, so she didn't say anything.

After a moment, Ruth went on. "I didn't mean for it to happen, but I wanted it to, does that make sense? I hadn't been planning on it but there was this charge, almost right away when we saw each other that first time, and it was, well, it was—"

"Fun?" Caroline said.

"Yeah, really fun." Ruth gave Caroline a slightly bashful look, as though she was attempting—and failing—to appear remorseful. "You know how you said I really needed to get a job? I think what I really needed was to hang out with Florence."

Caroline felt a little stung, as though her advice had been puritanical and nerdy. "But you're not really just hanging out," she said. "You're"—she lowered her voice—"you're having a physical relationship with her . . ."

"You think that's bad." Again the impish expression on Ruth's face. It was starting to make Caroline angry.

"Well, no. No, I don't think it's bad, but I don't think it's great, Ruth. I'm sure it's really fun—"

"Oh god, never mind," Ruth said, clearly annoyed. "I shouldn't have said anything. I thought you of all people would understand."

Caroline felt stunned. "Me of all people? Why? Because I seem like someone who's had an affair?"

"Because you're my friend," Ruth said.

Now Caroline felt terrible. "Of course I'm your friend," Caroline said. "And of course I understand, I mean, without a doubt I understand the impulse."

"But not acting on it. You think I shouldn't have acted on it."

"I don't know what you should have done!" Caroline said, exasperated. "Ruth, listen to yourself. You're being a little manic."

"That's how I feel!" Ruth said. "But weirdly not in a bad way, just in a jittery way, you know? Like an exciting, electric sort of way, like I'm wide awake."

"Yeah, well, I think that's how an affair makes you feel."

"It's not really an affair, I mean, we've only kissed once. Well, twice." Ruth had a sort of faraway look on her face then, as though she was replaying the moments in her mind.

Seriously? Caroline thought. Are you a teenager? Then Caroline remembered Siddha, and then Elliot. And for a moment, she understood what was happening with her friend, an understanding that made her feel a bit more compassion for Ruth, but also more worry. Ruth needed to stop what she was doing before she really fucked something up.

"No?" Caroline asked. "What is it then?"

"It's just—" Ruth shrugged, and seemed at a loss for words. "Oh, I don't know what it is. Maybe that's why I wanted to tell you. Maybe I wanted you to help me figure out what it is."

Caroline felt it then, the clutch of their collusion, their joining. It occurred to Caroline that a friendship was a sort of affair, really, or in some way that was what her friendship with Ruth had felt like to her. They had private jokes; they spent long stolen hours together. And even without attraction there was, at least for Caroline, a buzz, an energy. The wide-awakeness that Ruth was talking about now. Caroline felt it too. Her relationship with Ruth was separate from her marriage, and sometimes there were secrets. Not necessarily things that Mike couldn't know, just things she didn't really *want* him to know. Things that were just between her and Ruth. And it was enlivening, it was exciting. It was private. Which was maybe why Ruth's affair with Florence, her actual affair, felt like a betrayal. A betrayal, she realized now, on top of the betrayal—however unfair it was to see it as that—of not knowing anything about Elliot.

To make matters worse, her own relationship with Ruth was only half of what Caroline stood to lose. She thought of how it felt to be in Ruth's kitchen on a Saturday night, pleasantly buzzed on wine or some fancy cocktail Wyn had made, Mike making gumbo on the big stove, the music turned up or Caroline herself playing something on the piano, and the children, all the children. She thought—her heart swelling with love and pain—of just yesterday, when they'd been at Ruth and Wyn's for Thanksgiving oysters and champagne, their glorious iron-clad tradition of one festive hour together before they all went their separate ways to celebrate the holiday with family.

She could still taste and see it all—the sweet sea-watery oysters, the cold champagne, Wyn in her Carhartts, Ruth in her apron, the stereo blasting, the kids in the yard for one last jump on the trampoline before they all had to hit the road—Caroline's family headed to her father's place in Westchester, Ruth's family on their way to Wyn's brother's in Great Barrington. How could you fuck this up? she wanted to scream at Ruth. It's not just your family. It's my family too! And then she thought, But it is just Ruth's family, really. And that, well, that was the saddest part of all.

"Oh, Ruth. I love you like a sister." Caroline paused, aware in saying this that neither of them knew what it was to love a sister, or to be loved by one, and she wondered, was that the problem? Had they mistaken their love and loyalty? Was it nothing close to sisterly? "But I love Wyn, too. I mean, I can't know this and be in your house, all of us having dinner, hanging out. I wish I could, but I can't." She was angry, she realized, angry at what she stood to lose. Why had Ruth gone and fucked it up?

"This doesn't change anything about that," Ruth said.

"Are you going to tell Wyn?"

"No," Ruth said, firmly. "I'm not. And I don't want you to tell Mike. It doesn't need to involve our families."

"But it does, it already does. I can't have this kind of secret with you."

"I can't believe you're saying that. After you didn't tell me about Siddha's tattoo!"

Caroline felt slapped. "You said you understood!" she said. "You said you were glad to hear about it from her."

"Yeah, well, I actually heard it from Wyn, because Siddha doesn't tell me a fucking thing anymore."

Caroline reached out for Ruth, but Ruth pulled back, crossing her arms, looking away. For a moment, neither of them said anything. Then Caroline spoke. "Whatever you want to do with Florence, whatever it is you're doing, that's up to you. I just wish you hadn't told me."

"Yeah, well, that makes two of us," Ruth said.

The silence between them returned. Caroline hoped a child or two would come by, to break the tension, but no one did.

"You know," Ruth said, after a minute. "I think I should go."

"Okay," Caroline said. But she felt herself getting angry at the idea of having to clean up all this wrapping mess herself. "Actually, I'm going to go," she said. "You can finish up here." And with that, she left.

"YOU'RE HOME EARLY," Mike said as Caroline came in the front door. He was lying on the couch, looking at his phone. "No lunch?"

"No lunch," Caroline said. She sat down, took off her boots, rubbed her feet a little. She sat back in the chair, closed her eyes. "I think Ruth is having an affair."

Mike put down his phone. "You think she is, or she is?"

"She kissed Florence, so—?" And then, before Mike could answer: "I mean, it's more than that. She spends a lot of time with her. That's been going on for a while, but the kiss, I guess, was recent."

"And Wyn doesn't know."

Caroline shook her head. "No one knows but me. And now you. She told me not to tell you, but—" Caroline shook her head, annoyed. "How could I not tell you?"

"I mean, I get it," Mike said. "I get that she doesn't want people to know."

"Mike, you're not 'people.' You're my husband." She looked at him quizzically. "Wouldn't you tell me?"

"Maybe? I mean—"

Caroline didn't let him finish. "You think I shouldn't have told you."

Mike sighed. "I think now I know, and I wish I didn't."

"Yeah, well, me too!" Caroline said. "But I'm not going to be the only one."

"Okay, yeah, I get it," Mike said. "But it's kind of awkward, the whole family thing, I mean, me and Wyn—"

"Yeah, exactly," Caroline said, defensive. "Exactly. And that's Ruth's fault, not mine." She stood then, before Mike could say anything else, and stomped up the stairs.

27

On the second Sunday in December, Tobi's mom swung through Radclyffe for an unplanned but welcome visit. She'd been on her way to a wilderness school in the Adirondacks, where she was giving a workshop on wigwam construction, but a fast-moving snowstorm had rerouted her to Radclyffe at the last moment. This meant there were birch logs and animal hides strapped to the top of her Prius when she pulled up in front of the house, horn honking. Tobi opened the front door so the twins could run out to greet their nana, but she stayed on the porch. The sight of the logs made her a little uncomfortable. What would she say to the neighbors? That according to 23andMe her mom was ten percent Abenaki, so it was perfectly fine for her to drive around with a portable wigwam on the roof of her car? Tobi motioned to her mom to park around back.

Despite the wigwam, Tobi had to admit it was awesome to see her mom. She didn't visit that much, and it felt great for her to be here with her three grandkids, playing Apples to Apples Junior by the fire. Caroline had a concert, but Mike and Luca had rearranged plans so they could all have dinner.

"Let's do an early Lasagna Solstice," Mike had said, when Tobi called to fill him in on Lynne's visit. Lasagna Solstice was something the two of them had invented when they were in their twenties and looking for new holidays that didn't feel crappy and loaded the way Christmas did. They hadn't done one in years.

Tobi's heart soared at the suggestion. "Bolognese or béchamel?" she'd asked.

And just when she'd thought she couldn't be more pleased, Mike had said, "Both."

To get in his training run, Mike had jogged the five miles to their house while Luca rode his bike next to him, and the two of them had arrived sweaty and starving, which, Tobi had teased him, was the way Mike used to arrive pretty much everywhere. But then Mike had taken a shower, and Luca had drunk two mugs of hot chocolate and eaten a box of chicken nuggets, and now everyone was happy.

Evie was sitting on the couch, looking through fabric samples for a possible collab with a local textiles company and trying to get Mike to weigh in. "I like their palette, but this linen feels cheap." She held a napkin up to the light. "I mean, look at the weave." She handed it to Mike. "What do you think?"

"Mikey's more of a bar towel kind of guy," Tobi said.

"Yeah, I'm your man if you want to do a collab with the ex-cons over at the restaurant supply store."

"I might," Evie said. "You never know."

"We better start the lasagna," Tobi said, nodding to Mike and heading for the kitchen.

Mike got up. "Kitchen's closing, friends," he said. "Last call before dinner."

"Can we put on records?" Nina asked.

"Ask Mama," Tobi said.

"Ask Nana," Evie said, collecting her samples and getting up. "I'm going to run these upstairs and make a quick call."

"Yes!" Lynne exclaimed.

Tobi went right for the fridge and opened beers. She pulled off her sweatshirt and cracked the window over the sink, knowing the kitchen was about to heat up. Mike was orthodox when it came to lasagna. He made a béchamel. He made a Bolognese. He bought noodles from the Italian market, claiming he was obligated for reasons of heritage. Never mind that the heritage was Caroline's, and she didn't even eat lasagna because of a dairy allergy. What was it with Tobi's family and their love of other cultures? Of course, she herself had formally converted to one, so she had no leg to stand on. Which was why she dutifully stood at the stove, stirring milk into butter and flour and resisting the urge to turn up the flame and just get it done.

Mike was spooning his premade Bolognese into a saucepan to warm. Before he turned on the burner, he said, "Hey, I hope it's okay to say this, but I noticed you're, um—" He nodded at Tobi's chest.

"Semi-flat-chested?" Tobi said.

"Yeah," Mike said. "That. I noticed that. It looks cool. I mean, you look good."

"Thanks," Tobi said.

"Is it, like, a binder or something?"

"Listen to you, with the lingo."

"I googled," Mike said.

Tobi was touched. "It's just a sports bra. A sort of tight one. I've been wearing a binder sometimes, but it's awful. I mean like torturous. There's just no way I could wear it long-term."

"So you're doing the surgery?"

Lynne walked into the kitchen holding seltzer cans and an empty box of Wheat Thins. "What surgery?" she asked, alarmed.

"No surgery, Ma," Tobi said, glaring at Mike.

"I distinctly heard the word surgery. I have the ears of a bat. What is going on? Did you not get that mole checked? I told you to get the mole checked."

"Oh Jesus," Mike said.

"Oh Jesus what?" Lynne said. "Will someone please tell me what is going on?"

Tobi looked at Mike.

"I'm going to go check on the kids," Mike said.

"Stay," Tobi commanded. Mike stopped. "Ma, I'm fine."

Lynne was upset now. "You are not fine. If you are talking about surgery and you don't want to tell me—well, there's one thing I know, and it's that you're not fine. My god, Tobi. My god! What is it?"

"Okay, okay." Tobi sighed. There was no way to get out of this. Her mother knew her too well. "Look, Ma," she said in a very quiet voice. "I'm thinking—just thinking—about having breast reduction." She couldn't say "top surgery." Not to her mom.

Lynne looked stunned. "Breast reduction? You? Your breasts aren't big," she said. "You have my breasts."

"Actually, I have *my* breasts."

"You have the Gallagher breasts. They're absolutely perfect. Have been for generations." Lynne put her hands to her own breasts. "We have ideal breasts."

"Yeah, well, maybe for you. But either way, I'd really rather not talk about this right now. Okay? Now you know, and I don't want to talk about it anymore."

Evie came into the kitchen. "Talk about what?"

Tobi felt her stomach turn. She was going to be sick. She glared at her mother. "Not now, Ma. Not now."

"What not now?" Evie asked. For a split second she looked confused, and then she looked mad. "What's going on?" She looked at Lynne, and then at Mike. Neither of them said anything.

Tobi reached out her hand to Evie. "Hon, it's nothing, really."

Evie didn't take the hand. "It doesn't seem like nothing."

"You know what, could we talk about this later?" Tobi said. "Evie, please"—she was practically begging—"let's talk about it later. Seriously. Now is not the time, really. It's no big deal, I promise. Let's make this lasagna, and have a nice dinner, and we can talk later." Tobi looked at Evie with a look that she hoped conveyed how much she needed her to just give her a little time here.

"Sure," Evie said, in a cold voice. "Later is good. Later works for me. In fact," she said, a break in her voice, "I think I'll actually head out for a while, until later." She grabbed her coat from the hook by the kitchen door, and the hat under it. She pulled the hat over her ears. "Later," she said sarcastically and, thrusting her fingers into the air in a sort of aggressive peace sign, slammed out the back door.

Tobi leaned against the counter. "Shit shit shit."

"You're getting breast reduction, and you didn't tell Evie?"

"Ma! Seriously?"

Lynne threw up her hands and left the kitchen. Tobi leaned over the sink.

Lynne called from the living room, "I'm taking the children to the park."

Tobi ignored her.

"Thanks, Lynne," Mike said. "We'll have dinner when you get back."

28

The last week of the semester was always crazy for Caroline, but this year she felt herself almost floating through it, going through the motions of rehearsals and student recitals but not really paying attention. She'd sit down at her desk to send an email, then stand up fifteen minutes later, the email still unsent.

Since her fight with Ruth—and the conversation with Mike that had followed—Caroline couldn't stop thinking about loyalty. Mike's loyalty, to be exact. She kept thinking of the oddest, strangest moments, times when Mike had done something that hurt her, but in the tiniest, most inexplicable way. A hurt that, if she tried to explain it to someone, would make no sense.

The brightest, most vivid memory of this sort was of the weekend they spent in Radclyffe just after Caroline had been offered the job at Gorman College. They'd left Luca in Boston with Lynne and borrowed a friend's car to take the three-hour drive to Radclyffe. At first, Caroline had been nervous, anxious to leave Luca, but then after two hours on the Mass Pike, they'd ended up on a smaller highway that wound them through the upstate hills, and Caroline felt herself relax into the green fields, the blue sky.

They stopped at a little café whose parking lot bordered a field of sunflowers, where they ate the most delicious sandwiches and drank kombucha that tasted like flowers. They kept driving, but whenever they came to a town, they'd stop to eat something delicious and walk around. All day, Caroline went in and out of expensive-smelling stores with minimalist displays of linen napkins, ceramic bowls, hoop earrings, cookbooks, hand-woven baskets. Caroline loved every bit of it, and although they couldn't really afford to, she bought things: small gold spoons, nesting ramekins, a brass bracelet, a wooden rattle for Luca—all so beautiful, all so redolent of hope.

In late afternoon, they finally reached Radclyffe and the bungalow they were borrowing from a friend of a friend of someone Mike worked with. There was a key waiting for them under the mat, and as soon as they got inside, Mike headed to the bedroom for a nap. Caroline was too jittery to sleep, so she looked at some rental listings, made herself a drink with the house owner's booze, and walked around the house, looking in closets and kitchen cabinets and bookshelves. She reached for a cookbook from a shelf above the sink, and a leather journal fell onto the counter. She opened it, and saw that only the first few pages were filled, as was the case with everyone's journals. Had a journal ever, in all modern history, been filled?

The book had a few lists, something about life goals of some sort, a race to run, what sounded like a promotion at some kind of corporate job that might as well have been written in Russian for all Caroline knew of corporate-speak. She kept flipping, and there, with a few pages in between acting as some sort of palate cleanser, was a list: columns of names, dates, and in some cases, locations. *Monica 1991* was the first. Then *Liz, Kelly, Danielle, Natalie* and a large bracket, grouping them all as *1993*. The next name on the list was not a name, but rather *Asian girl at CBGB, 1994*—and then Caroline knew exactly what she was reading.

The list, which was long, was also current, and one of its last entries was *Leslie*, with a heart next to the name. This was Mike's friend's friend. Leslie. Which meant that this book belonged to Leslie's—husband? Boyfriend? But here was the part Caroline couldn't get over—there were more names! Only now the names were in groups. *Leslie, Tanya, Ben* (many). *Leslie, Joanne, Anna* (twice).

Oh my god, Caroline thought. And then, aloud: "Oh my god." She'd gone straight into the bedroom then, book in hand, to wake Mike. But when she'd woken him, and told him, and showed him the book—in disbelief, in horror, in what she later admitted to herself was a confusing but undeniable state of arousal—Mike didn't share any of her vast array of feelings.

"You read his journal?" he asked.

"It's not a journal," Caroline said. "It's a list of people he's had sex with!"

"In a journal," Mike said.

Caroline looked at Mike. "It's *crazy!*" she said. "Don't you think it's crazy?"

"I think it's private," Mike said.

Caroline playfully hit him with the book, but she wasn't really feeling that playful. "Is that your way of telling me you have your own list somewhere?" she asked.

Mike smiled mischievously and tapped his forehead. "All up here, baby."

"Yeah, well, I'm here to tell you that list is going to end with one name and one name only," Caroline said.

Mike pulled her onto him. "Yes, yes it is," he said.

Caroline sat up, not able to let it go. "It's just so smarmy," she said.

Mike started unbuttoning her shirt. "It wasn't there for you to read!"

"I feel like you're on his side," Caroline said, putting her hand over the buttons.

"I wasn't aware there were sides," Mike said, moving her hand, unbuttoning another button. "Also, I don't even know this guy's name."

"Brian."

Mike gave her a dubious look.

"I looked at a magazine subscription label."

"Okay, Brian. I'm not on Brian's side."

"But are you on my side?" Caroline asked.

Mike sat up then and rolled Caroline onto the bed. He got on top of her. "Technically, I'm now on top of you."

AT THE TIME, Caroline really hadn't understood why it was that Mike, in his reticence, in his disinterest, was so agitating to her. Later she would think of the word conspire, how it meant to breathe together, and in that moment, she added conspire to the list of things she would, if she could, add to her wedding vows. Will you promise to conspire with me? Because Mike, he wasn't conspiratorial. Mike saw all sides. Except that wasn't entirely true, and this was what sometimes made Caroline's stomach hurt and her head feel hot. Mike conspired with Tobi. She saw the way their heads bowed toward each other's, she heard how, when they were together, they took on the cadence of the other's speech, their mannerisms. She heard them talk about their past as myth and legend. She was startled by the intimacy of it. She was jealous.

Years later, Ruth and Caroline were at the lake with their kids, eating warm chocolate chip cookies out of a small metal tin Ruth had brought and watching the kids swim, when Caroline told Ruth the story of the notebook and its list. Ruth listened with rapt attention, exclaiming No! What? What the fuck! over and over. She wanted every single detail: what the house looked like, what sort of furniture they had, the dishes, the shampoo, the framed photographs, all of it. That afternoon, Caroline and Ruth created an entire narrative of this man and woman, their whole life together, and the tragedy that was certain to soon befall them if it hadn't already. Ruth had implored Caroline to remember their names so she could google. This is all I want, Caroline had thought. All I want today, and all the days of my life before, and all the days since. All I wanted was this. All I wanted was a friend.

CAROLINE TOOK HER final bow at the semester's last concert, the college's traditional production of the Christmas Revels. She threw open her arms to invite the crowd's praise, her eyes teary, her heart full with love for her students. Beautiful, beautiful, she whispered, knowing they could read her lips by now, and her face, knowing that they loved her as she loved them.

And it had been a beautiful concert. Every year, this was a beautiful concert. Caroline's colleagues in the music department always grumbled about how the Revels was the only concert that could fill the auditorium, the only one audiences outside the college turned out for in significant numbers, and maybe that was true, but who cared? And could you blame them? The concert, with its troupe of actors and dancers, its stage full of musicians, all of them singing and playing and rollicking together, it really was extraordinary. The college went all out with decorations, stringing grand cedar garlands and bunches of holly all around the auditorium, scattering tall, thick candles in brass holders all around the stage. And the words to the most well-known songs were printed in the program, so the concert had become something of a sing-along winter tradition among the pagans and non-churchgoing locals. Caroline loved to hear the great swell of the audience as they joined her singers for the Boar's Head Carol and "Lord of the Dance," and she loved—even more—the hush that fell over the auditorium as her students took the stage for the last time to sing the Mummers' Carol. She would never tire of teaching these songs, never tire of listening to her students play and sing them. This concert, every year, this was her Christmas.

After the show, backstage, Caroline hugged her students goodbye, told them to have a good winter break and that she would see them next semester. She was free now. For these weeks, she would pick Luca up from school, and they would eat dinner together—all together, the three of them—on the nights when she'd usually be teaching or giving a private lesson. She loved Christmas vacation even more than she loved the summer, which often felt too long, and by the end left her worried with the anticipation of getting back to the routine, how hard it might be for Luca. But a month was just long enough to be an actual break, short enough not to get in the way of her relaxation.

She was walking out to her car when she saw someone standing next to it, looking at their phone. "Evie?" Caroline called. "Hey, what are you doing here?" Had she come to see the concert? That would surely be a first; Evie hated Christmas and everything about it. She had a sort of wrathful anger about the holiday, which Caroline thought was mostly because Evie loved to be the best at anything that had to do with family traditions and aesthetics, and she couldn't be best at Christmas.

Evie looked upset. "Is Tobi having an affair?"

"What?" Caroline said. "Tobi?" For a moment she thought that maybe Evie was confused and had meant to say "Ruth," but then she realized she'd have no way of knowing about Ruth, and even if she did, she wouldn't care. She meant Tobi. "I don't know—I mean, no—I mean, why do you think that? Did something happen?" And why, she didn't ask, although she was thinking it, are you asking me?

"She and Mike and Lynne, they were all talking about something in the kitchen—something about Tobi, some secret she has—and Lynne was clearly upset, and when I came in, Tobi told her mom not to tell me anything, and then Lynne got more upset, but still no one was telling me anything, and so I just left."

"Maybe it's some kind of surprise," Caroline said, hopefully. "You know, something Tobi's planning for you, and she didn't want her mom to ruin the surprise, so she got mad. Maybe Tobi's taking you on a trip or some kind of secret like that."

"It's definitely not something like that," Evie said. "We don't keep those kinds of secrets; I mean we don't have the kind of life where we can surprise each other with trips."

Evie said this in a way that made it sound like she thought Caroline did, which was laughable. But this was no time for laughing, or even correcting her.

Evie went on, "I knew right away that it was something bad because Mike looked really sheepish. Like, he wouldn't even look at me. Like he knew, and he didn't want me to see that he knew."

"Oh, I don't know," Caroline said. "I think maybe he just didn't want to get involved. I mean, he's very conflict averse." Caroline was thinking now of what she'd told Mike about Ruth, about how she'd wanted Caroline to keep her secret, how Mike had asked her why she hadn't. Was this because he was keeping Tobi's secret? There were all sorts of things Caroline knew she was supposed to say now, things like, I know Tobi would never have an affair, or I know there must be some other explanation, but she couldn't seem to make herself say them.

"You could go home," she suggested weakly, "and just ask her."

"I'm too upset. I can't go home until the kids are in bed." Evie sounded like she was trying not to cry.

Caroline felt the closed door of her heart creak open for poor Evie. Maybe it was the concert, with its message of peace and goodwill, or the cold, clear air and the white lights strung on trees all around them. But most likely it was Caroline's anger and annoyance with Mike as of late and the sticky sweetness of this possible collusion with Evie. "Come on," she said, motioning toward the street. "Let's go to town. I'll buy you a drink." She pulled out her phone then, wondering if she might see texts from Mike, missed calls. There was nothing. She texted him *heading out for a drink with the department home late.* A few seconds later, the typing bubble appeared, then disappeared, then a heart popped up about her message. She put her phone in her bag.

"Should we walk to Sully's?" Caroline asked, buttoning up her coat and not waiting for a reply. "I think we could both use the fresh air."

29

When all the lasagna had been eaten, and the leftovers packed away, and the wine bottles taken to the recycling, and the salad tossed in the compost, and Tobi had scooped the last of the tiramisu out of the dish with a spoon she and Mike shared; when the floor had been swept, and the children washed and chased to bed, and the cats fed, and Tobi had sent her mother to bed in the apartment over the garage, the one that Evie had insisted on calling "the guest quarters," and not a "mother-in-law apartment," but which was only ever occupied by one or the other of their mothers-in-law—Evie came home.

"Hey," Tobi said. She was sitting outside on the front porch, wearing her coat. She'd been waiting for Evie.

"Hey," Evie said.

"Wanna talk?" Tobi asked.

"Not really," Evie said.

"It's not what you think, Evie."

"No? What is it then?"

Evie's voice was mean and cold, and Tobi understood, but still, it scared her. She also understood that she'd hurt Evie, and that even when she clarified, even when she cleaned up this misunderstanding, Evie would still be hurt.

Tobi sighed. "Look," she said, starting to speak, but not knowing what to say, she stopped. Evie looked at her, eyebrows raised. She was not about to help Tobi.

"Okay, look," Tobi said, trying to start again, "you know how the winter here is so long, eventually it starts to feel like it was never not winter? Like, winter is just the way the world is? And then one day you go into the grocery store, and there, right there in the front of the store, there are apricots, and you'd forgotten that there even was such a thing as apricots. And sure, they shipped them in from the other side of the world but still, there they are, and you'd forgotten, and it's so nice to be reminded."

Evie looked at her quizzically. "I thought you didn't like apricots. Every time I buy them, they go bad."

"I don't," Tobi said. "I mean, I don't like eating them. I like seeing them. I like what they represent. But anyway, that's not the point, the point is—" She stopped. She didn't know how to say this. "The point is, I just feel like I've been going along one way for so long, and it's been a fine way—I mean, a little hard, but whatever, the kids are little, we have the business—but then it's like I saw the apricots, and I remembered all these other things about myself, things that used to be true, and are still true."

"You saw Bex. Bex is the apricot. You're having an affair with Bex."

"I am not having an affair with Bex! Jesus, Evie. No, no, that's not it. But—"

"Oh my god, there's a 'but' to that?"

"I am not having an affair, at all, with anyone." Tobi looked at her, straight at her, trying to attune every cell in her body to Evie's, trying to talk to her in every possible language. Telepathy, words, eyes—all of it. She wanted every single bit of her to be telling Evie this total truth.

"Okay," Evie said, slowly. "So what's the 'but'?"

Tobi sighed. Was there a way to explain this without talking about Bex? "When I saw Bex, at Elliot's memorial—when I saw them, I just couldn't stop thinking that I wanted what they have, you know? That they have exactly what they want, and I—I keep not being able to get that, you know? To get what I want."

"You don't have what you want?" Evie said. "Welcome to middle age, Tobi, none of us have what we want."

"That's not true!" Tobi said. "You have what you want; Mikey has what he wants!"

"I thought what you wanted was to go back in the studio, and we did that, I—" Evie poked her own chest. "*I* did that. I made that happen for you. Like I always do." She shook her head. "Like I always make things happen for you."

This stung. "Yeah, well that's just it," Tobi said. "Did it ever occur to you that I might want something that you can't make happen, Evie? That doesn't have anything to do with you? I want top surgery."

"Oh my god," Evie said. "Oh my god. That's it?" She laughed, a sort of mean laugh. "That's what you couldn't tell me? That's what you told Mike? And your *mother*." She said the word with such disdain, such a bitter, acidic tone. "And you didn't tell me?" Evie started to cry. "Oh my god. I'm your fucking wife and you didn't tell me you want top surgery?"

"Well, maybe it was *because* you're my wife."

"Oh my god, don't throw that hetero 'marriage secrecy is normal' bullshit at me!"

"Jesus, Evie, you're the one who just called me your wife!"

Evie wiped a tear from her face. "But you told them first! You told both of them before you told me."

"I told Mike," Tobi said. "He told my mom. Just now. By mistake."

Evie shook her head. "I just can't believe that you told Mike and not me."

"I'm sorry," Tobi said. "I'm so sorry."

But here was the thing: Tobi wasn't sorry. She was, of course, so sorry that Evie was sad and hurt—but also, why couldn't she talk about this with Mike first? She felt the warm rise of loneliness and shame in her then, how she'd felt, always, so excluded from ties of brotherhood and of sisterhood, of fathers and daughters and even, in some ways, mothers and daughters. She'd always felt a little odd, a little off. Did that mean she was only allowed to have Evie? Did her fucked-up family, her boyish girlhood, her masculine femaleness, did it all preclude all familial bonds with anyone but Evie? The thought infuriated her. But then it also made her feel terrible, because wasn't Evie enough?

They sat for a while in silence. Evie crying, Tobi feeling, so much, that she didn't want to say, again, that she was sorry.

"I mean, I've noticed," Evie said, finally. "It's not like I haven't noticed the tight bras, and the way you don't want me to touch you anymore. I guess I just thought it was—oh I don't know. Honestly, I don't know what I thought. Maybe I just decided not to think about it."

"Sometimes I feel like you want to think about everybody else, but not me," Tobi said.

"What's that supposed to mean?" Evie said.

"You know what I mean. You're always thinking about other people, you're so curious about them, you're always analyzing—"

"You hate it when I analyze you! You have a literal physical aversion to it! You've been telling me to stop for the last twenty-five years!"

"Yeah, well—" Tobi didn't know how to respond to that. Evie was right, but Tobi knew she was too. People changed. "This wasn't how I wanted to have this conversation," Tobi said. She was angry. Angry at herself, at Evie. Angry, for some strange reason, at Bex.

Evie stood up. "Yeah, well, you should have thought about that before you kept this secret from me."

30

Marcia Glassie-Greene might have thought her couch was uncomfortable, but to Caroline it was perfect. She'd grown to love sitting on it, all alone. It felt luxuriously private and spacious, giving her the same feeling she had on the nights when Mike worked late, and she ate dinner right out of the pot, then fell asleep in the middle of their bed. Long ago, Caroline had known a woman who'd said, "Some women have diamonds, but I have therapy." At the time she'd thought that woman meant that diamonds and therapy both cost a fortune, but Caroline had come to realize that therapy was a luxury, a pleasure that belonged only to her.

Although this session, her first since the library sale, wasn't feeling particularly pleasurable. "I had a fight," Caroline said to Marcia after she'd run out of small talk and life updates. "With a friend."

"Oh?" Marcia said.

"You know her, the friend. Is it okay to talk about it?"

"It is. Unless you're planning some sort of vendetta, in which case I'd need to warn her."

They both laughed then, together, and Caroline felt the thrill of intimacy rise in her body, a great swoosh of love for Marcia, but not for Marcia the person, not exactly, or not just Marcia the person. It was love for the office, the tall paned windows with their view of the snowy mountains, the long cherry desk, the burgundy rug with its intricate gold patterns that Caroline liked to study when she had nothing to say, or when she knew what she wanted to say but was afraid to say it. She even loved the clock, with its graceful silver hands sweeping her toward the end of the session, reminding her not to waste her precious time. She loved it all.

Suddenly she was afraid of jeopardizing her relationship with Marcia, of telling her something that would make her take Ruth's side and think that Caroline was a bad person. "The fight's not really that interesting," Caroline said.

"Try me," Marcia said. "There's a broad range of things I find interesting."

Caroline smiled a little smile but didn't say anything. After what felt like several minutes but was just a few seconds, Caroline said, "I haven't gotten in many fights with a friend. Maybe not ever."

Marcia nodded but didn't say anything.

"I mean, I get in fights with Mike all the time. But I was thinking about it, and I was thinking, Have I ever gotten in a fight with a friend? I mean not since I was a little kid. And maybe not even then. Not a real fight."

"How did it feel?"

"Sort of terrible," Caroline said. She laughed a little. "I guess that's why I haven't done it before."

"But you've been angry with friends, in the past?"

"Oh sure," Caroline said. "All the time. But I never had a fight. I just sort of waited until the feelings passed, or the annoyance or whatever. And then, if it didn't pass, I'd just let the friendship go."

"Ghosting, as the youth like to say."

"Right," Caroline said. "Although it used to be much easier to do that. You know, before texting."

"But it wasn't like that this time, with this friend."

"No," Caroline said. "We had a fight." She paused for a moment. "I mean, I guess it was a fight? A disagreement? I don't know."

Marcia didn't say anything.

"I think my friend is having an affair. And when I told Mike, he said he wished I hadn't. That he wished I'd kept it from him."

Marcia nodded. "And do you wish your friend had kept it from you?"

"I wish she hadn't done it. Wasn't doing it, I mean."

"I can see that," Marcia said. And then, "What were you hoping Mike would say when you told him?"

"Oh, I don't know, I guess I wanted him to lead with, That's horrible, I'll never, ever, do anything like that."

Marcia nodded. "That sounds reasonable," she said.

Caroline couldn't tell if Marcia was joking. "But honestly, I didn't like that he didn't want to know. I mean, it was like he was accusing me of not being loyal to my friend. When all I was really doing was being loyal to him."

"That's an interesting word, 'loyal.' What do you mean, 'being loyal,' exactly? I mean, what do those words mean to you?"

Caroline looked at Marcia. "What does it mean? It means *loyal.*"

"Faithful?" Marcia suggested. "Consistent?"

Caroline waved a hand in front of her face in frustration. "I don't know! All these words, they're all just different ways of saying 'Don't cheat on your spouse,' and I'm always confused by that—I mean, there are a lot of other levels, you know? There are a lot of ways you can be disloyal that don't involve sex."

"Such as?"

"Such as not wanting to hear about someone else's affair!" Caroline said. She felt exasperated.

Marcia did not seem bothered by this exasperation. "Do you feel Mike's loyalty to you?"

"Mostly," Caroline said.

"But not entirely?" Marcia said.

"Mike is an extraordinarily loyal person," Caroline said. "I mean, it's a big part, maybe the biggest part, of why I married him. But . . ." Caroline stopped talking and Marcia didn't say anything. They sat in silence for a while.

Caroline went on. "I guess my mistake was thinking that a super loyal person would, when we got married, take all that loyalty and direct it just at me."

Marcia nodded. "I can see why you'd want that."

"But I was wrong."

Marcia nodded again, but she didn't say anything.

"He's loyal to me, of course, and to Luca, and to his co-workers, and his friends, and all that's great."

"So what's not great?" Marcia asked.

"Tobi," Caroline said, not believing she was actually saying it out loud. "His cousin Tobi. I feel like if he had to choose between me and Tobi, he'd choose Tobi. And I feel so stupid even saying that, because first of all he's not going to have to choose, and second of all Tobi is his blood relative, you know? She's basically his sister, and aren't we all supposed to choose our blood relatives?"

Marcia said, "Well, I'm not sure—"

"I don't have any blood relatives, that's the thing," Caroline interrupted. She was smiling then, a thin smile, one she used when she was trying not to cry—a sort of facial levee she'd built over the years, which held with varying levels of success, and was not, right now, working very well. She cleared her throat. "None. I mean, I have my parents, but that's different. I have no siblings, no cousins, no one. I have Mike. Mike is my person."

"He seems like a good person to have," Marcia said, kindly.

"He is. But I'm not his," Caroline said.

"You can have more than one person," Marcia said. "In fact, it's a wonderful thing, really, to have more than one person."

"I'm sure it is," Caroline said, a little bitterly. "I wouldn't know."

"You have your friend," Marcia said.

"That's not the same."

"It doesn't have to be the same to be wonderful."

"Yeah, well, we're having a fight," Caroline said. "As I already told you."

"You'll resolve it," Marcia said, as though that was all there was to say about what had seemed, to Caroline, an unclimbable mountain. "You know, you talk about Mike, how loyal he is, and I believe you, I really do, and I see it. But don't sell yourself short. You're loyal too, Caroline. I see it. I see it in your attention to Luca, and even the way you've tried to protect Mike from what you think might be my disapproval at his not coming back. You're steadfast. Your friend knows that, I'm sure. It's why she told you."

"She shouldn't have told me. It wasn't fair."

"No," Marcia agreed. "It was too much to ask. But sometimes too much is what we ask of the people we love most." She shrugged. "And it makes a mess. No doubt about it."

"I don't like this kind of mess," Caroline said.

"Very few of us do," Marcia said. "But you'll get through it."

"It's just that every time I think about talking with her, I sort of get this terrible, visceral feeling of dread. Like I just can't—I can't see myself doing it. But then, if I don't, how can we ever be friends again?"

"Maybe you won't talk about it," Marcia said.

"And then the friendship is over?"

"No, no," Marcia said. "Not at all. You know, I used to think that talking things out was always best, but I'm not so sure anymore." She smiled at Caroline. "Now I think there's really something to be said for letting things go, and just moving on. Wounds heal." She shrugged. "And the ones that aren't going to heal, well, they let you know. Either you'll talk it over, or you'll ride it out. Time will tell. You'll get through it, either way."

And there it was again, the way Marcia said something and made it seem like the easiest, most certain thing in the world. A done deal. She'd get through it. She'd ride it out, whatever that meant.

Caroline looked at the clock then and saw that her time was nearly up. She pulled on her coat, said goodbye, threw away her tissues, and took the two flights of stairs to the lobby. She pushed open the heavy glass door and took a deep breath. And when the door closed behind her, and the cold air hit her face, the certainty vanished, and Caroline was left, just as she had been when she walked in that door an hour earlier, with no idea what to do.

31

It was the Saturday before Christmas, and Ruth had a long list of errands. She'd woken early and taken a quick shower, hoping to sneak out the door before the kids were awake. But when she went downstairs, Abe and Siddha were sitting at the kitchen counter, eating cereal.

"Oh, hey there," she said. "You two are up early."

"Abie woke me up. He couldn't find the milk." Siddha made a dramatic glaring face at Abe.

"Abie, you could have asked me," Ruth said. She was fumbling with her earring, a large gold hoop. "Can you help me?" she asked, leaning in toward Siddha. "I can never close this right."

Siddha put down her spoon. "Hold back your hair," she said. "It's in the way."

Ruth scooped her hair back into a handheld ponytail and leaned closer to Siddha. She could smell Siddha's milky breath, the sweetness of her skin. The most familiar smell in the world, although it seemed like it had been months since Ruth had been this close to her.

"Got it," Siddha said.

Ruth gave the earring a tug and smiled at Siddha. "Thanks, doll."

She took a swig of cold coffee from a mug on the counter. "Okay, I'm out of here."

"Can we come?" Abe asked.

"Oh, it's going to be boring, hon. I'm just delivering toffee and mailing some packages."

"I like toffee delivery," Abe said.

"I think what you really like is sitting in the car and eating all the broken pieces," Ruth said. "Which you can just do at home."

The real reason Ruth didn't want Abe to come was that she was planning to stop by Florence's house. But then she had an idea. "How about if you both come, and after we deliver the toffee we can split up, and you two can do your shopping?"

"No thanks," Siddha said.

"Oh, please, please?" Abe said. "Please, please, please?" Abe came up close to Siddha and pressed his palms together under his chin like a choir boy, his eyes closed in fervent pleading. Siddha grabbed his hands and brought them to his cheeks. He opened his eyes and mouth wide, imitating Macaulay Culkin in *Home Alone*, Siddha and Abe's favorite movie. Abe loved to say he was just like that kid, despite never having been left anywhere at all, barely even left alone for a moment of his short life. No one forgot Abe, especially not Siddha, who loved him madly.

"Okay, Abie, twist my arm," Siddha said, and she held out her arm. He started twisting it, and then she jumped up out of her chair, grabbed his arms, tickled him, tried—and failed—to turn him upside down, instead knocking over the cereal box onto the floor, which brought the dogs running.

"*Okay!*" Ruth said loudly. "Let's go."

Abe wanted to take Siddha's car, and despite all the drama about the tattoo, Ruth had left the car situation alone, so when Siddha said, Sure, what the hell, I'll drive, Ruth just loaded the boxes of toffee into the back of the car and got in on the passenger side, all without a word.

Siddha let Abe play DJ, which meant the soundtrack of their ride to town was an eclectic mix of Stephen Sondheim, Taylor Swift, and Imagine Dragons.

"Maybe some Christmas songs, Abe?" Ruth suggested.

Justin Bieber's "Mistletoe" came blasting out of the stereo.

"Jesus, Abie," Siddha yelled, turning down the volume. "That's not even funny. Put on the oldies, the ones we like."

"Pull over there," Ruth said, motioning to an open parking space in front of the post office. She was opening the door before Siddha had even stopped the car. "Slow down!" Siddha said. "What is with you?"

"It's just a crazy day. Christmas is in a few days, and I've got a million things to do. I'm just kind of on overdrive."

"I can see that," Siddha said, putting the car into park.

AFTER THEY'D DELIVERED most of the toffee, Ruth said she needed to do one last thing. "I have to stop by a little party, just to say hello."

"Whose party?" Abe asked.

"That old friend who's helping me get Olive Street ready to sell." When Ruth had first reconnected with Florence, she'd imagined—in the spirit of a new transparency—that Florence and Siddha could meet, and that Siddha could talk with Florence about Elliot, about the person he'd been. But then Ruth had kissed Florence, and now transparency didn't seem like such a great idea. Going to Florence's house—having Siddha drive her there—felt risky, and secretive in the worst way, a shameful continuation of all the secrecy around Elliot. But Ruth couldn't help herself. Her desire was too powerful. "You two could go get a box of donuts to bring home, and Sid, you could help Abe pick out his presents for me and Mom," she suggested.

"Yeah sure, whatever," Siddha said. "Where's her house?"

Ruth gave Siddha Florence's address, and Abe turned up the music. When they arrived at Florence's, Ruth gave Siddha her credit card for Abe's gifts, pulled on her coat, and went up the driveway. She went into Florence's through the mudroom, calling out "Hello!" as she unzipped her coat and kicked off her boots. "It's freezing out there!"

Florence came in from the dining room. She was dressed in a red jumpsuit and chunky motorcycle boots.

"Wow," Ruth said. "You look . . ."

"Festive?"

"I was going to say 'hot,' but yes, very festive. I brought you toffee. Secret Huntley family recipe. Although for a price I can tell you what the secret is."

"Bourbon?" Florence asked.

"How did you know?"

"Wild guess. What was your price going to be?" Florence asked.

Ruth leaned in and kissed her.

"Was that a price or a reward?"

"Only you can decide that."

Florence raised her eyebrows and kissed Ruth again. My god, Ruth thought. Kissing. When had it ever been so extraordinary? It was as far as their physical relationship had gone, but its pleasures seemed endless, the thrill of the first kiss renewing itself every time their lips touched.

Florence pulled back after a few minutes, or seconds, who knew? "Enough of that," she said. She patted Ruth on the cheek. "I need to pull it together for my guests." She opened the toffee tin and took out a piece, popped it into her mouth, then poured the rest into a silver bowl and handed it to Ruth. "Will you put it on the table?"

Ruth looked at the engraving on the bowl. *Palm Springs Mixed Doubles, 1956.* "Was this your mother's?"

Florence laughed. "My mother's idea of mixed doubles was two Jack and Cokes. It's from an estate sale, like pretty much everything else I have of any value."

"Like that?" Ruth was gesturing to a footed cut-crystal punch bowl.

"Actually, that one's the real deal. The Howe family eggnog bowl. My grandmother saved her S&H stamps for ten years to get it. The Howe women are nothing if not patient."

Ruth smiled. "I appreciate that patience." When she felt the heat rising in her face, she waved her hand across the table laden with Bundt cakes and smoked fish and said, "So then, tell me, a poor wandering Jew, what is this all, exactly?"

"Isn't that a plant? Also, you're not poor or wandering."

Ruth shrugged. "I still don't know what's going on here."

"It's Eggnog Open House," Florence said. "Every Christmas Eve morning, my mother and her mother before her would cover the dining room table with a lace tablecloth, put out the punch bowl of eggnog, and slice up a coffee cake. Then at ten, all the women in the neighborhood would come over and drink a cup of nog, eat a piece of cake, and head back home, fortified for the days ahead. They came in wearing their aprons under their coats, right from their kitchens. No children, no husbands. The whole thing was over by eleven. The first time I was allowed to attend, I was eighteen years old."

"How did I not know this?" Ruth exclaimed, delighted by the idea of such an odd, WASPy tradition that the Huntleys didn't observe.

"I might have been in eggnog exile when we met," Florence said. "But then my mom and I reconciled. Maybe ten years ago? Just before she died. And she gave me the bowl. Of course, I've updated. My Eggnog Open House knows no gender. And I always plan it for the Saturday before Christmas. People are too busy on Christmas Eve."

"Oh, speaking of busy," Ruth said, "those floor guys can't come until the week of New Year's now, but I said fine. Right? That's fine?"

"I think so," Florence said. "I'm not in any rush." She smiled. "I'm glad you're here."

"I'm sorry I got the timing wrong," Ruth said, suddenly feeling flustered, that she'd made an error. She'd thought coming early was the right thing, was what Florence wanted. But maybe what Florence had wanted was just for her to come and drink some eggnog and make conversation with her neighbors. "The kids went to get donuts," Ruth said, aware that this was a strange non sequitur.

"With Wyn?" Florence asked.

Ruth was aware of how close Florence was. She shook her head. "No," she said, and felt the word catch in her throat. She coughed a little and said it again. "No."

Florence nodded. She tucked Ruth's hair behind her ear. "Your earring is falling out," she said, reaching in to fix it.

"Oh, it's always falling out," Ruth said, putting her hand to her ear, and meeting Florence's there. She took it, and for a moment held it, and then brought it to her lips. Florence pulled her hand away and kissed Ruth, a long deep kiss that Ruth felt all through her body.

Florence pulled away. She pressed her forehead against Ruth's. "Merry Christmas, Ruthie," she said.

"Merry Christmas, Florence," Ruth said. And then, quietly, "What are we doing?"

"I'm not sure." Florence leaned in, kissed her again, this time longer, slower.

Ruth opened the top button on Florence's jumpsuit. Florence didn't stop her, so she unbuttoned the next. Then Florence put her hand over Ruth's. "We don't have time," she whispered. "Not now." Florence touched Ruth's lips as though to quiet her, although Ruth hadn't said a word.

"Come in the kitchen," Florence said. She smoothed her own hair, but left the buttons of her jumpsuit undone. Ruth could see the lace of her bra, the pale skin of her breast. "Come talk to me while I finish."

Ruth leaned on the counter, facing Florence while she chopped. They chatted about this and that, nothing really, and every few minutes, Florence would put down the knife, and they would kiss. Just as Florence was scraping the last of the strawberries into the fruit salad, there was a knock on the back door. Siddha was looking into the kitchen.

Ruth felt her heart drop into her stomach. "Sid!" she said. She went to open the door. "Hi, hon." She hoped her voice didn't sound as strange to Siddha as it sounded in her own head.

"We need to go," Siddha said in a cold voice.

"You must be Siddha," Florence said. She was still standing at the counter, the buttons of her jumpsuit fastened again. Her eyes were shining, and Ruth knew she was trying not to cry.

"This is Florence," Ruth said.

Siddha gave Florence a half smile, then looked at Ruth. "I need to go. Now."

"Okay, okay," Ruth said brightly, slipping into her boots. She turned to Florence. "Flo, we have to run! Have a wonderful party!"

SIDDHA WALKED DOWN the driveway ahead of Ruth. "I texted you like twenty times," she said.

"I wasn't looking at my phone," Ruth said. She was still putting on her coat when they got to the car. "What's up? Where do you need to be?"

"Somewhere," Siddha said.

Ruth didn't push. She just got in the car. She turned to say hi to Abe, who was in the backseat with a box of donuts. She felt Siddha's eyes on her. "What is it, hon?"

Siddha looked away. She put the car in reverse and started backing down the driveway. "You lost your earring."

32

"Well," Caroline said, gathering pieces of ripped wrapping paper and stuffing them into a garbage bag, "Merry Christmas, one and all."

Luca was stretched out on the floor, studying the instructions to his Lego set. "Yep," he said, happy and distracted. "Merry Christmas, all and all."

"There's one more present," Mike said.

Luca popped up.

"For Mom," Mike said.

Luca flopped back down.

"But buddy, you're not gonna want to miss this," Mike said. "Both of you, come outside."

"I'm not dressed," Caroline said. She was still in her bathrobe.

"Just come out," Mike said. "It will only take a second."

So then out they went, the three of them, into the damp December cold. And there, in the driveway, was a red Vespa.

Luca shrieked. "You got Mom a motorbike!"

"It's a Vespa," Mike said. "But yeah, I did."

Caroline couldn't believe it. A Vespa? What in the world did Mike think she was going to do with a Vespa? "Oh wow." That was all she could say. "For me? Wow."

"When you didn't get the grant, well, I thought—well, that you could have a little bit of Rome right here. I've been working on it over at Tobi's, getting it running. It's a dream, Cece. You're going to love it." And then, in a bad Italian accent: "A motorino for my bella."

"Wow, Dad," Luca said, "you're really good at keeping secrets. There's no way I would have been able to keep this secret."

Mike avoided Caroline's eyes. Secrets were a bit of a sensitive topic. They'd had an argument that night after the concert when Caroline had gone out with Evie. Well, the argument had actually been the next morning, when, after driving Luca to school, Caroline drove back home to confront Mike. When she'd walked in the back door, Mike, who was sitting at the kitchen table drinking coffee, was startled.

"Shit," he said. "You scared me. What's wrong?"

Caroline then proceeded to tell Mike what was wrong, which was that she didn't know what kind of marriage they had if he was going to keep secrets from her, and that, honestly, she felt like a real fool, considering.

Mike looked confused. "Whoa," he said. "Back up. What secret did I keep from you?"

Caroline tightened her arms across her chest. "Tobi? Having an affair? And after everything I told you about Ruth, that you would just sit there, pretending you weren't dealing with exactly the same thing, up on your righteous high horse—"

"Caroline," Mike interrupted, holding up his hands. "Tobi isn't having an affair!" He looked at her then, confused still, but his face had the expression of someone who was figuring something out. "Did you talk to Evie?"

"Yes, I talked to Evie. A very upset Evie, who was waiting by my car after the concert."

"And she told you Tobi was having an affair?"

"Basically."

Mike rubbed his hands over his face. "Tobi is having top surgery," he said. "Or at least she's thinking about it. She's not having an affair."

Now it was Caroline's turn to be confused. "Top surgery?"

"Like a mastectomy," Mike said.

"Yeah, I know what top surgery is," Caroline said, annoyed.

"And she was keeping it a secret, until I fucked up last night and sort of told Lynne."

"So you knew and Evie didn't?"

"Yeah, I guess."

"She talked about top surgery with you and not Evie?" Caroline felt torn between satisfaction that Tobi and Evie were not as united as she might have thought and anger that Tobi had told Mike, who hadn't told her. In the end, the anger won out.

"Why didn't you tell me?" she demanded.

"Tobi asked me not to tell anyone."

"I'm your wife!"

"I still wasn't supposed to tell anyone!"

"That stipulation doesn't hold to spouses," Caroline said.

"Says who?" Mike said.

"Says me!" And Caroline turned then, and went out the back door. They hadn't spoken about it since.

WHICH WAS WHY, when Luca called the Vespa a secret, Mike firmly said, "No, no—it was a surprise, not a secret." He looked at Caroline then, apology in his eyes. Then he turned to Luca. "That's why I didn't tell you. I knew you'd spill the beans."

Before Luca could ask, Caroline said, "It means tell the secret." She looked at Mike and, melting a little, clarified: "Tell the surprise. Like the beans are the surprise, spilling out of—" Out of what? She'd never thought of that.

"Out of a beanbag!" Luca said. "But did you know it's not beans in a beanbag? It's little round plastic thingies. I cut one open once to see."

"Further proof that you could not have kept the surprise!" Mike said. "Dude, you have literally spilled the beans."

Caroline started to say Takes after me, but stopped herself.

"Mom!" Luca said. "Get on it! Ride it!"

"I'm in my bathrobe," Caroline said, as though that were the only reason she wasn't hopping onto this contraption in her driveway.

Mike put his arm around her. "Look, I know it's not the same as going to Rome, but I thought it might be fun. I thought you needed a little fun."

Seriously? Caroline thought. He couldn't be serious. He couldn't have possibly thought that a Vespa had anything at all to do with her trip to Rome, her disappointment, her loss, which still felt too big to talk about. Riding this thing was not her idea of fun. And anyway, she didn't need fun. She needed that damn Tate Fund grant. She needed to go to Rome! She needed Ruth back. She needed Luca to be okay. God, what else? Someone to deal with the roofers, a chest freezer for the basement, a new sink in the upstairs bathroom. A rug for her office. A dry cleaner who could get the stains out of her silk blouses. The list went on and on, getting longer and longer the more she thought about it. A Vespa was nowhere on the list. She did not, in any way, need a Vespa.

Mike went into the garage and came out with a helmet and goggles. "Want to try it out?" he asked. "It drives like a dream."

Yeah, like your dream, Caroline thought.

"Look, Cece, I know what you're thinking." Mike held the helmet against his chest. "You're thinking I got this for me, and not you. But I swear, I really think you'll love it. Just try it. Just take it for a little spin. I even got you a snowmobiling suit and special gloves, in case you want to ride it in the winter. I mean," he clarified, "when the roads are dry." He smiled. "Safety first."

Oh, Mike. Caroline leaned in and gave him a kiss. "Thank you," she said. "Truly. This is such a . . ."

"Strange present?" Luca suggested.

33

It was New Year's Eve, time for the annual Huntley New Year's bonfire, and the troops were tired. Ruth had wondered if they should skip it this year, but the look on Wyn's face—and all four children's—when she'd suggested it made her think otherwise. Ruth didn't really want to skip it either. It was a sweet tradition: everyone wrote their hopes for the new year on a piece of birch bark, and then threw the bark into the fire to send the wishes out into the universe. Or, as Wyn's ultra-religious brother's kids always said, "right up to Jesus."

It had been a long week, the first Christmas holiday they'd spent at home. When Wyn had floated the idea of staying at Sugar Hill for Christmas this year, Ruth couldn't believe what she was saying. For as many years as they'd been together, they had traveled to Nashville to spend the week with Wyn's family. Over the years Ruth had found the whole thing alternately charming and annoying, and she always found it over-the-top.

But her kids loved every minute of it: Grandma Rosalynn's twenty-foot eastern white pine in the center hall, the crystal candy jars filled with toffee and pralines, giant needlepoint stockings with each of their names sewn across the top in gold thread. There were rousing carol sings in the living room and cutthroat football games in the yard, late afternoon walks in the park down the road, long dinners and even longer games of Monopoly, charades, canasta. There were dogs, babies, kids, and in-laws of all ages everywhere. And everyone was always the tiniest bit drunk.

"Really?" Ruth had asked. "You want to skip Christmas?"

"Not skip it," Wyn said. "Just do it here, with the six of us. I thought I'd just leave everything to Bex, but then they got that gig, and I don't have anyone else to cover for me. Maybe by next year I can find someone, but—"

"So we can't leave?" Ruth interrupted. "Like, ever?"

"No, no," Wyn said. "We can leave. Bex will be back in February. We can leave. Just not this Christmas."

Ruth sighed. "Okay, well, sure." The thought of not traveling sounded very nice, she had to admit. "But I can't make Christmas happen," she said. "I've got Hanukkah to think about, and it's—"

"Eight nights of presents and food," Wyn finished. "I know, I know."

"We don't even have any of the stuff, no ornaments, no stockings. And what is your mom going to say? And don't you think the kids will be bummed?"

Wyn had kissed Ruth on the top of her head. "I've got it, babe, I've got it all."

AND IT WAS true, Wyn did have it all. Somehow she'd made Christmas happen, and it was, Ruth had to admit, really lovely. And other than the usual squabbles, the kids seemed to have a great time. Until today. Everyone was tired and hungry (but never at the same time) and the house was a mess. By early afternoon she'd had more than enough, and she sent everyone outside to get the fire going and collect the necessary pieces of bark. When she made her way out to the fire pit half an hour later, she could see that neither task was really in motion. Roz was sitting next to a sad little fire, staring into space.

"Roz, did you get enough bark for everyone?" Ruth asked. When Roz didn't answer, Ruth said, louder this time, "Roz! Get some bark!"

"Siddha went to get it," Roz said. "She's over by the creek. With Abe."

Wyn came across the lawn with a bottle of beer. Abe and Siddha came back from the woods, both their arms filled with curls of bark.

"Where's Gilly?" Ruth asked Wyn.

"I thought she was out here."

Ruth groaned. She got up, headed inside to find Gilly. "Does anyone want a blanket?" she asked, turned around again.

"Me!"

"Me!"

"Me!"

Ruth looked at them all, exasperated. "Then why didn't you get them before you came out?"

Wyn said, "Hey, Ru, will you also grab those pistachios on the counter? And that cheese?"

"Can you get my hat?" Roz asked.

"Anything else?" Ruth asked, sarcastically.

"We're good!" Abe said.

"No thank you!" Ruth and Wyn corrected in unison.

Ruth went into the kitchen, calling for Gilly, who didn't answer. She heard her phone ding with a text alert. She picked it up. It was from Florence. *happiest new year, my Ruthie. xx* Ruth held the phone against her chest for a moment, as though it were a letter and she a wartime bride. *You too, my love.* she wrote back. Then she deleted *my love* and replaced it with a heart emoji. Before she could change it again, she hit send.

"Gilda Grace Schwartz-Huntley!" Ruth yelled up the stairs.

"Coming!" Gilly yelled back.

When Ruth finally came back outside with the pistachios and cheese, Gilly behind her with a pile of blankets, everyone was sitting quietly with a piece of birch bark on their lap. Siddha gave Ruth a Sharpie and a piece of bark. "Thanks, sweets," Ruth said.

Once they had all written something, the time came to share. They began, as they always did, in reverse age order. "Abe?"

Abe cleared his throat. "In the new year, I hope to ride on a unicorn."

Everyone nodded solemnly, even Roz, which really said something about her commitment to the ritual's foundational commandment of "No commentary or judgment."

And they went on this way, around the circle. Roz hoped to be made captain of Scrabble Club, Gilly hoped to meet Taylor Swift. Siddha hoped to drive to South Carolina with Eliza for spring break. Ruth didn't say anything to that, just gave Siddha an artificial smile. Siddha gave one right back to her.

"Ruth?" Wyn said.

"This was a tough one," Ruth said with a sigh. "I have all the things I want."

"You always say that!" Abe said, smacking his forehead with his hand and theatrically tipping back on his log, both gestures he'd picked up from Alex P. Keaton, his new hero. Wyn had introduced Abe to *Family Ties* over the holiday, thinking the show might give Abe some pointers on how to survive in a houseful of sisters. Mostly what it had given him were a few darling new mannerisms and a lot of questions about Reaganomics.

"And it's always true," Ruth said. "Although I will say I wish for a trip to the beach. We haven't been to the beach in ages. Wyn?"

"Well, my wish is really more of an announcement," Wyn said. "I wrote that I hope to get a few dairy cows this year, and I just got an email that the two heifers I've had my eye on are pregnant. Looks like we're going to have a lot of cows around here this spring."

"So what are you wishing for, then?" Roz said. "This is wishes, not things that are already going to happen."

Oh Roz, Ruth wanted to say. It's time you learned something about your mom. She doesn't wish. She just does.

"Well, I guess what I'm wishing for is healthy calves and happy cows," Wyn said. "Yeah, I wish for happy cows!"

"Happy cows!" they all yelled, and everyone cheered, and then, on the count of three, they threw their bark into the fire. And then the kids wanted marshmallows, and Wyn said they'd have to find them, and Abe started whining because he was hungry and it turned out no one had given him lunch, so Ruth sent Gilly into the house for hot dogs they could roast over the fire, and for a moment she was so happy and wanted nothing, and in the next moment, quick as her next breath, there was not enough birch bark in all of Ulster County for what she wanted.

34

On New Year's Day, Mike asked Caroline about the scooter. "There's a shiny red Vespa in the garage waiting for a certain someone. Maybe today's the day?"

Caroline was still in her pajamas, sitting at the dining room table addressing envelopes for their New Year's cards (which always went out late) and eating stale panettone dipped in coffee. She'd just gotten a text from Ruth, asking if they'd all like to come over later for a little happy hour. Caroline was trying to think up a legitimate reason why they couldn't come, and had just settled on the lie that they'd love to, but were in the city. It was a small lie; they'd planned to still be in the city today—they always spent the holiday week in New York visiting Caroline's family—but at the last minute they'd decided to leave late last night, after her father's New Year's Eve party.

"Maybe," Caroline said, distractedly typing her text.

Mike shook his head. "God, I was so stupid! Tobi said you'd never want to ride it. I should have listened to her."

Caroline snapped to attention. She put down her phone, looked at Mike. "What do you mean, 'Tobi said'?"

"She was helping me, you know, fix it up, and she was right, I was just doing it for myself."

"She wasn't right," Caroline said. She stood up. "You know what? I'm totally ready. I'm ready to ride it."

Mike jumped up, clapping his hands together. "Awesome!" he said. "I'll go get her ready for you."

"It," Caroline corrected. "A Vespa is not a woman."

"Grab that snowsuit," Mike called, already out the back door. "I hung it in the closet!"

AND SO IT was that twenty minutes later a goggled, helmeted, and snowsuited Caroline was driving a Vespa through the quiet streets of Radclyffe. Everything around her looked so different at this speed, faster than a bicycle, slower than a car. The air on her cheeks was freezing but the rest of her was surprisingly warm, and after a while, her cheeks just went numb. She turned down one quiet street and then another, getting accustomed to the accelerator and the brake. It wasn't hard to drive, at all. In fact, it was pretty fun.

She headed for the center of Radclyffe, and at a stop sign, she turned and caught a glimpse of herself in a store window. She laughed out loud. Was that really her? Her head looked enormous. She kept driving, out past the playhouse, past the Hannaford. She made a right turn, climbing up the hill to the reservoir. Away, away from Mike and Luca. Is this what Mike knew? That happiness meant riding off in the opposite direction from the people who depended on you? She reached the reservoir, her gloved hands tired from gripping the handlebars, her stomach growling with hunger. But she still didn't turn back.

As she rode on, she thought not of Tobi and Mike, but of Marcia, and how much she loved her, even though she knew she wasn't supposed to, even though she knew it was just run-of-the-mill everyday transference. She didn't care because it was *her* transference. That was why she loved Marcia, because Marcia transformed all of Caroline's ordinariness into particularities. To Marcia, there was nothing predictable or monolithic about Caroline.

Where should I go now? she asked Marcia silently, this Marcia who had taken up residence in Caroline's mind. Anywhere! she heard Marcia say. Anywhere you want. She imagined Marcia seeing her on the scooter, and thought of how she'd tell her, next week, all about it, how it felt to ride. It would be lovely, telling her, it would be a joyful story, this story of her surprise, her bravery. And then, as though in service to the story, in the hopes of making it even better, even more fun to tell, Caroline pulled harder on the accelerator, feeling the scooter shift into its maximum speed, and she was flying, flying. At the turn to go back to town, Caroline headed left, up and away again, and thought, I will ride this thing forever.

But as it turned out, Caroline would not ride the Vespa forever. She'd forgotten that scooters, like cars, needed gas; she'd forgotten that Mike had told her the tank wasn't full, and that she'd told him no problem, she'd just take it out for a few minutes. And so, when the bike stopped being as responsive to her pulling back on the accelerator, and then started to whinny and whine and then stopped altogether, she was confused. But then she looked at the control panel and saw a gas gauge, the needle tipped all the way to empty. "Shit." And then, louder: "Fucking shit!"

Caroline could curse as loudly as she wanted. No one was going to hear. She was up at the reservoir, and no one was around. She quickly checked her phone and felt a flush of relief at the stairstep of bars. She also saw that she had a bunch of texts from Mike, checking to see if she was okay, and a missed call. He was worried about her. "All good!" she texted back, and then sent a selfie, thumbs up, her helmet on, smiling. "Home soon!"

Who, then, was she going to call?

EVIE GOT OUT of the car and went around to her trunk, pulled out a gas can.

"Hey," Caroline said. "Thank you so much for coming."

"Of course," Evie said. "Although my helpfulness ends here. I didn't even know how to fill this. I had to get the guy at the gas station to do it for me."

Caroline laughed. "I'm sure I can figure it out," she said. "I'm just grateful that you came. And didn't tell Tobi."

"Solidarity," Evie said.

Caroline was touched. She'd wondered if the night they'd spent at Sully's after the Christmas concert—when Evie had been worried about an affair and Caroline had reassured her of Tobi's love and loyalty—would change anything between them, and it seemed that it had. The thought gave her a burst of satisfaction.

Caroline found what she thought was the gas tank. She took off the gas cap and tilted the can into the opening. The gas can was heavy, and the angle was awkward.

"And besides," Evie said, reaching in to help steady the can, "I owe you. For the other night. I'm sorry for how I ambushed you."

"Hardly," Caroline said.

"You talked me off the ledge," Evie said. "Which was what I needed. And I guess you know that Tobi's not having an affair."

"I do," Caroline said. "I mean, Mike told me, but not until after that night of the concert. I didn't know anything before then."

"Oh, I know," Evie said. "I didn't think you were keeping anything from me. Honestly, I didn't think you knew, even when I came looking for you."

Caroline felt a little stung by this. "Because you knew Mike wouldn't tell me."

"I think so," Evie said. "I mean, that's what my rational brain was thinking, although I didn't have much access to it that night. I think maybe I just wanted to see you because you'd get it."

Caroline nodded, although she wasn't sure what Evie meant. She'd get what it meant that Tobi was having top surgery?

Evie went on, "There was something about walking into the kitchen, you know? With the two of them in there, and then how clear it was that there was something Tobi didn't want to tell me, and Mike knew, and I was just—I was just so fucking angry. And I wasn't just angry with Tobi. I was angry with Mike. I was jealous."

Oh, Evie meant that Caroline would understand the jealousy. Being on the outside. It was funny, she'd hardly considered this. Somehow it had seemed to her that it was different for Evie, but she saw now that it wasn't.

"I mean, ninety percent of the time, I'm glad she has him," Evie said.

"Totally," Caroline said, although ninety percent seemed a little high. Fifty, maybe?

"But that other ten percent, god it eats me. I mean, I have three sisters and I love them, but it's nothing like Tobi and Mike."

Caroline nodded.

Evie went on, "In the beginning I used to think it was their trauma bond, you know? But now—now I'm like, it's not that. It's something else. I mean, I think trauma can only get you so far. Although what do I know, I've had very little of it, as Tobi likes to remind me."

Caroline laughed. "Sometimes I feel like the hard part is deciding who I'm jealous of. Like, am I jealous of Tobi because of Mike's fierce love for her, or am I jealous of Mike, because he has Tobi? I don't really know. I mean, I'm an only child, and I'd thought Mike was an only child too, but he's not, not really. Early on when he'd tell me about his cousin Tobi, I thought it was so sweet that he had a cousin he loved. It took me a while to figure out exactly who Tobi was. I'd thought it was just him and me against the world."

Evie smiled. "I know that feeling."

"You know," Caroline went on, emboldened by Evie's candor, "I had this aunt who had these terrible in-laws, just awful people, and she was always over at our apartment, in the kitchen with my mom, talking about them. And one day she pulled me onto her lap, and she said, 'I have one piece of advice for you, Carolina mia'"—she spoke in an exaggerated Italian accent—"'marry an orphan.' And I remember my mother laughing and shushing my aunt, telling her not to poison me with her drama. But I also think I really held on to that advice. It came back to me when I married Mike. I thought, Aunt Maria would be so proud. I'm marrying an orphan. But my god, I was so wrong! Mike is so not an orphan."

"Yeah," Evie said. "You were really wrong."

Caroline sighed. She zipped the snowsuit up around her neck. She was cold. She couldn't believe she had to ride this thing back to town.

"And I was wrong about our kids," Caroline said. "They're not just cousins, either."

"No," Evie said. "They're not. Although that's a conversation for another day. You look very cold. You should get home."

Caroline reached into the snowsuit and pulled up her scarf. "Yes, I should. I'm freezing!"

Evie took the gas can and started walking toward her car. She stopped and turned. "Hey, do you want me to ride it? You could drive—I mean, we could meet up in the Hannaford parking lot and switch back. No one would ever have to know. You could turn on the heated seats."

Caroline was going to say No, no, that's okay, but at the sound of the words "heated seats," she caved. "Do you want to wear this snowmobiling suit?"

Evie laughed. "Kinda?"

"I could take a picture of you in it, for your GoldFynch Instagram."

Evie groaned. "Can I tell you how tired I am of all that? God, what did I get myself into? All that ridiculous image grooming, all those photo shoots."

"But you can't stop?" Caroline asked, zipping herself out of the snowsuit.

Evie shook her head. "It drives sales, like, crazily. Honestly what I really want is just to outsource it, hire someone to take over the accounts, but that seems impossible."

Caroline opened the back trunk of Evie's car and sat down to take off the suit. She handed it to Evie. "I might know someone," she said.

Evie didn't seem to hear her. She zipped up the suit, put on the helmet, and handed Caroline the car keys. "See you at the Hanna," she said.

"See you at the Hanna," Caroline said. "And thank you."

35

New Year's Day brought with it a terrible mood among Ruth's children. They were grouchy from too much sugar and too little sleep, and from the harsh withdrawal from presents and fulfilled wishes. Now it was just winter, and would be, for a long time. This was their first winter in the new house, which Ruth suspected the previous owners had wanted to sell because it was utterly, inhumanely freezing. She kept imagining them smugly snug in their New York City apartment, the radiators clanking and steaming and making them so warm they had to open the windows, laughing with each other about the fools who'd bought their upstate house.

The little kids had been wearing footed pajamas since Halloween, and for the last month they'd made a ritual of coming to the kitchen before bed, each of them clutching their own hot water bottle that Ruth filled from the kettle, then scurrying off like children in a Dickens novel.

Next year would be better, Wyn assured everyone. They would blow in insulation! They would install radiant floors and mini-splits! But none of that could happen until spring. For now, they would be cold.

Ruth had taken to wearing a wool blanket wrapped around her waist like a skirt. She wore a wool beanie to bed. She'd become as country as they came.

To fight off the day's grouchiness, and to get the kids some exercise, Wyn suggested they all go skating. "Do Caroline and Mike want to come?" Wyn asked.

"Oh, they don't skate," Ruth said.

"Really?" Wyn said. "I feel like I've seen Mike playing hockey there a bunch of times."

Ruth shrugged. "Maybe," she said. "But Caroline and Luca for sure don't." Ruth didn't really know if this was true, but Caroline's curt response to the olive branch text she'd sent earlier—the one inviting them all over for a New Year's happy hour—was confirmation of what she'd already suspected: they were not speaking. Or at least Caroline wasn't speaking to her. Ruth hadn't seen or even talked to her since their argument, although for a while she'd just been able to chalk that up to the craziness of the holidays.

The truth was, there had been plenty of time to reach out, and Ruth just hadn't. She didn't want to acknowledge their argument, and she didn't want to admit that she was still seeing Florence. But this morning, when Ruth had woken with a panic in her chest, a sudden fear that she was doing a terrible thing that she did not want to stop doing, it was Caroline she wanted to see. Not because Ruth wanted to talk things through with her, but because her presence was calming, a reliably warm distraction from worry.

Wyn was putting hot dogs in a thermos of boiling water. It was an old trick of her mother's, from hunting trips. The Huntleys thought it was genius. Ruth thought it was gross. But she didn't say anything. Her kids loved it now too. God, she wished she'd known how much of family life was your kids loving all the things you disliked about your in-laws.

Ruth finished packing up the food, the hot dog buns and ketchup, potato chips, pretzels, granola bars, dried mango, cashews, juice boxes, the thermoses of cocoa, of coffee. The kids came through the kitchen, swishing three pairs of snow pants, and then out to the mudroom, everyone (including Ruth) yelling about mittens and helmets and boots and water bottles and peeing one last time and where are Abe's skates, and just wear an extra pair of socks then, and don't swing your skates you'll cut someone and did anyone put the milk crates in the car, and does anyone know where the milk crates are? And then a protracted discussion of should they or shouldn't they take two cars in case anyone got cold. Wyn said No, we have to stop doing that, we have to stop taking two cars everywhere, and Ruth said, I think we should and besides, then I can get groceries on the way home. And then there was an argument about who was going in which car, and then Wyn promised to play the soundtrack from *Matilda*, which Ruth hated and Abe found frightening, so it was just Ruth and Abe in Ruth's car.

Finally, they were off. Soon the sun would set, but oh well. At least they were getting out. At least Ruth could blast the car's heater and finally get warm.

THE POND WASN'T as crowded as Ruth had expected. Pulling into the mostly empty parking lot it was clear that everyone else had had the good sense to stay home today, holiday or not. It was the sort of New Year's Day that Ruth disliked: gray and foggy and damp. She liked to begin the new year in the bright January sun, the sort of bracing, dry cold that invigorated even as it chilled.

It had been a cold December—much colder than usual—and there had been very little snow, which meant it was a good year for ice. From the shore Ruth could see its clear smoothness, etched only by skate blades. Someone had set up a hockey net and left a rain barrel of old hockey sticks on the ice.

"Can we skate across?" Roz asked.

"Yeah, I wanna skate across," Gilly said.

They were all sitting at the picnic tables by the shore, putting on their skates. Ruth was kneeling in front of Abe, tightening his laces. She looked up at Wyn. Abe wasn't a strong enough skater to make it to the other shore, and neither was Wyn. Ice skating was the one physical activity that Ruth was better at than Wyn, which meant that it was the one physical activity for which Ruth was assigned the role of what Wyn liked to call "varsity parent." (Not surprisingly, Ruth didn't share Wyn's affection for this term, but she went along with it so long as Wyn promised to never, ever refer to Ruth as "JV" when she was the one bringing up the rear with the less capable child.)

"Wanna play some hockey, Abie?" Wyn asked. Abe nodded and took Wyn's arm, and the two of them wobbled across the last edge of the snowy shore and onto the ice.

Ruth quickly laced her skates, zipped up her coat, and took off after the girls, who'd let go of the dogs' leashes and were skating together in a rare moment of holding hands. Ruth quickly caught up and then overtook them, which made them both shriek and skate faster. Then Gilly took a spill, and the dogs tackled her, and Roz, in true Roz form, kept skating on alone.

"*Roz!*" Ruth yelled, stopping to help Gilly and untangle the dog leashes. "*Wait for us!*"

Roz turned toward Ruth. She was yelling something Ruth couldn't make out. Ruth skated toward her, fast, so she could hear. "Someone's in trouble! Way over there, by the other beach."

And then Roz turned around again and took off at top speed.

"*Roz!*" Ruth yelled. "*Stop!* Come back!"

But Roz wasn't coming back.

She wanted to yell to Gilly not to follow, but she also didn't want Gilly skating alone. "Come on, Gil," she called, deciding that it was better for them to stick together. Ruth had great reverence for ice—she'd been skating on frozen lakes since she was three years old—and she knew that this ice was thick enough, this ice would hold them all and more, but she also felt every cell in her body tuned to what she was doing, skating across a frozen pond with her children.

"*Roz!*" Ruth yelled again. "*Stop!*" But of course, Roz wasn't going to stop.

Ruth felt her heart pound. She unclipped the dogs' leashes and told them, "Go, go to Rozzie," and she was reminded of a proverb her mother often quoted: "In skating over thin ice, our safety is our speed." It's not thin! she insisted to herself. Still, she skated faster.

"It's Siddha," Roz screamed, turning around to Ruth.

"Oh my god," Ruth said. She could see now that it was, indeed, Siddha, and she was running toward them across the ice.

"George and Teddy fell in!" Siddha yelled.

"What?" Ruth cried, panicked, looking around. She didn't see anyone. "Who are George and Teddy?" Were they kids Siddha was babysitting? No, she hadn't said she was babysitting. She'd said she was going to Eliza's. "Where's Eliza?"

Siddha just shook her head and said, "It's okay, it's okay, they're out! I got them out! They're on the shore, we were just screwing around over there, where it's marshy. We didn't have skates, so we were just staying close to shore, to be safe."

"It's not safe if it's marshy," Roz said, parroting what Ruth had told her and the other kids a million times. "You need a clear shoreline so the ice—"

"You're babysitting these kids?" Ruth broke in, still confused. "And you brought them here?"

"I'm not babysitting anyone!" Siddha cried. "I'm just hanging out with them. It's George and Teddy. Elliot's kids." She looked straight at Ruth. "My brothers."

Ruth felt numb.

Siddha went on, "They're both wet, and I think George cut himself. His head is really bleeding. And I think I left my phone in the car." She was frantically rummaging in her fanny pack, as though the more she rummaged, the more likely her phone was to appear.

Gilly caught up with them. Ruth grabbed her with one hand and Roz with the other. "Now, you listen to me," she said to them. "Take the dogs and go back. Go back and tell Mom what happened, and that everything is fine, but I need to help Siddha."

Roz opened her mouth, and Ruth squeezed her arm, tight.

"Ouch," Roz said. "Okay, okay. But you don't have any shoes."

Ruth looked down. "Fuck," she muttered. "Okay. Go back, and I'll be there in a minute. Go!" She gave each of them a little push, then turned back to Siddha, who was crying, hard. "Siddha, listen to me. Stop crying. You need to hold it together. Do you understand me? Take a breath. Hold it together. Siddha, you need to get off this ice. You need to find your phone, call their mom, and tell her to meet us at the ER. I'm sure they're fine, but that head needs to get looked at."

Siddha nodded and turned back toward the shore. Ruth followed Siddha as she slid across the ice, but soon enough the ice became too cracked and warped for Ruth to skate over. "It's too uneven now," Ruth said. "You're going to have to go without me. Just drive around to the other parking lot, and I'll meet you. You can follow me to the hospital."

"Okay," Siddha said. "But can you call Hope?" Her voice was tentative.

Ruth looked at her. She was so angry. "I don't know Hope. I don't have her phone number."

"Mama, I need your help."

Ruth grasped both of Siddha's arms. She looked right at her. "I am going to help you. Everything is going to be fine. But I'm not calling Hope. Walk back, get them to the car. Blast the heat. Then call Hope, tell her what happened, and that she needs to meet you at the Radclyffe ER. Tell her everyone is fine."

Siddha started sobbing again. "I can't, I can't, I can't call her, she'll be so mad."

Ruth was angry at how careful Siddha was being with Hope, how cautious. She knew why, but it still made her angry. "Hope's the mother of twin boys," Ruth said. Not to mention Elliot's wife, she thought. "This kind of drama is nothing new for her."

WHEN THEY GOT to the ER, a woman that Ruth assumed was Hope was waiting at the entrance. She was wearing a long down coat over basketball shorts and old clogs without socks.

Ruth parked, and Siddha pulled in next to her. Teddy and George spilled out of the car, and Hope came running over. "Playing on thin ice?" She grabbed Teddy, and then George, and then Siddha, hugging them all at once. "Seriously, what is wrong with you three?"

Ruth turned away so no one would see her smile. Ah, so this was the woman who could handle Elliot.

"I'm so sorry, Hope," Siddha said. "I'm so so so sorry! The ice seemed so thick, I mean, people were driving snowmobiles on it, I mean—"

Hope put her hand on Siddha's face. "It's okay, doll. Really, it's okay."

Siddha didn't pull away from Hope's hand. Ruth, in all her life, had never been so jealous, or so grateful.

"I'm Hope," Hope said, letting go of the kids and offering her hand to Ruth. "A strange but fitting way for us to meet."

Ruth took her hand. "I'm Ruth." She didn't know what else to say. Thank you? I'm sorry? I hope you understand why I took my child away from your husband?

"Let's go," Hope said, beckoning to the boys. "Let's go in and get you checked out." They all walked toward the entrance.

Ruth gently reached for Siddha's arm. "I think we can head home. Hope has this now."

Siddha yanked her arm away. "I'm going to stay," Siddha said. "I'll be home later."

"I think you should come now," Ruth said.

"I don't think I'm going to."

Hope turned and looked at Ruth, and gave her a little nod. Ruth reached for Siddha's arm again, this time less gently. "Sid, can I talk to you for a minute?"

Siddha looked at Ruth's hand, and Ruth felt her flinch under her grip. The panic and pleading of just a short while ago had been replaced with stoicism and anger. But even so, Siddha followed Ruth around the side of the hospital building. Ruth looked up at the sky, squinting. Then she looked at Siddha again, but she didn't speak.

"How long?" Ruth asked, finally. "How long has it been?"

Siddha didn't hesitate. "Since that party," she said. "That Sukkot party. That day you had a party instead of taking me to Elliot's memorial."

"Sid, we had no idea—"

Siddha interrupted. "I don't care. I really don't care. You asked how long it's been, and that's how long. That night, I went to Barton Falls Hardware. I drove over there because I wanted to see it. And Hope was there, and she offered me a job. She offered me a job, and I took it. And then I started hanging out with Teddy and George, and with Hope too. With all of them."

"And that's where you've been. After school, and on the weekends. You've been in Barton Falls. You've been working at Elliot's hardware store."

Siddha nodded.

"Not babysitting, or studying with Eliza?"

"I mean sometimes, but no . . ." Siddha shook her head. "Not really."

"You could have told us. We wouldn't have been mad."

Siddha made a face. "You think I didn't tell you because I was afraid you'd be mad? Seriously? You thought I'd care if *you* were mad at *me*?"

"Look, I know you're angry—"

"He! Was! My! Dad!" Siddha pounded the beat of the words on her chest with her closed hand. "And you, you were such a fucking liar, all the time saying he was just a donor, never telling me his name, never telling me you knew him, never telling me he was right here! And what—I'd just meet him when I turned eighteen, like the other kids? Great plan, except then he died, and now I can never meet him, and I'm stuck with you and Mom, and all the stupid things you say to make yourself feel better about all the stupid things you did—"

"*Enough!*" Ruth yelled. "That is enough. You cannot talk to me like that. I *tried*"—Ruth pounded on her own chest now, and her voice broke—"I tried so hard to do what was best for you."

"You don't know what was best for me. And now it doesn't even matter, because he's dead. Which is probably a huge relief for you."

Ruth felt as though she'd been hit in the stomach. Would her own sadness always be a secret? Would losing Elliot never be allowed to matter because of what she'd done to Siddha? "No, Siddha, it is not a relief. Not at all. It's a terrible tragedy, and I'm so, so sorry. But the thing is— Elliot, the Elliot I knew—he was a mess, Siddha. He was a real mess. He was in no condition to be a father."

"Shut up," Siddha said. "You're just trying to make yourself feel better."

Ruth felt rageful. "I'm happy to shut up, Siddha. But why don't you ask Hope about it? Have you asked Hope? Has she told you who Elliot really was? Or are you too busy telling her how evil I am? How controlling?"

"You know what, I will ask Hope. And we'll have plenty of time to talk because I'm going to stay at her house. I'm not coming home."

Ruth glared at Siddha. "Great," she said. "Enjoy your time with her."

"I will!" Siddha said, and she took off, running toward the ER entrance.

Ruth's heart was pounding when she got into the car. "Damn, damn, fucking shit, damn," she said aloud. She rested her head on the steering wheel for a moment, then pulled out her phone. There was a text from Wyn. *All okay?*

Ruth burst into tears. No, Wyn, all is not okay. Not for Siddha, not for me, and not for you. *Yes* she texted back. *All okay, thank god. Will explain everything when I get home.*

RUTH PARKED IN Florence's driveway and went in through the back door. Florence was sitting at the kitchen table, her glasses on, reading the paper. "Oh, hey, beautiful," she said. "What a nice surprise."

Ruth sat down. She started to cry. Florence took off her glasses and sat back in the chair.

Ruth wiped the tears from her cheeks. "Siddha found Hope, and Elliot's kids. She's been working at the hardware store. She's been spending all her time over there. Every time she wasn't home, when I thought she was babysitting or with her friends, she was with them."

"Oh. Oh, Ruthie."

"I know," Ruth said. "I've been so dumb."

"You haven't been dumb. You've been grieving."

Ruth nodded. "I can't do this, this thing we're doing. I can't do it anymore."

"I know," Florence said.

Ruth groaned. She put her head in her hands. "I can't believe I'm going to lose you again. I can't believe I could have had you as a friend, and now I can't have you at all."

Florence smiled. "I liked it this way. And anyway, we both have plenty of friends."

Ruth looked up at her. "Well, it was fun, wasn't it?"

"Very," Florence said. "But not as fun as it might have been if you weren't so in love with Wyn."

Ruth wanted to say, I'm in love with you too, but she knew it wasn't true.

Florence leaned in then, and Ruth kissed her. They kissed for a little while, and then they stopped, because Ruth was crying again. Florence laughed and handed her a napkin.

Ruth blew her nose into it and stood to put it in the trash. She stood at the counter, her arms crossed. "Siddha is sleeping at Hope's house." Ruth shook her head. "I don't understand how we got here. I don't know what is happening. All these years I lived with this buried, secret fear that I'd lose her to Elliot in some way, and then he died, which should have meant that fear died too, but now here I am, losing her anyway."

"She'll come home," Florence said. "Not tonight, maybe. But she'll come home. I can promise you that. I promise you haven't lost her."

"She's so mad."

"I know."

Ruth leaned her head back, looking at the ceiling. Hot tears rolled across her cheeks. I have never, ever been this sad, she thought. "I should have kept you, for Siddha. I mean, if we hadn't done this, she could have known you, you could have been her connection to Elliot."

"She has Hope for that," Florence said. "And the boys. And the Elliot they knew, that's the Elliot she needs now. You and I are the only ones who need to remember our Elliot. And it's been so sweet, Ruthie. Remembering with you. It's been the sweetest."

Florence stood. She hugged Ruth.

"I'm going to miss smelling your hair," Ruth said. And then she laughed, and cried a little more, and laughed a little more, and felt genuinely crazy.

"Oh, doll," Florence said, pulling her closer for a moment before letting her go. "I'm going to miss everything. And I will see you around when—"

"Say hello," Ruth said, emphatically interrupting her. "I mean, if you see me, always say hello, please. We wasted so much time not saying hello."

"Of course," Florence said. "I'll always say hello."

BACK IN THE car, Ruth was desperate to get to Wyn. But she knew that she couldn't go home, not yet. If she went now, she'd tell Wyn about Florence, and she did not want to tell Wyn about Florence. She would not set off that particular bomb in their lives. Nothing good would come of it. That much she knew. She knew almost nothing right then, but she did know that.

Ruth drove to Olive Street. There had been workers there all week, refacing the kitchen cabinets, so the heat was on and the house was warm. She went right upstairs without even taking off her boots. She rummaged around in a drawer and found a beach towel, and she turned on the bathtub tap, sitting naked on the toilet while she waited for it to fill.

She slid into the hot water and heard herself groan, in pleasure, in relief, in sadness. For years and years all she'd wanted was to get into the bath—this very bathtub—in a quiet house, this very house! With no chance of being interrupted: no Roz crying outside the door, no Abe begging to get in with her just this once, no Gilly wanting to play her the song she'd just learned on the recorder, no Siddha wanting to come in and paint her nails, no Wyn asking if she could please hand her the toothpaste.

Ruth closed her eyes and leaned her head back against the tub's cool porcelain lip. "This wasn't what I meant," she said, to no one in particular, to no one at all.

36

The annual GoldFynch warehouse sale was an idea that had once seemed genius and now was a total nightmare. What had started as a jolly winter day spent in the parking lot of their first studio—drinking hard cider and spiked hot chocolate and catching up with friends who stopped by to say hello and devotees who had arrived two hours early for the chance to get discounted pots—was now a chaotic, hectic ordeal involving timed tickets and a rent-a-cop who had to be paid double overtime because it was, per tradition, always on January second.

The date had been Evie's idea: a seconds sale on January second. When Tobi said Isn't everyone broke on January second? Evie said no, their credit card statements wouldn't have arrived yet, and they'd still be in that holiday delusion of bounty. They had to clear their shelves—and boy, did this sale clear them. The discount was only twenty percent, which wasn't that steep considering these were pots they couldn't sell at full price. They had small defects, a little warping or too many glaze crawls, all things that no one who wasn't a potter would really notice. The goal was to bring their inventory of seconds as low as possible because seconds didn't make them any money. Or much money. At this point the sale barely paid for itself. But they weren't about to stop now.

Tobi was in the back, helping unload stock, and Evie was in front, conferencing with a store manager who was having trouble getting the credit card system online. They'd been avoiding each other all week. They split the shifts with kids and at work, and when their date night came around, Evie texted Tobi to tell her that she'd be working late and Tobi could do whatever she wanted. Tobi felt like they were communicating mostly through the kids and the little things they left around the house. Evie, who was a fastidious cleaner, had left her fried-egg pan in the sink all day, and if fried-egg pans could talk, this one would have said that Evie was not coming back to clean it, and if Tobi wanted to fry herself an egg, she'd need to wash this first.

Tobi was mad. She was mad, but she didn't know if she was allowed to be mad, which was a confusing feeling. She'd had it many times before in arguments with Evie, who was an accomplished arguer, having been raised by a public defender and a history teacher. When they fought Tobi often got turned around, unsure of what was happening, or if she was even making sense. But this time was different. She knew what was happening. Evie was being ridiculous. And she felt, in a way that both saddened and angered her, that she'd somehow lost hold of this thing, this desire that had, for those few expansive, frightening months, felt like it was entirely hers.

Now here they were, at the goddamned seconds sale, and there was no way to escape each other. And so the whole day they worked, and sometimes talked to each other, and at the end of the day—when everyone was gone, and they'd sold all the pots and sent the staff home, and it was like the old days, the two of them there alone—Tobi, who was angry, and tired, and tired of being angry, carried a box to the back room where Evie was sorting, and she set the box down, and crossed her arms over her chest, and said, "I'm really, really tired of this, Evie."

Evie looked at her. Really looked at her. Steely-eyed. Evie was angry, but—and this was what frustrated Tobi—more than anything she was hurt. Tobi wanted to say You can't be hurt! This is about me! Not you.

But she couldn't say those things, because of the way she'd handled all of this.

"I am sorry," Tobi said. "I am sorry that I didn't tell you. I am sorry that I kept it a secret, and that I hurt you."

Evie looked at her.

"But—" Tobi said, and Evie groaned, and Tobi held up her hand. "But you're going to have to forgive me. And we're going to have to move on. Because I need you for this."

"And what is 'this'?" Evie asked. "I mean, I know, I know you've said it. It's top surgery. But is there more? I mean, is this about, is it about wanting—" Evie didn't finish.

"To transition?" Tobi asked. She knew she had to say the word. She knew Evie wouldn't say it, but she knew that somehow, even though it wasn't what she wanted to do—what she needed to do—it was a word they would have to be able to say. "No," Tobi said. "No. That's not what I want. And honestly, that's part of why it's been so hard to get my head around what I wanted. It's part of why I haven't wanted to talk about it, because I'm just not sure if I'm even allowed to want it, you know? But I think I've accepted the fact that there's no perfect cocktail of hormones for me, so I might as well stick with what I've got. Same with changing pronouns, or my name. I'm not doing either of those things."

"Well, either way you don't need a new name," Evie said.

"Yeah, I know, Evie. I know." Tobi sighed. "I know I don't need a new name. I just don't want these anymore," she said, putting her flattened palms on her breasts. "It's so hard to explain."

"Not to Mike. You could explain it to Mike."

"No," Tobi said. "No, I couldn't. That's just it. I couldn't explain it to Mike. But Mike didn't need an explanation. That's why I could talk to him. I didn't need to have it all figured out."

"But I would have needed an explanation?" Evie said.

"Yeah, you would have. Am I wrong?"

Evie didn't say anything.

"The weird thing is, I thought you knew. Or at least suspected. I was wearing a binder in those photos for *Hudson Quarterly*. I thought, well—I thought that's what you liked about the pictures."

Evie started to cry. "God, I feel so stupid," she said. "I just thought you looked confident. I thought you looked happy. I thought you looked like you were finally sort of easing in, you know? Claiming your power." She laughed, a bitter sort of laugh. "I thought it looked like you'd arrived. It was sexy."

"Well, I sort of had," Tobi said. "I think that's the point."

Evie nodded, a sad look on her face. "Right." She looked at Tobi. "Have you talked to a surgeon?"

"No," Tobi said. "But I have an appointment."

"And you were going to go do it without me?"

"No," Tobi said, emphatically. "I wasn't. I really wasn't. I was going to tell you before then, I swear."

Evie pushed her glasses into her hair, wiped her eyes with a Kleenex. "God, Tobi, why didn't you give me a chance? You didn't even give me a chance to do the right thing. Maybe I would have."

Tobi smiled at her. "Maybe," she said.

Evie looked at the ceiling. "But probably not," she said.

"Probably not," Tobi said. She pulled Evie toward her, and Evie found her place in her arms.

"I love your breasts," Evie whispered into Tobi's shoulder.

Tobi pulled back. "No, you don't." She laughed a little.

Evie punched her gently and settled back in against her. "I mean, I know that they're not—they've never been our *thing*, exactly."

"It's been hard to compete," Tobi said, reaching for Evie's breasts, which had been, and would, she hoped, always very much be their thing.

"I get that they don't make sense to you. Maybe that's what I love. Like, there you are, butch and tough, and then your shirt is off, everything is off, and it's all there, just for me. It's all your secrets." She started to cry again. "They're just mine. They're the thing you don't let anyone see but me."

"Evie, come on. All of me is just yours."

"No," Evie said. "That's not true. And it's okay, I mean, it's not supposed to be like that. But that's not true."

"I'm all yours, Evie."

"You don't need to be all mine. That's not what I'm trying to say. What I'm trying to say is that—oh, I don't know. I want the best of you."

"My tits are not the best of me," Tobi said. "They're kind of the opposite, really."

"I want your secrets, Tob. That's all. That's what I want. And your breasts were your secret. And I know—I always knew—that was because they were troubling. They were incongruous. I always knew they weren't really right. I did." She paused for a moment. "And then they became a much bigger secret."

"I didn't know what I wanted. And I needed to know what I wanted."

"Without me."

"You're not unbiased."

"Yeah, well, neither is little Bex."

Tobi laughed. "Wow. You don't need to hide your disdain."

"It's not disdain."

"What is it?"

"Annoyance?"

"Okay, well you're not hiding it well."

"Oh please, why should I? It's not like Bex and all the Bexes of the world are hiding their annoyance with me."

"I don't think they're annoyed," Tobi said.

"You're right, they're not annoyed. They don't even have the energy to be annoyed. They're just oblivious. I mean, we're totally invisible to them, which is fine—"

"It doesn't seem fine." Tobi was laughing now.

"Yeah, well I guess I'm just wondering, where's the gratitude? That's what I'd like to know. Where's the fucking gratitude for everything we did, everything we fought for? I didn't lie down in the street so they could just ignore me."

"I don't remember you ever lying down in the street."

"You know what I mean! We were taught to respect our elders. We owe everything to them. Adrienne and Audre. Kay and Barbara. Do you think Bex and their crowd have any idea who Kay and Barbara even are?"

"No," Tobi said. "But hon, I didn't know who Kay and Barbara were until you told me. I'm gonna guess most lesbians don't know who Kay and Barbara are. Not everyone writes a college thesis on the Daughters of Bilitis. But they know themselves! They know who *they* are, and what they want."

"Because of us!"

"Well then, that's all the more reason I should follow Bex's lead," Tobi said. "All the more reason that I deserve to do what I want. And for you to get behind it."

"I just don't know when we lost sight of liberation," Evie said, glumly.

"Come on, hon. You're the CEO of a multimillion-dollar company. I don't think dykes getting top surgery have drifted any farther from liberation than you have."

Evie leaned back into Tobi. "Please just never stop using the word 'dyke.' Even when you don't have tits. That word is important to me."

"I promise," Tobi said. *Even when you don't have tits.* Tobi felt her heart flip. This was going to happen.

"You're going to have to give me a new secret," Evie said, slyly. She pulled Tobi toward her.

"Maybe I'll get a new tattoo," Tobi whispered.

Evie made a face.

"Or not," Tobi said.

"No, no, a tattoo would be cool. It would be good. Maybe I'll get one too."

Tobi rolled her eyes.

Evie, ignoring the eye roll, pointed at her. "But no phoenix-rising shit. No Celtic symbols of rebirth. No Celtic anything."

"For someone who's dedicated a lot of their life to bodily autonomy, you're really controlling."

Evie blew her nose into a paper towel and threw it in the compost bin. "I need a beer."

"I've got some in the studio, on the fire escape. Come on." Tobi headed for the door, and they went down the hall and outside together. It was funny—even though they both worked there, had worked together every day for as long as either of them could remember, Evie rarely came to Tobi's new studio. They walked in silence. Tobi felt a great weight had been lifted. Evie knew. She put her hand to her chest. She could do this now, she thought, elated. It was as good as done. The worst was over.

Later, much later, there would be incisions and pain, bandages, nausea from painkillers, physical therapy—all of this and more—and Tobi would laugh, or try not to laugh, remembering how that night she'd thought it was as good as done when the reality was she hadn't even begun. This was before the first consultation, and the second; before Tobi decided on a different surgeon; before strange, confusing fights with Evie, and doubting herself, and holding her ground anyway. This was long before Tobi did the hardest thing she'd ever done. But also, she had been right. It was, in some ways at least, as good as done.

She went ahead of Evie into the studio and, without turning on the light, went out the window to the fire escape. Evie followed her. They squeezed in together on the bottom step. Tobi opened a beer, handed it to Evie. She opened one for herself. She tapped her bottle against Evie's. "I love you," she said.

Evie took a long drink of her beer. "I know."

Tobi laughed. "And you?"

"Oh, Tob," Evie said. She sighed, took another drink of her beer. There were tears in her eyes. She touched her hand to her face, the bottle to her forehead. "More than I should." She took another drink. "When I thought, for even that little while, when I thought—"

Tobi could hear the sob in Evie's throat. She took the bottle from Evie's hand and, shaking her head, whispering Shush, whispering No, whispering Never, she kissed her, hard, and Evie kissed her back, harder. She climbed onto Tobi, opened her coat, then let it fall to the cold and dirty grate, where it knocked over Tobi's beer, which rolled across the metal step and fell through the railing, shattering on the pavement with a crash that Tobi ignored, and Evie—if she noticed it, she didn't let on.

37

"I'm going to run to the store," Caroline said. "I was thinking we could make pizza for dinner, and everyone could do their own toppings? And then we could make brownie sundaes for dessert? Or is that too much dairy? Are the twins lactose intolerant? I don't want to give anyone a stomachache."

Mike came up behind Caroline, and kissed her neck. "No one is lactose intolerant, babe."

"Jacob Neff is," Luca said. He was sitting at the kitchen table, eating waffles. "He ate three cupcakes and then threw up all over the roller rink at Elsa Lutton's birthday party. Boy, am I glad I didn't get invited to that one."

Caroline looked at Mike, trying not to laugh. How good it felt, to have to stifle a laugh and not a sob.

"You really dodged a bullet there," Mike said.

"A bullet of puke!" Luca said, and then pretended to throw up.

"Okay, okay," Caroline said. "I've got it." She reached for her coat. "I was thinking we could go to the school sledding hill this afternoon? I also read there's a show at the planetarium, which is a little more of a drive, but we could do that tomorrow morning, maybe?"

"Sure," Mike said. "Anything. But we could also chill here. The kids could just Xbox or whatever."

Caroline made a face. "I highly doubt that Nina and Jules are allowed to Xbox or whatever," she said.

"That's what would make it fun!" Mike said. "The thrill of the forbidden." He kissed her.

Caroline didn't want to admit it, but she was nervous about this weekend. On Wednesday, Evie had called to ask her a favor. "And you can totally say no," she'd said.

Caroline had tried not to laugh. Did Evie not remember the last time she'd said that to her?

"We need a night away," Evie said. "Just a little break from all the crazy. Could the twins stay over at your house on Saturday night?"

"Of course! Bring them over anytime!" Caroline had said. She wondered why Tobi hadn't just asked Mike, but she was also thrilled—thrilled—that Evie had asked her instead.

Now she gathered the canvas grocery bags from the hook by the back door. "Okay, I'm going. Text me if you think of anything else."

Mike saluted. Luca imitated him, but instead of holding his hand parallel to his eyes, he held it perpendicular. Mike wrestled him onto his lap. "Oh, kid," he said. He looked at Caroline then, quickly, apologetically. She rolled her eyes, but smiled. He blew a raspberry kiss on the back of Luca's neck. "Oh, my sweet boy."

CAROLINE WAS IN the produce section when she saw Ruth. Before she could turn and walk the other way, Ruth called to her.

"Oh hey!" Caroline said, hoping she sounded surprised.

"I thought that was you," Ruth said. She leaned in to hug Caroline.

"I've been meaning to call," Caroline lied.

"It's a crazy time," Ruth said.

Caroline nodded. "It really is."

Ruth pointed at Caroline's cart. "That's a lot of fun food you've got there."

"Nina and Jules are staying with us."

"Oh my god, really? That's great. Are Tobi and Evie going to the Bahamas or something?"

"Something like that," Caroline said with a laugh that sounded more nervous than she wanted it to. "They just needed a little getaway." There were so many things Ruth didn't know! It pained Caroline—in an actual, visceral way—to think of all the things they hadn't talked about since their fight.

"I get that," Ruth said. "Hey, why don't you all come for dinner? The kids could sled on our hill, and we could make a fire, and Wyn could do chili or something, and the kids could watch movies in the attic, we could even have a big sleepover—we've made the attic into a rumpus room for the winter."

Caroline felt herself start to sweat. She unbuttoned her coat, hoping she didn't look flushed. "Thank you," she said, trying to smile in a way that didn't look fake. Did she want to spend the evening at Ruth's? Of course she did. But she couldn't let herself say yes. "I think we're pretty set with plans."

Ruth looked hurt and Caroline felt a horrible mix of guilt and pleasure.

"Oh, yeah, sure," Ruth said. She smiled at Caroline. "I'm glad. That's so nice for all of you."

Caroline nodded. "Listen, I've got to dash. Let's talk soon."

"Very soon," Ruth said, eagerly. "I want to hear all your news."

Caroline pushed her cart into the next aisle. She felt nauseous. My god, Caroline, she thought. What are you trying to do here? Was she trying to punish Ruth for having an affair? She wasn't Ruth's wife for god's sake. Why did she care so much?

Because I'm jealous, she thought. That's it, I'm jealous. All these feelings Caroline had been having—the anger over the secret, the worry about losing what their families shared—they were all real, but the realest feeling of all was jealousy. She was jealous of Florence. Because

Ruth's attachment to Florence, her crazy affair with her, it was all tied up in Ruth's secret past, a time of Ruth's life that was fundamentally, wildly important but that Caroline had known nothing about.

And Florence knew everything! Caroline had had all these years of intimacy with Ruth, all these years of thinking there was nothing she didn't know, and then this? What she'd wanted to say, ever since that morning at the pond, was Why? Why oh why didn't you ever tell me? Caroline felt tears begin to well in her eyes. Afraid that she'd run into Ruth at the checkout and that she'd see her crying, she abandoned her cart in the aisle and left the store.

After a good cry in her car, Caroline drove to the grocery store on the other side of town and raced through the aisles to make up the time she'd lost. She didn't want to explain to Mike why she'd taken so long. When she got home and went into the living room, it was clear that no one was thinking about how long she'd been gone. All the cushions were off the couch and Luca was wearing one of Mike's ties around his head. Nina was riding on Mike's back as though he were a toy pony. Jules was standing on the coffee table. Luca was jumping up and down with what was clearly euphoria.

"Oh hey, Cece," Mike said. "We're just horsing around," and then he made a whinnying sound and rose up like a mustang, dumping Nina onto the pile of couch cushions. She shrieked with delight.

"I must rescue my brucksin!" Luca said, and jumped off the couch and into the cushions next to Nina, who proceeded to wrestle with him.

"What's a brucksin?" Caroline asked.

"A brother cousin," Nina said. "I'm Luca's cuzster. That's a cousin sister."

"Oh," Caroline said.

"I suggested 'sibling,' but with a hard *c*," Mike said. "But then Luca pointed out that it sounds too much like sibling if you say it wrong"—Caroline raised her eyebrows—"and they all decided they wanted something more interesting."

"I get it," Caroline said. (But did she?)

There was no time, that day or the next, for mulling the semantics.

My god, Caroline thought, three children was a lot of children. They made pizzas, they made pillow forts, they put on a concert, they went sledding, they built Lego towers, they built block towers; they built, somehow, a stuffed-animal tower. "How about a movie?" Caroline kept asking, but there were no takers, which was really something if you considered how little screen time these kids were allowed to have. The twins followed Luca up and down the stairs, in and out the back door. He was a pied piper and Nina and Jules were a two-person band of travelers.

"Oh. My. God," Caroline said, when, on Sunday morning, they had finally convinced the three of them to watch some TV.

Mike was lying on the living room floor, his eyes closed. "Yeah," he said.

The front door opened then, and Evie and Tobi came in, bringing the cold with them. Tobi took one look at Mike and started laughing.

"Has Gulliver been felled by our Lilliputians?"

Mike groaned.

"Sit," Caroline said. "Or, if you want, there are waffles and coffee in the kitchen. We can't get up."

"That bad?" Evie said.

"Oh no, no," Caroline said. And then she smiled at her. "That good, actually."

Evie smiled. Tobi came back from the kitchen with coffee.

"Did you have fun?" Caroline asked.

"It was the best," Evie said.

Tobi nodded her agreement. "Thank you guys, so much, honestly. It was a lot, I know. How can we repay you?"

"No need," Mike said.

"Truly," Caroline said. And she meant it. "But," she said, hoping that what she was about to say wasn't going to give Mike a heart attack, "there actually is this one thing I've been wanting to ask you."

38

Ruth wanted, so badly, to fix things with Caroline. She'd felt such a pang of longing when she'd seen her at the store. In the two weeks since New Year's, not a minute had passed without her wanting to talk to Caroline. Standing there in front of a tower of pomegranates, Ruth had wanted to embrace her, to tell her about Siddha, about Florence, about everything. She wanted to say she was sorry. Why, then, had she not been able to say any of those things, but only stupid, frantic things?

Ruth needed Caroline as much as she needed Wyn. Every bit as much. She knew this wasn't supposed to be true, but it was. And of course it was different—in all sorts of ways—but a best friend was a lifeline. A best friend was hope. A best friend was how you got through the day, how you stayed married, stayed sane. A friend had faith in you, and was optimistic for your future. She gave you the bigger half of the donut, and made you want to give her the bigger half, too. Ruth had read something once about how there was a study that showed that a good friend was a better indicator of happiness than a happy marriage, and she'd thought, Seriously? We needed a study to tell us that? A friend, a friend was—well, what was the old line? A friend was a second self. But that wasn't really even it. A friend was a better self. A friend was, always, a bit of a thrill. A friend, Ruth had come to understand, was the real affair.

But then how could a friendship be so easily derailed? She and Caroline, they'd talked about everything. They'd discussed sex and bodies, mothers, children, spouses—all of it—without batting an eye. They'd laid bare their souls. And yet, here they were, unable to bear their anger, their misunderstanding? Why were their feelings about each other the only feelings they couldn't discuss? Why was anger the one feeling out of reach, the bridge too far? And is that what friends do when they get angry? Do they just burn the bridge? I won't, Ruth vowed to herself. I just won't.

Still, she hadn't called Caroline, and she hadn't texted her, and then—there they were in the grocery store, an awkwardness between them that Ruth could not believe, would never, in all her life, have imagined could be possible.

WHEN SHE WAS sitting in the bathtub in the house on Olive Street on New Year's Day, Ruth had wanted, more than anything, to pick up her phone and call Caroline. Instead, she read back through months of their text chain, the freneticism of it, the jokes, the shorthand, and she felt bereft. She wanted to call Caroline to say, I ended things with Florence, and Siddha is staying with Elliot's wife, and I'm going home without her, and can you tell me that it's going to be okay? Because that, really, was what they did for each other. They said, over and over, in all sorts of ways, that it was all going to be okay.

But Ruth didn't call Caroline that night. She drove back to the house once she was certain all the kids were asleep. She walked in through the mudroom, kicked off her boots, sat down at the kitchen table, and cried. She cried for Siddha. She cried for Elliot. Wyn sat with her, reassured her. Ruth could feel Wyn's sympathy, but also her frustration at all the reassuring she'd had to do since Elliot had died, and this made Ruth angry, and she told Wyn so.

Wyn drank some scotch then, and Ruth took off her coat, and they moved to the living room, near the woodstove. Wyn said she was mad too, furious, actually, that Ruth had never—not even once—stopped to think about how Elliot's death and Siddha's sudden attachment to him—to the idea of him—made Wyn feel. How vulnerable it made her, how left out. She told Ruth that she was tired of Ruth's negativity, her endless complaining. I am so tired of it! Wyn yelled. Ruth wanted to say *You're* tired? But she didn't. Instead she said she was sorry—so sorry!—that she'd been ignoring Wyn's feelings about Elliot.

Ruth wished she could apologize to Wyn for her affair with Florence, because Caroline had been right, she'd been having an affair. Ruth wished she could explain how inevitable it had been, that she'd needed Florence for all sorts of reasons, some that made sense, and some that didn't. She'd needed Florence for the things that Wyn couldn't give her, and although those things had, for a little while, been essential, they weren't now, and it was over. It was all over. But Ruth didn't say any of this. She knew that nothing good would come of confessing a betrayal that she didn't regret.

They were wide awake then, despite all this talk of exhaustion, and Ruth felt in the air between them a strange sort of magnetism, not of desire, but a feeling that she belonged, at least at this moment, wherever Wyn was. It was a peculiar feeling—why didn't she want to go upstairs and go to bed?—but there was no getting out from under it. It felt imperative. And there was also the electricity of Siddha's absence, the live wire of knowing she wasn't home, and wouldn't come home, and that was a thought Ruth couldn't let her brain touch, and so she had to stay away, and she needed Wyn near her.

They went outside and checked the water in the barn, and Wyn said, I could make a fire? And Ruth said, Sure. She went back inside for a bottle of wine while Wyn brought kindling from the barn. They sat close to each other and to the fire, too close, much closer than they ever let the children sit, and Ruth finally understood how a fire could make you warm. She unzipped her coat. Ruth told Wyn she was getting a job, any job, to get out of this house. Wyn said, Fine. And when not even the fire could keep them warm enough, they went back inside, and

Wyn said, the smallest beads of tears in her eyes, Why are you always avoiding me, now that I'm finally around, now that we finally have time? Ruth didn't say anything, but when they were warm again, they took off their coats and went to the downstairs guest room and had sex which was not gentle, but was, in its roughness, necessary.

Around midnight, they ate leftover chicken curry and laughed at things that weren't really that funny, because they were tired and a little drunk, and the sex had loosened something in them, but had not untangled it entirely.

Ruth, all this time, did not say one word about Florence, even after the sex, even after they'd drunk another bottle of wine. Ruth didn't even mention her name, not once. Around three in the morning, Ruth scrambled some eggs and they talked about taking a trip to Kiawah Island in February, and Ruth imagined them all together there, even Siddha, especially Siddha, and that thought was too much to bear, and Ruth longed for baby Siddha in her bathing suit, running on the hard sand of Kiawah that first year they'd taken her to meet Wyn's parents.

Ruth remembered how Rosalynn had fallen in love with Siddha, and how Ruth had felt a great exhale, there in the warmth and the wealth of Rosalynn's matriarchal embrace, and she saw now that her annoyance with Rosalynn, her disdain for her, was an act of loyalty to her own dead mother, when in truth she loved Rosalynn, she always had.

After they'd eaten the eggs, they had sex again, and this time it was gentle, this time it was slow, and when they were done, they slept. When the sun came up, Wyn rose and pulled on her pants and her sweatshirt and her hat, and Ruth said, There goes my farmer, and for the first time, there was no sarcasm, no taunting in her voice. And she thought, This ice is breaking too, which made her think of Siddha.

Wyn left the room, and Ruth heard her fill the dogs' food bowls, heard her open the back door, and she lay back down on the bed, and cried for Siddha and for Florence, and for Elliot. And for Caroline. Oh, she cried for Caroline. For all the things she wanted to tell her. Because had any of this even happened if she couldn't tell her best friend?

39

Tobi was running late. She hadn't bothered to text Evie to tell her. They both knew she'd be late, as much as they both knew she hadn't forgotten. It would be hard to forget something she was dreading as much as this. She found a parking space on Masonic, and when she turned the corner onto Main Street, she saw Evie waiting for her.

"Sorry," Tobi said.

"It's okay," Evie said.

"Are Mike and Caroline already here?"

Evie nodded. "They went upstairs."

Tobi looked up at the second-story window, as though she'd be able to see them. She took a breath. "Okay, well, here we go."

Mike and Caroline were sitting on the couch when they went in. A woman sitting opposite them rose to greet them. "Come on in," she said. "I'm Marcia." She had a warm smile and a pleasant, symmetrical face that was framed by full gray bangs. She was barely five feet tall.

"Please, please, sit down," she said, taking her seat in an Eames chair. She motioned toward the couch. "I apologize, it might be a little tight for the four of you. After Caroline called me and asked if we could do this appointment, my only reservation was, where will they all sit!" She laughed. "As Caroline and Mike will attest, I am a bit challenged in the furniture department!"

"It's a beautiful office," Evie said.

"Thank you," Marcia said. She took a sip from her coffee mug, which Tobi immediately recognized as one of hers from Few&Far. Tobi looked at Evie. Do we say anything? she asked silently. Evie didn't respond, silently or aloud. And since Tobi had vowed not to speak unless absolutely necessary, she didn't say anything.

Marcia spoke first. "I know something about Mike and Caroline's family, but Evie? Tobi? Tell me about yours. I know you have twins, but remind me, how old?"

"Five," Evie said.

"Well, as they say, you have your hands full."

"Very," Tobi said. "And we run a company."

"Oh, wow," Marcia said. Tobi imagined that Marcia's next question would be about the company, and they could all have a fun laugh over the mug, but Marcia asked, "And the twins' names?" And with that, the door seemed to close, with a final slam, on mug small talk.

"Nina and Jules," Evie said. "Well, Julian. But we call him Jules."

"Lovely," Marcia said. "I've always been fascinated by twins. Such an interesting way to sail the sibling ship. What's their dynamic?"

Tobi looked at Evie. Evie said, "It's sort of always changing, you know?"

Marcia nodded. "A sign that you're doing a good job."

Evie seemed emboldened by this praise, because she said, "Right now it's a bit tricky because Nina is so much more, well—" She paused.

"Capable?" Marcia offered.

"Yes," Evie said. "Exactly. More capable."

"And how is that for Jules?"

"Oh, it's fine," Tobi said, breaking her vow. "He's our little bodhisattva."

"I'd say he's more like our little bulldozer," Evie said.

Tobi looked at her.

"I mean, he's a doll," Evie said. "He's the absolute best. But he's a five-year-old boy." She laughed a little, a light, dismissive laugh. An if-you-know-you-know kind of laugh.

"Nothing wrong with that," Tobi said.

"Well, that's certainly true," Marcia said. And then, again with that small smile, that tiniest of smiles: "What does it mean to you, the both of you, being a boy?" She made a small gesture toward both of them, as though she were handing them a dictionary so they could look up the word. "What is it, exactly, that you're saying when you say that? Are there things, or people, you think Jules needs because he's a boy?"

Tobi and Evie looked right at Marcia, and said, in unison, "No."

"Definitely not," Tobi said.

There was a moment of silence, and then Evie, with her hand on Tobi's leg, said, "There have been some feelings about Jules having a dad. Or not having a dad."

Really? Tobi telepathed to Evie. You're going there?

Marcia nodded. "Jules's feelings, or your feelings?"

When Evie—who seemed to have received Tobi's message—responded with just a soft smile and a shrug, Marcia smiled kindly at both of them and said, "We can come back to that."

Marcia turned her gaze to Caroline and Mike. "And Luca? I know a lot about him, but I don't know how he feels about Mike's role in the twins' lives. How did you explain it to him?"

"Well," Caroline said. "That's sort of the thing, we haven't explained it much, or very well. We haven't been clear."

"And that clarity, that feels essential to you," Marcia said.

"It does," Caroline said. "I mean—actually, no—I mean yes, I mean—" She laughed. It was funny, Tobi thought, to see Caroline so unsure of herself, and so relaxed. It wasn't a side of her Tobi recognized, but she liked it.

Caroline went on, "I think we were pretty clear for a while, but the thing is, now—well, now it's not so easy to be black-and-white about it. It seems like Luca is ready for the complexities, but we're not."

"I think they're all ready for the complexities," Evie said. Tobi put her hand on Evie's leg. Not a competition, babe.

"Sure, of course," Marcia said. "Quite honestly, I'd say the kiddos were ready for the complexity all along; it was the four of you that weren't."

None of them said anything.

"This, of course, has nothing at all to do with your limitations and everything to do with how we've been conditioned to think about families. There's some rigid thinking that can be hard to soften."

"Well," Evie said, "as a queer family, we're pretty adept at that."

"I'm sure you are," Marcia said. "And in order to both make and protect that family, you've had to make some agreements. One of those was with Mike and Caroline. Agreements are so important, aren't they? But life really does get in the way, doesn't it?"

Marcia continued, clearly not wanting answers to either of her barely rhetorical questions. "That can be the problem. Although, you know—honestly, I don't want to use that word here. I don't want to call this—any of this—a problem." She smiled at them, shifted in her seat. "Because ultimately this, this—situation, and it *is* challenging, I don't mean to diminish the challenges, not at all—but ultimately what we're talking about here is ties that bind. Familial, biological, emotional. It's about your pasts"—she gestured to Mike and Tobi—"and healing those pasts."

What does she know about my past and how does she know it? Tobi wondered.

Marcia went on, "It's about taking care of the people we love. It's all the reasons we're here, all the best of being human. So then, really, I think, the true question is just—what's the message? Not what's the plan, or what's the arrangement, or what's the story, or what should everyone feel or not feel, because all those things are going to change over time; there's just no getting around that, no matter how settled you felt when you made this agreement. It's fluid."

She shrugged. "I'm sorry to have to say that, because I know how nice it can feel to think we can have certainty about these things, but we can't. But what you can get clear on is the message." She folded her hands in her lap. "So then that, I think, is our work. That's what I might be able to help you with. The message. What is the message?"

Caroline spoke. "That Mike donated sperm to help Tobi and Evie conceive the twins." Marcia made a face that suggested she was thinking over that answer, although Tobi suspected she was just waiting for an appropriate amount of time to pass before she spoke again.

"I'd say that's more of a fact," Marcia said. "I'd say that was the arrangement, or the plan. That was the action you all took. But you're a little beyond that now, in terms of lived experience. That is, in many ways, the past. Past action taken by people who have new information. And new people! You've got these three little beings, with their own feelings and desires, and they're going to need more than a repeated recitation of that fact."

"So . . . what, then," Caroline said, "we tell them they're all siblings?"

"Is it your intention to raise them as siblings?" Marcia asked.

"No!" they all four answered in unison.

"Okay then," Marcia said. "I'd most definitely not tell them that. What exactly was your intention, all of you?"

"Ours was to have children," Tobi said. "Well, a child. We got lucky."

"And yours?" Marcia looked at Mike and Caroline.

"To help out," Mike said.

"All right, okay. Now we're getting somewhere. Now we're getting closer to the message, the part of this whole thing that abides." She brought her hands together to cradle an imaginary ball. "Tobi and Evie wanted children to love and care for, and Mike and Caroline wanted to help them, because they're family. Love and care. Helping. Family. That's the message. Not 'father,' not 'brother and sister.' Just 'family.' And families help each other. Families are made up of children and adults. People who care about each other and are committed to each other's well-being. That's clearly what you all are to each other. Committed to each other's well-being. And so that's the message."

"But what do we say to Jules when he wants to call Mike his dad?" Evie asked.

Mike looked alarmed. "He wants to call me Dad?"

"He has," Tobi said. "Sometimes, a few times, not that often, I mean—"

"When Jules tells you he wants to call Mike his dad, you ask him why," Marcia gently interrupted. "You ask him what he loves about Mike. And what he thinks about dads, what a dad means to him. You get curious, and you get brave."

"Which," she said, turning to Caroline and Mike, "is what you'll need to do too. You'll need to listen to Luca, and ask him what he thinks. Maybe someday he'll want to call Jules and Nina his siblings. Maybe he'll want to play around with how that feels, and maybe he'll decide it's what makes the most sense to him." Marcia shrugged. "If that day comes, you'll need to meet it with that same curiosity and bravery, knowing that there's absolutely nothing wrong with those desires, those feelings. You'll ask him what he loves about Jules and Nina, and what brothers and sisters mean to him. You'll tell him you understand. And then, maybe someday down the road you'll all laugh about that time when he wanted to call them that."

"I don't know if I can do that," Caroline said.

"I know you don't," Marcia said. "But you can. I'd guess there are lots of things about being a parent that you didn't think you could do that you've done beautifully. And the same for Jules and Nina," Marcia said, turning her gaze to Tobi and Evie. "When they come to you with their feelings about Mike, or their ideas about dads, it's your job to just listen. Maybe they want to call Mike their dad for a while." Marcia tapped her pen on the table next to her chair. "Well, then maybe they do. That would be a great time for you to ask them what they like about calling him that, what the word means to them, what they like about it. You're going to have to throw open the curtains on this one, all of you. You're going to have to tolerate some of your own discomfort for the sake of your kids. But honestly, no more than you already have, so many times, over and over. This one feels loaded, I get it. So then, unload it! Take off the weight of society and language and expectation. Let it just be about your kids."

Marcia paused for a moment, and none of them spoke, and then she went on. "You know, it's all so beautiful, what you're doing. Honestly, it brings tears to my eyes. I mean, I know it's hard as hell. And it seems like you've got a lot of forces working against you, but it's the best of being alive, right here. It's love and care. And that," she said, clasping her hands together at her heart, "well, that's your message."

THE FOUR OF them stumbled out onto the street.

"Thank you," Caroline said.

"Sure thing," Tobi said at the same time Mike said, "No problem."

Evie glared at both of them. "No, thank *you*, Caroline. For knowing just what we all needed."

Caroline squeezed Evie's arm.

"Too early for a drink?" Tobi asked.

"Definitely not," Caroline said, and to Tobi's surprise—to her pleasure—Caroline took Tobi's arm, leaned her head for a moment on Tobi's shoulder, and led her, and all of them, down the block toward town.

40

Siddha's self-imposed exile had incited a complex range of emotions in Ruth, although, try as she might, she hadn't been able to conjure any genuine anger at Hope. Even though Hope was, as Ruth had said to Wyn, harboring a fugitive (Wyn had rolled her eyes), Ruth still couldn't feel anything but goodwill toward her. Whenever she tried to feel annoyed, she'd think of the weight of Hope's sadness, and then, on top of that, the weight of her young sons and her store. But for all the goodwill she felt, Ruth realized she'd never sent a condolence card, or reached out in any way at all after Elliot died.

This was why, on a Saturday morning two weeks after the chaos at the pond, Ruth stopped at Nuttleman's Flower Shop on her way to Hope's hardware store. She bought a small planter of paperwhite bulbs that were just beginning to sprout. As she drove to Barton Falls, she thought of what she could say to Hope, what would be appropriate. How do you thank someone for taking care of your runaway daughter, especially when you once took legal action against that person's now-dead husband?

But Ruth didn't need to worry about it, because when she walked through the door, Hope, who was ringing up a customer, saw her and put her hands over her heart, then motioned wordlessly to the back of the store. Ruth, afraid she might cry, just mouthed her thanks, put the paperwhites on the counter, and kept walking.

"Hey," Ruth said.

Siddha was crouched near the floor, sorting window cleaners. "Hey," she said, not looking up.

"Want to come outside for a minute? I have burritos, from Ojala."

"I'm working," Siddha said. "Hope needs me to finish this."

"It's fine!" Hope shouted. "Go!"

Siddha smiled a little, and Ruth felt her heart swell. "Come on," Ruth said.

They went outside. There was a picnic table past the far side of the parking lot, on a little flat spot next to the creek. "Let's go over there," Ruth said. "I can grab blankets from the car so our butts don't freeze."

Siddha didn't say anything. Ruth looked at her, in her little red apron with the pockets, her printed name tag. It nearly broke Ruth's heart, but she admonished herself to stay strong. She'd already talked about it with Wyn, how she'd need to not be emotional, not cry or let her feelings seem outsized. This was about Siddha, her sweet kitten. This lunch was a plate of milk set out to lure her home.

"How do you like working at the store?" Ruth asked. She put the burrito bag on the picnic table and handed Siddha a fleece blanket.

"I like it," Siddha said. She arranged the blanket like a little cushion on the bench.

Ruth opened the bag, handed Siddha a burrito and a napkin. She took out the other burrito and smashed the paper bag flat, slid it across the table in front of Siddha, offering it as a plate. Siddha put her burrito on it, but she didn't unwrap it.

"Mom says hi," Ruth said. Wyn had actually said, Tell that kid I fucking love her, but Ruth was trying to play it cool.

Siddha nodded.

Ruth took a bite of her burrito, a sip of her water. She looked down at the creek, which was frozen in spots, running in others. There was a January thaw, and the sun was bright and warming.

"I brought you something," Ruth said. She reached into her purse and handed Siddha a photograph. Siddha looked at it for a moment, and then looked at Ruth, and then at the photo again.

"It's Elliot and me. And you."

The photo was of Ruth, her hair thick and wild around her face—much like Siddha's was now—holding her T-shirt up, her arms crossed over her breasts, her pregnant stomach exposed. And Elliot, dressed in overalls, was kneeling at her stomach, both hands around it, his face bright. Ruth's head was thrown back; she was laughing.

"He called it communing," she said. "He was convinced you could hear him in there."

Siddha held the photo. She was letting herself study it now, intently. "His hair was so red," she said, finally.

"It was," Ruth said. "He was a real redhead. Before you were born, I wondered if you'd get it."

"But I didn't," Siddha said.

"No," Ruth said. "You got my hair. And my eyes. A lot of me." And then: "But a lot of him too."

Siddha nodded.

"I'm sorry, Sid," Ruth said. "I'm so sorry he's gone."

Siddha spoke then, but she didn't look up from the photo. "He wasn't in good shape then," she said.

Ruth didn't know what to say, other than a silent prayer of thanks to Hope, who must have told Siddha a few things about Elliot. "No," she said. "He really wasn't. I wanted him to be. I really, really did. I gave him lots of chances, Sid."

"He did get it together," Siddha said. "Later."

"Yeah, he did."

"But you didn't care."

Ruth took a breath. "I didn't really know, Sid. And the thing was, I couldn't afford the risk of finding out. You were—you are—too precious." That word, how true it was! How it made Ruth want to climb over the picnic table and hold Siddha in her arms. But Ruth stayed still. "He really, really loved you."

Siddha nodded.

"Siddha," Ruth said, trying to keep her voice steady. "If I'd known, if I'd known this was all the time you'd have, I would have—"

"You would have what?"

Ruth felt a sob in her throat, the rush of tears. "No," she said, shaking her head. "Actually, no. I was about to say I would have given him another chance, I would have seen if he could handle it, but I don't think I would have. That's the truth. And I'm so, so sorry. That's really what I want to apologize for. That even now, if I could do it again, even knowing that he was going to die so young, I still would have tried to protect you. I would have tried—and failed, clearly, as we see now—" She laughed a little. "I would have failed. I would have failed to keep you from being disappointed, from suffering an enormous loss. I wish that weren't true. Maybe that's what I'm so sad about. I wish that knowing what I know now, I would have done it differently. I'm fierce when it comes to you, Siddha. I am fiercer for you than I am for any other human on this planet. And that blinds me, it does. And I'm sorry."

"I feel like I can't forgive you," Siddha said. "And that makes me really scared. Like if I can't forgive you, I'll never feel better."

Ruth felt a puncture of anxiety. She was desperate to mend things with Siddha, desperate to be forgiven. But she knew that wasn't how this was going to work. She was going to have to be brave. She was going to have to sit with the terror of not knowing how, or when, she and Siddha would heal. "It's okay!" Ruth said, wiping her eyes. "You don't have to forgive me. You really don't. I mean, I hope that someday you can, but even if you can't, it's okay. You will feel better. I promise. But you don't need to force it, the feeling better or the forgiving. That will just make you more angry. Trust me, I speak from experience."

Siddha smiled at her, a real smile, an old smile, and Ruth thought, for a moment, that she would not survive the love she felt for this child.

Ruth took a long drink of water, to steady herself. "You know," she said, then paused, sure of what she needed to say but having no idea how to say it. She wanted, somehow, to acknowledge that Siddha had seen her with Florence in the kitchen that day, and while Siddha hadn't seen them kiss—Ruth had gone over the logistics of the scene in her head a million times and was certain she hadn't—she also knew that

Siddha had felt the charge between her and Florence, the energy in the room. Ruth and Siddha—Ruth and all her children, but especially Siddha—were keenly attuned to each other's moods and emotions, and there was no denying that Siddha knew something. Ruth went on. "Elliot's death, it made me a little crazy. It made me sad, and crazy. And I'm sorry. I'm so sorry."

"Well at least you didn't get a tattoo," Siddha said.

Ruth laughed. How good it felt to laugh! "Oh no! Are you having regrets?"

"No, not really," Siddha said. "Well, maybe? I didn't do the best job."

"Oh, Sid," Ruth was really laughing now. "At least it's not permanent."

Siddha groaned. "But I'm actually thinking of getting another."

"Oh?"

"Yeah. A morning glory."

Ruth put her burrito down on the picnic table.

"Don't cry," Siddha commanded.

Ruth closed her eyes and nodded.

When Siddha was young, three or four years old, and couldn't fall asleep, Ruth would crawl into her bed to rub her little back and whisper to her. Ruth would tell her that one September day, long ago, when Siddha was a baby and the two of them were living in a house *just* big enough for the two of them, with a backyard *just* big enough for the two of them, they were sitting in that yard early in the morning, and Siddha, who loved—had always loved—the fresh air, was sad. So Ruth bounced her and sang to her, and waited for the sun to come up. And as it did, as it hit the brick wall of their building, a tangled vine of morning glories opened their blue trumpets to the day. "And I held you up to those flowers," Ruth would whisper, "and you stopped crying. You just watched them. And those flowers told me that they had opened just for you."

And Siddha would say, sleepily, "The flowers told you that?"

And Ruth would say, "The flowers told me that."

Now, Ruth looked at Siddha. "Will you come home? Everyone misses you so much. It's not the same without you."

"Yeah," Siddha said. "I'll come home."

41

Caroline sat on her front porch steps in the cold air. She'd just been out for a long walk which had felt twice as long as it actually was. Usually when she walked she was either with Ruth or talking to Ruth on the phone. She'd tried listening to a podcast, and then an audiobook, and then a playlist of possible new pieces for the spring's student ensembles. None of it had interested her in the least, so she took a shortcut home across the park.

But when she'd arrived home, she'd sat down on the steps, not yet ready to go inside. All she really wanted to do was talk to Ruth. She thought of what Marcia had said, about how maybe they'd talk through their anger and maybe they wouldn't, and either way would be okay. Caroline wasn't really sure she believed this, but before she could talk herself out of it, she took out her phone and texted Ruth.

Mike got me a moped for Christmas, WTF?
And then, quickly:
I made Evie and Tobi go to therapy with me!
Also I have Tobi gossip
And a plan to get you out of the house

Call me?

Caroline clicked off her phone and slid it into her pocket. She pulled her coat around her. She felt brave. She felt scared. She missed Ruth so much.

And then, just as Caroline's head began to swim with the anxiety that she'd made a big mistake, that there was no way to just start up again, that Marcia was wrong, of course she was wrong, Caroline felt her phone vibrate in her pocket. She took it out. It was a call from Ruth.

"Ruth!"

"Tell me everything," Ruth said. "Leave nothing out."

Caroline nearly jumped off the steps. She pulled out her earphones, put them in her ears, buttoned her coat, and headed off down the block. For a moment she wished she had her gloves—the day had suddenly gotten colder—and she thought maybe she should have gone to the bathroom, but she wasn't going back inside, no way. Mike would ask what the dinner plan was, and Luca would want to tell her something very, very important. And right now, Caroline could not be interrupted. There was, at this moment, nothing more important in the world than this.

42

Ruth was in the kitchen when she heard a car in the driveway. She looked out the window above the sink and saw that it was Siddha. She stood watching, not moving. She watched as Wyn came out of the barn and, opening her arms wide, yelled, "*Siddha!*" And she watched as Siddha ran to Wyn, and jumped into her arms, wrapping her legs around her, and Wyn, because she was so strong—because she was Wyn—absorbed the full force of Siddha without so much as a wobble, and she held her for a long time.

And then she yelled—again, because she was Wyn—"Siddha's here!" and the other kids ran out of the house. Gilly and Abe stopped to pull on their boots, but Roz was in stocking feet in the snow, the three of them tackling Siddha, hugging her. Wyn swept Roz off the ground so her feet didn't freeze, and Abe wrapped his arms so tightly around Siddha, and Gilly turned back to the house and yelled, "*Mama! Siddha is home!*" and for a moment Ruth thought she should just wait for Siddha to come inside, that she should give her some space, but then she thought better of it and ran out the door.

THREE MONTHS LATER

It was the first day of May, and there was going to be a party at the hardware store. Hope and Siddha had been planning it for weeks. There would be free hot dogs and an ice cream truck, and a thirty-percent-off sale on lawn bags, grass seed, and vegetable starts. It would be a celebration of spring, and of Elliot's birthday; he would have been fifty-one years old that day.

It had been a cold winter, but everyone and everything was warming, even Wyn and Ruth's farmhouse. Partially because of the warmer temperatures, but mostly because Bex and their buddies were helping Wyn install solar panels and a new furnace.

"Is Bex even real?" Caroline asked, standing on the ground next to Ruth as they watched Bex on the steep roof, suspended in a harness, bouncing around the eaves. "I mean, they don't seem entirely real."

"Honestly, I don't know," Ruth said. Ruth had released all her hang-ups about Bex—all her antipathy, and certainly her jealousy, she had no leg to stand on there—and welcomed them into the fold. Ruth even asked them to sing sometimes. They were beautiful to look at, there was no question. "No wonder Tobi wanted to have top surgery," Ruth had said to Wyn one night after Bex came over for dinner. "Bex makes *me* want to have top surgery."

Wyn had grabbed Ruth's breasts then, in mock—but also authentic—horror. "Perish the thought!" she said and slid her hand under Ruth's shirt.

There was a time when Ruth would have batted her hand away, laughing, scolding, but that time was not now. She pulled Wyn in, bit her ear gently, and whispered, "Never."

THE MAY DAY party had been Hope's idea. She'd run into Wyn and Ruth at Bread Euphoria one afternoon in early April, the two of them sitting on a bench outside, sharing a sandwich. Wyn had come into town to have lunch with Ruth, as she did sometimes now that Ruth was working at GoldFynch as the social media manager.

"Hey, Mamas," Hope said, approaching Wyn and Ruth.

"Hey, Mama," Ruth said.

"I'm glad to run into you," Hope said. "I've been cooking up a plan I want to run by you." She explained about the party. "The thing is, I don't have any money." She laughed. "So we'll need to sort of home grow it."

For a moment Ruth was worried that Wyn would offer to pay, no price too high, and that would embarrass Hope. But Wyn just said, "We could do hot dogs? Set up grills in the parking lot? Buy everything at Costco?"

Hope agreed that this sounded like a great plan and suggested they hash out the details over dinner on Saturday. They had family dinners with Hope and the boys now; it was a new tradition they'd started after Siddha came home.

They'd also gone to the lawyer's office, to finally see what Elliot had left for Siddha. Ruth hadn't really known what would happen—she'd only seen will readings in movies—but it was very casual. After a little small talk and a few signatures, the lawyer presented Siddha with a small enamel box and a letter. Siddha read the note that was taped to its lid. "Siddha, there are fifty-one quarters in this box. I'm going on good faith that your mom is still alive when you're reading this, and that she can explain their origins." Siddha looked at Ruth. "Can you?" she asked.

"I can," Ruth said. She smiled at Siddha. "But maybe read the letter first?"

The lawyer gave Siddha the letter. She read it silently, and then handed it to Ruth. Ruth held it so both she and Wyn could read together.

> *Dear Siddha,*
>
> *The lawyers who give you this box will know how to contact my wife, Hope, and my sons. They are your brothers. They will take care of you, although if you're anything like your mother, you won't need much taking care. But you will need company and as much family as you can get. Remember that—there's no such thing as too much family. And if you want to know anything about me, anything at all, just ask them. But there's one thing I can tell you right now, Siddha: I loved you from your first breath until my last. And there's one more thing. Please don't be hard on your mom, especially if she's an old lady when you're reading this. But even if she's not, be gentle. She did the right thing.*

EARLY ON THE morning of the party, Wyn drove to Costco and bought hot dogs and buns, ketchup and mustard, and bottles of Mexican Coke. Siddha's friend Eliza set up a face-painting station outside the hardware store, much to the delight of the children and the annoyance of their parents. Ruth thought that at the end of her life, what she'd really want back were the hours she'd spent in face-painting lines.

By noon, the party was in full swing. Wyn grilled, and Ruth put on a red apron and helped box up people's plants, taking instruction from Siddha, who was working the outside register. Caroline rode all the way from Radclyffe on her Vespa, and when she arrived, Siddha gave her a red apron too. Evie came by with the twins and Luca, who'd slept at their house the night before. Ruth saw Caroline open her arms at the sight of him, then watched as Luca just waved at her and went off to get a hot dog. And then Ruth saw Caroline smile, and she knew the sweetness of Luca's indifference, how for Caroline there was nothing bitter about her boy in motion, away from her. Mike and Tobi were the last to arrive, the two of them wearing river shorts and Tevas, their noses sunburned from a morning on the lake. "They're still training for the Rod?" Ruth asked Caroline.

"I have a feeling they'll be training for that thing for the rest of their lives," Caroline replied.

The afternoon went on, in the way of pleasant spring afternoons. Kids chased each other across the grass. Toddlers in strollers fed hot dogs to actual dogs when their parents weren't looking. Those parents talked to each other about new restaurants and old TV shows and asked each other if they were ready for the summer crowds to arrive (no one was). Florence came by and bought a flat of pansies. She called hello to Ruth, who called hello back.

When the last of the hot dogs had been grilled, the last pansy sold, Siddha, George, and Teddy stood up on a picnic table, each of them with a Coke bottle in their hand. "Hello!" Siddha called.

"Hello!" the crowd called back.

"We'd like to make a toast to Elliot, our dad," Siddha said, "who loved hot dogs, and loved this store, and loved all of us."

Everyone raised their hot dogs and Coke bottles. "To Elliot!"

Ruth looked around at this sea of faces turned toward Siddha, all of them flush with love, and it occurred to her then that this party was for Siddha. Siddha, who had missed the memorial; Siddha, who had missed so much. This day was for her. And it was a gift from Hope, and from Wyn and Ruth too, and from all these people who loved her, and knew what she'd lost. How proud Ruth was to think of Siddha knowing this, and knowing how to stand—however wobbly, however shy—in these beams of love.

"And now we have a surprise for you," Siddha said. She jumped down from the table and motioned for everyone to follow her and her brothers down to the creek. And there, waiting, were all their kids: Gilly and Roz and Abe, Luca and Jules and Nina, standing behind a row of laundry baskets filled with origami paper boats.

"We made a flotilla," Siddha said. "All of us, together. We made a hundred boats for Elliot." She picked up a boat and motioned for people to do the same. "Everyone, take a few boats, and we'll send them into the water." She handed out the boats. "The paper is biodegradable," she added cheerfully. "So no one needs to worry!"

"Actually, it's water soluble," Roz said. Siddha tackled her in a hug.

The kids joined Siddha in distributing the boats to everyone. Ruth looked at Wyn, then Hope, silently asking Did you know? They both shrugged. Caroline gave Mike the same silent look, and Tobi and Evie gave it to each other. None of them knew how or when their children had made a hundred origami boats, together.

Everyone waded into the shallows of the creek. They balanced on rocks, and on each other, and a few kids fell in, but everyone managed to hold on to their boats until Siddha gave the command. And then the creek was alive with the brightness of the floating paper, bright like candles, like lanterns lit by the sun. Everyone was silent as the boats floated, tumbling into each other, capsizing, righting—and then, when the last boat had disappeared around the bend of the creek, everyone cheered.

ACKNOWLEDGMENTS

Thank you to Claudia Ballard, my intrepid and brilliant agent, for making my dream come true. Thank you to Whitney Frick, my peerless editor, for being that dream. Thank you for seeing the heart of this book, and for bringing it to life with your tenacity and love.

At The Dial Press/Random House, thanks to Talia Cieslinski, JP Woodham, Erika Bruner, Maria Braeckel, Avideh Bashirrad, Debbie Aroff, Corina Diez, Michelle Jasmine, and Andy Ward.

Thank you to the Minnesota State Arts Board for their generous support of my work through an Individual Artists Grant.

For their encouragement and support, I am grateful to Emily Abeln, Kelly Anderson, Heidi Bryan and Carol Burling, Essie Chambers, Pete Garber, V. V. Ganeshananthan, Alison Rogers, and Karin Wallestad. Special thanks to the early readers of this manuscript: Jodi Ayres, Heather Bray, Sally Franson, and Kate Galle. Thank you to Mark Gaddis for teaching me about motorcycles.

To Jenn Halvorson and my fellow masters at Solcana Fitness, thank you for letting me be the Ferdinand amidst your awesome ferocity.

Curtis Sittenfeld, thank you for your excitement, right from the start and all the way through. You made all the difference.

Thank you to Heather Abel for every day and every word.

There is no family like my family. Boundless thanks to my parents, Catherine and Jerry White, whose love for me and for this world are my life's greatest gifts. Thanks also for the gift of my siblings, DB and Rebecca. You two are the absolute best.

Grace and June, my darling girls. What a joy it is to be your mother.

And the greatest, deepest thanks to Chris, my wife. Oh, how I love that word! Oh, how I love you.